Murder in the
CHILCOTIN

Murder IN THE Chilcotin

Roy Innes

NeWest Press

COPYRIGHT © ROY INNES 2010

Library and Archives Canada Cataloguing in Publication

Innes, Roy, 1939 –

Murder in the Chilcotin / Roy Innes.

ISBN 978-1-897126-69-1

I. Title.

PS8617.N545M865 2010   C813'.6   C2010-903641-7

Editor: Diane Bessai
Cover and interior design: Natalie Olsen, Kisscut Design
Author photo: Laura Sawchuk
Proofreading: Caroline Barlott and Deanna Hancock

NeWest Press acknowledges the support of the Canada Council
for the Arts, the Alberta Foundation for the Arts, and the Edmonton Arts Council for our publishing program. We acknowledge
the financial support of the Government of Canada through the Canada Book Fund for our publishing activities.

#201, 8540 – 109 Street
Edmonton, Alberta T6G 1E6
780.432.9427

NeWest Press   www.newestpress.com

No bison were harmed in the making of this book.
printed and bound in Canada   1 2 3 4 5 13 12 11 10

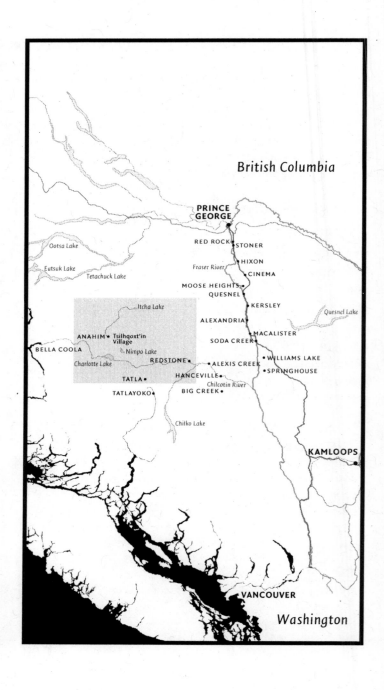

PROLOGUE

He stood with the women. No men came. He was barely thirteen, but old enough to watch, they said. Strong enough to help carry out the bodies.

The people from the town were there: 250 of them, according to the newspaper. Many were sitting — in chairs, wagons, buggies — waiting for the show.

They were led out, one at a time, up the steps of the gallows. A white man priest followed behind, moaning some foreign words. Five trips in all. Five warriors: one the boy's uncle, another, a cousin, just sixteen; a cousin more like a brother. The boy remembered days together, hunting, fishing, riding like the wind.

Only one spoke before the noose went round his neck: Klatsassin, their leader; their chief.

"We are prisoners of war," he said, "not criminals."

The boy couldn't hold back a gasp when the first dropped through the trapdoor, but he didn't cry. None of them cried, nor did they turn away. But some of the white women did.

When it was over, the crowd dispersed. No one met their eyes. An aura of shock and shame surrounded them.

The doctor made his last trip into the shed below the gallows. They'd simply pushed each body aside as the next one was hanged, so as not to offend the white crowd's sensibilities seeing the dead men. Finally the Mountie sergeant came over to where they were standing.

"Okay," he said. "You can take them away."

The boy climbed onto the wagon seat and gave a light tap with the reins to urge the pony forward. He pulled up to the door of the shed and got down. Two of the women entered first and then him. They shielded the light a bit, but not enough.

They were ugly in death; heads flopped over, crotches wet from urine and feces, hands bound behind their backs. Warriors once. Now pieces of meat lying on the ground, waiting to be taken away for burial. White man's prisoners of war.

The shock didn't lift for days, but when it did, a hatred built in the boy's heart that he vowed would never leave. The story would be passed on ... and the hate. The white man would pay for his injustice.

1

RAVENS WHEELED ABOVE THE GRAVEL ROAD, screaming their displeasure at one another, fighting for dominance over this tiny bit of Cariboo sky. A half-kilometre south lay B.C. Highway 20, a strip of asphalt running halfway across the province from Williams Lake to the Pacific coast. A curl of smoke rose on the western horizon from a small gypo mill on the outskirts of Anahim Lake. It was too soon for the smell of death to reach the great black birds, but the inert form lying on the road below held promise for them.

Two men were beside it. One stood, a tire iron clutched in his hand; the other knelt, searching for signs of life in the prostrate body. When he was sure, he rose and spoke to his companion.

"Sheessuss. Yuh kilt 'im. Yuh kilt a Mountie."

"He mad' me mad."

Their voices were soft, almost childlike, and neither face showed a trace of emotion.

Silence followed, both men seemingly lost in thought as they gazed down at the dead policeman. Finally, the killer turned, walked back to a battered old pickup parked just ahead of the RCMP cruiser, and threw the tire iron into the box.

"Got ta dump 'im," he said.

The other man hesitated for a moment, then grunted his agreement. "Yess. Got tah ditchem fer shur."

They worked quickly, efficiently, as though the whole thing had been planned. With considerable effort, they managed to drag the body to the cruiser and lift it onto the passenger seat where one held it in the sitting position, while the other buckled the seatbelt to hold it there. Next, they erased traces of the scuffle with buck brush switches pulled from the side of the road. That completed, and satisfied nothing had been left to attract attention, one man got into the pickup, the other the cruiser. They started the vehicles and drove about a hundred metres before turning onto an old abandoned logging road. Within seconds, the tiny caravan disappeared from view, hidden by the dense second-growth timber covering the hillside.

Quiet descended again on the gravel road. The ravens dispersed, flying elsewhere to search for their daily fare; but, momentarily, soft hoofbeats and the jangle of a bridle broke the silence as a figure emerged from the pines.

The horse, a small pinto, shook its head, annoyed perhaps by standing in the shadows for so long while its young rider watched the scene unfold below them, not moving until the men had gone.

The boy urged the animal across the ditch and onto the road, finally pulling up where the Mountie's cruiser had been parked. In one of the tire tracks, a metallic gleam caught his eye. He dismounted, keeping a firm grip with one hand on the reins, picked up the object and blew the dust off it. It was a pen: shiny metal at one end with the figure of a Mountie on a horse, and a bulbous red grip on the other. He quickly stuffed it into his pants pocket, looked around a bit more, then climbed back on his horse and rode off at a gallop, heels pounding against the pinto's flanks.

INSPECTOR MARK COSWELL, satiated from his morning breakfast orgy at The Dutch Pancake House, gazed with annoyance at the message light flashing on his office desk phone, and grumbled, "Who in hell needs to talk to me at seven-thirty on a Monday morning?"

He picked up the receiver and stabbed the message button. A beep, then a familiar voice came from the speaker. "It's me ... Blakemore. I need to speak to you ... pronto."

Pronto? His former corporal, newly promoted to sergeant, had left Vancouver just a few months before to head the RCMP unit in the West Cariboo district—cowboy country all right, but not as yet American. Pronto, indeed.

He punched in the number left at the end of the message. The fledgling sergeant answered on the first ring—not a good sign.

"Thanks for getting back to me right away," Blakemore said. "I've got a problem up here."

Coswell sighed. Blakemore and problems seemed to go together. "For heaven's sake, you just got there. You couldn't possibly be in trouble so soon."

Blakemore ignored the comment. "One of my rookies, Brent Hansen, was found dead over the weekend inside his burnt-out cruiser at the bottom of a ravine. Poor bugger. His very first posting. Hasn't been here any more than a couple of months."

"Accident?"

"I don't think so. I drove in with the coroner after he got the call. Crime scene was a mess. The native police crew and half the population of the reserve were there. Tire tracks everywhere. They'd even pulled the cruiser up from the ravine. Had to, they said, to douse the wreck with enough water so the fire wouldn't flare up again."

"Go on. Why not an accident?"

"The head trauma. Back of the skull caved in by a narrow object. The airbags were burnt up but they had deployed. And even if they weren't effective, any injury should have been to the front of his head, not the back. No. I think he was dead before the vehicle ran into that ravine."

"The coroner agree?"

"Yes—on the drive back to Williams Lake. He didn't say a word at the scene."

Coswell exhaled through pursed lips. Yes. Blakemore had done it again. It was four years, almost to the day, since the murders in the Monashees,* the first mess Blakemore got him dragged into.

"Okay. Now give me the bad news," he said. "You know how to handle a murder investigation. Why call me?"

"Complications."

"Like what?"

"The First Nations Police Force. They're stonewalling me."

"I didn't know they had a force in the Cariboo, and even though they obviously do, a dead Mountie equals Federal, not local—end of argument."

"Easy to say, but you haven't had to deal with the Tsanshmis. Tough as boot leather and stubborn as hell. Race relations up here aren't so good."

"I get the picture, but where do I fit in?"

"I'd like you to speak to Ward. His kind of political clout is the only thing that's going to give me the authority I need in this case, and you know how to talk to our revered leader."

Chief Inspector Ward was lord of the provincial RCMP and Coswell's immediate boss—a man with the same characteristics that Blakemore just used to describe the Tsanshmis.

"All right. One of our own is down. Someone has to pay. Now what, exactly, do you want?"

"It would be best if Ward did a face-to-face with the miserable bastard who heads up the native force—Chief Daniels. He's not the band chief. That's Chief Isaac who's two hundred years old and as communicative as a rock. Daniels runs the show."

---

* *Murder in the Monashees*, NeWest Press 2005

Coswell winced. He knew damn well that Ward wouldn't leave his Vancouver ivory tower to go to the Cariboo unless Queen Elizabeth happened to be touring the place. He'd send a delegate and Coswell knew just who that delegate would be.

✳✳✳

Blakemore was waiting for him the following morning at the Williams Lake airport terminal. The fifty-five-minute flight from Vancouver had been mercifully smooth. The dread of being stuck in an eighteen-seat turbo-prop airplane, not much more stable than a kite, in Coswell's opinion, had made for a restless night's sleep.

"You okay?" Blakemore said, remembering the green, motion-sick inspector who'd flown in to the Kootenay airport years before.

"I'm fine ... and hungry. It's lunchtime. Take me to the best steak house in town. I know they grow cows up here. Let's see if they know how to cook them."

"No problem there. Wife's gone to Vancouver, so I've been batching." To Blakemore, "batching" meant dining in restaurants.

Steaks at the Quarter Horse Cafe easily satisfied both men's standards — inch-and-a-half-thick sirloins smothered in caramelized onions, with huge baked potatoes on the side.

"Hold the greens," Blakemore told the waitress. "I don't want to overeat."

Business didn't commence until dessert and coffee were served. Coswell paused halfway through a forkful of saskatoon berry pie.

"Okay. Give me the whole story, and remember, I'm here as a consultant. This is your case."

Blakemore laid down his fork and leaned forward, looking around before he spoke. "They want to do the investigation themselves. They say it's on their land, so it's their right."

"Bullshit. I told you the federal laws take precedence. What's the problem?"

"Sam Hansen is the problem. Father of Brent, the dead rookie. He's kind of a god among the ranchers here. His grandfather literally opened up the Anahim Lake region in the early 1900s."

"And was hated by the natives for stealing their land?"

"You got it, even though it was all legal, fair and square. Federal government at the time gave out land grants to anyone willing to set up viable ranching."

Coswell laughed. "You mean the government stole their land. Well, that should have smoothed everything over."

Blakemore didn't laugh. He frowned and continued, speaking in a low voice. "Hansen found out right away about us getting pushed aside by the Tsanshmis and he raised hell. Came into the station boiling. Thank God the coroner kept his mouth shut about the cause of death or it would have been ten times worse."

Coswell shook his head. "When will people learn? Pissing everyone off gets you nowhere, but you did the right thing calling me in. I've got no axe to grind—I'll just lay down the law. You concentrate on solving the case. Leave the power brokers to me."

Blakemore gave a sigh of relief. "I thought you'd say that, so I've already arranged a couple of meetings. First one's this afternoon ... with Sam Hansen. Getting him off my back will be a great start."

Coswell nodded, then looked pensive. "I'm wondering. How did your rookie get assigned here? First posting's never in home territory."

"I told you. His old man's got power."

Despite his determination to let Blakemore handle the case, Coswell's years of being in command took over.

"I presume the boy grew up on the homestead. Must have

gone to school, mixed with the native kids. You might want to start looking there."

"I've already thought of that. Unfortunately, I have to get by the elders first—both native and white."

"Okay. Let's get going, but first we'll stop off at your station. I'll change into my uniform. Nothing like a little brass to impress the locals, much as I hate to wear the damn thing."

✱✱✱

Blakemore offered to hire one of the local logging helicopters to fly them in to Anahim, but Coswell would have nothing to do with it.

"We'll drive," he said. "I've never been to the Cariboo and I want to have a good look. I checked, and it should only take us a couple of hours. I noticed a number of reserves along the way. We might stop in at a few to let me get the flavour."

God knows where he checked, Blakemore thought. The drive would take closer to three or four hours and there was no telling what the inspector planned to get out of the local flavour. Reserves were not on the list of fun places to be for an RCMP officer, official visit or no.

Coswell drove. He'd correctly predicted the gut-wrenching curves along the way and had no wish to test his queasiness as a passenger. Blakemore did not suffer from motion-sickness but the inspector's apparent disregard of the posted speed signs gave him considerable trepidation. When the needle touched 120 kph, he could remain silent no longer.

"Jeesh, Inspector. Ninety's the limit on this road. We don't have to make it in two hours. Better to get there alive and without an embarrassing citation."

"Relax. We're on official business. Besides, I concentrate better when I drive fast. It's a lot safer that way and this is a great road. I'm enjoying it."

After two more curves, the coefficient of friction almost

reached zero on the back wheels, prompting Blakemore to try once more.

"See those red splotches every so often?"

"Yeah. Some animals got hit at night, I guess."

"Not just at night and some of the big ones are moose. You hit a moose and we're dead. Those long legs put the mass up about windshield level."

Coswell slowed to one hundred and ten. "Keep your eye out," he said.

They drove for a while in silence. Blakemore eventually became accustomed to the speed, although he did keep a constant lookout for anything that might dash in front of them.

"I've been thinking," Coswell said. "Why are the Tsanshmi so reluctant to allow an RCMP investigation? They couldn't possibly have the training or forensics to deal with something like this."

"Two reasons: one, the killer or killers could have been members of the band. There's enough bad blood around here to make that a real possibility. Checking it out themselves keeps the game on their turf."

"And then they can avoid the white man's justice. Is that it?"

"Maybe. They do have a different sense in that regard than we do."

"What? A couple of sessions with the healing circle? I've read about that."

"I don't know," Blakemore said. "I guess it depends on the circumstances and who did it."

"Like the killers were being abused by your rookie? Or maybe the Chief's son did the deed?"

"Could be."

"You said 'two reasons.' What's the second?"

"Sam Hansen has been mouthing off, spreading the word that Tsanshmis murdered his son. There's even a little vigilante talk going around I hear."

Coswell whistled. "You've got to be kidding. This isn't Mississippi north, is it?"

Blakemore shrugged. "Maybe closer than you think, and I'll bet the war paint started coming out of the closet the minute word got to the reserve about Hansen's raving."

"Great," Coswell said. "We're headed straight for enemy territory and I'm not even armed."

"Riot gun's mounted beside the emergency brake and I've got my sidearm," Blakemore said.

"I've never had to use either and don't plan to start now. We'll talk our way out of trouble. Trust me."

Blakemore didn't reply.

***

Coswell's interest in touring a reserve ended when Blakemore pointed out the first one, a series of dilapidated dwellings amidst what appeared to be an automobile graveyard.

After kilometres of intermittent barbed wire fencing and Black Angus cattle roaming in green fields, the entrance to the Hansen spread loomed on the right—a massive, weathered-pine arch with The Running H Ranch burned into the wood at its apex. As Coswell manoeuvred through the potholed dirt track leading to the ranch buildings, he silently blessed the Force's decision to supply rural units with decent suvs instead of the clunky city sedans.

"Have a heart, for heaven's sake. Slow down," Blakemore pleaded. "I've only got the one set of kidneys."

The main house looked as though it had been built a hundred years ago—log construction, small windows, and a traditional, full-length porch. An incongruous, late-model 350 Dodge Ram diesel with auxiliary lights from bumper to cab top, sat parked in front.

"Now there's a man's truck," Blakemore said. "Four-wheel drive and enough torque to pull a mountain. God, I wish I could afford one of those."

"Suitable on a ranch," Coswell said. "But just a big toy for you. You're better off with one of those little Suzuki Jeeps like you drove in Vancouver. Remember?" *

"I remember. Japanese sardine can. The claustrophobia gave me nightmares."

Coswell pulled the cruiser up behind the Dodge.

A small corral occupied what in the city would be the front yard. A lone figure leaned against it, one foot resting on a railing. He was hatless, his full head of white hair ruffled by the breeze — tall, lanky, wearing a denim shirt and jeans. A single black stallion ran about the enclosure, snorting its disapproval of the cruiser and the cloud of dust that came with it.

"Where the hell is everyone?" Coswell asked as he shifted the car into park.

Blakemore shrugged. "Mounties heading up your driveway tend to make some people around here scatter. The guy over there, by the way, is Hansen."

The man didn't move, seemingly ignoring his visitors, and didn't speak until Coswell and Blakemore stood beside him. Even then, he continued to watch the stallion pawing the dirt at the far side of the corral.

"That's Brent's animal," he said. "Best quarter horse in the whole damn country. Never told the boy that. Nobody could ride him except Brent. Useless to me. Useless to anybody now."

"We are sorry for your loss, Sam," Blakemore said, "and I'm also sorry to have to bother you, but Inspector Coswell here has come from Vancouver to help."

Hansen turned and looked at them, finally settling his gaze on Coswell. His pale blue eyes showed no sign of grief, only anger ... and resolve.

"Much appreciated," he said. "But I don't have a lot of faith

---

* West End Murders, NeWest Press 2008

in police right now. My son didn't run that car off the road. He drove a tractor when he was nine. Hauled hay with a pickup at fourteen. Never an accident, even in high school when the rest were raising hell. Nope, somebody murdered my son and I plan to find out who."

In just those few minutes, Coswell had a complete picture of the man. He was hard and unyielding, with standards probably only he could live up to—regretting now that he hadn't been easier on his son and seeking vengeance to make up for it.

"You'll have a much better chance of finding out what happened if you work with us," Coswell said. "We've got the necessary licenses, so to speak. People *have* to talk to us."

"They'll talk to me, too," Hansen said, and, realizing he'd said too much, changed the subject. "You could probably use a coffee about now. Let's go sit on the porch and I'll have Maggie bring something out for us."

As they walked to the house from the corral, Coswell wondered why this Maggie person hadn't appeared when they drove up. Surely the sound of the cruiser doors slamming would have carried into the house.

Hansen pointed to a row of rustic lounge chairs set in the shade of the overhang. "Get yourself comfortable," he said, then pulled the door open and shouted inside.

"Coffee time, Maggie. We've got two visitors. Bring some of that bannock you made ... and fixings to go with them — butter and jam."

To Coswell's dismay, Hansen took a chair beside Blakemore. All three now faced the yard, their expressions and body language largely hidden — not exactly conducive to productive interviewing. Hansen continued to stare straight ahead, only occasionally finding something interesting on the toe of his boot to alter his gaze.

Coswell got the talk going. "Sergeant Blakemore filled me

in on the situation here, particularly in regard to the Tsan-shmi problem, and—"

"A problem only to you," Hansen said, cutting him off. "I don't have to kowtow to those bastards. If they want war, I'll give it to them."

"These aren't the 1800s," Coswell said. "Taking the law into your own hands will just get you into deep trouble. Please, let us deal with this."

Hansen calmed down. His voice took on a sly undertone. "You've confirmed that my son's death was murder ... haven't you?"

Blakemore took the initiative. "We believe it was," he said.

Hansen merely nodded.

"Which makes it even more imperative that we handle it," Coswell said. "And I can tell you that the sergeant and I have a pretty good record solving cases like this. Give us a chance."

The door opened, interrupting the proceedings. A woman stepped out, carrying a basket covered with a calico cloth. She was very young, with pronounced native features: skin a burnished bronze, eyes almost black, shiny raven hair pulled into a tight horseshoe-shaped bun at the back of her head. Her ancestry was North American Indian, no doubt, but not west coast, more the chiselled features of the prairie or eastern tribes. She wore a white shirt, sleeves rolled down, buttoned at the wrists and tight-fitting jeans that accentuated perfect curves. In short, she was gorgeous.

Coswell watched, fascinated, as the woman dragged over a bench with her free hand, set the basket down, and began to serve its contents. She moved with the grace of a cat, each motion deliberate, her face expressionless, never once making eye contact.

She handed each man a cup of steaming coffee and offered bannock wedges neatly arranged on a china plate. The meal was tempting, but the men's attention remained focused on the girl.

"That's fine, Maggie," Hansen said. "We can handle the rest."

She turned and, without a word, went back into the house, pulling the door shut behind her with a faint click. Hansen pointed to the basket.

"Help yourselves," he said, and as they reached forward, "I can see that she made an impression on you, but don't be fooled. That girl's beauty is only skin deep. She's the last of Anne's projects, my late wife, before cancer ate her up last summer. Anne collected Vancouver street kids like other people rescue dogs from the pound. Maggie's a drug addict ... still on treatment, by the way—a job I plan to get rid of as soon as it can be arranged. Doling out methadone's not something I enjoy."

"I thought only physicians could do that," Blakemore said.

"The rules get bent a bit this far from civilization."

Coswell began to wonder if *any* rules applied this far from civilization. He felt as if he'd just been transported to the Old West, but he pulled himself sharply back to the present and got on with the business at hand — getting Hansen to back off the case.

"Have you considered that your son's killer might not have been a local, but just someone passing through — a fugitive, a drunk, or your everyday wacko psychopath? That happens not infrequently, you know. Nothing's safe for a policeman, not even a simple roadside check."

Hansen thought this over for a minute, but didn't buy the argument. "No. Whoever ran Brent's vehicle into that ravine knew the territory. Anyone else would have just hightailed it. Probably a spur of the moment thing, fit of temper and all that, but Brent's killer is right close by. Mark my words."

Coswell tried to think of a reasonable rebuttal but couldn't come up with one.

"Can you give us some names?" Blakemore asked.

"You can start with your drunk and abusive regulars. Check your own lists. I'll keep mine to myself. Don't want word to get out that the big bad whitey is looking for someone in particular. It's bad hunting practice to announce yourself."

That brought an end to the questioning. Coswell recognized the futility of trying to cool Hansen's thirst for vengeance. Time to move on. He took the last big bite from his piece of bannock, washed it down with a swallow of coffee, and stood up. He motioned to Blakemore.

"Time to mount up, Sergeant," he said, slightly embarrassed by his choice of words. "We've got a lot of ground to cover today."

Blakemore, having already finished his bannock, palmed another piece as he rose.

"We appreciate your talking to us," Coswell said, "and please pass on our thanks to your lovely Maggie for a delicious coffee break."

"I'll do that," Hansen replied. He got up from his chair but remained on the porch while the two Mounties returned to their cruiser and prepared to leave.

"Not a handshake kind of guy, it appears," Coswell said, turning the key in the ignition.

"You got that right," Blakemore said and began eating his purloined treat, scattering crumbs on his lap as he did so.

★★★

As they drove west, the country changed abruptly from huge tracts of green grass and alfalfa fields to scrub pines and untamed wilderness.

"They run out of barbed wire?" Coswell asked, noting the absence of fencing.

"We're on reserve land," Blakemore said. "Indian cattle roam free. I'd suggest you slow down a bit."

He'd barely gotten the last statement out before they rounded a curve and Coswell slammed on the brakes.

"Jesus! There are cows all over the road," he said. "That's got to be against the law on a major highway. Someone could get killed running into one of those things."

"No law says you have to fence your land up here. Onus is on the drivers and I can tell you if you hit any of that beef, you'll have to pay for it."

"Damn. Now what do we do? They're moving around like they own the place."

He leaned on the horn, but the cattle—steers, cows, and a multitude of calves—barely paid any attention, continuing to graze on either side of the highway, crossing unpredictably back and forth.

"You get out and shoo them away," Coswell said.

"Not a chance. Cows with calves can be real ornery. I'm not into getting myself gored."

Coswell hammered the horn a couple more times and tried to ease the cruiser forward with little success. Finally, the solution came to him. He turned the dial on the siren to full blast and flicked the switch.

Stampede! The herd split up and thundered into the bush on both sides leaving the road clear. Coswell pulled the gearshift into first and burned rubber for fifty metres before slipping it into drive.

"I hope the tribal police didn't hear that," Blakemore said. "They'll think we're infringing for sure."

"Bugger them. If they let their cows run loose like that they deserve a little infringing."

"So much for diplomacy."

"Never mind. Last sign I saw said we're just forty klicks from this place with the unpronounceable name—T-s-i-l-h-q-o-x-t'i-n. How the hell do you say that?"

"Chilcotin," Blakemore said.

"Really?"

"Used to be called Coxton, named after some gold commissioner from way back, but when the Tsanshmis chose it as their band office, the name got changed quick. There's a bit of a nasty history around that — white men slaughtered, deception, warriors hanged — a real mess. Called the Chilcotin Wars."

"Ah. An amateur historian. You surprise me."

"I do read, you know," Blakemore said, miffed. "And I wanted to get some idea as to why there's so much racial friction around here."

"Get different cultures and religions together in close quarters anywhere in the world and there'll be friction, especially when one of them arrived first. But I admire your efforts."

***

As they approached Tsilhqoxt'in, a church, perched halfway up a dry hillside on a dinky, bulldozed landing, caught Coswell's eye. A long set of stairs led up to it. The building was tiny, but a disproportionately high steeple topped with a wooden cross rose from its roof, making the whole thing look top-heavy.

"I wonder if they do funerals up there," Coswell said. "Must have to dig a couple of extra graves to allow for heart attacks."

The village was set back from the highway a hundred metres. The potholes in the dirt access road were even deeper than those at the Hansen ranch. "Main Street" consisted of three buildings, all facing the highway: a garage with two pumps, a ramshackle building sporting a Coke sign on the door, and a long park-type trailer. Coswell made out a sign reading BAND OFFICE above a door at one end of the latter and one reading TRIBAL POLICE over an identical door at the other. The residences, twelve in all, were simple, un-adorned boxes, most in need of repair, but each with a television satellite receiver. Derelict vehicles and kids' toys supplied most of the landscaping. A few young children loitered at the side of the dusty road. There were no sidewalks.

The police cruiser, parked in front of the band office, ap-peared identical to the one he and Blakemore had driven up in, complete with a blue and red light bar, but TRIBAL POLICE replaced RCMP within the logo.

Blakemore led the way up the office stairs. Coswell trailed, still looking around. "God knows how this place rates bold print and a dot on the map," he said. "There can't be more than fifty people living here, although I can see why. The amenities leave a lot to be desired."

"Pretty close guess," Blakemore said. "Most of the popula-tion lives out on the land, small ranching and the like. They do their shopping in Anahim or Williams Lake."

He hesitated for a moment at the door, debating if he should knock, but then decided to go right in.

Two men were seated in the office, both in uniform. One, much younger and slimmer, sprang from his chair when the Mounties entered. The other, a man of about fifty, give or take ten years, remained seated in what looked like an armchair on wheels. Twenty pounds of extra fat filled out his frame and face, erasing what otherwise would have been wrinkles.

"Didn't hear a helicopter," he said. "You drive?"

"Yep," Blakemore replied. "This here's Inspector Coswell from Vancouver."

The man's eyes flickered with amusement. "Bringin' in the big guns, eh?"

He nodded to Coswell and cocked his head towards his associate.

"That's Richard. Don't let the uniform fool you. He's just an intern helping out while my deputy's on holidays. Still in school learning to be a cop. I'm Chief Daniels."

Richard bristled.

"I'm in my last year of criminology at Simon Fraser University," he said.

Daniels shrugged. "Whatever. But these men have come for a heavy talk about territorial matters, Richard. Chief of police-type talk. Why don't you take the cop-mobile out there for a spin? Come back in an hour or so."

He might as well have slapped the young man across the face, judging from his reaction. Richard stood for a moment and then bolted out the door.

"Was that necessary?" Coswell asked. "Not much of an internship if he's chased away from discussion of a policing matter."

"He's a little too keen at times. Gets these hifalutin scientific ideas that only cloud the picture. Better we do a man-to-man and keep everything straight."

Coswell recalled Blakemore's "stonewalled" expression. Chief Daniels had a game plan, all right ... chiselled into stone.

3

RICHARD DELORME SLID into the front seat of the tribal police cruiser and slammed the door, his handsome features distorted by anger and embarrassment. He shifted into reverse and started to back up.

"Look out!"

He jammed on the brake just as a tiny figure on a pink tricycle appeared in his outside rear-view mirror — a child, and he'd almost run her over! His anger melted in an instant.

The shout came from farther away. He looked to his left

and spotted the source: a boy about ten years old standing in front of the store clutching a sketch pad.

Richard gripped the wheel hard for a moment, then reached forward and turned off the ignition. He got out of the cruiser and walked over to where the boy stood.

"Thanks, Jimmy," he said. "That was close."

The boy looked down at his feet.

"Dumb sister," he said. "I'm supposed to be looking after her, but she don't listen."

"Little kids are like that. You can't watch them all the time and if anyone's at fault, it's me."

Jimmy continued to look down; the scare still fresh on his face … along with the guilt.

"No school today?"

"Teachers' holiday."

Richard laughed. "A professional day, you mean."

The boy nodded.

"What are you drawing?" Richard asked. "May I see it?"

The boy shyly handed the pad over. He'd sketched the cruiser.

"That's really good, Jimmy, and I mean it. You've done it all in pen. That makes it hard. No rubbing out the mistakes."

The squeak of a tricycle, badly needing oil, announced the arrival of Jimmy's little sister, who was about five years old.

"He done it with his new pen," she said.

"Is it a special kind, Jimmy?" Richard asked.

"Nope. Just ordinary."

"Is too special," the girl said. "Got a picture of a Mountie on it and a red handle."

The boy glared at her.

An image flashed across Richard's mind: he remembered a pen just like that — Brent Hansen's pen. He'd kidded his friend about it. "Worried about getting blisters from all the tickets you're going to write," he'd said.

"Let me see the pen, Jimmy."

"Don't have to."

"Yes, you do. I'm telling you as a policeman. Now, hand it over."

The boy looked for a moment as though he might turn and run, but slowly shoved his hand into his pocket and drew out the pen. Richard took it and knew instantly that it was Brent's.

"Where did you get it?"

"Found it on the road."

"What road?"

"I forgot."

Richard reached forward and grasped the boy's shoulder. "I know who this pen belonged to, Jimmy, and he's dead. I need you to tell me exactly where you found it and when. If you don't, a whole lot of serious trouble is going to land on your head. Now give."

Jimmy began to cry. His sister followed suit, but Richard merely tightened his grip.

"If you tell me," he said. "You won't be in any trouble. I promise."

The boy looked up, tears streaming down. "Yes I will. They'll hurt me."

Richard let the boy's shoulder go. Through the tears he could see terror. "They?" he said. "Mounties don't hurt kids. You know that."

Jimmy hung his head. "Not Mounties ... them."

Richard could hardly breathe; his heart raced. The boy had witnessed Brent's murder!

"Jimmy. Who were they? Who killed the Mountie?"

"I got to go home now," the boy said. "Mom will be mad if I don't. Come on, Cindy."

Richard let them go. He'd talk to Jimmy again, but not out in plain view where them might be watching. Now all he had to do was decide whether he'd let that asshole Daniels in on his discovery. A gut feeling told him to keep the information quiet for the time being.

He went back to the tribal police car and started it up again. This time he carefully checked his rear-view mirror before he pulled away. A cruise up the highway would give him time to think.

THEY WERE GETTING NOWHERE. The tribal police chief blocked them at every turn.

"Everything points to murder," Coswell said. "Blow to the back of Constable Hansen's head. C'mon. That didn't come from an accident. And why would he even be up that road? Sergeant Blakemore tells me it's nothing more than a trail."

"Found a hunting rifle on the floor of the wreck," Daniels said. "Figure the boy saw a big buck and chased it with the cruiser. Probably had the rifle in the back and when he went into the ravine, it came flying forward and hit him on the back of the head ... tragic accident."

For a moment, Coswell couldn't speak. Did this rube really think he was going to buy that?

"Yep," Daniels said. "A real tragic accident."

Obviously he did.

Coswell exploded. "Listen, you poor excuse for a lawman. One of our men has been brutally murdered — a cop-killing, for Christ's sake. Where's your sense of duty?"

Daniels remained placid. "Duty's done," he said. "Report's been filed. Case closed."

Coswell leapt to his feet and turned to Blakemore. "Let's get out of here, Sergeant," he said. "Talking to this man is a total waste of time."

Blakemore rose from his chair, bewildered by the turn of events, and shocked at seeing Coswell lose it. He almost regretted bringing him in on the case.

Daniels didn't move from his chair. Coswell paused at the door and turned back to face him.

"I'm going to turn this God-forsaken place upside down until I get answers, and if you raise just one finger to stop me, I'll bring Ottawa down on your head so hard you'll be lucky to get a job as horseshit sweeper at the local rodeo."

With that, he stomped out, Blakemore right behind him.

Back in the cruiser, Coswell didn't say a word, his face grim. He started the engine, backed up, and swung onto the access road at a speed that would have bounced them off their seats if not for the seatbelts. Blakemore reached frantically for anything that would steady him — dashboard, door handle, roof.

"Whoa, Trigger," he pleaded. "You're going to bust an axle."

He caught a glimpse of Coswell — grinning from ear to ear. "Got to keep up the charade," he said.

"Charade?"

"Fear, my man, fear. We'll get cooperation from that complacent lout, I can assure you ... indirectly. He's just witnessed a hornets' nest stirred up and there's a good chance he might get stung. Having two pissed-off Mounties combing the place will force him to check how well his ass is covered. I'm going to drop you off in a minute and I want you to hoof it back there and watch him."

"What are you going to do?"

"I'm going to find that intern and have a talk with him. He's out on the highway somewhere and I've got a fifty-fifty chance of running into him by going west. If he's gone in the opposite direction, try to intercept him before he turns into the village. Get yourself a spot where you can see the station and the highway east."

"You think he'll cooperate?"

"I have no doubt. He's mad, and rightfully so. You don't get loyalty from bright, ambitious people like that by putting them down. The boy's on his way up in the world and he knows it. Daniels is a fool."

When he was sure he couldn't be seen, he pulled the cruiser to the side of the road and let Blakemore out.

"We'll rendezvous at the gas station in an hour. If I'm not back by then, try going over to the police trailer and use the 'good cop' routine on Daniels. Maybe you can get him to let his guard down a bit. Oh, and by the way, I've decided to extend my time up here. You need help. We'll be a team again."

Blakemore watched the cruiser pull away. He didn't like the feeling of humility that had come over him when he realized how cagey the inspector had been. The brand new sergeant's stripes on his shoulder felt slightly uncomfortable. With a sigh, he turned and started back toward the village, cutting through the bush until he found the perfect spot to start his vigil.

✳✳✳

Coswell decided that twenty minutes would be enough of a drive in one direction. He reasoned that the young intern, Richard, should have turned back by then. Daniels had told him to return in an hour or so. Very little in the way of traffic appeared on the highway: one or two semi-trailers, a few logging trucks and a number of pickups, most of the latter driven by natives. When the twenty minutes had passed, he slowed to a crawl and spun the steering wheel, pushing the cruiser into a tight u-turn.

He barely got up to speed again when red and blue lights flashed in his rear-view mirror.

"Shit!" he said to no one as the cruiser bore down on him. He flicked on his flashers. The vehicle slowed and pulled in behind him. Coswell recognized Richard behind the wheel. He turned off the flashers and when he saw the intern do the same, he rolled down his window and stuck his arm out to signal a right turn.

At the first side road he came to, Coswell made the turn and drove fifty metres before coming to a stop. Richard followed, pulled up behind him, and got out. Coswell did the same and waited for him to walk over.

"Didn't want to create a scene back there while you wrote me out a ticket," Coswell said.

The young man looked confused for a second until Coswell began to smile. Richard grinned in return.

"I don't have the authority to give you a ticket, anyway," he said. "Just a warning. Besides, I'm not into power-tripping. This internship's strictly a way of getting as much as possible on my CV when I apply to the RCMP."

"You're going to follow in Brent Hansen's footsteps?"

"Yes," he replied, with such conviction that Coswell knew he had an ally.

"Tell me about it," he said. "Did you know him very well?"

"Since elementary school. He was a couple of grades ahead but we got to know one another through horses and rodeos. We became best friends, actually."

"What kind of person was he?" Coswell asked.

"Great guy. Nothing like his bigoted old man or some of the other white ranchers' kids. Didn't look down on anyone ... even an Indian. Everybody liked him."

Uh-oh, Coswell thought, *another saint*. But saints weren't immune from enemies. He could think of a few who met rather gory ends, including the Messiah Himself.

"Unfortunately, somebody didn't like him," he said. "He was murdered, you know."

"I know."

"You do? Chief Daniels doesn't think so."

Anger again. Coswell waited. Finally, Richard let go. "He wouldn't listen to a thing I said. I took the forensics option at school last year and I've done a lot of reading. That crime scene could have been preserved. We came up right behind the fire truck. He did nothing when he saw the cruiser burning—just stood back and let the fire guys at it. They asked him if they should haul it up and he told them to go ahead. And he made no effort to keep the gawkers back. They tramped around everywhere."

"Did he do anything inside the vehicle before Sergeant Blakemore and the coroner arrived?"

"Yes he did, even though I said we shouldn't disturb it."

"He told us a rifle had been found."

"News to me. He must have found it while I was trying to move the crowd back. But it's no surprise that Brent had a rifle with him. He was nuts about hunting, and deer season started on Saturday."

"Daniels thinks that was the cause of death, hit on the back of the head when it came flying forward."

Richard thought for a moment. "I don't think so. I didn't see any sign the vehicle rolled. Looked like it slid down nose first. Also, I find it hard to believe that Brent would take a police vehicle up that poor excuse for a road just to chase after a deer. And even if he did, his rifle would be beside him. Stop, get out, and walk around the back to get the gun? No way. The deer would have been long gone. One more thing doesn't fit either, if he was road hunting."

"What's that?"

"The seatbelt. No one hunts with his seatbelt on."

Coswell whistled. "Wow. I'll bet you're acing those criminology courses. That's fine deductive reasoning."

Richard shrugged. "Just common sense."

"Nope, that's deductive reasoning. Welcome to the world of practical investigation. We're glad to have you."

The young man glowed. "Thanks," he said. "I don't get much praise around here."

Coswell could hardly contain his delight. He'd found the mother lode of local information and he wasn't about to let it get away.

"Let's go sit for a while. My legs aren't what they used to be and maybe you'd like to get a look inside our state-of-the-art cruiser. Nothing but the best for our district sergeant."

Richard perked up like a bird dog. Coswell guessed that the tribal vehicle contained only the basics, but he wasn't sure; the interior of a police vehicle was so familiar to him that he took all the gadgets for granted. Richard, however, raved about it.

"I've heard about these inboard computers," he said. "Not much use out here but I'll bet they're a godsend to city police." He laughed. "I'm surprised Willy's Pond rates one, though."

"Willy's Pond?"

"That's what the locals call Williams Lake."

Coswell pressed his advantage, satisfied that he'd established a good rapport. "I must confess to you that your Chief Daniels has been less than helpful to our investigation. He's obviously thinking along different lines from us. I'd like you to join Sergeant Blakemore and me on this ... officially. What do you say?"

"Officially?"

"I'll arrange to have you made an auxiliary RCMP constable. That will look even better on your CV and the pay's probably as good as your internship. Blakemore and I will be your sponsors. You've already got a uniform that's close enough."

Richard hesitated briefly. Coswell knew the young man was too bright to miss the obvious snow job, but the offer was too good to turn down.

"I'd like that," he said. "And I get no pay as an intern; just the privilege of working with Daniels."

"Great. Let's start right now. Give me your take on all this. I'm particularly interested in who you think might be the guilty party in Brent Hansen's murder."

Richard smiled. "I can't answer that exactly, but I'm a hair's breadth from finding out." He related the incident with the boy, Jimmy.

"My God," Coswell said. "You've just made my day."

✸✸✸

Richard and Coswell, engrossed in their conversation, paid no attention to the pickup that slowed briefly when it came abreast of them, and then sped off along the highway heading east, its two occupants disturbed by what they saw.

"Jeesh, dat's Richert talkin' to a white cop."

"Yess."

Five minutes of silence passed before either spoke again.

"We neetah go huntin'."

"Yess."

✸✸✸

Hunger pangs stabbed at Blakemore and he prayed that Coswell wouldn't take much longer. Without his rifle and the anticipation of a big, fat buck coming into range, bush-sitting offered no satisfaction. His view wasn't the least inspiring: the Tribal Police office and the highway occupied the east-side view; nothing happening in the former and just a bit of local traffic on the latter—no sign of the intern.

He gazed west. A vehicle appeared in the distance. Coswell? He watched it approach, but instead of a police car, an old rattletrap of a pickup appeared. It turned into the village, bounced through the potholes and came to a stop in front of the Band office. Two men got out. Both wore cowboy hats, denim pants, and jackets. He couldn't see their boots, but they hobbled along like they'd just got off their horses. At first, he thought they were going into the office, but they continued on to Daniels end of the trailer and disappeared through the door.

Ten minutes later, they came out, got back into the pickup and returned to the highway heading west just as the two police vehicles came into view, putting Blakemore in a quandary — should he flag the cruisers down or remain hidden? He chose the latter. The young intern might not be favourably impressed by an RCMP sergeant spying on his community from the bushes. He waited until he saw both men enter the tribal police office before he emerged and began the dusty walk to join them. He'd just reached the parking area when the door to Daniels office flew open. First Coswell appeared, then Richard, both looking grim. Coswell's wink let him know that the charade continued but he wondered what was happening with the intern.

"Come with us," Coswell told Richard. "Coffee's on me and I'm badly in need of a doughnut. Can you recommend somewhere close?"

"Yes. Gramma's. She doesn't do doughnuts, but she'll have something just as good and it won't cost you a cent."

They piled into the cruiser. Richard took the back seat.

"What happened in there?" Blakemore asked.

"Whole lot of manure hit the fan," Coswell replied. "Say hello to our new colleague, by the way: Auxiliary RCMP Constable Richard Delorme."

Blakemore's eyes widened. "Can you really do that?" he said.

"Just a matter of a little paperwork, but I'll make it effective as of today."

Blakemore smiled. Another Coswell manoeuvre.

"How did Daniels take the news?"

"Not well. Apparently our Richard was more valuable to

him than he let on. Moaned about the work he's got to do now all on his lonesome."

Richard grunted. "Load of crap. Brent's so-called accident is the biggest thing he's ever had to deal with. Mostly all he does is hand out tickets to people speeding through the reserve. Says the money goes into tribal coffers, but I've been with him, and a lot of those tickets don't get written. Cash up front at fifty per cent of the full fine is a deal and most folks don't pass it up. I'd love to see the books on that."

***

In sharp contrast to the dusty village, Gramma's property, less than five minutes away, displayed a profusion of colour and a sense of pride in her surroundings — flowering shrubs, roses, a neatly trimmed, lush green hedge. Her house was a whitewashed log cabin set off by flowerboxes stuffed with red geraniums under each window. The only sign of dilapidation was a dented pickup of questionable vintage parked in the gravel driveway. Coswell pulled the cruiser alongside.

An elderly lady stepped out onto the front step, her kindly brown face offset by thick snow-white hair. She hurriedly unfastened her apron and held it in her hand. Coswell immediately thought of his own grandmother, who would have understood: never greet a visitor with your apron on.

"I want you to meet Gramma Birch," Richard said. "The lady who raised me from a runt."

"Ya wurnt no trubble," the old lady said. "Cum in 'itch yur frenss, Richert."

The interior of the house reflected the outside — neat and even more colourful. Intricately designed blankets served as throws over much of the seating; bright pictures of mythical native creatures lined the walls and on every available shelf sat finely woven baskets.

"Gramma is Coast Salish, as you can probably tell,"

Richard said. "Aside from some carving and beadwork, there's not much in the way of artistic artefacts in the Chilcotin. Ranching, I guess, didn't allow for much creative time."

Whatever communication took place between Richard and his grandmother went unspoken, but the old lady hustled into the kitchen to brew tea and put together a plate of cakes and cookies. Gramma didn't do coffee, obviously.

Once all had been served, Gramma took her leave. "Goin' fer a smok," she said. "You men tawk."

They watched her pick up a can of tobacco and a package of papers from the kitchen table and then go out the back door. Richard smiled.

"She does that even in the winter," he said. "Just for me. I don't know where she heard about secondhand smoke, but she did."

Coswell wanted to know more about this young man and his grandmother, but business came first. After two swallows of the excellent tea and one and a half poppy seed cakes, he began.

"Anything to report, Paul?"

"Nothing, except for two over-the-hill cowboys paying a very brief visit to Daniels. You must have passed them. They pulled out just before you drove in."

"Didn't notice them," Coswell said, but Richard had.

"Bill and Art Johnson," he said. "Sons of Chief Isaac, our Tsanshmi Band chief. They've been hunting partners of Daniels' for years. It's getting near the rut now. They were probably arranging a hunt."

"In ten minutes?" Blakemore said. "They literally came and went."

"Never mind," Coswell said. "Richard is about to break the case wide open."

Blakemore almost spilled his tea. "He what?"

Coswell told him about Jimmy, the boy who likely witnessed the killing.

"That's assuming I can get him to talk," Richard said. "He's a scared little fellow right now."

"We'll definitely leave that up to you," Coswell said. "Meanwhile, the two of us have need of a hotel close by. We'll set up shop here. Williams Lake is too far away."

"I'm afraid what few hotels there are shut down this time of year," Richard said. "The tourists have all gone home." Then, after a moment's thought. "If comfort's not too important, there is the Anahim Hotel."

"Sounds fine to me," Blakemore said. "Beats camping out under our emergency blanket."

Coswell shot him a glance. "We'll check it out," he said.

***
***

Comfortable now with Gramma's tea break in their stomachs, Coswell and Blakemore continued on toward Anahim.

"Let me know when we get to the turn-off to your crime scene," Coswell said, scanning the highway far ahead for more cows.

"It'll come up pretty quick," Blakemore said. "There's an old gravel logging road that parallels the highway all the way to Anahim. Serves as an access to a number of properties. The trail to the crime scene branches off from it. But do you really want to go up there? I took pictures of everything and the wreck's gone."

"Of course it's gone, presumably to Williams Lake, awaiting forensic examination."

Blakemore squirmed. "Actually it's at a garage in Anahim. Daniels called up a tow truck from there to come get it. I just haven't gotten around yet to arranging the transfer."

"And you think no one will touch it? Isn't scavenging a way of life in this country?"

"Not much left to scavenge. It's burned pretty bad."

Coswell didn't look reassured. "I do want to go up to the site," he said. "But first thing when we arrive in Anahim is check out that vehicle, burned to a crisp or not."

Blakemore was saved further embarrassment when the road to the crime scene appeared just ahead.

"That's it to the right," he said. "There's a short stretch of gravel, then it gets primitive. No better than a wagon trail. You'll really have to drive slow on that."

"Just keep watching for moose."

"And cows."

"Right. And cows."

Blakemore needn't have worried about speed. The vehicle strained with the tighter switchbacks and increasing slope, forcing Coswell to use the lowest gears. He marvelled that logging trucks had once negotiated the route.

Ultimately, the road dead-ended on an abandoned landing.

"This is it," Blakemore said and pointed to the front edge. "He went over there."

Coswell brought the cruiser to a stop and got out. Blakemore followed.

"You can see what Richard and I meant about the crime scene, eh? Tracks all over the place. When the coroner and I drove in, most of the spectators were gone, but half the population must have come up here."

Coswell didn't reply. He merely glanced down to confirm Blakemore's comments before walking to the edge where the car had gone over. He gazed down the slope.

"Not so steep. My guess is the killers lit the vehicle on fire. We'll check the wreck and see if the gas cap's off. Maybe even find some ash residue from the rag they used."

Blakemore nodded. "No use going down there," he said. "I had a look while the coroner packed up. Bootprints everywhere again. The volunteer firemen helped the tow truck operator hook his cable to the back bumper."

Coswell stood for a moment longer, then turned and walked back to the cruiser.

"Well, we know one thing for certain. Hansen was right. The killers knew the area. Nowhere lower down could they have staged a scene like this. Narrows the search, for sure."

✱✱✱

They spoke little on the way back to the highway. The return route, all downhill, allowed Coswell to amuse himself again by taking the hairpins at the cruiser's limit, ignoring Blakemore's white-knuckle grip on the door handle.

"Always liked off-roading," Coswell said. "First car of my own was an old Jeep my father gave me. Didn't give a damn what I did to it, so I put it through its paces. I'll bet there are still tracks of mine in the Okanagan bush that nobody can match."

Blakemore didn't reply until they pulled back onto the pavement.

"I believe you," he said.

✱✱✱

A two-runway airfield announced the suburbs of Anahim Lake. Coswell's spirits rose.

"Good. First sign of real civilization since we left Williams Lake. This is more like it."

Blakemore decided to let the bubble burst on its own.

"Good God," Coswell said when they drove in. "This can't be it. A double big dot on the map and a sign that says 'Hub of the Chilcotin.' Christ, there are bigger hubs on a golf cart."

"This is it," Blakemore assured him. "Anahim Hotel's right over there."

"You mean that replica of a saloon from a low-budget western?"

"Quaint, isn't it?"

Coswell groaned. "I'm feeling faint. I need food, but I suppose you're going to tell me this is the only place in town to eat."

"Took the words right out of my mouth. No need for restaurants around here. The bar downstairs in the hotel serves good food and there isn't much of a gourmet crowd for anything fancier."

The lack of gourmet cuisine certainly hadn't affected the hotel's business. There wasn't a parking space to be had for an entire block ... except at the fire hydrant directly in front. Coswell manoeuvred the cruiser into it.

Both Mounties ignored the momentary hush that came over the bar when they walked in, accustomed to the reaction after their years in the Force. But the waitress, a husky young woman carrying a full tray of beer mugs, didn't bat an eyelash when she saw them; instead, she pointed with her free hand to a corner table, still littered with plates and glasses.

"Take that one," she said. "I'll clean it up in a minute. Menu's on the board."

They made their way to the table, eyes watering from the smoke in the room.

"What happed to the no smoking in a public place law that exists everywhere else in this province?" Coswell said when they sat down.

"Pretty hard to enforce it up here," Blakemore replied. "And no one truly gives a damn. I kind of like it. Gives the place atmosphere."

"You're sick."

The food was good, smoke or no smoke: cheeseburgers, generous with the beef, and potato wedges, crisp and delicious. Coswell asked for a side of mayonnaise to dip his in.

"Weird," their waitress said, but she got it for him.

Blakemore ordered a pint of lager.

"What wines do you have?" Coswell asked.

"Both ... red and white."

She spoke with a touch of pride, not humour, so Coswell didn't pursue the subject.

"I think I'll have a beer too. See if you can find something brown."

***

They didn't hurry their meal. Both ordered wild strawberry pie with ice cream for dessert, then coffee. By the time they finished and checked into the hotel for the night, dusk had fallen.

"Damn," Coswell said. "We should have checked out your rookie's cruiser first thing. They probably roll up the sidewalks in this town at six. Garage will be closed."

But it wasn't. The owner came out the minute he saw the cruiser drive in and welcomed them. "Thank goodness," he said. "Somebody to tell me what to do with this thing. Daniels, the bloody useless Indian, gave me no instructions other than to haul the mess here."

Coswell found the statement remarkable since the owner appeared to be native himself.

"I'm Tom," the man said. "Tom Porter."

The wreck, still tied down on a flat-deck trailer, looked surprisingly intact, aside from the blackened surface and gutted interior. The headlights were smashed, the grill pushed in, and the windshield shattered, but the bumper had minimal damage. The doors were all shut. Coswell gazed at it for a moment, then turned and spoke to the garage owner: "We'll need this transported to Williams Lake. I'll give you a signed authorization tomorrow morning after I've had a chance to look it over in better light. Meanwhile, I don't want anyone to lay a finger on it. Understood?"

"You're the boss," Tom said. "And nobody has touched it since I got it here. Who would want to anyway? Nothing worth taking."

As the two officers walked back to their vehicle, Tom had one more thought. "I don't suppose you could sign a cheque at the same time, eh?"

Coswell smiled. "Payment on delivery," he said. "But don't worry. Ottawa's good for it."

"I've heard that before," the man muttered.

5

RICHARD YAWNED. Seven o'clock. Way too early. Normally he didn't leave his grandmother's house until eight-thirty. Daniels never got in before nine and the walk to the village took only twenty minutes.

He marched along, swinging his arms in the cold morning air, telling himself to wake up. Jimmy would be leaving his house shortly for the school bus and he wanted to intercept him as soon as he stepped out the door. He knew the boy would be alone; his only sibling, the sister, was too young for school and the village parents almost never walked their children to the bus. He remembered when his grandmother insisted on seeing him off on his first day of school, embarrassing him. When Gramma moved safely out of earshot, the other kids called him a sissy. They were lucky she didn't hear or she'd have cuffed their ears.

He contemplated school-bus life for the kids. The elementary school in Anahim was fifty minutes away; the high school in Williams Lake, two hours. No wonder so many dropped out.

Brent Hansen had made the trip more bearable for Richard, he remembered. Bullying at any level came to a quick halt when Brent and his sister got on the bus. Brent wouldn't tolerate such behaviour, and since half the kids' fathers depended on Sam Hansen one way or another, either working for him or using his influence to market their cattle, no one challenged him.

Richard asked him once why the sensitivity, since the bullying rarely involved him.

"It's cruel," he said. "And it hurts."

When not in use, the bus remained parked at the gas station. The village kids boarded it there, arriving at the last minute, squeezing that extra few minutes of bliss from their warm beds. The drivers, over the years, were never natives. Too unreliable, according to the school board. Mostly they were loggers or cowboys injured in some accident, too crippled to do anything else. They drove in each morning, parked their personal vehicles, gassed up the bus and had it warm for the kids when they arrived. Their only fault, if they had one, was their total lack of concern for anything going on in the seats behind them. The load, from their point of view, needed no more attention than the logs or cattle they had formerly transported.

Frank, the present driver, stood at the gas pump watching the meter tick off the gallons. Litres hadn't arrived yet at the village. Richard gave him a wave.

Jimmy's family lived in one of the boxes behind the main street. Richard vaguely remembered the father, a shiftless fellow who deserted them a few years back. His wife Gertrude spent most of her day watching TV, smoking, and drinking beer.

He waited at the end of the sidewalk in front of the house. Best to avoid any conversation with Gertrude first thing in the morning. The previous night's drinking would have left her in a foul mood. He watched the children emerge from the houses up and down the block, funnelling like ants down to the gas station—all but Jimmy. The heat generated from his brisk walk began to wear off and a chill settled in. Eventually, the bus pulled away and he had no choice but to go up to the door and knock, hoping that Jimmy might answer. No such luck. Gertrude, looking like the wrath of God in her ratty housecoat and ridiculous bunny slippers, opened the door instead.

"Richard," she said. "What do you want?"

"I want to talk to Jimmy," he said.

Her eyes narrowed. "What for? He's a good boy. Whatever they said he done, he didn't."

"He didn't do anything, Gertrude. I just want to speak to him."

Any normal mother would have gone on from there, but Gertrude apparently didn't care as long as it wasn't a police matter.

"He's sick," she said. "You'll have to come back some other time."

"How's he sick? It'll just take a minute."

Gertrude didn't budge. "Gut ache. Now go away, Richard. I'm not feelin' so hot either."

The door closed in his face. He debated pounding on it and demanding to see the boy. After all, his new RCMP status should give him that right, but an angry mother standing around would not make for a good interview. He didn't want to disappoint Inspector Coswell, but it would be better to wait a day for Jimmy to recover, or go over later in the afternoon when Gertrude, at least, would be feeling better, courtesy several beers.

He turned and started the long walk back to his grandmother's. She'd be happy to see him. His leaving without breakfast did not sit well with her. The thought of bacon and eggs with homemade bread, toasted and saturated with butter, cheered him. He'd phone the Anahim Hotel from there and talk to Coswell.

***

"Good timing, Richard," Coswell said, speaking on the hotel phone. "We just finished a remarkably wonderful breakfast in the bar of all places and I've had a great night's sleep. It's like a tomb here at night. I could barely hear Blakemore's snores at the other end of the corridor."

Richard told him the bad news regarding his abortive interview with the boy.

"No matter. You've done the right thing waiting for better circumstances. Meanwhile, why don't you come up here? We're going over to check out Brent's cruiser at the garage. A criminologist's eye would be useful."

Coswell could almost feel the young man's enthusiasm. "I'll be there right away. I'm at Gramma's."

"Will that old pickup I saw in the yard get you here?"

Richard laughed. "No problem. It runs better than it looks."

"Okay, but don't break any speed limits. Your Chief Daniels might be out on highway patrol. Also, Sergeant Blakemore and I have to do some long distance check-ins with our respective offices before we leave the hotel."

"Chief Daniels will barely be out of bed," Richard said. "I'll see you shortly."

***

Tom Porter appeared to be disembowelling a large tractor when they walked over to his garage. He stopped working only long enough to acknowledge their presence.

"Mornin'," he said. "Got no time for chitchat right now, but you men have at 'er. Just let me know when you're finished so I can roust somebody up to drive it to the Pond."

They went around to the back and stood for a moment surveying the burnt wreck.

"Fire damage concentrated at the rear," Coswell said. "That's consistent with the gas tank being the incendiary."

A smile tugged at the corner of Blakemore's mouth. "Only one little problem."

"What?"

"The filler door's shut."

"So it is."

They'd made only one lap around the flat deck when Richard pulled up in a cloud of dust. He gave a wave in Tom's direction and came over to join them.

"Have I missed anything?"

"No," Blakemore replied. "We just got started. Nothing much useful to see so far."

"True," Coswell said. "But let's get on with it. We'll open the driver's door first."

Blakemore reached for the handle. Coswell stopped him. "Whoa," he said. "Fingerprints."

"Fingerprints? You've got to be kidding. There are probably ten sets on that door—firemen, cops, tow truck operator ...."

"And the killer who drove it up to that landing," Coswell said.

Richard joined in. "Still worth a try," he said. "It would take a lot of sorting out, but it's possible. There may even be some DNA."

"Gloves, please," Coswell said.

Blakemore, disgruntled, fetched three pair from the cruiser.

As soon as he'd put his on, Coswell opened the door and looked inside. He peered around for a minute or so and then reached under the dash, found a lever, and gave it a yank. "See if that released the gas tank door," he said.

Richard was closest.

"Yep. It popped," he said.

"Open it and tell us what you see."

Richard carefully extended one gloved finger and pulled the door back. "Cap's gone," he said, "and there's some fine ash around the top. Remains of a wick?"

"Good thinking," Coswell said.

Blakemore needed more convincing. "Then how did the door get shut? The killer sure as hell didn't do that after he lit it."

"Good question," Coswell replied. "One of the firemen down below? Or maybe someone on the landing when they pulled the wreck up."

"But why bother? There wouldn't be any gas left."

Richard answered before Coswell could reply.

"Then it was someone who knew the significance of an open tank and wanted to hide it, hoping no one else would notice."

"Daniels?" Blakemore said.

"Who else? It certainly wasn't me."

"That's all speculation, of course," Coswell said. "But I think we can now effectively squelch any accident talk about this."

Blakemore moaned.

"And I guess some poor soul has to search the bushes for the gas cap with the killer's fingerprints on it. He probably just winged it, and if he didn't do that right away, we'll never find it. There's way too much road between the landing and the highway to cover, even with a metal detector."

"I'll do it," Richard said, "on my way back to the village."

"Needle in a haystack," Blakemore said. "So don't waste too much time looking. But thanks for volunteering."

Coswell didn't proceed immediately to examine the rest of the interior. Instead, he crossed his arms and stood gazing at it. "Before we go further," he said. "Let's picture the scenario. I'll describe what I think took place. Feel free to interrupt me at any point."

Blakemore looked bored, but Richard was fascinated.

"I visualize two men in a vehicle. Brent stops them for

whatever reason. A fight ensues and Brent is struck from behind. The killers now have to dispose of the body, the cruiser, and do it quickly before they're seen. They stuff Brent into the cruiser. One of the men drives it up into the hills, the other follows. At some point, they get the bright idea to stage an accident to hide the murder. Upon arrival at a suitable site, they move the body to the driver's seat, strap it in, set up the gas tank fire, and push the cruiser over the edge into the ravine. The moment it goes up in flames, they jump back into their vehicle and drive off."

"One person could have done the killing and then towed the cruiser," Blakemore said.

Coswell shook his head. "Not likely, unless he drove a proper tow truck. Pulling the cruiser with a single chain up to that landing? Impossible."

"How about a hitchhiker?" Richard said. "People bum rides a lot around here—sometimes they want to save on gas money or they've been grounded by a drunk driving conviction. It would be typical of Brent to stop for someone like that."

"And Brent knew the individual," Blakemore added, "because no policeman would let an unknown sit in the back seat, and that's the only way he could have been struck the way he was."

"Good thoughts all," Coswell said. "But a thorough going-over by forensics for fingerprints, blood traces, and so forth should give us some answers. At this point, however, I think we can proceed on two assumptions: Brent Hansen was murdered, and the killer or killers are local. Okay, let's have a look."

Their examination produced nothing more of note except for one item.

"There's no rifle here," Coswell said. "Front or back. Where is it?" He looked at Blakemore.

"Daniels didn't spring that rifle business on me until the

day after the coroner and I examined the body, and then only by phone," Blakemore said. "I told him it should have been produced up front as a cause-of-death item, and definitely not removed from the vehicle. But he just passed it off."

"Well, he won't pass it off now," Coswell said. "It's part of a murder investigation, and we'll add that to a few other questions our tribal police chief had better start answering."

"What's next?" Blakemore said,

"I'll sign the authorization note for Tom Porter to get this hauled to Williams Lake and then we'll have an early coffee break at the hotel before we head back to the village."

★★★

When they walked into the hotel bar-restaurant, it looked as though the breakfast crowd hadn't left. If anything, there were even more customers including one group sipping glasses of beer at a corner table.

"What a wonderfully nutritious breakfast that is," Coswell commented.

"One of the evils around here, I'm afraid," Richard replied.

They had only a few minutes to wait before a table became free.

"Coffees all round," Coswell said to the waitress when she came over. "And are those fresh cinnamon buns I smell?" She nodded. "The sergeant and I will have one for sure. And you, Richard?"

"Just coffee," he said. "I had a big breakfast."

"You'll never fill out that way," Blakemore said. "Basic training will be easier on you if you bulk up a bit."

Richard just grinned.

Coswell surveyed the room while they waited for their coffees. Two tables were pushed together against one wall and eight young men sat there, all First Nations. One got up and made his way over to them. He nodded to Coswell and

Blakemore before speaking directly to Richard.

"Sorry about Brent," he said. "Tough to lose a friend like that. He was a good guy. That's from all of us."

"Thanks, Allen," Richard said. "Thank the guys, too. I appreciate it."

Allen stood for a moment as though he had something more to say, then turned and rejoined his friends.

"That was touching," Coswell said, "and I think a lot got said there. Perhaps you could do some canvassing on your own without a couple of millstones around your neck like the sergeant and me."

Richard nodded. "Okay," he said. "I'll hang around with them a bit after coffee and see what I can dig up."

The waitress arrived with their order. "I'd hate to be the woman trying to fill you two up," she said, looking at Blakemore and Coswell. "Swore I just got through serving you breakfast."

"We're still growing," Blakemore said.

"I can see that." And with that, she hurried off to serve other customers.

"I love them like that," Blakemore said. "Cheeky."

Richard smiled, then became serious. "There's another person you might want to interview, and you'll have a lot more luck than I would."

"Who's that?" Coswell asked.

"Chief Isaac."

Blakemore laughed. "You've got to be kidding. I've been told he speaks only to the gods and definitely not to some white man in a uniform."

"That's the word, all right, but in truth, Chief Isaac probably knows more about what goes on in this community than anyone else, including Daniels. He's got sources everywhere and they keep him informed."

"The godfather?"

"Something like that. He's traditional, for sure, and the elders support him."

"What about the young?" Coswell said. "I don't think there's a society anywhere that isn't rebelling against the old guard to some degree."

"Things are changing, but that old guard is tenacious. Look at fundamentalism around the world—Muslims, Catholics, Jews, Orientals, all holding onto power through tradition. Seniority still dominates and First Nations in this country are no exception."

"But some of your traditional values are good. Look at the conservation movement, the parks and all that. First Nations seem to be the only people truly slowing the mad scramble to extract every natural resource this country has."

Richard's jaw tightened. "Spoken from the other side of the tracks," he said. "My generation is well aware of our land assets. We can read the real estate flyers, the commodity prices, the Americans' hunger for water resources. We're sitting on billions, but any cashing in has been stymied by the fairy tale wishes of our fathers, or more specifically, our grandfathers. Preserve the untamed wilderness? For who? Stick us in hovels, live off the land using bows and arrows, serve as tourist attractions? Why should we be the joe-boy stewards? Who's going to benefit from our lands being turned into parks? I can tell you it won't be us."

The two Mounties had actually stopped eating as Richard went on with his rant.

"But we are integrating into white society, slowly but surely. Did you notice the speech differences in two generations? That squishy talk just labels us as Indian. My contemporaries want to compete nose to nose and be recognized for doing so. Let the elders eat the smoke in those old huts. We want to live like everyone else, in modern surroundings and give the same to our children." He stopped suddenly and became sheepish. "Whoa. I got carried away, didn't I?"

"Never apologize for stating your convictions," Coswell said. "It shows the man you are. But I must say, you've opened my eyes."

"Ditto,' said Blakemore, who returned to munching his cinnamon bun.

"And I guess now you can see why I'm not a personal favourite of Chief Isaac or any of the other elders for that matter, Gramma excluded, of course. This isn't the first time I've run off at the mouth."

"I understand," Coswell said.

"You know, it started for me when some bright bureaucrat suggested elders come to the school and talk to the kids about the old ways."

"That was a bad thing?" Blakemore said.

"My class lucked out getting the Johnson brothers, chips off the old man's prejudicial block. They started by scaring the daylights out of us about the Chilcotin Wars and then painting an unbelievably bad picture of the white man. You can imagine what that did in a mixed classroom. I told Gramma about it and she insisted right away on coming to talk to us. Teacher agreed. But one whole hour trying to reverse the harm, which included labelling the brothers a couple of dinosaurs, didn't work. Kids still considered them bogeymen."

He paused and looked around for a moment.

"You know, at this time of day those two are usually with the beer drinkers over there. I suppose they're off hunting, but it's a bit early." He frowned. "Bogeymen ... I wonder."

Coswell picked up on it instantly. "The boy."

"Yes," Richard said. "Jimmy's bogeymen."

✯✯✯

It took Coswell just seconds to rattle Daniels when he and Blakemore charged into his office.

"We have proof now that Brent Hansen was murdered," he said, "and the killer is most probably a local. This puts you in doo-doo up to your eyeballs for tampering with a crime scene."

"What?"

Coswell, still standing, placed both his hands on Daniels' desk and leaned forward, his face just inches away from the startled chief.

"Murder of an on-duty RCMP officer comes under full Federal jurisdiction, which, at this point, is Sergeant Blakemore and me. If we don't get every ounce of your cooperation, I'll have the sergeant put the cuffs on you, and the cells in Williams Lake will have a new occupant. Now let's hear exactly what happened when you got to the scene."

Daniels sank back in his chair, deflated. "Just trying to protect my people," he said. "A little booze drives some of them crazy. Sober, they wouldn't hurt a fly. I figured Brent Hansen was just in the wrong place at the wrong time. There's a lot of bad blood here. Goes back a hundred and fifty years."

"You said that right," Coswell replied. "One hundred and fifty years. But this is today, and there's no excuse for what they did. Now, I think you know who the killers are, so give!"

Daniels recoiled even further and his voice went up a full octave. "I don't," he said, "and that's the God's truth. I thought it might be the Johnson brothers, but they're a couple of sixty-year-old crocks. Brent Hansen could take them both on with one hand tied behind his back. And they weren't even around when the killing took place. They dropped in here yesterday. Told me they'd just got back from visiting relatives in Bella Coola."

"Where are they now?" Blakemore asked.

"That's why they came by — to tell me they were going hunting. I sometimes go with them. Don't know if they've left yet. You'd have to ask their father, Chief Isaac. They live with him."

"Perhaps you could ask him for us," Coswell said, his tone cool.

"You'd probably do better. The Chief's never been happy that I got this job without his personal consent. Damned unfair of him. I lobbied hard for the position, direct with Victoria."

"We will, then. Now, where is that rifle you said you found in the wreck?"

Daniels rose and walked over to a large steel cabinet with a combination lock. He opened it and reached inside.

"Don't touch it," Blakemore said. "I'll get it."

He pulled the rubber gloves that he'd used at the garage in Anahim out of his pocket and donned them before he lifted the charred 30.06 from the cabinet.

"We'll need a set of your prints to go with this," he said.

"No problem. I'll make one up for you now."

Daniels sat back down at his desk, flipped open an old-fashioned ink pad used for rubber stamps, and methodically pressed each finger on it and then onto a sheet of white paper. When he was finished he handed it to Blakemore.

"The rifle was on the floor, just like I said. I guess I just wished that's what killed him."

He looked so pathetic with his ink-stained fingers and hang-dog expression that Coswell took mercy on him and ended the interview.

"Okay. That's all for now. Just draw us a map so we can find your Chief's place."

***
***

Coswell noted that the road into Chief Isaac's property branched off just a few kilometres from Anahim.

"Is this all reserve land?" he said.

"No," Blakemore replied. "Isaac, the old devil, is actually squatting on Crown Land. Probably settled there just to show that he doesn't believe the Queen legitimately owns anything in the Chilcotin."

"This guy sounds tougher by the minute," Coswell said.

"We'll soon see, because there it is, straight ahead."

Coswell expected some sort of ranch, but all he saw were a small log house, a horse barn, a chicken coop and a privy set in a small clearing surrounded by dense pine forest. No attempt had been made to grow anything—vegetables, flowers or even hay for the horses. Dry buffalo grass, thistles and various weeds covered the property. No power. A rusted pickup sat parked beside the barn.

"Whoa," Blakemore said. "Better stop here for a minute. I recognize the truck. That's the one I saw the Johnson brothers driving when they went to see Daniels. Maybe they haven't left on their hunting trip yet."

Coswell braked to a halt. "Ambush?"

"Possible. Remember those poor buggers in Mayerthorpe? One nutcase kills four of our guys doing a routine check at his farm. We could be facing two loonies here."

Coswell thought it over.

"A high-powered rifle would have nailed one of us by now right through the windshield. But I agree—we should be cautious. I'll drive up to the front door; you keep me covered and I'll do the knocking."

Coswell drove the hundred metres to the house at a crawl, both officers looking ahead, ready to duck behind the dashboard at any sign of movement.

He parked the cruiser nose-first in line with the front door. They sat for a moment, waiting for someone to appear, but all remained still. They got out and left the doors swung open. Blakemore had the window rolled down on his side. He drew his pistol and stood, using the door as a shield. When he felt ready, he nodded at Coswell to go forward.

The inspector showed none of his usual blasé manner as

he proceeded slowly up onto the small porch, the hair rising on the back of his neck. He rapped on the door. No answer. He rapped again. Still no response.

Blakemore joined him, pistol in hand. "Going in?" he asked.

"No. We've got no warrant and really no justification to barge in. Let's just look around ... and put that pistol away."

They peered in the front windows. "Looks like nobody's home," Blakemore said, "but I see breakfast dishes for one still on the table."

"We'll check around back."

Coswell noticed it first: a wisp of smoke rising from what looked like a giant beehive at the very edge of the tree line.

"What's that?" he asked.

"Ah," Blakemore replied. "Our revered chief is in his sweat lodge."

***

A well-beaten path led to the lodge, but their trousers acted like magnets to the overhanging hound's-tongue, the noxious local weed. They arrived with their legs covered from the knees down by sticky burrs.

The lodge consisted of a framework of willow wrapped in canvas with a four inch stovepipe sticking out one side. A stack of small wood rounds lay at the entrance, a simple tent flap. Blakemore, remembering the old Vancouver steambaths, guessed that the occupant or occupants were nude, and so he announced his presence in a loud voice.

"Police," he said. "We'd like to talk to Chief Isaac."
Silence.

He said it again, but still no response. He turned to Coswell. "Now what do we do?"

Coswell reached forward, pulled the flap back and stuck his head in the opening. "Good morning, Chief," he said.

"Feels nice and warm in there. May we come in?"

A voice, more like a growl, answered.

"Yess, but quick. Yer makin' me colt."

They were forced to get down on their hands and knees in order to crawl into the four-square-metre structure. When the flap closed behind them, it was dark save for a bit of light that filtered through the canvas and the glow from wood coals heating a washtub filled with rocks. Fortunately, they sat so close together that facial expressions could still be made out.

Blakemore had guessed right. The man sat cross-legged, totally nude, in front of the fire, and he did look two hundred years old. Shoulder-length snow-white hair framed a face marked with wrinkles upon wrinkles. His parchment-like skin hung in folds over his chest and belly. Not a drop of sweat.

That wasn't the case with Blakemore and Coswell, however. Within seconds, the heat opened every pore, soaking their uniforms.

"You wouldn't consider moving our conversation to the house, would you?" Coswell said.

"Tawk here," the chief said.

They had no choice. Knees drawn up, leather boots pulled back from the hot embers, shoulder to shoulder, the two Mounties began what both later conceded was the strangest interview they'd ever done.

"We're looking into the death of Brent Hansen," Coswell said. "You're aware of that by now, I'm sure."

A barely perceptible nod.

"He was murdered."

No reaction.

"By someone local," Blakemore said.

Slight narrowing of eyes.

"We understand that not much happens around here that you don't know about," Coswell said, "which is why we've come to talk to you. We hope you will help us."

"He wuss a cop."

Coswell's turn for narrowed eyes.

"If by that you mean his murder should be no surprise, you'd better explain your answer. We're not talking a buck in hunting season here."

Coswell's combative tone had no effect. The chief sat unmoved.

The claustrophobic atmosphere, the heat, the sweat streaming down his chest, and the uncooperative interviewee finally got to Blakemore. "Your two sons are prime suspects right now," he said, "and you are not doing them or yourself one damn bit of good sitting there like a bump on a log. If you continue zipping your lip, it makes me think they're guilty as sin and I'm going to work doubly hard to prove it."

Coswell glared at him, but Blakemore couldn't be stopped.

"And when I do, I'll make damn sure you're charged with abetting. In a cop-killing, the judge will put you away for the rest of your miserable life."

Finally, a frown.

"My boyss don' ki'l people."

"Where were they, then, last weekend?"

"Went ta Bella Coola."

"To do what?"

"Visitin'."

Coswell, happy now with Blakemore's approach, interjected. "Visiting who?"

"Fren's."

"What are the friends' names?"

"Dint say."

Blakemore's turn: "Where are your sons now? I see the truck parked outside."

"Huntin'."

"Hunting where?"

"Itchass. Tuk horssess."

Coswell could no longer suppress the urge to return to open spaces and breathable air. "That will do for now," he said. "But we will be back and if you're in this rat's bladder when we drive up, get your ass over to the house. We've had enough of your games."

They walked back along the path, single file, sucking in the delicious clean air and holding their arms away from their sides to cool dripping armpits.

"I shouldn't have lost it back there," Blakemore said. "Now they know we're on to them, but that old bugger's attitude just made me boil over."

"Don't apologize. It worked out okay and from the looks of this place, I doubt if they're travelling with cellphones. Also, I think you rattled him enough to make him slip up on the visit alibi. I'm sure the sons coached him or vice versa, but remember what Daniels told us? They were in Bella Coola visiting relatives, not friends."

"Right. I'm going to enjoy checking that out when we finally corner them, but where do we go from here?"

Coswell turned and looked back at the lodge. He pondered for a moment, and as he did so, a gnarled hand appeared from inside the lodge, grasped two pieces of wood, and pulled them inside.

"Time to do a little unofficial search," he said. "We'll start with that truck."

It took them no time to find the tire iron, which was still lying in the box where it had been thrown. Blakemore pulled on a rubber glove and picked it up. He held it at one end with two fingers and eyed it closely.

"Blood and hair," he said. "We got it—the murder weapon.

These guys are dummies for sure. I can't believe they didn't wipe this off."

"Stow it carefully in the cruiser," Coswell said. "Forensics will bless us. They shouldn't have any trouble tying this to the victim and I'm sure the fingerprints will match the ones on the wreck. This is almost too easy."

"Want to go back and confront the old bastard?" Blakemore said.

"No. That won't get us any further and we don't want to fire up the jungle telegraph any more than we've done already."

They returned to the cruiser with their prize.

"I don't suppose I should ask about warrants or anything on this," Blakemore said.

"No. Don't. Let's go find Richard. I don't feel like waiting 'til these two come back from their hunting trip. We'll go after them."

"A manhunt in the wilds of the Chilcotin," Blakemore said. "This is getting better all the time."

"Giddy-up, cowboy. You've been reading too many westerns, Blakemore. Personally, I can't wait to get back to Vancouver restaurants where they offer a little more than 'red or white.'"

RICHARD SPENT AN HOUR IN THE BUSH around the crime scene, searching in vain for the gas cap. His conversation with the group at the Anahim Hotel had been equally fruitless. No one offered any reasonable suggestions as to who the killers might be and the mention of the Johnson brothers drew a blank. Tired, scratched, and discouraged, he returned to his pickup and headed back to the village. Jimmy remained his best bet to impress Coswell and Blakemore. The boy had the answer they needed to solve the murders, he was sure of it. To hell with the mother. He'd demand to see the boy and threaten to call in a higher authority if she didn't cooperate.

On the drive back, however, his confidence waned: it was a problem he'd had for as long as he could remember; a Pavlovian response, he'd decided, from generations of white man's dominance. Pretty hard to be confident when you're just another dumb Indian.

His depression still hadn't lifted when he pulled into the village, and rather than charge up to Jimmy's house, he decided to stop in at the Tribal Police office. Daniels, much as the man annoyed him, was a fellow Tsanshmi. Time to make amends.

***

"What brings you here, Richard?" Daniels said, tilting back in his chair. "I thought you'd be hobnobbin' with your Mountie friends."

Richard slumped into one of the visitor's chairs. "Don't be like that." he said. "You know it's a chance for me to get ahead."

Daniels paused before he spoke, his voice softening. "You're right, Richard. Get yourself out of the Chilcotin. You won't get anywhere with a second-rate tribal cop."

Richard looked up, surprised, and then he understood. "They gave you a pretty rough time, eh?"

"I deserved it."

Richard laughed bitterly. "Right. Put yourself down. Isn't that the way of our people? Your working explanation of Brent's death was reasonable. No need to apologize."

"Thanks, but the truth is, I stepped way over the line in this and may have let someone get away with murder. That's wrong, and if there's anything I can do to help your investigation, just name it. The guilty party needs to be caught, no matter who it is."

Richard couldn't help being suspicious of such a reversal in character, but he welcomed the change, temporary as it might be.

The thump of boots on the front steps made them both jump. The two Mounties entered without knocking.

"Saw your truck outside, Richard," Coswell said, ignoring Daniels. "How did it go?"

"No luck, I'm afraid, but I'm about to go over to — "

Coswell cut him off. "No need to — or at least, no need right now. Maybe later, but I think we found enough answers at Chief Isaac's to proceed."

"You got him to talk?" Richard said, amazed.

"Let's just say the visit proved most productive, but we do need some information from you, Chief Daniels."

The chief sat up. Coswell continued.

"The two Johnson brothers are persons of interest to us and we want to talk to them. Unfortunately they've gone off hunting somewhere called the Itchas. They left on horseback sometime in the last forty-eight hours. Maybe you could give us an idea just where they might be at this point."

"They're going after caribou. The Itchas are the mountains north of here. But a hunting trip like that could take a week or so. You'll have a long wait."

"We contemplated visiting them on site."

Daniels whistled. "That's a tall order. Lot of territory to cover; all thick forest. You'd have to go in on horseback yourselves and a guide would be a must. Personally, I've never gone up there. When I go with them, we road hunt down low for moose." He turned to Richard. "The north end of the Hansen ranch goes well back there. Had you ever gone caribou hunting with Brent? Maybe you could be the guide."

Richard shook his head. "I'm no hunter. Never could kill anything. I think it was those animal-god stories Gramma told me when I was little kid. I did go up there with Brent a few times but that was quite a while back."

He paused, an idea forming. "You know," he said. "The person who's most familiar with that country, for sure, is Sam Hansen. The Itchas have been the Hansens' hunting grounds for generations."

Blakemore looked at Coswell. "What do you think?" Blakemore said. "I see no harm in asking him. He wants his son's killers found as much as we do."

"Hmm," Coswell said. "I'm not sure that's a great idea, but I suppose we'll be close enough to rein him in if he gets carried away. All right. Let's go see him."

The two Mounties turned to leave; Richard remained seated.

"Go with them," Daniels said. "Maybe you can soften the old bugger up a bit. You were Brent's friend, after all."

"Never rated very high with his father, though," Richard said.

Coswell, standing at the door, heard the remark.

"You can't be less welcome than us," he said, "and maybe you'll improve our luck. Come along." And then with a grin. "That's an order, Constable."

Richard went.

***

"Wow. Looks like nobody's home this time," Blakemore said as they drove into the Hansens' yard. "Even the pickup's gone. Wonder where they went."

Coswell parked the cruiser and all three walked to the front door. Blakemore did the knocking. No answer. Two more tries but still nothing.

"They can't be gone long," Richard said. "There's smoke

coming from the chimney."

Coswell tried the door. Unlocked. He pushed it open. There, in the hallway, stood Maggie, the native girl, looking like a deer caught in headlights. Her pupils were huge.

"It's just us," Coswell said. "Friendly visit. We've come to see Mr. Hansen."

She remained tense, guarded. "He's gone to the funeral," she said.

Coswell heard Richard curse behind him. "Just like the old bastard not to let anyone know."

Coswell hurriedly carried on with the girl. "Oh, I'm sorry," he said. "I should have considered that. It's been a few days now since his son's death, hasn't it?"

No response and she hadn't budged an inch. Blakemore and Richard shifted uneasily on the porch.

"When do you expect him back?" Coswell said.

"Should be here by now. The funeral was early this morning and he said to expect him home for a late lunch. I've got it all ready. He's bringing Bonny with him."

"Bonny?"

"Brent's sister," Richard said.

Coswell considered that.

"We really must speak to him," he said. "May we come inside and wait? Our vehicle is a little cramped for the three of us and it's still a bit cool in the wind out there."

She paused, seemingly reluctant to make a decision, and then turned aside to let them file past. "Go sit in there," she said, pointing to a room behind French doors. "I'll bring you coffee."

One step into the room and they felt a feminine hand. None of the stuffed moose heads, bear rugs, or mounted guns one would expect in a log house. The furniture was French provincial, Persian carpets lay about the floor, the paintings on the walls shouted Old World, and Coswell counted at least four Tiffany lamps. He and Blakemore looked down at their dusty boots. Richard, however, had eyes only for the girl. To Coswell's amusement, his new deputy seemed totally smitten.

After a short wait, Maggie came in bearing a similar tray to the coffee-on-the-porch episode with Sam Hansen—strong brew and bannock. She apparently had an endless supply of both.

After setting the tray down, she turned to leave, but Richard spoke up quickly.

"Please join us," he said. "I don't think we've met. Are you from around here?"

What a line, Coswell, thought. Obviously they hadn't met and Richard knew damn well she wasn't local, but it worked. She sat down on a chair beside his.

"I'm from Hobbema," she said.

"Ah, Alberta, Cree," Richard said. "I'm Tsanshmi, from here." Brilliant conversation.

Silence.

Blakemore finally noticed Richard's infatuation and decided to help out.

"Hobbema. My first posting. Helluva introduction to policing. Lucky I got out alive."

A flicker of a smile at the corner of the girl's mouth. "Lots of trouble there, for sure," she said.

Richard proceeded to put his foot in his mouth. "What brought you out to this part of the world?" he asked.

"Probation," she replied.

Richard's dark skin didn't hide his embarrassment. Coswell quickly changed the subject: "I wasn't aware that Brent had a sister."

"She lives in Vancouver," Maggie said. "A lawyer. A nice lawyer. Helped me a lot."

Obviously, the girl had a complicated story: Hobbema with its racial problems, Vancouver's drug scene, and finally ending up with the Hansens. But that held only passing interest to Coswell — intercepting the Johnson brothers took priority.

"I'm having second thoughts about this horse chase," he said. "Maybe calling in our helicopter is a better idea. We could use a bullhorn to request they return to the village."

"I think that would just drive them farther into the bush, even if we do spot them," Blakemore said.

Richard nodded in agreement. "The helicopter eventually runs out of gas and those two could live out there indefinitely."

The sound of the front door opening halted their discussion. Sam Hansen strode into the sitting room before anyone could get out of their chair.

"Maggie," he barked. "Go give Bonny a hand with her luggage."

The girl hurried from the room. Hansen shot a quizzical glance at Richard, but focused on Coswell.

"Not a good time for you to show up," he said. "Unless you've caught my son's killer."

"I'm afraid not," Coswell replied. "But we do have two likely suspects."

Hansen's frown lessened. "That is good news. What are their names?"

"Bill and Art Johnson."

Hansen's face clouded over again. "I might have known. Those two should have been garrotted at birth. White man haters of the worst variety."

"Who should be garrotted, father?"

A woman stood in the doorway — a very tall, slim woman dressed in a dark business suit, her hair a deep shade of auburn. Coswell guessed her to be in her late twenties. She radiated an aura of authority. Hansen answered her immediately.

"Those bastard Johnson brothers. They killed Brent."

"Whoa," Coswell said. "We haven't proven that yet. At the moment they can only be considered suspects."

"Strong suspects, from the sound of it," the woman said as she marched across the room, hand extended to Coswell. "I'm Bonny Hansen."

He took her hand, surprised at the strength of her grip, and introduced Blakemore. He was about to do the same with Richard, but she interjected.

"Ah. Richard. How you've grown. Brent told me you were planning to join the RCMP. I see you've succeeded."

Richard blushed. "I'm just auxiliary," he said.

She turned back to Coswell. "My father is old school. Hang 'em high, eh, Pops?"

Hansen mumbled something unintelligible.

"You and I know how complicated our justice system is, Inspector, but I am interested, of course, in knowing how you've proceeded so far. Are your suspects in custody?"

"No," Coswell replied. "And that's why we're here. They've gone caribou hunting in the mountains on horseback and we need help tracking them down."

"You've come to the right place, then. My father is the best tracker in the Cariboo. Aren't you, Daddy?"

She put her hand to her mouth and spoke sideways to Coswell. "Little Indian blood in there somewhere, I think."

"Bonny!" Hansen barked. "That's not funny."

Blakemore struggled to wipe the grin off his face.

"I'll help you, of course," Hansen said. "And Bonny is right. I've hunted those mountains for years. I know every trail." He paused for a moment. "When did they leave?"

"We saw them in the village yesterday afternoon," Coswell said. "They probably left shortly after that."

Hansen began thinking out loud. "They would have cut over to Hobson's trail from their place. That takes them into the high country. The game people say the main caribou herd is above Itcha Lake right now. They won't be in any hurry. I'm guessing they'll take a day or so to get there and then camp out on top."

"How long from here?" Coswell said.

"Half a day at the most. We have a giant shortcut that goes straight to the top from my back pasture and it's easy riding. I let a couple of outfitter friends of mine use it. They keep it well packed. If we leave at dawn tomorrow, we can head them off."

"Let's do it," Blakemore said.

Coswell smiled at his colleague's enthusiasm. He doubted that a Vancouver West End boy from modest means had spent any amount of time on a horse; and compulsory riding for RCMP recruits ceased in 1966. Coswell's father, however, had felt that riding skills were essential to manhood and his suffering son knew the meaning of saddle sores.

"It would be best if you stayed here, tonight," Hansen said. "That way there'd be no worry of getting up in time or vehicle problems. We have more than adequate accommodations — my wife's response to falling beef prices. She had visions of turning this place into a dude ranch."

"Those were good visions," Bonny said. "Mom knew how to bend with the wind."

The point struck home and Hansen frowned, but he continued to order the arrangements. "Maggie. You get Bonny settled in her old room and then take towels and whatever over to the guest cottage. I'll go with Inspector Coswell and Sergeant Blakemore to the stables and measure them up for saddles."

"And Richard," Bonny said.

Hansen hesitated just for a second. "And Richard," he said.

Maggie looked strained. "I have lunch all ready."

"Later," Hansen said.

***

When they went out into the yard, a scene was unfolding in the corral that formerly held the black stallion. A herd of cows and calves were being driven into it by three comic book cowboys — slouched, black hats, bandanas, chaps, and spurs. Two were First Nations, heavy-set individuals. But the third appeared to be white; he was a leather-faced man who could have been anywhere from fifty to seventy, lean and ramrod-straight in the saddle.

Hansen shouted over to him. "Garret! Let Andy and Verne finish that up. I need you over at the stables."

Garret touched his hand to the tip of his hat and trotted his horse over to a large barn where he dismounted and led the animal inside. When he emerged on foot a few moments later, he appeared to have shrunk. He was a small man, probably no bigger than five-six. He stood in the barn doorway, pulled a pack of cigarettes out of his shirt pocket, popped one up with a quick shake, and with practiced ease, drew it out with his lips. From his jeans pocket, he produced a classic Zippo lighter and lit the cigarette, snapping the lid back with a satisfying click after he'd done so.

"We're setting out on a one-day ride tomorrow morning, real early," Hansen told him. "I want you to fit these men up with something they can handle." He turned to Coswell. "You'll have to excuse me. I have some business to attend to in my office before we eat, but come back inside when you're finished here. I'll have Maggie serve lunch then." With that, he walked quickly back to the house, leaving them with Garret, who eyed them curiously between drags on his cigarette.

"I know you're a rider, Richard, but what about you two?" he said, looking at the Mounties.

"Don't worry about me," Coswell replied. "I rode a lot when

I was young. Might be a bit rusty, though. I'd prefer something on the docile side."

Blakemore, surprised that he was the only inexperienced one, wanted that well understood. "I've never been on a horse," he said. "Docile sounds good to me too."

"Not many of those around here," Garret said, and then after a moment's thought, "Outfitters have a couple of their packhorses pastured with us right now. Clydesdales. Quiet animals and they're used to carrying weight. Also, I'm told they can handle any trail like a mountain goat. Surprising for something so big and clumsy-looking."

"I like the sound of those," Blakemore said. "Put me down for one."

Coswell hesitated briefly but nodded. The reference to weight wasn't lost on him. Compared to Garret's skinny frame, he and Blakemore were definitely Clydesdale material.

"They'll do," he said.

Richard was next.

"You want to try Spook?" Garret said. "I remember you were up on him once."

"And off him almost as fast. Gave Brent a great laugh, remember? That's a one-man horse."

"I remember," Garret said. "But I also remember you got back on him and stuck."

"Thanks but no thanks," Richard replied. "My butt's softened up too much with all that university stuff."

"Okay. I've got the picture. Everything will be ready for you in the morning and I'll be here to help. Maybe the boss wants me along, too. Where are you going, by the way?"

"On a manhunt," Blakemore said, now well into the spirit of the adventure. "We're going after a couple of murder suspects."

Garret tipped his hat back. "You don't say. Anyone I know?"

Blakemore hesitated, wondering if he had said too much,

but Coswell gave no indication he cared. "The Johnson brothers," he said.

Garret's eyes narrowed to slits. "They killed Brent? The boss was right. Goddamned Tsanshmis." He quickly realized his gaffe. "Nothing personal, Richard."

Richard didn't reply, his face grim. Coswell eased the tension.

"There are bad eggs in every society," he said, "Now, if you don't need us any longer, Garret, I've been told lunch awaits us."

Maggie hadn't returned from the guest cottage when they got back to the house. Hansen and his daughter were upstairs, and so the men retired to the sitting room to wait.

"That Garret chap would be perfect for a cigarette ad," Blakemore said. "Is he as tough as he looks?"

"Tougher," Richard said. "Garret Parker's been foreman on the Hansen ranch for as long as I can remember. I've heard he had his own spread at one time but it went belly up. Tried to go it alone — no wife or family to help. There were a lot of rumours about his cattle getting rustled. Naturally he blamed the Tsanshmis. No love lost there, for sure."

"He seems to tolerate you okay," Coswell said.

"Only because of Brent. He's as prejudiced as Sam Hansen otherwise."

"And Bonny?"

"Hard to tell. She's always kept her feelings to herself."

"And continues to do so, it appears," Coswell said. "She seems awfully composed for someone who just lost her brother. Were they not close?"

"No two people were ever closer. She was his protector. Poor Brent could never live up to his father's expectations, but Bonny sure did. She could stand toe to toe with him on just about anything."

"What about their mother?" Blakemore said.

"She gave up, I think, and lost herself in charity work. When she died and Bonny went into full-time law practice in Vancouver, Brent had a hard time. He couldn't wait to join the Mounties. No way did he want to hang around here under his father's thumb."

"On another note, Richard, my young friend," Coswell said with a smile. "How did you manage to miss meeting that delectable creature, Maggie?"

"I stopped being a regular visitor to the ranch when Sam Hansen began to make it pretty damn obvious he thought his son should mix with a better class of people. Brent never said anything about her either, which is strange. It's not like he didn't notice beautiful girls."

Maggie returned first. She came into the room to remove the remnants of the coffee and bannock.

"Those were lovely appetizers," Coswell said, "and I believe we're joining you for lunch."

The news didn't faze her in the least. "Lots of food," she said.

Richard had risen from his seat when she entered and offered to help. A trace of a smile gathered at the corners of her lips. "No," she said. "Best I do it all. I hear the Hansens coming downstairs."

She left just before father and daughter came into the room. Bonny had changed into jeans and a white blouse, open at the collar.

"Two o'clock," Hansen said. "Time to get something substantial in our stomachs. That Indian hardtack won't fill you up." He called down the hallway: "Maggie! Is it ready?"

"Don't shout at her like that," Bonny said. "She's a human being, for heaven's sake."

Maggie's answer from the kitchen cut off a reply. "Yes, Mr. Hansen. I'll serve it in the dining room."

The dining room was smaller than Coswell expected, furnished in the same manner as the sitting room—beautifully upholstered chairs around a dark mahogany table that sat eight. Only five places were set, however. Maggie and the hired men, it appeared, ate elsewhere. "Simple" would best describe the fare—beef stew, boiled potatoes, string beans, and great slices of sourdough bread.

"Meat and potatoes," Bonny remarked. "That's about as exciting as father's taste ever gets, but it makes life easier for Maggie."

"Nothing wrong with it," Hansen said. "Sits in your gut a lot longer than that health food crap your mother was so keen on."

Lunch proceeded in that vein, with Bonny occasionally interrupting her polite chitchat to take pot shots at her father. Both Mounties sensed the tension in the room and Richard appeared to feel it the most. He hardly said a word, even though Bonny tried to draw him into the conversation. Only the occasional appearance of Maggie bringing food and clearing dirty dishes got a rise out of him. Bonny picked up on the attraction immediately and watched with amusement.

After a blueberry pie dessert and yet another coffee, Coswell announced that the three of them had to leave.

"We'll pick up our toothbrushes," he said, "and more suitable apparel for our ride tomorrow. Would nine o'clock be all right for us to return?"

"That would be fine," Hansen replied.

Blakemore wondered where the hell they were going to get "suitable apparel." He hadn't seen anything resembling a clothing store since they left Williams Lake. Richard followed, taking a backward glance towards the kitchen.

When they stepped out on the porch, a deafening cacophony emanated from the corral. In one corner, the two First Nations cowboys squatted at a fire stirring the coals with iron rods. Backed up against the fence on the opposite side were the cows and their calves. Garret, on horseback, approached them, lazily swinging a rope. Suddenly a calf bolted and in an instant Garret's rope snaked out. The noose dropped over the animal's neck. Simultaneously the horse skidded to a stop and the line snapped tight, jerking the calf off its feet. It fell into the dust with a thump. Garret calmly urged his horse to back up and drag the bawling creature along the ground to the waiting cowboys who pounced on it.

In less than five seconds, one man's knife flashed, the testicles came off, and the wound was mopped with a black paste. The second man, ready with the branding iron, rammed it against the calf's rump. The sizzling sound carried all the way to the porch. Richard paid no attention to the proceedings but Blakemore was mesmerized.

"Jeez, doesn't that make you want to cross your legs?"

***

None of them spoke until Coswell pulled the cruiser onto the pavement and turned west toward the village.

"What now?" Blakemore said.

"I've decided that the young Indian boy's testimony is worth obtaining. I know it's a trauma to the lad, but there may be some difficulty in court with the forensic evidence."

"Obtained without a warrant," Blakemore said.

"Possibly."

"A good defence lawyer could make mincemeat out of Jimmy's testimony as well," Richard said. "He's only ten years old."

"Ah, but it adds to the stack. A jury will take it all in. I think a little insurance is worthwhile and I know I'll embark on this manhunt with more purpose, making doubly sure we have our culprits."

"All right," Richard said. "But drop me off at the tribal office. I don't want to attract any undue attention."

"Done. Meanwhile, we'll go on to Anahim and shop for something comfortable to ride in."

"The general store has jeans and shirts," Richard said. "They might have something your size."

Coswell ignored the innuendo. "We'll pick you up at your grandmother's at eight-thirty. Hopefully you'll have good news for us."

JIMMY'S MOTHER ANSWERED THE DOOR, still wearing her housecoat. "Jesus, Richard. Haven't you got anything better to do than bug us?" She reeked of stale beer and cigarettes.

Richard decided to take a more aggressive approach. "Get off your high horse, Gertrude," he said. "I just want a minute with Jimmy. I'm not going to hurt him."

"He said you were going to get him into big trouble. Wouldn't tell me what trouble, but the kid's not dumb so I got to listen to him."

"Sit in with us if you want. Stop me if you think I'm giving him a bad time."

She seemed to run out of steam at that point. "Oh, what the hell. I'm watching Oprah. Go in and talk to the little bugger. He's in his room." She stood aside and pointed down a short hallway.

Richard winced at the filthy state of the place, although he wasn't surprised. Like many of the single mothers in the village, she'd given up. Dirty dishes were stacked in the sink, her little girl was on the floor playing with a motley collection of abused dolls, and a hamper overflowing with dirty laundry stood in a corner by the back door. The girl was lost in her own dreamworld and paid only fleeting attention to Richard. Gertrude returned to a moth-eaten chair in front of the TV and flopped down, a half-empty bottle of beer in one hand and a smouldering cigarette in an ashtray beside her.

The door to Jimmy's room was open. Richard knocked on the jamb. "May I come in?" he asked.

The boy was lying on an upper bunk, reading a comic book. More ragged dolls were scattered on the lower bunk. Both beds were unmade. Jimmy glanced at him briefly and then resumed looking at his comic book.

A single chair, which appeared to serve as a clothes hanger, offered the only place to sit other than the bunks. Richard walked over to it, pulled the clothes off, and tossed them onto the bed. He sat down, tilted the chair back, and regarded Jimmy.

"Feeling better?" he said.

"No."

"You look better."

"I'm not. Still sick."

Silence.

"I don't think you're sick at all," Richard said. "I think you're just scared."

Silence.

"We'll get them, you know. They've run off into the mountains, but we're going after them and when they're caught, they won't be able to hurt anyone. Jail's where they're going and I can promise you that."

"You sure?"

"Cross my heart."

Silence.

"What happened, Jimmy? I need you to tell me. We know

it was the Johnsons you saw do the killing, but we don't know the details."

The boy continued to look at his comic book as he spoke.

"The big one hit him on the head when he turned around. Fell like a dead steer."

"Then what?"

"They loaded him in the cop car. The ugly one drove it. The big guy drove the truck. I didn't come out of the bush 'til they were gone."

The big one was Art Johnson. The ugly one was his brother Bill, who had a face pitted with acne scars.

"Could you see them clearly, Jimmy? Maybe someone who looked like the Johnsons?"

"I know them," Jimmy said. "No mistake."

Richard breathed a sigh of relief. This child wouldn't seize up in court.

"Thank you, Jimmy," he said. "But I want you to keep our talk just between us, okay? Don't even tell your mom. It's safer that way."

Jimmy looked at him, and fear flashed once more in his eyes. "You promised," he said.

"And I'll keep that promise. Don't you worry."

Gertrude sat staring at the TV when he walked past her on the way to the front door.

"Happy now?" she said, not looking away from the screen. "I told you he was a good boy. Only trouble he gives me is with that damn horse of his shitting all over the backyard. His father left it for him. Jimmy would have a fit if I got rid of it."

"He is a good boy," Richard said. "Surely that horse is a small price to pay for his staying that way."

"Easy for you to say. I don't have a grandmommy to keep a roof over my head."

Richard went out the door and slammed it.

"Bitch," he said. "Miserable Tsanshmi bitch."

***

On the drive back to the Hansens, Richard related his interview with the boy. Coswell noted a surprising flatness in the young man's tone.

"Why the glum face?" he said. "You've broken the case wide open and you've done so with first-class police work. Congratulations."

"It'll take me awhile to ignore the personal element," he said. "But thanks."

"And," Coswell went on, "we are about to return you to young Maggie. I've noticed your interest and I can't say I blame you. She is quite beautiful."

Richard smiled. "She is, isn't she?"

"You do know that her history appears to be somewhat tainted."

"She's a drug addict," Blakemore said.

"Tactfully put," Coswell said. "But it is true; Sam Hansen told us. She is, however, on a methadone program."

"I'm used to addiction around here," Richard said. "Granted, it's mainly an alcohol problem, but there are cures, and if Brent's mother steered Maggie in the right direction, she'll recover."

"I hope so," Coswell said, although the phrase *love is blind* popped into his head.

***

Garret met them in the yard when they drove in.

"Bring your kits," he said. "I'll take you over to the guest cottage, then Sam wants us all back at the house for nightcaps."

The guest cottage was more a live-in suite with a complete kitchen, generous sitting area, two bedrooms, one with a double bed, the other with two singles, and an outsized bathroom

84

boasting both a tub and a shower. Coswell checked out the bedrooms.

"I'll take the double," he said. "I'm not used to company when I sleep."

"What about Richard?" Blakemore said. "He sleeps alone, too."

"I doubt if he'll make that a lifetime habit. Listening to you snore will toughen him up for when he's married."

Blakemore grinned and turned to Richard. "I get the bed closest to the door, "he said. "That's the shortest distance to the whizzer. When you're over forty like me, you'll know why."

On their return to the house, Coswell noticed a smaller cabin set well back in the trees behind the corral. Garret saw him looking.

"That's mine," he said. "Nice and private."

***
***

The atmosphere had mellowed considerably when they went back into the house. Father and daughter were upstairs in the den, a total contrast to the formal front sitting room downstairs. It was a "man's room," complete with mounted animal heads, framed photos of old ranching scenes, a large gun cabinet, great leather chairs with a well-beaten patina, an enormous chesterfield of the same material and an old roll-top desk in one corner.

Sam Hansen was well into a bottle of Glenfiddich which he had placed on a wood burl coffee table in front of him. Bonny sat in one of the chairs sipping a glass of white wine. Coswell, Blakemore, and Richard fit easily onto the chesterfield. Garret pulled over a straight-back chair from the desk, but didn't sit down right away.

"What can my good foreman pour for you gentlemen?" Hansen said.

Bartending appeared to be part of Garret's job description.

"Just a beer for me," Blakemore said.

"What is that white you're drinking, Bonny?" Coswell asked.

"An Nk'Mip chardonnay," she said. "It's excellent. Comes from a very successful First Nations vineyard in the south Okanagan."

"I'm quite familiar with their wines," Coswell said. "You've got good taste, Sam."

"I brought it up from Vancouver," Bonny said. "My father doesn't know wine from horse piss."

Coswell wondered how many glasses she'd drunk. Her language had definitely slipped a bit.

"Indian wine," Hansen said. "Wouldn't be surprised if it *was* made from horse piss. Too lazy to pick grapes."

Garret gave a great guffaw. Coswell could sense Richard's muscles tighten.

"You can see the level of culture around here, Inspector," Bonny said. "Cowboy equivalent of locker-room humour. How quaint, father."

Coswell heard the words, but the sarcasm seemed a weak protest to the racist remark. He couldn't help wondering how much of the father existed in this sophisticated lady.

"I'll have a glass of the chardonnay," he said.

"What about you, Richard?" Garret called over.

"Nothing, thanks. I don't drink alcohol."

Coswell just caught Hansen's smirk and imagined what he was thinking: Indians can't handle alcohol, ergo, Richard wouldn't risk embarrassing himself.

Garret just shrugged and walked out to the landing at the top of the stairs. "Maggie!" he shouted down, "We need a couple of beers out of the cooler and one more of those white wines."

They hadn't seen Maggie in the kitchen when they came in, but obviously she was on call until the night's drinking ended. Bonny's concern for anyone shouting at the girl appeared to have vanished. She said nothing.

"What weapons are you bringing along tomorrow?" Hansen said. "I'll take my 30.06 and Garret's coming with us. He'll pack his 30.30."

Blakemore didn't miss a beat. "I have a Smith & Wesson nine-millimetre and there's a riot gun in the cruiser we can bring."

"Gentlemen, gentlemen," Coswell said. "This all sounds like a troop movement. Let's not forget we're going up there to interview a couple of suspects, not engage in a firefight."

"Better safe than sorry," Hansen said. "Besides, we might run into a grizzly or two. Always carry a gun in this country."

Coswell knew that further argument would be futile, but later he would tell Blakemore to leave his bloody riot gun in the cruiser.

Maggie could be heard coming up the stairs. In a moment she came into the den carrying a tray with two frosted mugs full of beer and a tall glass of white wine. Garret grabbed one of the mugs as she walked by.

"The other one's for the sergeant," he said. "Inspector drinks wine and nothing for the kid."

Hansen poured himself a refill of his Scotch as Maggie delivered the wine to Coswell. She paused in front of Richard. "Can I get you something, too? Coffee? A pop?"

Richard got up. "Coffee sounds good. I'll come downstairs with you. No need your making another trip."

Maggie didn't object and they left together with four sets of eyes following them out.

"Now there's a match made in Hell," Hansen said. "More fetal alcohol infants for society to look after."

"Jesus, father!" Bonny said. "Must you wave your bigotry like a friggin' flag? We have guests, you know."

"Facts of life," Hansen muttered into his Scotch.

***

Richard hadn't returned to the den when Coswell decided it was time for him and Blakemore to retire for the night.

"We'd better hit the sack," he said. "That long ride tomorrow might be a bit hard for a couple of greenhorns."

"I'll roust you up in lots of time," Garret said. "No need to set an alarm."

"We're going to stay up for a while," Bonny said. "The three of us need to do some more reminiscing about Brent. Maybe ease the ache a bit."

Finally, Coswell thought. *Some indication the woman wasn't made entirely of ice.*

"See you all in the morning," she said. "Sleep tight."

"Yep, see you then," Hansen said, slurring his words.

Maggie and Richard were in the kitchen, sitting across from one another in a small breakfast nook.

"Us old folks are going to bed," Coswell said, "but you needn't hurry Richard, and don't worry about waking us. I'll have my door closed and I suspect that Blakemore could sleep through an earthquake."

Bright halogen yard lights lit the way to the cottage, but they were hardly necessary. A full moon in a cloudless sky illuminated the whole countryside.

"Look at those stars," Blakemore said. "Nothing like that in the city. Takes your breath away."

"It's the cold that's taking mine away. The temperature must have dropped ten degrees. Hurry up. I need warmth, not starlight."

***

Coswell lied to Richard. He'd never been a sound sleeper, bedroom door closed or not. He heard the young man come in, almost without a sound, but the slight click of the door latch wakened him. He pressed the night-glo light on his wrist-watch — it was midnight. As usual, it took the better part of an hour for him to get back to sleep.

He woke once more — or half-woke — to the sound of a horse whinny, but he was too tired this time to even bother looking at his watch, and promptly fell back to sleep.

It seemed as though he'd just closed his eyes when Garret pounded on the door. "Rise and shine, men. It's going to be a beautiful day for a ride. Breakfast's waiting up at the house."

"Aaargghh," came from Blakemore's room. "It's still dark."

"We leave at dawn, remember?" Garret said. "That's just a half hour away. Better hustle."

Blakemore called out, "You awake, Inspector?"

"Barely. What about Richard?"

"I see movement, but I tell you what — you can have the bathroom first. I'm just going to close my eyes for a second."

"I will use the bathroom first, but get your ass out of bed and be sure Richard's wide awake. I doubt if our host tolerates tardiness and I want to start out on the right side of him this morning. I think his head may be hurting a bit."

***

But Hansen looked the least hungover of everyone. Maggie, who'd prepared the breakfast, appeared dog-tired. Richard gave her a sympathetic smile.

"Good," Hansen said, as though he were addressing the troops. "We'll be ready to move out bang on time. Garret's at the stables getting the horses fed, watered, and saddled up. We've both finished breakfast, so choke down some of this and we'll be off."

The two Mounties looked forlornly over the array of scrambled eggs, toast, jams, bacon, sausages, and a gigantic pot of coffee. Blakemore estimated that he could happily spend an hour enjoying the fare.

"I must apologize for Bonny's absence this morning," Hansen said, rising from his chair. "Her door was shut tight and I sure as hell wasn't going to wake her. She's not a morning person at the best of times and today she'd be a real bitch. Better to let her sleep in."

✦✦✦

Light was breaking when they went out into the yard. The two Mounties shivered in the morning cold, having neglected to add warm jackets to their clothing purchase. Summer tunics gave little insulation and they envied Richard's sheepskin coat. Hansen and Garret wore light denim jackets but Coswell figured they were padded inside.

"You'll warm up once we get going," Hansen said, "and the sun will be out soon."

Garret led over the two gigantic Clydesdales, their great hairy feet kicking up the dust.

"Take your pick," he said. "They're both geldings. Gentle as a couple of hairdressers."

Coswell noted the gay reference. Blakemore couldn't help but visualize the gelding procedure they'd seen earlier; he felt the urge to cross his legs again.

Richard swung easily up onto his mount, a spotted Appaloosa. Coswell took considerably longer. In fact, if Garret hadn't given him a boost, he might never have made it. The Clydesdale's back was a long way up for the height-challenged inspector.

Blakemore's six-foot four frame gave him the advantage. Once settled in the saddle, he looked over with some disdain at Coswell's ungainly scramble to mount up.

Hansen led them out on his Arabian stallion, followed by Garret riding a quarter horse, then Coswell, Blakemore, and, finally, Richard. The order proved fortuitous. Blakemore's smugness vanished the moment Hansen sped up to a trot. He found it virtually impossible to keep centred on his animal. Bounce, bounce, slide to the left. Overcompensate. Bounce, bounce, slide to the right. Coswell ahead looked really smooth, like he had shock absorbers in his butt. Blakemore tried to emulate him, but failed. Bump, bump. His teeth rattled. Richard rode up alongside.

"You're too tight," he said. "Just relax and go with the motion of the horse." That helped, but it still felt like his vertebrae were coming apart. Mercifully, Hansen slowed his horse to a walk when they began to climb. The warmth from the rising sun and the effort to stay balanced on the horses, especially on the steep sections, quickly drew the chill from their bones.

No one paid much attention to the scenery, although it was truly spectacular: huge grassy fields gave way to cedar and hemlock forests, followed by spruce and subalpine fir as they rode higher. The Itcha Mountains loomed ahead, snow already crowning a few of the peaks. Creeks and waterfalls tumbled down. Squirrels darted across their path and periodically, grouse exploded out of the thickets when they rode by.

Almost no grass grew on the trail, unable to survive the pounding of horses' hooves, despite an adequate supply of fertilizer. Coswell noted that some of it looked fresh.

After two hours of riding, Hansen stopped at one of the rare level patches of ground.

"We'll take a piss break here," he said. "I don't know about the rest of you, but that morning coffee's hit the end of my pecker."

He had company. All five dismounted and watered the bushes.

"Don't see you packed much in the way of firepower," Hansen said, zipping his fly. "I was serious about the grizzlies. Horses can sense them a mile away, so if those Clydesdales start to get antsy, you'll be wishing you had something to defend yourself."

"The bear would have to get through you and Garret first," Coswell said. "By then my intrepid Sergeant Blakemore will dispatch the beast with his trusty pistol. He's a deadly shot."

Hansen laughed. "You obviously don't know grizzlies. Horses go crazy when one's around. Pretty hard to get a shot off when your animal rears and the bear's coming toward you at twenty-five miles an hour."

"Oh," Coswell said.

Blakemore grinned. He felt perfectly comfortable in the wild. He had hunted for the entire three years of his old posting in the Kootenays. Bears didn't frighten him, and he enjoyed seeing Coswell's concern.

"Just play dead, Inspector," he said. "A grizzly might maul you a bit, but they don't usually eat a human ... unless it's old and can't take down anything else."

"Thank you, Sergeant," Coswell said. "That's very reassuring."

***

The forest ended as abruptly as it began. They rode out into the most remarkable stretch of natural grassland on a high plateau just below the mountain peaks. Hansen pulled his horse to a halt.

"Caribou country," he said. "They stay up top during the day but come down early morning and late evening to feed. Some hunters climb after them, but most camp down here and wait. The Johnsons will be waiters, for sure."

"I don't see anyone camping," Coswell said.

"It's early in the season. Anyone hunting around here right now is down lower looking for moose. If you delay a month or so, the snow drives the caribou down, making for easier pickings. The Johnsons coming up here at this time is a pretty damned good indication they're looking for a place to hide out."

"What do we do now?" Blakemore said. "My ass could use a bit of relief."

"There's a cabin at the top where Hobson's trail ends. It's just below that ridge ahead. Snowmobilers keep it up, but it's open to anyone on a first-come, first-served basis. If the Johnsons have ridden up that far, they'll have stopped there for sure."

"Then we'd better approach with caution," Blakemore said.

"I agree," Hansen said. "So what we'll do is this: You people stay here. I'll ride over to the treeline and work my way down on foot to where I can see the cabin. If it looks deserted, no horses tied up, I'll give a wave and you can ride on."

"And if someone's there?"

"I'll come back here. Don't worry."

They watched Hansen canter his Arab across the field and dismount at the treeline.

Hansen tethered the horse, pulled his rifle from its scabbard, and disappeared. Coswell's heart jumped as he watched the scene unfold. "I'm not sure I like this plan," he said. "I think we should all go down there."

"Boss isn't some sneaky Pete," Garret said. "He'll do what he said. We'll wait here."

Coswell bridled. "Garret, my man, I think you are under a misconception as to just who is in charge of this expedition and—"

Crack! Crack! Crack! Three shots rang out from below.

"Holy shit!" Blakemore said. "He's shot them."

"Hold on," Richard said. "That came from much farther down than the cabin and the shots were timed a couple of seconds apart. That's a distress signal. Some hunter's in trouble."

They'd barely started across the field when Hansen reappeared and got back on his horse. He joined them just as they crested the ridge. Smoke came from the chimney of the cabin, but two green ATVs were parked there, not horses. Standing beside the all-terrain vehicles were three uniformed men, all busy putting on helmets and gloves. They stopped when they saw the riders appear.

"Game wardens," Hansen shouted as he led the way down and pulled up beside the machines.

"I have three RCMP officers with me," he said to the man closest to him. "Better talk to them first before you do anything."

The man removed his helmet and looked at them in amazement. "What in God's name are you doing way up here?" he said. "But no matter. Someone's in trouble down there and we're going to help."

Coswell, arriving last, struggled to catch his breath. "Wait," he said. "We're after a couple of murder suspects. It could be them. Better let us go down first."

"Murderers? You're damn right you can go first. In fact, you can take this machine. I'll follow in the other with the medical kit ... well back."

"Okay," Coswell said. "And I am familiar with these machines. My father had a couple at our vineyard. The sergeant and I will go down first. Richard, you ride with this gentleman. It's too early in your career to get shot at. Wait 'til you graduate."

He looked directly at Hansen and Garret, who appeared ready to go down with them.

"Don't even think about it," he said.

They both glared at him, but Blakemore looked the most pained. "I guess there's no chance of me driving," he said. "I've been on one of these a few times myself."

"No."

They donned the helmets, but only Coswell pulled on gloves. Blakemore reached into a breast pocket and drew out a clip of nine-millimetre cartridges. "Never travel with a loaded gun," he said. "Unless you have to."

He unsnapped his holster, drew out the pistol, and slammed the clip in place. After a quick check that the safety was on, he slid it back and snapped the flap shut.

"Okay. We're off, but don't dump us, for Christ's sake."

"Just hold on tight," Coswell said. "And look out for moose. Shout if you see one."

***

They hadn't gone two hundred metres when below them they saw a man running up the trail, a daypack bouncing on his back and a high-powered rifle in one hand. Coswell braked the ATV to a halt. Blakemore got off, pulled out his pistol, and held it in a two-handed grip, pointed at the runner. The man stopped and looked up at them. He'd obviously heard the noisy engines.

"Let's just make sure he isn't the mad trapper," Blakemore said, and then shouted, "Police! Put down your rifle."

The man obeyed immediately and held up his arms. "No, no," he shouted. "I'm not the one you want. Please help. I've just seen a massacre."

Coswell got off the ATV. "We'll walk down," he said. "Keep your pistol handy."

The man had dropped to his knees when they got to him. Sweat streamed down his face and he gasped for breath. "Thank God you're here," he said. "I thought I might be next." He twisted and pointed back down the trail. "It's right around that first turn. Two guys shot to death. One in the face."

"Okay. Calm down. You're safe now."

Coswell helped him to his feet. "Now take a deep breath,"

he said, "and tell me what happened. But while you're doing that, maybe you could show me some I D."

The man quickly produced his wallet and handed it to Coswell.

"Take one of my cards. My name's Wes Baxter. Me and two buddies are camped over at Itcha Lake. We've been hunting up high for caribou over a week now and no luck. Today's our last day, so we spread out this morning, looking for moose. I won the draw, lucky me, to come this way; it's only a half-hour hike back to the lake. The rest went the other way. Probably too far away to hear my shots."

Blakemore holstered his pistol and picked up Wes' rifle, noting that the safety was on.

"Nothing in the breech," Wes said. "Maybe you can pull out the clip for me. I'd have done it when I saw you but there wasn't enough time."

Blakemore nodded, pushed the release button, and grabbed the clip as it popped out. After he had racked the bolt a couple of times to be certain the breech was empty, he placed the clip and the rifle into the hunter's trembling hands.

"Nice to see good gun safety out here," Blakemore said.

Coswell looked up and saw that the second ATV had arrived and parked behind theirs. Richard and the game warden were still sitting on it looking down at them. "Richard," he called out. "I want you to come here, but I'd like both of those machines taken back to the cabin." He turned to Wes. "Do you think you could drive one back?"

"No problem."

"Okay. Off you go then, but I want you to wait there 'til we return."

"Fine with me. That cabin's pure luxury."

He watched the man scramble up the trail, barely nodding as he passed Richard on his way down. The enthusiasm on the young man's face as he approached brought a smile to

Coswell's face and memories of his own rookie years.

"Right then, Richard, almost-criminologist," he said. "Shall we charge down there and investigate?"

Blakemore stood, amused at the inspector's bait, but Richard didn't bite. "No. We should start right here."

"You passed," Blakemore said and pointed to a footprint. "This is our hunter's boot. Let's see who else walked this trail recently."

They proceeded with painstaking care, but saw nothing except hoofprints going in either direction. There were two piles of horse droppings that Richard said were relatively fresh.

"Not warm-fresh," he said. "But nothing's got at them yet. Horseshit's a delicacy for birds and beetles."

The tent came into view first, its white canvas standing out among the greenery. They approached cautiously, careful not to disturb the ground.

Wes had described the crime scene well — a massacre. Both victims were crumpled side by side at the entrance to the tent, one face down, the other on his back. They were completely nude.

They'd chosen an excellent campsite: a tiny glade in the forest just off the trail, level ground, and a small stream nearby. The remnants of a campfire still smouldered inside a circle of stones, and a stack of dry branches lay alongside ready for rekindling in the morning. An empty whiskey bottle had been thrown carelessly to one side.

"A liquid supper," Coswell said.

"No," Blakemore said. "They'd have eaten, all right, but made damn sure they cleaned up any trace of it. A tent isn't much protection against a sniffing grizzly."

"Horses are gone," Richard said. "Someone let them go. I can see the saddles and bridles over there."

"Footprints," Blakemore said. "The killer had to have left footprints."

Coswell nodded. "I agree, but we're in a bit of a quandary. In Vancouver, this whole area would be surrounded by yellow tape and no one would move in until forensics went over it. But what the hell do we do here? It would take forever to get the crew and all their equipment from Vancouver helicoptered in."

"All we've got, I'm afraid," Blakemore said, "is the coroner in Williams Lake. The game wardens can radio him for us. Hopefully the logging helicopter's still available. There is a forensic kit at the precinct office along with a decent camera. I'll have somebody take it over to the pad."

"While we're waiting for him, we can go over the area ourselves," Richard said. "Set up a grid and search it together. I've got a pen and notebook to record everything we see."

"Both good suggestions. But let's just pause here for a moment and envision what happened."

They stood silent for a full minute.

"Okay," Blakemore said. "I'll start off. It's pretty obvious that these two wouldn't be standing out in the cold in their bare skin unless someone made them. Questions: Did the killer come with them? If not, were they followed up or did someone come down from above?"

"Chief Daniels is the only one I've ever heard of that went hunting with them," Richard said. "Their father, maybe, when he was younger."

Blakemore tried again. "There was fresh horseshit on the trail above. Maybe the killer or killers came from there."

Coswell shook his head. "I doubt it. Sam Hansen said the Johnsons probably planned to stay at the cabin. I could see them riding up, spotting the feds ensconced there, and then turning back to here. The shit's most likely from their horses."

"What, then?" Blakemore shrugged.

"Time of death will be an important clue," Richard said. "I can do that now for you ... to a degree."

"Go to it," Coswell said. "We'll stay here and watch but I suggest you approach from behind the tent and I needn't remind you of the footprints. A shell casing or two would be nice."

They watched Richard work his way through the brush, finally reaching the victims. "I wonder how many dead bodies he's seen," Blakemore whispered.

Richard heard. "Lost that bit of squeamishness over in Vancouver," he said. "Year one."

He squatted beside the body that was face down. First, he wiggled the arm slightly and then slid his hand under the armpit. Next, to their amazement, he pulled a buttock aside and inserted his finger as far as he could reach into the rectum.

"Helluva thermometer," Blakemore said.

Coswell called over. "What do you think?"

Richard grabbed a handful of moss and wiped his finger, then stood. "Axilla's cool, but the core is still slightly warm and rigor mortis in the arm is mild. I'd estimate time of death eight hours, maybe even less. It must have gone down to freezing last night with that full moon. That would favour less."

He looked over at the bloodied face of the second body. "Nothing's attacked those eyes yet," he said. "I'm saying six hours, give or take."

Coswell looked at his watch. "It's not quite nine. That means they were killed before we left the ranch. I wonder why the shots didn't wake up the game wardens. They heard Wes' rifle okay."

"Wes' gun is a 30.06 with a high muzzle velocity," Blakemore said. "Makes one helluva crack when it goes off. The noise from a lower velocity, like some of the older carbines or a pistol, doesn't carry as far. Could get lost in the normal forest snap, crackle, and pop."

Coswell thought that over. "A pistol, eh? If it was a revolver, there won't be any shell casings. Let's hope the killer used a semi-automatic or a single-action rifle. I can't see the shooter hanging around to beat the bushes looking for the spent brass that flies out of those weapons."

They finally remembered the men waiting up at the cabin. Blakemore volunteered to walk back and fill them in, as well as start the ball rolling with the coroner.

"No," Coswell said. "I'll go. I want to contact Chief Daniels. Get him to sweep the lower part of the trail on horseback. No use barging down there with ATVs. Any guilty party would hear them coming a kilometre away. I'll also notify the coroner. What's his name?"

"Dr. Basra. Try the hospital, but he can't always come to the phone. Spends a lot of time in the operating room."

"Okay. Now you two scour this site. Stick something on your shoes so we can separate your footprints from anyone else's."

***

Coswell had noted the trail's steepness when he drove down on the ATV, but the climb back up let him know his appalling level of fitness. He stopped at the top to catch his breath and survey the cabin scene. To his delight, all the men were inside and the horses tethered at the back. He hurried over to the latter, walking as soundlessly as he could.

He approached Hansen's Arab and stroked it gently for a moment before he checked the saddle. The only item attached to it was the rifle in its scabbard; there were no hidden compartments in which to hide a pistol. He moved over to Garret's horse and repeated his inspection. Again, the 30.30 sheathed, but in addition, a saddlebag was strapped to one side. It opened easily but contained only rags and some fencing tools. He closed it again and walked around to the cabin entrance.

When he went in, all six men were gathered around a plank

table in the middle of the room, drinking coffee. A modern, airtight woodstove blazed away in one corner, split rounds neatly stacked beside it. The spacious kitchen area sported a stainless steel sink with a water reservoir above. Coffee brewed in a large pot sitting on a propane stove. Cupboards top and bottom contained pots, pans, cups, dishes—enough to supply a small army, it seemed. Double bunks, complete with thick foamies, lined the remaining walls. Sleeping bags were laid out on three of the lower bunks.

Hansen spoke up first. "I gather our hunt has come to an end."

"One hunt, maybe. But another has just begun," Coswell said. "Two men have been brutally murdered down there and I plan to find out who did it." He turned to the warden who had offered the ATV. "Do you have a radio that can get me patched through to Williams Lake?"

"Better than that. We've got a satellite phone. You can call direct. I'll get it for you."

Coswell began his calls with the coroner. The hospital switchboard operator put him through to a speakerphone in the operating room.

"Can't get up there today," Dr. Basra said when Coswell explained the situation to him. "The helicopter's gone to a camp in the Charlottes. Won't be back for three or four days."

"There's a lake close by here that a group of hunters flew into. Itcha Lake. Can you come in by float plane?" Coswell asked.

"I doubt it. There's a fog moving in down here that'll have planes grounded soon. The alternative, of course, is to drive, but this surgical case I'm dealing with right now is going to go on another couple of hours at least. Cancer patient. When I'm done, I can tell you, I'll have no desire to pound up there in a vehicle and then ride a horse in the dark all the way up that mountain. Think about it."

Damn, Coswell said to himself, but he couldn't argue. There were limits.

"Okay, then. We'll move the bodies this afternoon to somewhere safe from scavengers. I'll call you in the morning and check on flight conditions in your area."

"Not before eight," Basra said.

Coswell cut the connection. Hansen got up from the table and signalled for Garret to do the same. "Sounds like you're going to be here a long time," he said. "Unless you need our help, I'd like to get back to the ranch. It won't run without us. Richard can lead you back."

"No," Coswell replied. "We have enough manpower without you. By all means, go. I'll see you off."

He followed them out to their horses, scanning their clothing for anything heavy bouncing in the pockets. He saw nothing and decided he wouldn't do a pat-down, but when they got ready to mount their horses, he made a request.

"I'll ask you to leave your firearms with me, please."

"What do you need our guns for?" Garret said. "I'm not handing mine over. Might meet a grizzly on the way back."

"Surely you don't consider us suspects," Hansen said. "We were with you, remember?"

"We've ascertained that the killing took place some time ago. I can't rule anyone out at this point and holding your guns is a routine procedure, I can assure you. But wait just a minute."

He hurried back into the cabin and emerged a few moments later with a rifle. "Here," he said, handing it to Garret. "On loan from a games officer. We'll arrange to have it returned later."

Garret tried to object again, but Hansen cut him off. "Take it, then give him yours," he said, pulling his own from the scabbard and handing it over. "We've got nothing to hide."

Garret glowered at him, but obeyed. Hansen swung into

the saddle, wheeled the Arab about, and set off at a fast canter. Garret followed, clutching the borrowed rifle.

Coswell leaned their guns against the cabin and went inside. He began by commandeering the wardens and their machines to help bring the bodies up from the crime scene. Also, they had an excellent digital camera with them.

The head warden's name was Frank Crawford. "No problem, Inspector," he said. "We're all volunteer first responders back home. Scraped our share off the highway both sides of Quesnel."

Wes was not so enthusiastic. "Count me out," he said. "I just want to get back to my buddies and forget all this."

Coswell couldn't think of anymore questions to ask the man, and let him go. "Don't leave the area, though," he said, "without contacting me or Sergeant Blakemore first."

***

Reaching Chief Daniels took longer than Coswell expected. The phone number of the tribal police office in Tsilhqoxt'in wasn't terribly familiar to the young lady handling the 411 line. Eventually she found it in the Williams Lake directory and put him through.

Daniels almost choked when Coswell told him what had happened.

"What? Art and Bill murdered? By who?" Then a revelation. "*Hansen!* He did it, sure as God made little green apples. If you don't arrest the bastard, I will."

"Whoa, Chief. That's way beyond even a wild assumption. But don't worry; he's right here with us and I'm on top of it. Meanwhile, there's a very important job I'd like you to do and it has to be done quick."

"Name it."

"The killers could be coming your way down that Hobson's trail the Johnsons took. I'd like you to roust up a couple of men to sweep that as far as you can. I don't have to tell you to be careful."

"I'll do it," Daniels said, "But don't let Hansen out of your sight."

"Like I said, don't worry, but I want you to promise me one thing: no gunfire."

"We'll do what's necessary."

Coswell hung up, feeling a bit uneasy about turning Daniels loose, but he couldn't think of an alternative.

***
***

Blakemore and Richard were still investigating when Coswell and the three wardens brought the ATVs down the trail and stopped fifty metres away.

"Don't disturb the tracks we've marked," Blakemore shouted up.

Coswell noted a series of twigs stuck in the path around the hoofprints.

"Wait here," he said to the wardens. "I'll go first and pick a safe route for us but I'd like whoever's going to be the photographer to come down with me."

That proved to be Frank Crawford, the wardens' crew chief.

"I hope you've got lots of room in that camera," Coswell said. "I want pictures of everything. Start with a long shot of the trail, and then focus on the hoofprints. Do them in order. You'll notice they all have numbers beside them."

He waited for a moment until Crawford got started on his picture taking. Satisfied, when that appeared to be going as directed, he proceeded to walk carefully down the trail, staying well away from the prints. Blakemore and Richard waited for him below.

"Good work, men," he said when he got there. "But I'm afraid I've got bad news. Our coroner's not coming. Williams Lake is fogged in."

"Damn!" Blakemore said. "Those fogs sometimes hang around for days. But why can't he drive up?"

"He didn't sound keen on doing that, so I'm afraid we're on our own. But we have lucked out some. Our chief warden over there is going to photograph everything. One of you should go over and supervise."

"I'll do it," Richard said. "I think Sergeant Blakemore and I have done about as much as can be done under the circumstances. But it's too bad we don't have something more than a camera. I'm sure our killer left signs in the tent or at least on the flap."

"We can dismantle the whole thing if need be and send it to forensics," Coswell said. "But for the moment, we'll just have to make do. Now tell me what you've found."

Richard pointed to Blakemore and then went over to where Frank Crawford knelt, carefully photographing each of the marked prints on the trail.

Blakemore gave the report. "First off: the whole campsite's covered in a thick layer of needles, twigs, and general plant debris — not exactly sand on a wet beach. We couldn't distinguish any footprints other than horses'. There were a few cigarette butts around the fire — tailor-mades."

"How about shell casings?"

"None, and we looked damned hard for them."

Coswell pointed to the tent. "What about inside there? I see you've pulled the flap open."

"With a stick," Blakemore said. "I didn't want to go inside and disturb anything before our forensic equipment arrived, but I guess we might as well now. You can see from here that the place was ransacked."

"You've got your gloves on, so go ahead, but maybe slip off your boots ... and don't move anything until we get a photo of it."

Blakemore did as ordered, stepping carefully over the body at the entrance.

"I can tell you there's no doubt someone cleaned them out," he said after a brief look inside the tent. "Rifles gone and I see a trucker's chain hanging from the ass of one of their jeans without a wallet attached. Pockets turned inside-out also."

"Robbery? Way up here?" Coswell said. "I don't believe it."

"Remember the movie *Deliverance*? Bunch of hunters hi-jacked by a family of weirdos? No cops in the general vicinity to worry about. Great place for a robbery."

Richard and Frank Crawford, having finished their trail photography, came over to stand by Coswell. Richard had heard the robbery comments.

"That's not too far-fetched," he said. "Some guys do get kind of primitive out in the bush with rifles in their hands."

"If that proves to be the case," Coswell said, "Chief Daniels and his men may end up apprehending our killers on the trail."

"Or they're still up here somewhere," Blakemore said. "But how do we find them? Maybe have a talk with that hunting group over at Itcha Lake?"

"I guess so, but I wish we could call in a helicopter right now. Much better chance of spotting them from the air. We could also get the bodies flown out. The longer they sit around here, the poorer the forensic analysis."

"Well, wishing isn't going to get us anywhere," Blakemore said. "So what are we going to do?"

Coswell didn't know what to do, but a slight drone off in the distance caught his ear. Presently it got louder — it sounded like a low-flying plane.

"What the hell is that?" he said. "I thought everything was grounded."

"Not out of Nimpo Lake, obviously," Frank Crawford said. "That's a small town on the main highway about eighty kilometres due south. Chilcotin Air's based there: small two-plane outfit. Survives by flying hunters and fishermen in and out of the lakes around here."

"Ah, yes," Coswell said. "I remember on the drive from Williams Lake. Another dot."

As they listened, a Beaver float plane suddenly appeared directly overhead, no more than a hundred feet up.

"He's coming down on Itcha Lake," Frank said.

Blakemore was ecstatic. "Bonanza! I can conscript him to take the bodies out. There's bound to be coolers for game storage back at their base: perfect morgue and there should be lots of room. Sounds like Wes and his group are going to be skunked."

"I can confirm the coolers," Frank said. "We check them out occasionally, but Chilcotin Air flights aren't cheap and the company's not shy about charging government people to the hilt. Hope your department's good for it."

"No problem," Coswell said. "I'm on a big expense account. The sergeant here will be the escort."

"Okay. I'll radio up to the cabin and get one of my men to motor over there and fix it with the pilot."

★★★
★★★

After every square inch of the campsite had been photographed, everyone pitched in to load the bodies onto the ATVs and transport them over to the shore of Itcha Lake, where the pilot waited impatiently, worried about the possibility of evening fog settling on Nimpo Lake.

Coswell interviewed the hunters, but quickly ruled out all three as suspects. They were businessmen from Vancouver on their very first trip to the Cariboo. Their previous annual hunting expeditions had been to the Kootenays. They saw no other hunters and heard no shots.

"The pilot who flew us up here said we should have the whole area to ourselves," Wes said. "He even made a couple

107

of big circles to show us where we'd be hunting. Didn't see a sign of anyone."

That narrowed the possibilities. If someone had arrived in the area before the Johnsons, the Vancouver group surely would have bumped into them or seen their campsite. A much more likely scenario would be that the killers had followed the brothers up the trail from below. But investigating that would be a Herculean task, even with Richard's help — they'd have to cover the village, the ranches, and even Anahim. Daniels' involvement, much as Coswell hated to admit it, would become a necessity.

By the time all was loaded — Wes and his buddies' mountain of equipment, the Johnsons' bodies, Blakemore and the three hunters — the afternoon had disappeared. The pilot, now visibly agitated, jumped into the cockpit and prepared to take off.

Beaver aircraft have been the preferred choice of bush pilots for decades. Their massive radial piston engines give them remarkably short takeoff and landing capabilities with significant load weights. Tiny Itcha Lake, however, stretched those capabilities — barely seven hundred metres of water, then trees rising abruptly from the shoreline.

The pilot backed the plane up until the tail just touched the willows at the edge of the lake. He stayed there for a couple of minutes and then pulled back the throttle. The engine revved up to a deafening roar before the plane began to move. Coswell held his ears and watched, fascinated, as the plane charged across the lake, lifting off just in time to clear the treetops by what seemed bare inches. He shuddered to think of the view from the passenger's seat.

Frank Crawford had no trouble persuading them to stay in the cabin overnight ... or at least it was easy persuading Coswell.

"It's dangerous riding a horse over these trails at night,"

Frank said. "Too easy for an animal to trip and maybe even break a leg. It's also prime time for cougars and grizzlies to be out and about."

"We'll stay," Coswell said.

***

The cabin proved to be even better equipped than it had appeared at first glance. Stored in lockers below the bunks were blankets and pillows sealed in heavy plastic. Previous occupants had filled a pantry near the sink with cans and cartons of food, all neatly dated with an indelible marker.

Frank pointed out a gas line that led outside from the stove. "Stack of twenty-pound propane cylinders out there, all hauled in on Ski-Doos in the winter. This is a no-motorized-vehicle area in the summer—government machines excluded, of course."

There were flashlights, batteries, axes, saws, decks of cards, maps, magazines, pocket books, and in one corner, a plug mounted with a cord leading out the window.

"Solar panel on the roof," Frank said. "You can charge cellphones, laptops, GPSs—even our satellite phone."

"How do they keep from getting stuff swiped out of here?" Coswell said. "I notice there isn't even a lock on the door."

"This is a heritage building. Government property. Old Hobson, the man who homesteaded here in the '30s, built it. Between us, the Parks Board, Forestry, Fisheries, and so forth, the place is watched pretty closely. Also the individuals who stay here are solid citizens—hunters, riders, snowmobile people. They respect the territory."

"Someone down below didn't."

"Yes, and that really shocks me. I've never heard of such a thing. Sounds like something from the gold rush days. Folks who come up here now are pretty well-heeled. They don't need to rob anybody."

EVERYONE SLEPT WELL IN THE CABIN: the wardens because they were accustomed to camping out, Richard because he was young. Even Coswell, exhausted from the activities of the previous day, drifted easily into a sound sleep .

Frank rose first. He started the woodstove to take away the morning chill and put on the coffee. The rest got up shortly after, each automatically taking on a chore — gathering breakfast fixings, setting the table, hauling in water. Coswell asked to use the satellite phone to contact Blakemore, who was staying overnight at the Chilcotin Air Lodge. To his surprise, Blakemore came on the line almost immediately.

"Thought I'd still be in bed, didn't you?" he said.

"That did cross my mind, but I assume the smell of hunters' breakfast starts early down there."

"You bet and it's a dandy."

"Enjoy," Coswell said. "Now what's happening in Williams Lake?"

"Still fogged in. The guys here checked, but no problem really. The Johnson boys are comfortably cool in the meat locker. Dr. Basra will be happy we moved them here." Blakemore gasped. "Wow! You should have seen that. Fish just jumped out in the lake. Had to be three pounds at least. I've got to bring the wife up here. This place is heaven. Lake full of fish, great food, and a bed with one of those wonderful memory foam mattresses."

"I'm so happy for you, but get back to work," Coswell said. "First, be sure you secure that locker where you put the bodies, and get a temperature reading. Next, contact Dr. Basra and tell him to send a meat wagon to pick them up. I want those bullets dug out of them ASAP and ready for ballistics analysis."

"Will do."

"Good. Now it's way too early for Daniels to be in his office, so I want you to get a lift to the village and find out what happened on his trail hunt."

"Okay. I tried to get the pilot to fly that way but it's in the opposite direction to Nimpo Lake and he was definitely in a big hurry to land before the fog rolled in."

Coswell hung up and took a deep breath. He'd saved the most dreaded call for last: headquarters in Vancouver. Chief Inspector Ward did not take the latest turn of events well.

"How could you possibly allow things to go from bad to worse up there?" he shouted. "Three days absent from your duties here and now you want more time?"

"Not my fault all this happened, but I've got to admit it's a real mess," Coswell said. "One dead Mountie and now two murdered sons of the tribal chief. The press will have a field day." He knew that would shift Ward's gears.

"Hmm. How far has it gotten to this point? The press, I mean."

"Nowhere. So far, the majority of the locals think the Mountie's death was accidental and this latest slaughter's too fresh for word to have gotten around. It will, though ... and soon."

"All right. You stay there and get it all settled. I don't want any negativity directed at the Force. Damn reporters love to scream incompetence and they'll just love the First Nations angle."

"Sergeant Blakemore and I will work day and night on this, sir," Coswell said. "And we'll get results much sooner by working as a team."

"Some team as I recall, but keep me informed."

Coswell gave a sigh of relief when Ward finally cut the connection.

***

The wardens continued to be generous with their time. Coswell and Richard took down the tent, but Frank and his men hauled it up and tied it to Blakemore's Clydesdale, along with Hansen's and Garret's rifles. The Johnsons' saddles and bridles, they decided, could be temporarily stored in the cabin.

They left right after breakfast. Richard had the horses ready. Coswell said goodbye to Frank Crawford and his crew, thanking them for their help.

"Don't forget this," Crawford said, and handed Coswell the memory card from his camera. "I've got a couple more, so keep it. We're scheduled to stay here for four days and then we'll ride back to Quesnel."

"To Quesnel on those machines? That's one helluva long ways."

"Sixty-four kilometres, to be exact, but there's a cutline that runs dead straight most of the way, so the riding's not too tough."

"I find that hard to believe," Coswell said. "But while you're up here, I'd appreciate your letting us know if you see any suspicious characters moving about. The desk clerk at the Anahim Hotel will take any messages for us."

"Will do, Inspector, and good luck. I've had to deal with Tsanshmis a few times on conservation issues. Not pleasant."

***

The ride back to the Hansen ranch took longer and proved more uncomfortable than the ride up. The horses picked their way down the steep grade with great care, and leaning back in the saddle put considerable strain on Coswell's back. He called Richard to a halt three or four times so he could dismount and ease the pain. Richard appeared to need the break as well.

"I guess you've ruled out Sam Hansen as the killer," Richard said at their first stop.

"No," Coswell replied. "I agree that it's unlikely he's our man. But if you think about it, a good rider could make it from the ranch, do the killing, and be back before dawn. There was a full moon last night and a clear sky—making for good light, as you'll recall."

"But he'd really tied one on with the Scotch. I can't see him functioning well enough to pull that off."

"Ah," Coswell said. "It appeared that he'd drunk a lot of Scotch, but did we actually see him doing so?"

Richard shook his head. "Good point. He could have been faking. I never thought of that."

"Experience, my boy, experience. It will come to you. Be patient."

Their next stop was at the bottom of a sandy slope.

"Tie the horses up to something," Coswell said. "I'm going to do a little forensic work here and I want you as a witness."

Coswell got off his horse, handed the reins to Richard, and walked around to Blakemore's Clydesdale, where he pulled off the two rifles.

Richard tethered the animals to a couple of gnarled pine trees and joined him.

"Hold this," Coswell said, handing him Garret's gun. He ejected the clip from Hansen's 30.06 into his hand while simultaneously opening the breech. "Empty," he said, "and the clip's full." Then, to Richard's amazement, he jammed the clip back and cranked a round into the chamber.

"What on earth are you doing?" he said.

"Plug your ears."

Coswell fired a loud round into the sandy bank and turned to Richard. "Dig that out, would you?"

Richard laughed. "Well, I'll be darned. A ballistics test."

Coswell repeated the procedure with Garret's rifle. "Now I can give them back," he said. "We'll have nice rifling marks on both those slugs. Don't mix them up, though. Put them in different pockets along with a label."

***

Hansen greeted them when they rode into the yard. "Welcome back to civilization," he said, his tone friendly but wary. "How did your investigation go up there?"

Garret appeared at the door of the stable. Hansen waved him over.

"It went well," Coswell said. "We've gathered considerable forensic material. It appears that the victims were slain in the process of a robbery and the killers most likely came up the trail from the village."

"Indians robbing Indians," Garret said. "Been going on for hundreds of years."

Coswell spoke quickly, squelching any comment from Richard. "Give these men their rifles back, would you? We won't be needing them now."

Richard obeyed, although he glared at the foreman.

"Why don't you come inside?" Hansen said. "Maggie can roust you up some coffee and nibbles. Bonny's gone to visit a friend."

"Thank you," Coswell said, ignoring the hopeful look on Richard's face, "but we must be off. Sergeant Blakemore's waiting for us at the village. He flew to Nimpo Lake with the bodies. Williams Lake is socked in."

"I heard," Hansen said.

For a brief second, Coswell wondered if the rancher had managed to listen in on all the satellite calls he'd made, but then dismissed the thought. Hansen was too old-fashioned to know how to do that.

Richard led Blakemore's horse over to the cruiser where he and Coswell lifted the tent into the back hatch.

"Evidence?" Hansen said.

"Routine," Coswell replied. "The coroner couldn't get to the scene, so we're bringing as much of the scene to him as we can."

Hansen looked puzzled by the remark but said nothing.

Garret returned the horses to the stables. Richard and Coswell went to the guest cottage and collected theirs and Blakemore's overnight kits. Hansen waited in the yard and followed them to the cruiser when they returned.

"We'll be back, I'm sure," Coswell said, climbing into the driver's seat. "But thank you for your hospitality, Sam."

"Any time. The door's open."

Coswell smiled as he drove the cruiser out of the yard. "He could come to regret that invitation."

***

Daniels' cruiser was gone when they drove up to the tribal police office. Blakemore came to the door.

"You have no idea how boring it is here," he said. "Hunting magazines lose their appeal after a dozen or so. I should've arranged to meet you at the Anahim hotel."

"Where's Daniels?" Coswell said.

"Left almost the minute I got here. Said he had to get out on patrol."

"What? Has he lost interest in the murder investigation?"

"Probably went to spread the word about the Johnsons. He only had time to notify Chief Isaac yesterday, aside from the two he deputized."

"Okay. What did he report to you?"

"Not much," Blakemore said. "He and his men passed the Johnsons' horses heading back to their stable. They just let them go and continued on up. Claimed there wasn't a soul on the trail except for some local right at the bottom just before they rode back into Anahim."

"What local? On horseback?"

"He didn't say, but I guess the guy must have been clean or he'd have gotten more excited about him."

"I'm not impressed with the chief's excitement level. I'll have a talk with him when he gets back."

Blakemore's shoulders sagged. "Couldn't we just check in at the hotel for a minute? I had a really early breakfast and nothing since."

"We can stop off at my Gramma's," Richard offered. "She'll give you something that'll tide you over 'til supper."

Coswell relented. He also had an ulterior motive: Gramma, being an elder, would have some useful information about the Johnsons. For the past four years at least, Richard had spent most of his time away from home at his studies in Vancouver, so his finger wouldn't be on the pulse of the community. But his grandmother's would.

"What are we going to do with that tent in the back?" Blakemore said. "It's beginning to smell awfully smoky in here."

"You can leave it at Gramma's," Richard said. "She has a greenhouse without much in it right now."

***

Gramma produced tea and salal berry muffins on a big plate with a half a pound of butter nicely softened in a bowl. On a separate tray were cream, sugar, spoons, and butter knives.

"I hope you're going to join us this time," Coswell said. "I'd like to ask you a few questions."

The old lady showed a glimmer of surprise, but she went back into the kitchen and brought out a well-used mug for herself. She drank her tea straight.

"I guess you've heard about the Johnson brothers," Coswell said.

"I hert," she replied, then nothing.

"I'd really appreciate it if you could tell me something about them. We're a long ways yet from identifying their killers."

"Dumb guyss," she said. "Too lazy tah leave der dad."

"Did they have jobs?"

"Juss sometimess. Most dey liff off de lant — ders and utters."

"They have a reputation for rustling the odd animal from neighbours," Richard explained.

"Yess. Meat eaterss fer sure. Dem and dat ole Isaac."

"I gather you don't think too highly of the band chief," Coswell said.

"Full uff hate, him … an' hiss fadder an' hiss fadder before. Dey not forget."

"Local history again, Inspector," Richard said. "1864, the Chilcotin Wars. Klatsassin, a chief, and some of his warriors took exception to prospectors and their like invading the territory. They declared war and shot a few, which brought white man's justice down on their heads. The presiding judge didn't see it as a war. He declared them common criminals and ordered a public hanging in Quesnel. Our people considered it a terrible insult and some, mainly the relatives of the condemned, have carried on a hate campaign ever since; Chief Isaac being the latest in the line."

"Hmm. That would explain Brent Hansen's murder but not theirs. Can you give me any idea who might want them dead? How about some of the people they stole from?"

"Mahbe 'ansen, eh?" she said. "Ded son, big loss."

"I told her," Richard said, embarrassed. "Sorry."

"Don't be," Coswell said. "I'm sure Chief Daniels is spreading the word with great efficiency."

The old lady remained silent for a moment and then spoke. "Tom Porter. Doss boyss hurt 'im bad."

"The garage man? What happened there?"

Richard interrupted. "Now, Gramma, Tom Porter is no killer."

"He wants ta ranch," she said.

Richard looked at Coswell. "That is true. He leased a small piece of land beside Chief Isaac and tried to make a go of it, but couldn't work with his father at the garage and keep an eye on his stock. Claimed the Johnsons kept harassing him, stealing from his property. He complained to Chief Daniels, but nothing ever got done about it."

"Is he still trying to ranch?"

"I doubt it. When his father died last year, he had to take over all of the garage work. Probably let it go."

"Still hass it," Gramma said. "Keeps 'is hoss's terr."

***

Coswell hesitated for a moment before firing up the cruiser. Blakemore sat up front beside him; Richard was in the back.

"Okay," he said. "We'll see if Daniels is in his office. If he isn't, I think it's time we did some long-distance research."

"What's that?"

"Get my corporal in Vancouver to see if there are rap sheets on a few people—the Johnsons and our friend, Garret Parker. There's something about him that makes me suspicious. And, although I know you'll disagree, Richard ... Tom Porter."

Richard just gave a shrug.

"And while the good corporal is at it, I'll have him contact the National Gun Registry back east. It would be most interesting to know what arsenal exists at the Hansen ranch. Maybe a pistol or two?"

***

When they got to the village, they found Daniels back in his office conversing with someone on the phone.

"Talk to you later," he said to the party on the other end.

"Business just walked in." He pointed to the chairs. "Take a load off your feet," he said.

They all sat down.

"You've given your report to Sergeant Blakemore," Coswell said, "but I'd like to know more about the local you met on the trail: his name, whether or not he was on horseback, and where exactly he turned off."

"Nothing for you there, Inspector. Just Tom Porter out for a walk with his dog. He comes up to that so-called ranch of his after work to tend his horses. Stays overnight a lot since his dad died."

"How much of the trail did you actually cover?"

"As much as possible, considering the distance and the late start, but enough to catch anyone in a hurry to get down."

He held Coswell's gaze. "I didn't think we would find anyone," he said. "Art and Bill's killer is sitting back real comfortable in that big ranch his daddy gave him."

Time for a little truth-bending, Coswell decided.

"We haven't let Sam Hansen off the hook, if that's what you're thinking," Coswell said. "But facts don't support his being guilty. We were with him at the time the murders took place."

"Well, then, he paid someone to do it. Either way, he's guilty."

That ended the meeting. Coswell had had enough of Daniels stubborn bias.

"Time to go," he said. "Thank you for your help."

"Anytime," Daniels said. "But no more trail rides. I put my nag out to pasture when I got the cruiser. A lot easier on the back."

✳✳✳

"Where next?" Blakemore said when they got back to their vehicle. "Too bad about that Porter business. Sounded promising there for a while, but there's no way the man could have ridden all the way up that mountain and gotten back again in one day."

"I agree, and I must say, things are looking bleak. All I can suggest is poking around Anahim and the village. Talk to people. Maybe get some leads."

"Try Chief Isaac again?" Blakemore said. "He should loosen up a bit now. After all, we're his best bet for finding his sons' killers. And having Richard along with us might help."

"I doubt it," Richard said. "Remember what I said about me and the elders? Also, I think he has the same mindset as Daniels. But it probably would be worth talking to him. He'll be thinking vengeance and I'm afraid he has enough connections to pull that off."

"To Isaac's house we go, then," Coswell said. "But we'd better have our kid gloves on this time. He has lost two sons."

***

The pickup truck was still parked beside the barn, but no smoke came from either the house or the sweat lodge. Blakemore knocked on the door. Silence. He peeked in the front window.

"Nobody home again?" he said, and then to Richard, "Would you go and look in the sweat lodge? Maybe he died out there."

They watched while Richard went over to check it out. He pulled back the flap, peered in, then turned to them and shook his head.

Coswell tried the door. Unlocked.

"Good suggestion saying that he might have died," he said to Blakemore. "Gives us a reason to go inside. Maybe he's lying cold in his bed."

The place reeked of smoke—wood and tobacco. The table in the kitchen area had been cleared, but the sink contained at least three meals' worth of dirty dishes. An old-fashioned hand pump was mounted on the counter beside it. In the living room area, three chairs were lined up in front of an old Pioneer woodstove: one a reasonably new La-Z-Boy recliner, the others secondhand store rejects. Tobacco tins filled with sand sat on the floor between each chair, the cigarette butts in various stages of decay. Decorations were sparse: a black bear hide nailed to one wall, a gun rack beside it containing a single lever-action rifle. A couple of calendars with western scenes adorned the other wall.

But the most striking feature hung above and to the right of the woodstove: a blown-up photo of a seated Indian wearing an animal fur hat and a jacket, likely of deerskin, with long fringes hanging down over his chest. His pants could have been denim, but he wore leggings that extended to his knees and moccasins rather than boots. His facial expression projected anger, pure and simple; the corners of his mouth couldn't have extended any lower. Not a comforting image.

"Chief Klatsassin," Richard said, seeing Blakemore and Coswell staring at the picture. "Instigator of the Chilcotin Wars, First Nations hero, and a symbol of white man's injustice."

"Wouldn't want to meet him alone in the woods," Blakemore said.

"No you wouldn't," Richard agreed.

Blakemore looked around the seating area. "I wonder what they do for entertainment. I don't see any reading material and no TV."

Richard laughed. "When they weren't occupying a table at the Anahim bar, Art and Bill spent most of their time in that old pickup nosing around. The chief, however, holds court. People come to him—like an emperor of sorts. I'm a bit nervous that he isn't here. I hope he hasn't organized a war party."

"Surely that's not possible," Coswell said. "We're talking the real world here."

Richard didn't reply.

The rest of the house consisted of two bedrooms. One obviously belonged to the chief; it was furnished with an old brass double bed, a wooden crate with a gas lamp on it, and a set of dresser drawers against one wall. On the other wall, spikes had been driven into the logs to serve as clotheshooks.

"Wow," Blakemore said. "This place is depressing."

"You should take a tour of the village houses," Richard said. "Aside from having electricity, they're not a lot prettier."

The second bedroom, much larger, contained a double-mantle Coleman lamp hanging from the ceiling, an electric cable spool that served as a shared bedside table between two cots, a relatively modern organizer-type closet against the wall beside the door, and a large steamer trunk wedged under the only window.

Coswell glanced into a tobacco-tin ashtray sitting on the bedside table. "I can see one form of entertainment the boys partook of," he said.

Blakemore and Richard, still in the chief's room came over. Coswell held up a roach. "A little happiness on the old homestead, eh?"

In unison, the men looked over at the steamer trunk.

"Be my guest," Coswell said. "But try not to disturb anything."

Blakemore undid the latch and lifted the lid. A strong odour of mothballs rose from inside. He paused for a moment and then began pulling aside a layer of folded blankets that served as a poor disguise for what lay beneath them. "Well, well, well," he said. "A veritable treasure trove of nicely packaged weed. I think our boys were in the business." He looked at Richard. "You hear any rumours about this from the young and the restless?"

"Not a one," Richard said. "But the crowd I hung around with weren't into drugs — using it or growing it." He continued to stare at the stash. "There's way too much here for personal use. They're obviously selling the stuff, which would explain how they paid for their booze, cigarettes, and, I hear, a few trips to experience the nightlife of Vancouver."

"And if this *were* Vancouver," Coswell said, "I'd instantly start looking for an unhappy competitor protecting his territory."

"A drug killing? Here?" Richard said. "I find that hard to believe."

"Only a thought. I doubt there's a local market big enough to warrant such a thing."

"Don't speak too soon," Blakemore said. "There's Williams Lake, Quesnel, and even Prince George — 75,000 people live there. Keeping supplies this far from the narc squad would be a smart move. Maybe our boys shortchanged the wrong people."

"Send an assassin way out here?" Coswell said. "Highly unlikely. Better to get them at delivery time."

"I disagree. There'd be less chance of getting caught if you bumped them off up on that mountain. Maybe they hired someone local — a druggie."

"You are not cheering me up, Blakemore," Coswell said. "How are we going to find such a person?"

"Daniels?"

"Maybe. Letting him handle the pot find might bring him onside, but I wouldn't get my hopes up. He appears to have a mind that can only move in one direction."

Richard and Blakemore nodded in agreement.

"We'll head over to Anahim," Coswell said. "I'll phone Daniels about the marijuana and then get in touch with my Vancouver office to start the records search. You and Richard take in the happy hour at the bar and sniff the wind. I'll do a quick hike over to Tom Porter's garage and have a chat with him. He might know the comings and goings of the Johnson brothers in a little more detail."

***

The garage appeared to be closed for the day when Coswell got there; the huge roller door was down and the lights illuminating the gas pumps were switched off. He was about to turn back when he noticed a glimmer through the front window. He peered in and saw that the light came from an inner office.

He rapped on the door. Tom appeared, holding a pen in his hand.

"Good evening, Inspector," he said. "Just balancing some accounts in the back. Come in and have a seat."

His office consisted of a plain metal desk pushed into a corner behind the door and an old-fashioned swingback wooden chair. "A hundred years old, that chair," Tom said. "Belonged to my grandfather. He bought it at an estate sale in Victoria right after he started the garage. Said a successful businessman needed a bank manager's kind of office chair."

Coswell looked around and noted that three generations who'd all worked in the same business hadn't produced much in the way of progress. There were three pumps outside — two gas and one diesel. Inside was a single bay with an old-fashioned columnar hoist, presently unoccupied. On the walk over, he'd also noticed that there wasn't much in the way of work parked in the yard.

Tom insisted Coswell sit in Grandfather's chair. He found what looked like a padded piano stool on rollers and pulled it over for himself.

"I got that wreck over to the Pond for you okay. Hauled it there myself. Figured the day was a writeoff so I stayed the night. Had a few beers and watched the strippers at the Palomino. Took my time coming back too. I'm a bit hungover."

A lot of unasked-for information, Coswell thought.

"Business slow?"

"Dead slow. That tractor you saw me working on is the last good paying job I've had in a while. Most ranchers are cheap buggers and do their own repairs. The rich ones take their fancy machines into the Pond."

"That's a nice-looking towing outfit you've got out there, though. I notice it's a Dodge Ram 350 with a Cummins diesel. Same vehicle Sam Hansen has. Few grand in that, for sure. It looks new."

"It is. Got some money when dad died, and between that and the bank, it's mine. Always wanted one." Tom shifted on his stool. "You didn't come here just to hear about my garage business," he said. "What can I do for you?"

Coswell smiled. "You're right. I presume you know what happened to the Johnson brothers."

"The whole town knows. You can't have a piss around here without someone telling someone else about it."

"I gather you weren't exactly on friendly terms with them."

Tom gave a harsh laugh. "That's an understatement. Worst neighbours you could ever have. I don't mind saying I'm glad somebody snuffed them. Couldn't happen to two nicer guys."

That lowered Porter as a suspect in Coswell's mind. Murderers weren't that open.

"What can you tell me about them? We're looking for any kind of lead."

"The killer should be given a medal, not a jail cell, but I guess you have to appease the white-haters. Wouldn't want another Chilcotin War."

"I've heard a lot about that war lately," Coswell said. "Amazing that it's hung on so long."

"You're right about that, but it gives some people around here a purpose in life. Maybe one of them did it. Nothing better than a couple of martyrs to keep the pot boiling."

"Interesting suggestion, but right now we're leaning more towards a drug-related motive. I hope you'll keep this confidential, but it appears the Johnsons were involved in dealing marijuana."

"Big surprise," Tom said. "With beef prices fallen the way they have, cattle rustling doesn't paying what it used to. Drug-running would be right up their alley."

"Did you notice anything on their property that might suggest that?"

"You mean bikers and hopheads? Nope. Nothing like that and if they had a grow-op, it must have been way off in the bush somewhere." He paused for a moment, thinking. "For a couple of lazy buggers, they did a lot of trail riding out back. Could have been tending a crop."

"Can you give us any names to check out? Associates? People who would be as happy as you seeing them dead?"

"Not really. They fly under old Isaac's wing, sons of the chief and all that bullshit." He smiled. "If detesting the bastards is why they were killed, I guess I'm your best bet."

***

Satisfied that nothing more useful appeared to be forthcoming from Tom Porter, Coswell returned to the Anahim Hotel and joined Blakemore and Richard who were seated at a corner table in the bar, their expressions glum.

"Not a happy happy hour today," Blakemore said as Coswell pulled up a chair and sat down. "I think poor Richard here has become the town pariah. Being seen with us has not done his social standing much good."

"Doesn't worry me," Richard said. "I don't plan to have my life dictated to by Chilcotin prejudices. Screw them."

"Now, now," Coswell said. "When all this is over and justice has prevailed, you'll be back in everyone's good graces again."

Blakemore wasn't impressed. "Right. Everyone loves a cop. Better get used to it, Richard."

Coswell related his conversation with Tom Porter. "Not much help," he concluded. "But the drug angle does make more sense."

"It would be nice if you could convince the locals of that," Blakemore said, noting the furtive glances in their direction. "How did Daniels react when you told him about the marijuana find?"

"Pretty cool. Just said he'd deal with it."

Their outspoken waitress came by at that point. Her good spirits hadn't lagged a bit.

"Welcome back," she said to Coswell. "Love ya or hate ya, you guys are good for business. What'll you have?"

"I think I'll try a glass of your red."

"Rickards. Just a glass?"

Coswell turned to Blakemore. "Rickards?"

"Rickards Red. It's a beer."

Coswell sighed. "Make it a pint," he said. "And more of these cholesterol sticks."

"Cheezies," Blakemore told her.

She hurried off, swinging her hips and tossing off remarks to patrons who tried to intercept her. Coswell renewed his conversation with Blakemore.

"You know, you've given me an idea. Richard has made me a little nervous about hostilities in the community and I must say the atmosphere in here reinforces that."

"Yep. We're as popular as coons in a henhouse, all right."

"Let me run this by you, Richard. What do you think of my calling an information meeting somewhere appropriate? Say a community hall or whatever. Do you think we'd get a crowd?"

Richard brightened. "I think that's a great idea. The school's the best place to hold it. I can talk to the principal. And people will come, out of curiosity if nothing else. I'll get my Gramma to go. She'll draw a crowd by herself. Folks around here say she'd be tribal chief if she wasn't Salish."

"Might stimulate a few leads, too," Blakemore said. "Let's do it."

"Okay," Coswell said. "We'll leave you to do the organizing, Richard. Post a few notices, word of mouth … things like that. If you get at it early, maybe we can run the meeting tomorrow evening—say, seven-thirty?"

"Shouldn't be a problem. I'll get started right away."

"Good."

"Meanwhile, what are you and I going to do?" Blakemore asked Coswell.

"Nothing but eat a good dinner tonight. Tomorrow morning we'll hang around the hotel until my corporal gets to his desk in Vancouver. He should have most of the information I asked for by then. That may point us somewhere. I also think another visit to Chief Isaac is imperative, followed by one to Daniels. I don't want either of them stirring up trouble."

"Good luck," Richard said.

THE NEXT MORNING STARTED WELL. Coswell rose at six-thirty, shaved, dressed, and went downstairs. He was tempted to wake Blakemore, who was snoring away in his room, but decided to let him sleep in. The desk clerk hadn't come on duty yet, but he saw one of the staff wheel a cart out of the service room, a native girl about twenty years old. He gave her a wave and hoped she might be a university student like Richard, working to escape the reserve life. He would have stopped to talk to her but he needed a coffee and something to quiet his grumbling stomach. He chuckled to think that the Anahim Hotel must have the only bar in the province that opened at seven in the morning for breakfast.

He was first through the door at seven, but four burly men came in right after him and settled in a corner booth. Loggers, he thought, judging by their clothing: bare heads, macs, broad suspenders, padded pants, and work boots. Only one, the youngest of the group, paid any attention to him and then only briefly. None were native. They spoke in deep, rough voices. Hard men.

The waitress served him first. She was considerably older than the afternoon girl but had a similar personality. A big lady with breasts that Blakemore would describe as two watermelons near ready for picking.

"What's tickling your fancy this morning, chief?" she said. "And where's that big hunk that came in with you yesterday?"

"Getting his beauty sleep. He needs it."

"Wouldn't kick him out of my bed for eatin' crackers."

Coswell ordered the Hungry Man Special. Mealtimes were becoming too unpredictable not to stock up.

"I thought the logging industry had pretty well shut down in the province," he said. "I'm surprised to see the men over there. They are loggers, aren't they?"

"Yep. Fallers, the lot of them. Going after pecker poles before the bugs get them all. Government's giving big incentives."

"Pecker poles?"

"You know. Skinny trees."

"Don't elaborate," he said. "I get your drift."

She rolled over to the kitchen and clipped his order onto a carousel, giving it a good spin when she did so.

"Don't do that!" the cook shouted from the back.

"Eff off, Charlie," she said and gave it another spin before heading over to the loggers' table.

Blakemore came in just as Coswell finished his breakfast and was onto his second coffee refill. "You should have woke me up," he said. "Now I've got to hurry."

"No. Take your time. My corporal will just be getting into the office. I'll finish my coffee and then give him a call. We might as well meet back here."

"Good, now let me see that menu."

Coswell passed it over. "See those four guys in the corner over there?" he said.

Blakemore looked over at them. "What about them?"

"They're loggers. Fallers, the waitress said."

"So?"

"More people in the bush. And as I recall, fallers work well ahead of everyone else. Any operations going on along that Hobson's trail?"

"I don't know. But dammit, we're going to end up suspecting everyone if we start thinking that way."

"Just a thought," Coswell said. "Okay, you eat your breakfast and wait till I come back."

"Don't hurry. I want nothing on my plate right now but bacon and eggs."

***
***

Coswell phoned Vancouver from his room. Corporal James answered his extension on the very first ring.

"Thanks for hanging around on a Saturday morning," Coswell said. "Were you able to get that information for me?"

"Got it all and it's ready to send," he said. "Do you have internet up there?"

"I doubt it," Coswell replied, "but this hotel does have a fax machine. Give me ten minutes to go down to the office and receive it. I sure as hell don't want that information in the public domain."

"Right, sir. I'll start timing as of now. Ten minutes." But before Coswell could hang up, the corporal had a final thought. "Should I transfer you over to Inspector Ward? He came in this morning too."

"Don't you dare."

"Yes, sir."

The golf courses must have been rained out, Coswell surmised, or Ward had to put in extra time to make up for his absentee homicide inspector. Either way, Ward would be in a bad mood.

***

"That was too quick," Blakemore said when Coswell returned. "I'm not even halfway through yet."

"Don't bitch. We'll go over this together."

"You go over it. I'll listen carefully."

Coswell remained silent for a few minutes while he sorted out the five-page fax. "The Johnson brothers. Not much considering their reputation. A few DUIs. Interesting that Art Johnson was still under a driving suspension when he died. Maybe that's why Brent Hansen stopped them."

He read on.

"Couple of drunk and disorderlies in Williams Lake dating back a few years. Oh, and I see they hit the big time in Vancouver. Hauled up before a judge for beating up a prostitute. She laid charges but they got off. Nothing at all on Garret or Tom Porter."

"What about the gun registry?"

Again, Coswell read for a minute before replying. "Much more interesting. Our Sam Hansen is a most obedient citizen. He's registered every one of his guns, it appears, and guess what?"

"What?"

"He owns a Colt .45 revolver."

"Doesn't every cowboy? What about Garret?"

"Even more interesting. He's registered nothing."

Blakemore whistled. "Now we're getting somewhere," he said. "But it's my turn to get on the phone. I'll see if Dr.

131

Basra's dug out those slugs yet. A little ballistic evaluation might just clear this whole thing up."

He came back three minutes later.

"He's sick, for Christ's sake. How can a doctor be sick? His nurse said maybe this afternoon. Sounded like he'd have to drag himself off his deathbed just to do a little autopsy."

"That is disappointing," Coswell said. "But I'm sure he'll get at it as soon as he can. I hope you passed on how important that information will be to us."

"Told her to tell him the whole case is hanging in the balance."

"Good. That may not have been an exaggeration. In the meantime, however, I think we should pay another visit to Chief Isaac and hope he isn't in his sweat lodge. We might have trouble bullying him out of it, what with his dead sons and all."

***

"The chief seems to have abandoned his court," Coswell said when they drove onto Issac's property. Once again, there was no answer to his knock and nobody in the sweat lodge. They entered the house.

"Someone's cleaned up," Blakemore said. "The dishes are gone out of the sink and the whole place looks tidier. I can't imagine old Isaac doing that. He must have maid service."

The bedrooms, too, had been straightened out and the beds made. Freshly laundered clothes were stacked on each one. Coswell went straight to the steamer trunk and opened it.

"Pot's gone ... Daniels?"

"Must have been. I wonder if the maid was part of the program."

"Good thought. We'll squeeze her name out of Daniels."

They returned to their vehicle and headed to the village.

A hundred metres along the access road from Isaac's driveway, Coswell noticed a metal gate on the same side with a PRIVATE PROPERTY — KEEP OUT sign bolted to it.

"Another pot plantation?" Blakemore said, noting the inspector's interest.

"Maybe, but it could also be Tom Porter's property. Let's have a look."

Blakemore got out and unlatched the gate for Coswell to drive through, then closed it before returning to the cruiser.

In keeping with the neighbourhood, trees screened the view into the clearing where the buildings were located, such as they were: a tiny shack, an outhouse, and a small stable with a corral. Two quarter horses looked through the railing at them.

Blakemore went over to the shack and peered in the window. "God, what a dump. Looks like some hermit's abode." He tried the door. It was unlocked. "Should I go in?" he said.

Coswell didn't answer. He was standing beside the cruiser, apparently mesmerized by the horses.

"You gone cowboy or something?" Blakemore said. "Nothing special about those two nags."

"No. Not the horses. Look what's parked behind — that black thing."

Blakemore looked. "It's a horse trailer. Not a big surprise, I'd say."

Coswell walked quickly over to the shack. "You stay outside," he said, "and shout if you hear anyone coming."

Before Blakemore could comment, Coswell disappeared inside, but in just a few minutes, he came back out and closed the door.

"It's Porter's place, all right. Some truck magazines with his name on the address label."

"Unless you found a gun or another stack of weed, I'm not impressed."

"I found neither. But don't you see ... the trailer?"

"The trailer?"

"Porter could have driven one of his horses to a road that would get him well up the mountain towards the Johnsons' camp. I'll just bet such a road exists, and that truck of his could pull a train up there."

Blakemore shook his head. "Loggers and trailers. You really are reaching," he said.

"Stranger things have happened, and this is strange country. Don't pooh-pooh the idea so fast. I'll check with Richard. Also, I should have included Tom Porter in that gun registry search."

"You'd have wasted your time. Porter's an aboriginal. Aboriginals boycotted the registry," Blakemore said. "Along with a good number of ranchers, farmers, trappers, and grampa's-gun-in-the-attic people. We were lucky to get that data on Hansen. Someone obviously nagged him."

"You are such a wet blanket," Coswell said.

***
***

For the second time, flashing red and blue lights appeared behind Coswell after he accelerated out of a turn onto a straight-away section of the highway. Blakemore laughed. "Didn't I warn you?" he said. "Ninety klicks up here and that's an obvious spot for a speed trap."

"Don't nag. That bastard knows it's us. Why doesn't he turn the damn flashers off?"

And they didn't go off, even after Coswell pulled over and stopped. He watched in the rear-view mirror as the tribal cruiser came up behind him and parked. They waited, but no one got out.

"Now what's he doing?" Coswell said.

"Running us through his stolen vehicle list?" Blakemore said.

"You are getting on my nerves."

Finally, the door opened and Daniels' lumbering figure emerged. With maddening slowness, he walked over to Coswell's side of the cruiser, citation book in hand. Coswell rolled down the window.

"Clocked you at a hundred and ten," Daniels said, "and rising. Couldn't be speeding officially, unless I've gone blind and deaf. No lights. No siren. Tsk, tsk." His arrogance had returned with a vengeance.

"Give me the damn ticket, then," Coswell said, and to his astonishment, Daniels wrote one out and handed it to him.

"You have a nice day," Daniels said.

Coswell snatched the ticket and tossed it onto the dash. "Now it's my turn," he said. "I want a formal meeting with you regarding our murder investigation."

"No problem. Just follow me back to the village. I might go a bit slow for you, but you'd best stay behind me."

With that, he returned to his cruiser, started it up, and pulled onto the pavement. He drove by them, eyes straight ahead, and didn't turn the annoying red-blue lights off until he'd gone a hundred metres down the highway. Coswell followed.

"He didn't put his turn signal on when he pulled out," Blakemore said. "Want to flash him?"

"Piss off."

***
***

If anything, Daniels smug demeanour got even worse back at his office. He leaned back in his chair, hands behind his head and gazed at the two Mounties.

"All right, gentlemen. Let's get at it. I've got things to do and places to go."

Coswell choked back his irritation. "First," he said. "It appears that the Johnson killings have raised the hostility level in this neighbourhood to a dangerous level, which, in my opinion, obliges you to cool it down."

Daniels face hardened. "I don't need advice from big-city Mounties to tell me how to treat my own people. And, in my opinion, you've added to the problem by poking around here instead of concentrating on the Hansen bunch."

To his annoyance, Coswell found himself on the defensive. "Concentrating anywhere means we've pretty well made up our minds who the guilty parties are, and in a homicide investigation, that's unprofessional. Now let's move on."

Daniels folded his arms across his chest. Stubborn.

Coswell turned to Blakemore. "Go ahead, Sergeant," he said.

Blakemore, mildly surprised to be shoved to the front, took over. "We see that the pot's been removed from the trunk at Chief Isaac's ... you?"

"Yes. I entered the premises and extracted the illegal substance. I didn't need a warrant, of course, knowing it was there. I presume you had an equally legal reason for entering?"

Blakemore, taken aback by Daniels' sudden sophistication, told himself to be careful. "We were investigating the residence of two murder victims."

"Owned by Chief Isaac. One would have thought it wise to obtain his permission first."

Coswell ran out of patience. "Oh, cut the bullshit, Daniels. Are you going to cooperate or not?

"Would I do anything but?"

The chief's smirk infuriated Coswell, but he let Blakemore carry on. "We'd like to know the name of the person who cleans Chief Isaac's house."

"Esther Martin, his daughter. She works at the post office in Anahim."

Lovely, Coswell thought. The odds of her spilling the beans on her dead brothers would be a big fat zero.

Blakemore continued. "Speaking of Chief Isaac, where is he at this moment?"

"Gone to Williams Lake. Someone conveniently ordered the bodies sent there before he could see them. His only sons. Shame, really."

"Enough of this game-playing," Coswell said. "We're leaving."

As the two Mounties headed for the door, Daniels gave them a parting shot: "If there's anything I can do to help you gentlemen, just ask."

✦✦✦

Coswell stopped the cruiser at the intersection of the village road and the highway.

"This is ridiculous," he said. "I literally don't know which way to turn. Until we find out what calibre of gun did the shooting, there isn't much point of barging in on the Hansens. I think it needs to be timed perfectly."

"Maybe we should track Richard down," Blakemore said. "Without us cramping his style, he might have heard something around town."

"Good idea. I'm surprised we haven't seen him yet this morning. I wonder where he is."

The answer to his question came just after they had started down the highway toward Anahim, and spotted Richard's pickup turn onto the pavement heading their way. Coswell pulled onto the shoulder, rolled down his window, and waited. Richard stopped his truck across from them and rolled down his window. He wasn't alone. His grandmother sat beside him.

"Just taking Gramma to the village," he called over. "Her craft group meets today at the tribal centre. Great place to spread the word about our meeting tonight. Where are you going?"

"Back to the hotel."

Gramma said something to Richard. He listened, then called back out the window. "She told me not to worry about picking her up. She's going to walk back to the house when she's finished. No arguing. I'll meet you at the hotel."

"That's some lady," Blakemore said. "No wonder Richard's become what he is."

"Yes. Love and attention can beat down some awfully tough barriers. I wonder how many more like her live around here."

***

"I'll reserve us a seat in the bar," Coswell said, when they got back to the hotel. "You go check for messages."

"Okay, but order me a coffee and a piece of that carrot cake I saw on the counter this morning."

Richard came in just as Blakemore disappeared into the lobby. Coswell waved him over. "Hope you beat your former boss to the highway. He's handing out tickets like party favours."

"Don't tell me he gave *you* a speeding ticket. That's rich."

"Rich is right. Damn near two hundred bucks. I'll have to do some creative accounting to sneak that through the budget."

The door from the lobby burst open and Blakemore strode in, looking uncharacteristically deep in thought.

"News?" Coswell said.

Blakemore sat down with a thud. "Maybe I should order a beer instead of coffee."

"What happened?"

"Well, I must have impressed the hell out of Basra's nurse. She got him up and moving. He went to the morgue and extracted the slugs."

"And?"

"They weren't from a .45."

"What, then?"

"A .38, of all things."

Coswell's eyes widened. "A Saturday night special? That's a city punk's gun."

Richard joined the conversation. "Not necessarily," he said. ".38 revolvers go way back: World War I and before. Even the old North West Mounted Police had them as standard issue."

"You don't have to go back that far," Blakemore said. "That's the pea shooter I got when I graduated from Regina in the mid-nineties. Thank God the Force switched to nine-millimetre semi-automatics right after. Gave us a fair fight with the bad guys."

"Interesting," Coswell said. "But I don't think the Johnsons were shot by a Mountie. Now let's try to get a handle on this. Who on earth would be running around in the outback with a .38 revolver?"

Silence.

"What about insurance against bears for hikers or people who work in the bush?" Coswell asked.

"Like your loggers?" Blakemore replied. "They'd be pretty stupid. A .38 would only work if you'd rather shoot yourself in the head than get mauled to death by a grizzly."

"Perhaps a young city lad came up here for a job. I understand there's some sort of rush to get the trees cut and hauled out before the bugs get them. Must be a need for extra workers."

"And brought his convenience-store-robbing .38 with him?" Blakemore said. "That's a big stretch."

"When the forensic lab in Vancouver gets the bullets, you'll have some answers," Richard said. "They can identify the manufacturer and even the age of the gun to a degree. Little changes in barrel design over the years show up on the slugs."

"I sure as hell hope so, because I'm running out of ideas," Coswell said.

Silence again, but this time it was broken by Sam Hansen entering the bar. He saw them and came directly over to their table.

"Just in town fuelling up," he said. "I saw your school meeting notices. Don't know if that'll lessen the local heat, but I applaud the effort."

"Part of the job," Blakemore said. "Keeping the peace."

Hansen laughed. "King Solomon himself couldn't do that in this neck of the woods," he said. "We need a generation or two to die out first."

Blasting the Johnsons away represented a good start, Coswell mused.

"Bonny's heading back to Vancouver tomorrow," Hansen said. "She's arranged an afternoon barbecue as one of those celebration-of-life things for Brent. Nothing big. Just a few of her friends and us. Would the three of you like to come? You'll have lots of time to get to your meeting."

Richard and Blakemore looked at Coswell, whose mind had just jammed up at the unexpected invitation. Why was Hansen doing this? To get an inside track on their investigation, most likely. But an informal visit to the ranch could be to their advantage as well. Garret was still a person of interest and perhaps a .38 pistol could be found on the ranch somewhere. Also, once a few drinks had loosened them up, the friends might reveal some useful information.

"We'd be delighted," he said. "Thank you for asking. For some reason, policemen aren't at the top of most people's invitation list."

"No. It's fitting," Hansen said. "Brent was overjoyed to be a Mountie. He'd have been pleased you attended."

He declined their invitation to join them for coffee. "I have to rush back," he said. "The shindig starts at two and I've left

Garret minding the spit. Prefers his beef burnt to a crisp, so I need to be there to take it off." He looked at Blakemore's carrot cake. "Don't fill up," he said. "Besides plenty of beef, the girls have put together a big spread."

After he'd left, Blakemore voiced his delight. "A real Cariboo barbecue! Does life get any better?"

"I'm looking forward to it as well," Coswell said. "But don't forget to keep your eyes and ears open. The answer to our murder mystery may well end up being at that ranch."

"Nice he included me this time," Richard said. "But I'll bet Maggie and I'll be the only First Nations blood there."

"Isn't that enough?" Coswell teased. "Maggie, I mean."
Richard blushed.

"I presume we're going to dress casual," Blakemore said. "Leave the uniforms off."

"Right," Coswell replied. "The guests will know we're Mounties, but we want to look as off-duty as possible. Better hit that store again, I think. Those denim shirts looked quite smart."

"What about ten-gallon hats and string ties?"
"Very funny."

✳✳✳

They pulled into the Hansens' driveway a few minutes after two and realized they were probably the last to arrive. A half-dozen vehicles were parked in front of the house, but something going on in the corral drew their attention. Dust rose in the air above it and people were hanging on the railings. As they neared, they expected to see another calf-branding session but the corral was empty except for a single rider pulled up at one end, head turned, gazing intently down at a chute below. The rider looked familiar.

"It's Maggie!" Richard said. "I'll be damned. She's a roper. Stop for a second, would you? I want to watch."

She was indeed a roper. A calf exploded from the chute. Her horse took off like a shot right behind it. A lasso whirled, then snaked over the calf's head. In one motion, the horse jerked to a stop, the calf flopped down, and Maggie was on top of it, a rope clenched in her teeth. She gathered three flailing hooves, pulled the rope from her teeth, and wrapped it round the animal's legs twice before giving it a tug. The whole process took only seconds. She stood, hands raised in the air.

"Wow," Richard said. "She's good."

"I'll say," Blakemore agreed. "Wouldn't want to run away from that filly. Better be careful, Richard."

Coswell started the cruiser up again and parked at the end of the line of vehicles. Hansen and his daughter came over to greet them.

"What do you think of those Hobbema girls?" Bonny said, looking at Richard. "Aren't they something?"

"Wish she could cook as well," Hansen said. "Time for her to get back to the kitchen. We'll be eating soon."

"Oh, don't be such a grump," Bonny said. "She's entertaining the group and it's all ready anyway. I can cook a little, you know." She told them to go introduce themselves and watch the fun. "I'll bring you something to drink. You'll enjoy the riesling I've opened, Inspector. Another lovely Nk'Mip wine," she said, looking mischievously at her father. He frowned.

"Just a beer for me," Blakemore said. "Anything made from hops."

"And for you, Richard, I have a non-alcoholic punch."

Aside from Garret, who was supervising the event, most of the observers were in their twenties, Brent's age. They all knew Richard, who started to perform the introductions, but Coswell cut him off, fearing he'd refer to them as "Sergeant" and "Inspector."

"I'm Mark," he said, "and my linebacker friend here is Paul." He saw Blakemore suck in his gut.

They were received with nods mostly, but a couple of the men shook their hands.

"Who's next?" Garret called out, obviously bored by social conventions. He was sitting high on the railing, operating the chute.

A chorus of "Richard, Richard" followed. Richard shook his head.

"You're not going to let some Alberta cowgirl win the ribbon, are you?" Garret said, his eyes taunting.

"I'd be quite happy to have her win the ribbon," Richard answered back. "I'm out of practice."

They would have none of it. Boos and hisses.

He climbed through the railings. Maggie was still standing there, holding her horse's reins. She handed them over with a shy smile. "Don't get hurt," she said.

She might as well have injected testosterone straight into his veins. He returned her smile and mounted the horse. "Just watch and learn," he said.

He kicked the horse into a trot and circled the corral a couple of times, lazily swinging the lasso before stopping next to the chute. He leaned forward in the saddle, grasped the pommel with his left hand, and shouted "Go!" Garret opened the gate and a calf shot into the ring.

From Blakemore and Coswell's point of view, Richard seemed to do exactly as Maggie had done, but there were subtle differences: the lasso snaked out a moment sooner, less line played out before the horse jerked to a stop, and the calf was still in the air when Richard leapt from the saddle. There were no flailing hooves. He had three legs gathered and tied before the calf regained the wind that had been knocked out of it. Maggie watched him through the railing. Still on his knees, he faced her and raised his hands. His face broke into a smile ... and then he winked at her.

"Jeesuzz," Blakemore said. "If that's out of practice, I'm Queen of the May."

Maggie's laugh startled Coswell, standing beside her: the spontaneous laugh of a young girl who didn't have a care in the world. But the joy lasted only seconds before her face clouded over. She turned and hurried back to the house.

That ended the contest; no one else wanted to try. They began to move en masse toward the wonderful aromas wafting from the barbecue. Richard offered to help Garret return the calves to the pasture. "No," Garret said. "I can handle them by myself, but it would save me a trip if you'd take Rusty back to the stable and tie her up. I'll deal with the saddle."

Surprisingly, Blakemore hadn't moved with the crowd toward the food, and before Richard could get back on the horse, he called to him. "I don't suppose I could do that, could I? I've been dying to feel what it's like being on a genuine riding horse. That Clydesdale I rode didn't really cut it."

"Sure, why not?" Richard said. He opened the gate and led the horse through.

Blakemore, feeling confident after his cross-country ride, swung himself into the saddle and adjusted the reins.

"A little warning," Richard said. "Rusty's a quarter horse, which is kind of like the dragster of the equestrian world. See how she's built — all rump and it isn't fat. You'd better just walk her."

"Sounds like an old girlfriend of mine, but I'll be careful."

Richard didn't head up to the house. He had a premonition, and in a moment it came true. Garret, on another horse, was moving the calves away from the corral in an orderly line, but the sight of Blakemore, who had quickly urged Rusty into a canter, caused one young animal to veer away from its brethren.

All of Rusty's instincts and training kicked in. Her massive hindquarters exploded into a takeoff worthy of an Olympic sprinter. Blakemore instantly found himself looking straight up at the sky, the back of his head on Rusty's rump and his feet still in the stirrups, pointed straight ahead. Try as he might, he could not right himself. He heard Garret thundering up beside him.

"Hold on," he said.

But Blakemore had nothing to hold onto. He'd let go of the reins. There was a whistling noise, then a thump as Rusty skidded to a four-point halt. Blakemore, however, did not. He flew forward and slammed his face onto the horse's neck. Blood spurted from his nose.

Garret jumped to the ground and removed his rope from the calf's neck. "Figured that was the best way to stop her," he said, "without getting you slewed into the dirt.

Blakemore tried to thank him, but his hand squeezing his spouting nose prevented an audible response.

Richard came running up. "Are you okay?"

Blakemore nodded his head vigourously and slid to the ground.

"I think I'll lead her the rest of the way," he said, releasing his nose just long enough to get the words out. He looked back at the house. It appeared that no one had noticed his performance ... except Coswell, who stood looking his way and shaking his head.

***

The barbecue looked like something out of a boilermaking foundry: a two-hundred-gallon oil tank cut in half and hinged. The huge lid opened and closed with minimal effort thanks to a large counterweight. What appeared to be half a beef carcass turned on the spit over a bed of wood coals.

Guests circulated through the dining room, filling their plates with salads and vegetables but leaving room for giant slabs of beef that Sam Hansen carved outside on a butcher block table.

As he stood in line, Coswell noted two uncorked bottles of red wine set on a small table beside a washtub filled with cans of beer on ice. After he'd gotten his chunk of perfectly cooked meat, he returned to the dining room for the red wine. A plump young woman with dark hair was already there, reading the label. Coswell looked over her shoulder.

"Bonny seems to be supporting our First Nations' winery," he said. "I'm Mark Coswell."

She turned and faced him. "Inspector Coswell, I've been told. Pleased to meet you. I'm Jean Neiborg." She pointed to the wine. "I just read the blurb on the bottle, but how do you pronounce N-k'-M-i-p?"

"Inka-meep. Wonderful vintages. You'll enjoy their Merlot. Let me pour you a glass."

She laughed. "Thank you, but I'm no connoisseur. Coming from here and being a student leaves me in the plonk class."

She stood, plate of food in one hand, wine in the other, and looked around for a place to sit. He knew that she'd prefer being with her contemporaries, but this was too good an opportunity to miss.

"Why don't you join me?" he said. "I really don't know anyone other than the Hansens and they're busy tending to guests. This country fascinates me and I hope you can give me a little history." A look of reluctance crossed her face, but he persisted. "I see most are eating out on the porch but I prefer inside away from the hovering insects, don't you? Let's try the sitting room?"

Good manners prevailed. "Okay," she said and followed him.

The room was deserted.

"My two colleagues will join us shortly, but meanwhile, let's get started at this magnificent food."

She didn't need a second invitation, obviously enjoying food as much as he did. Blakemore appeared at the door, unseen by the woman. Coswell gave him a "go away" glance and hoped the sergeant would find an equally promising interviewee. Richard, he knew, would be hanging around wherever Maggie was, and so, after sharing a few murmurs of pleasure over the food, he began his questioning.

"I guess being from around here, you knew Brent pretty well?"

"Not that well. He was the little nuisance brother. Bonny and I are the same age. Best friends."

"And you're still in school?"

"Doing my Ph.D. at UVic ... in psychology."

She returned to eating. Coswell had to time his questions between mouthfuls—his and hers.

"Is your family into ranching as well?"

"No. My dad's in the logging business. Machines are his thing, not horses. In my early teenage years, that almost broke my heart. I loved horses. Bonny, bless her, came to my rescue and got her father to let me ride theirs." She thought for a moment. "In fact, I probably made a pest of myself. I practically lived here 'til we both went off to university."

Bonanza. He had struck gold.

"Bonny is holding up well, considering she's just lost her only brother," he said. "Nuisance or not, they must have been close. There were just the two children, I believe."

"I should have said he was a nuisance to me. Bonny protected him like a mother hen."

"From whom?"

She paused, weighing her reply. "Sam Hansen, if you haven't noticed, has a rod up his ass. Nothing Brent did lived up to his expectations. Bonny, on the other hand, could do no wrong—Daddy's perfect princess. She adored Brent and hated the way his father rode him. She stepped between them so many times you wouldn't believe it."

"I'm surprised. I've heard that even the First Nations community admired Brent. Around here, that has to say something. And I understand from Richard that he hunted and competed in rodeos. Surely that would be manly enough for anyone."

"Not old born-in-the-saddle Hansen. First Nations folk are not on his list of people his family should be intimate with, and he considered calf-roping a girl's sport. I suppose if Brent had killed himself getting thrown off a bronc or gored by a bull, his old man would have been happy. Those are 'man' sports."

"Did their mother not interject on her son's behalf?"

"A wonderful woman, Anne Hansen, but she was old school when it came to obeying her husband. That dominant male tradition is still alive and well around these parts … Bonny excluded, of course." She laughed. "I'm really sounding like a psychologist, aren't I? How boring."

"Not boring at all. There's a lot of psychology in my line of work."

She laughed again. "Then we're talking shop. Thank goodness no one's listening." Suddenly, her eyes narrowed. "Bonny's told me you strongly suspect that the Johnson brothers killed Brent. You're on the right track there, for sure. Those two were bags of bile, just like their father."

"I have heard that from other sources, but what Bonny told you is true. It's a little early, however, to let that out. We're still awaiting forensic reports."

"No one will hear it from me," she said. "My lips are sealed. But tell me more."

Coswell smiled. "Do you say that to all your patients?"

"Caught me," she said. "But I am interested in criminal behaviour. Puts a little spice in my usual diet of nice neurotics."

Coswell was beginning to warm to this lady. "Well. Here's

a thought for you. I think Brent's murder was an accident. Someone got provoked, a manslaughter rating at most, but the Johnsons were killed in cold blood. That's murder one. A horse of a completely different colour, if I may use the local vernacular."

"Oooh," she said. "Do you have anyone in mind?"

"I thought *you* might have a suggestion. You're much closer to the ground on this."

Yet another laugh. "Turned the table right around. I should have you as one of my profs instead of that old wood I've been assigned as mentors in my Ph.D. program."

"I've been in the business a long time," Coswell said.

"Okay, but I can't really help you much. I don't even spend the summers at home anymore. But, speaking clinically, I guess you have to consider vengeance as a motive. Sam Hansen in particular. Having his son murdered by Indians would strike him to the core—and he's not a man to cross, even with minor matters."

"We have considered him, of course, but he has an excellent alibi. Both he and Garret were with us when we found the bodies, and the time of death makes it unlikely he could have done it."

"Good. Much as I dislike the man, I'm glad for Bonny's sake. But where do you look now? I'd suggest the reserve. Sam Hansen isn't the only one who hated those two. I remember an incident one summer between semesters when I was home. Tom Porter got a real mad going at them. Said they were rustling his cattle and threatened to shoot on sight if he caught them at it."

"That's a name we've been given already, but can you think of anyone else?"

"I'm afraid not. Like I said, I've lost touch with the local scene."

Coswell had one more avenue to explore. "I understand

that there's been a resurgence of logging in the area. Your father must be pleased."

"Is he ever! His business just about went under, like most of the ranchers around here."

Coswell tucked that latter bit of information away for future reference and continued his train of questioning. "It must be hard for your father to get crews together. I presume the slump in the industry forced most of the regular loggers to find work elsewhere."

"You got that right. I've seen some of the types he's had to hire lately. I think he gets them straight from jail." She caught the inference immediately. "Ah. Perhaps the Johnson slayers weren't local at all. Good thinking, and my father has operations all over those hills. Bonny told me where their bodies were found."

"Do you think he'd be willing to help us?"

"Absolutely. My dad's a great guy, but give me a little time to set it up for you. He lives and breathes work these days. Doesn't spend much time at home."

Coswell gave her one of his cards. "We're staying at the Anahim Hotel. They're good about taking messages for us."

Suddenly, Bonny swept into the room. "There you are," she said. "Come on out to the porch. I'm going to give a short toast to Brent's memory. Fill your glasses."

Coswell detected a note of annoyance in her voice and wondered if she was displeased that he'd cornered her talkative friend.

When they went outside, Coswell saw Richard and Blakemore gathered with the rest. Richard stood beside Maggie; Blakemore still eating. Bonny called them all to attention.

"Brent hated speeches and I'm going to make this short, but I just want to say out loud what most of you know. My brother was a credit to his family, his community, and his profession. We've all lost something precious."

Her voice caught, and she simply raised her glass.

"To Brent," everyone said.

Conversations resumed, although in a more subdued tone. Jean Neiborg went directly to Bonny after the toast and gave her a hug. A few more joined her. Coswell saw Sam Hansen disappear into the house and quickly followed him. He guessed that the father's emotions had boiled up as much as his daughter's and sought the privacy of his den. Perfect opportunity to corner the man, alone and maybe vulnerable.

***
***

He was sitting in one of the leather chairs, the wineglass replaced with a highball glass filled to the brim with Scotch. There were no tears. Defeat more than grief etched his face.

"We have to leave shortly," Coswell said. "I wanted to thank you for inviting us today and again offer our condolences for your loss."

"Thank you."

Hansen appeared to shake off his mood and regain his composure. "Have a seat," he said. Coswell sat. "Your meeting tonight. I presume you'll spread the word that I'm not involved in the Johnsons' murders?"

"I will most certainly suggest that there are other possibilities."

Hansen smiled. "I'm still on your list, then?"

"Right now, everyone's on my list, including the members of this household."

"This household? Who else besides me?"

"Garret, maybe. We have a reasonably accurate time of death now and a good rider could have made it from here, do the shooting, and return before dawn."

Hansen frowned. "I don't think so. Garret and Brent were close. Probably a better father to the boy than me, but he's not a violent man despite his demeanour."

"Never any clashes with the Johnsons? Add some fuel to the fire? I understand they ruffled more than a few feathers among the populace."

"No. Their activities didn't extend this far. We heard about it all, of course, but since it didn't affect us, we never got our backs up."

"Is Garret from around here?"

"He's originally from Chicago. Doesn't talk about it much. I think he had a tough childhood. My father took him on years ago. We grew up together in an arm's-length sort of way. He picked up ranching skills even faster than I did."

"An American," Coswell said. "No wonder he didn't register any of his guns. That would be totally alien to someone from the right-to-bear-arms U.S. of A."

Hansen chuckled. "You ran us through the gun registry? How clever."

"Routine."

"Would you like to inspect my arsenal? My feelings won't be hurt."

"Just your pistols."

"The Johnsons were shot with a pistol? Amazing."

He got out of his chair and went over to the gun cabinet and opened it.

"Well, that lets me off the hook. I have only one and I'm quite happy to hand it over to you. It's my father's. I use it occasionally to kill an animal from our herd when we need to restock the freezer."

It took Coswell only a glance to see that the pistol was a .45. Long guns filled the rest of the cabinet. "No. The murder weapon was a .38 revolver."

"A girl's gun? Believe me, you won't find Garret with a .38."

"Perhaps not, but .38s are common in Chicago and they're not exclusive to girls. Maybe he brought one with him."

"Point taken," Hansen said. "But if he has one, I've never

seen it, and over all these years, that would be unusual."

"Does Bonny own a gun?"

Hansen almost convulsed. "Bonny! That'll be the day. She can't even stand seeing a chicken beheaded. No. Bonny stays as far away from guns as she can get."

Coswell rose. "Thank you for cooperating like this," he said. "I know it's a bad time for you."

Hansen's smile vanished. "It is. I think I'll stay here a bit longer. Goodbye, Inspector, and good luck with your meeting."

Coswell turned to leave.

"And good luck with Garret," Hansen said.

***
***

Getting Blakemore and Richard to leave the party took some persuasion. Richard didn't want to leave Maggie, and Blakemore, despite the discomfort of his swollen nose, had settled in to the food and drink. Coswell finally managed to drag them away and led them back to the cruiser. Ignoring Blakemore's grumbling, he drove off before they'd even fastened their seatbelts.

Once back on the pavement, when they could hear one another, he took reports.

"I noticed you didn't circulate a lot, Richard," Coswell said. "But don't apologize; she really is a doll. Did you find out more about her, though?"

"A little," he said. "She's had a rough life."

That appeared to be it. Richard didn't elaborate and Coswell didn't push him.

"What about you, Paul? I hope you didn't forget why we were there."

Blakemore bristled. "Of course not. I want this damn case settled as fast as you do. Our respective precincts are going to start howling soon with us being absent for so long."

"Oh, don't be so sensitive. What did you find out?"

Blakemore, only partially mollified, gave his report. "There is logging going on close to where we found the bodies. One of the young friends has a summer job up there."

"I've got that lead, too. Anything else?"

Blakemore looked disappointed. "A tiny bit about the drug scene here. Seems pot is a flourishing industry in the First Nations community. One young fellow I spoke to implied that a lot of the ranchers' kids get their supplies from the reserve. Not him, of course."

"Go on."

"The same kid also told me he thought Daniels had a hand in the business, that he was buddy-buddy with the Johnsons."

"Wow," Richard said. "I've heard nothing like that."

"Maybe Chief Isaac isn't the only one who considers you a maverick," Blakemore said. "Your contemporaries might worry about being squealed on by a guy who wants to be a Mountie."

"Damn," Coswell said. "We should have done an inventory of the marijuana in that trunk. We literally gave it to Daniels. There must have been a couple hundred packs of the stuff."

"He'd be pretty stupid not to turn it in, though."

"I wouldn't put anything past that man."

They all pondered that for a few moments before Blakemore moved on. "What did you find out from that roly-poly lady you were talking to in the parlour?" he asked Coswell. "Looked like you were having a cozy little tête-à-tête."

"Plenty."

He related his conversation with Jean Neiborg.

"Now we're cooking with gas," Blakemore said. "A whole flurry of leads and we've still got old Garret to go. When are you going to talk to him? "

"Soon, but not in a crowd of people, and before I do, I plan to have our colleagues in the US run a records check on him."

"Okay. What's the order now?"

"Meeting tonight at the school, Jean Neiborg's father tomorrow morning, and Garret some time after that."

They drove on, all three encouraged by the new leads.

10

THE ANAHIM SCHOOL TURNED OUT TO BE much larger than Coswell expected.

"Grades one to eight," Richard informed him. "Kids are bused in from a long ways away. Next public school is Bella Coola, a hundred and fifty kilometres west, or Tatla Lake seventy-five east.

"My god. And high schools?"

"Williams Lake and that's it. It's a hundred-and-fifty-kilometre bus ride, morning and afternoon, regardless of weather —we have a very efficient snowplowing system."

"That's obscene," Blakemore said. "I used to bitch about my two-block walk to high school in the West End because it was uphill coming home. And if they even thought it might snow in Vancouver, the schools would be closed."

"Good way to separate the wheat from the chaff, though," Coswell said. "Any kid that can put up with that and still want to go on has a good chance of succeeding. You, the Hansens, and Jean Neiborg are good examples."

"Unfortunately, a lot of potential gets blown away in that chaff," Richard said.

Coswell changed the subject as they turned into the school driveway. "It looks as though we'll have a lot of empty chairs for our meeting, Richard. I see a grand total of two cars parked in the lot."

"And one's the custodian's. The other belongs to Miss Eklund, the principal, but don't worry. Arrival at meetings in this community is a last-minute affair. Usually people come in order of prestige, so Gramma and her group will likely be last. Miss Eklund, by the way is another survivor of our school system. Her family's run the general store in Anahim for ages."

In Coswell's eyes, Miss Eklund looked far too young and stunning to be the principal of a school. Her attempt to disguise her youth and beauty with an unflattering business suit, dark-rimmed glasses, and blonde hair pulled back in a bun failed miserably.

"We've set up the auditorium for you," she said. "The seating in the classrooms is a bit uncomfortable for some of our people."

"Fat asses," Blakemore whispered to Richard.

"That will be fine," Coswell said. "I have no idea how many will come, but it doesn't matter. Any number will do. I gather word of mouth is a very effective way of spreading information in this community."

"Too true," she said.

***

They began to arrive, exactly as Richard had described, except all were First Nations — not a single white face to be seen. The first group consisted of younger women, some carrying infants, a few leading young children. Hardly any men came with them, although Coswell recognized Richard's friend Allen from the bar, and a smattering of teenagers. The two Hansen ranch hands, Andy and Verne, were there sitting off to the side in the very back row. Next came the elders — men first, almost a dozen strong. They sat together, isolated from the rest and well back from the front. No sign of Chief Isaac or Tom Porter. Lastly came Gramma's group, all matriarchs of the grandest variety. Whether by design or accident, the entire first row of seats was left vacant for them. Gramma led the way. She sat down at precisely seven-thirty.

Coswell had no problem with public speaking. In his role as an RCMP inspector, he had even given talks in some of the schools. But the audience staring at him now in this small auditorium, unsmiling and totally silent, almost unnerved him. There was none of the usual hum from pre-speech conversations. Even the children were quiet.

He planned to begin with a bit of humour to loosen everyone up, but this audience didn't look as though it could be loosened by a bomb. He walked over to the lectern that had been provided, and cleared his throat.

"Thank you all for coming," he began. "I know it's customary for police nowadays to be close-mouthed about their investigations, and there's a reason for that—technicalities that can get a criminal off. But I'm going to do things differently here. I think you people have a more down-to-earth idea of what's right and what's wrong, so I'm going to be completely open with you. I hope once you've heard the facts, you'll help us gather information that will solve these dreadful murders."

Still no response. Stone faces.

"We have a number of leads in the Johnson killings and we are looking seriously at each one. I know there's a feeling that Sam Hansen is responsible and we have considered that possibility, but recent information is pointing in another direction—the illegal drug trade. I'm sure you're all aware of the violence that's associated with that."

A few of the teenagers looked at one another, and Coswell was certain he saw an eyebrow or two raised ever so slightly in the elder group.

"Early forensic results indicate that the killer or killers came up Hobson's trail from below and attacked the Johnsons in their camp."

More raised eyebrows.

"They could, of course, have also run afoul of someone already in the area—people not from this community."

He paused, grasped the lectern on either side, and stared hard at the crowd.

"We will solve these murders, but we need two things from you. One, keep an open mind about this. You can see that a number of possibilities exist. And two, please come forward with any information that could help us, no matter how small."

Silence.

"Do you have any questions?"

More silence. Then, Gramma stood up.

"Gut tawk," she said, then turned and headed up the aisle to the exit followed by her entourage. This appeared to be the signal for everyone to leave and after some general shuffling, the rest filed out behind them, leaving Coswell still clutching the lectern, astounded.

Blakemore came over. "I don't smell a fart. I wonder what you said to cause the mass exodus."

Coswell relaxed. "Not exactly a standing O, I have to admit," he said.

Richard and Miss Eklund, who had been sitting at the rear of the auditorium, joined them. "You did great," Richard said. "We might get some information, and I think you've defused a situation that could have gotten out of hand."

"I hope you're right," Coswell said. "But those male elders didn't look like I impressed them one little bit."

"Maybe not. They're all Chief Isaac's cronies, but they're not immune to reason. I think you softened them up."

Miss Eklund seemed quite happy with his performance as well. "I know how you feel, Inspector," she said. "My first get-to-know-the-new-principal meeting went just like that, so far as the First Nations attendees were concerned. Not one of them said a word, and they'd known me since I was a little girl."

"Respect," Richard explained. "You'd become a teacher, a

professional, someone who should be listened to, not questioned. Very old-fashioned. A fault, really, but nice in a way."

She smiled. "I do remember more than a few questions from you, Richard."

"I'm an aberration," he said.

Coswell thanked her for arranging the meeting and, before he could stop himself, reached forward to shake her hand and said, "I hope we meet again."

Blakemore flashed him a look as they filed out, but Coswell preempted any comment when they got back into the cruiser.

"I was dying to throw in the fact that we're almost one hundred per cent sure the Johnsons massacred Sam Hansen's son," he said, "making them a couple of sons-a-bitches, not two glorious warriors."

"That might have backfired on you," Richard said. "To some of those old buggers, one less Mountie is no great loss. And Chief Isaac's sons have status."

***
***

They went back to the Anahim Hotel bar. Coswell decided that the meeting had been a success after all and wished to have a small celebration. He was also curious to see if some of the meeting crowd had spilled over there, particularly the male elders. Booze helped loosen tongues and release inner feelings.

The bar was busy, but the elders had obviously gone elsewhere. Some of the younger set were there, however, including Richard's friend, Allen. He glanced their way for only a second. Coswell noted also, that despite the fact they were all wearing their uniforms, the usual hush when they entered hadn't occurred.

"I think we're getting to be a fixture in this place," Blakemore said. "I feel downright at home."

"Your kind of place, all right," Coswell said. "But there's nowhere to sit except at the bar."

"Why not sit there? Afraid of someone getting the drop on you?"

"No. But I might want to order something to eat and I hate to compete with you for elbow room. I presume you'll be eating."

"I'm not hungry," Richard said. "That'll give you some extra room." He took a stool to Coswell's right.

No one appeared to be tending the bar.

"I see only one waitress in the whole place," Blakemore said. "A real cutie. Beats hell out of the weightlifter we had the first night here. But surely she doesn't have to tend the bar too."

In fact, she did. Returning with a tray of empty glasses, she plucked three cardboard coasters from a stack and dropped one in front of each of them before setting the tray down, her pretty young face showing the strain.

"I don't know whether to thank you guys or curse you. That meeting brought in a pile of extras."

She quickly unloaded the used glasses into a long steel tub, already overflowing, and shouted through the window to the kitchen, "Roger, you lazy bugger, get out here and haul these empties away."

Coming back, she fixed them with a no-nonsense look. "Kitchen's closed. You'll have to do with stuff in a package. No mixed drinks. What'll you have?"

"Whatever handle's closest to you, my sweetie," Blakemore said. "A mug of draft."

"I'm not your sweetie," she said. "My grandfather's younger than you."

She poured the mug and thumped it down on Blakemore's coaster.

Coswell smiled. "He's so uncouth," he said. "I really admire your looking after this whole place by yourself. Could I trouble you for a glass of red wine? Beer gives me the vapours." Blakemore almost choked mid-gulp.

She eyed them for a second, then bent down and pulled a litre bottle of red from under the counter. "Don't get much call for wine," she said. "You're the first out of this bottle. Should be good."

She unscrewed the cap, found a glass that looked more like a miniature brandy snifter, and filled it three-quarters full. Coswell estimated he was looking at almost eight ounces of a questionable vintage.

"Coke," Richard said, when his turn came. "Straight up, no mix."

"You got it," she said. But it didn't come in a can or a bottle. She reached into a metal bucket, pulled out a handful of ice cubes, and dropped them into a beer mug. This was followed by a spray of brown, foamy liquid from a hose with a nozzle attached.

"Perfect," Richard said when she set it down in front of him.

Then, before they could say another word, she grabbed her tray and was off.

"Damn," Blakemore said. "I at least wanted some potato chips or beer nuts."

"I'd wait my opportunity if I were you," Coswell said. "You haven't made a good impression."

"Yeah. Too bad I don't get the vapours like you do."

Coswell swirled the wine in his glass, surprised to see it actually had some legs to it, and a sniff confirmed that it was a passable Merlot.

"Do you have to do that?" Blakemore said. "You're embarrassing us."

Coswell looked up at the big mirror behind the bar. No one was paying them any attention, but before he could respond, he saw someone slide onto the stool beside Richard —the friend who'd been at the meeting. He could barely hear their conversation.

"Hey, Richard."

"Hey, Allen. How goes it?"

"Okay ... you?"

"Okay too."

Silence. Coswell started to lose interest, but the exchange quickly picked up.

"That drug thing's been going on for a while, you know," Allen said. "But just weed, no hard stuff."

"Pretty big supply for the local market."

"They exported."

"Grow it themselves?"

"No. There's a bunch came up as tree-planters a few years ago. Saw the potential for hiding a big grow operation in the area. They're the suppliers."

"How did they hook up with the Johnsons?"

"I'm not sure who approached who. Could have been either way, but having two Indians as mules worked out good for all parties."

"How do you know so much about all this, Allen? You and I never got into anything like that."

"Kid sister. Fifteen years old, for Christ's sake. I caught her smoking the stuff and threatened to tear the hide off her if she didn't tell me where she got it from. I did some heavy research after that."

"Did you speak to anyone about it?"

"Daniels. But that was a waste of time and I should have known it. He and the Johnsons are as close to kissin' cousins as you can get. Told me a little weed didn't hurt anyone."

"Why didn't you report them to the Mounties at the Pond?"

"Daniels put me off. I got the distinct feeling I should keep my mouth shut and you know how things go on this reserve. Those buddies of Chief Isaac at the meeting tonight are probably reporting to him right now. You're lucky being away. I've got to live here."

"Then why are you telling me?"

"I probably shouldn't be. They're dead now, but someone else will just pick up where they left off. Maybe you can stop it."

Neither man looked at the other during the entire conversation and when the waitress returned, Allen got up abruptly and left the bar.

"How are you guys doing?" she said, unloading yet another tray of empties. It appeared that she really didn't want an answer, having ascertained at a glance that they weren't yet ready for refills, but Blakemore spoke up.

"Our bodies need junk food in the worst way. How about giving us a couple of big bags of nacho chips and three or four of those beer nut packages? They're small."

All were clipped on a big wire frame with clothespegs. She expertly ripped off the desired items and piled them in front of Blakemore.

"Thanks," he said. "You truly are a sweetie."

This time, she smiled. "You're welcome, Gramps."

The moment she left to serve other patrons, Coswell turned to Richard. "Good job," he said. "Couldn't have done better myself."

"What happened?" Blakemore said. "I couldn't hear a thing."

Coswell filled him in.

"Wonderful," Blakemore said. "Now we have to beat the bushes looking for pot growers."

Richard looked slightly pained. "I'm kind of tied up tomorrow morning," he said. "Gramma's a dedicated churchgoer, and when I'm home I always attend with her. It's a tradition."

"And a good one," Coswell said. "She's proud of you and it's a chance to show off her fine grandson. Take the day off. We'll check in with you later if anything comes up."

*** ***

Their opportunity to beat the bushes, as Blakemore so aptly put it, came up sooner than expected. Richard had left for home in his pickup and the two Mounties headed to their rooms. Gerald, the front desk clerk, stopped them.

"Bert Neiborg wants you to call him right away. Here's his number. You can use this phone if you like. Nothing much doing here right now."

Coswell dialed. A deep, raspy voice came on the line. "That you, Inspector? Daughter says you want to talk to me about some of my crew."

"I would," Coswell said. "And I very much appreciate—"

Neiborg cut him off. "Got a better idea. If you think some of that riff-raff did a bad deed, you can talk to them direct. Got a copter hired to fly in parts to a busted skidder up there. You can go along. Lots of room. I'm going up too. Time I did a little checking of my own, which will take a couple of hours or so. Pilot will wait and fly us back."

"Excellent," Coswell said. "When and where should we meet you?"

"Gerald will give you directions. Liftoff's at six. See you there."

The line went dead. Coswell hung up.

"I didn't get a chance to ask him how long the flight was," he said, contemplating his queasy stomach.

Blakemore reacted only to the time. "Six in the bloody morning! Where will we get breakfast?"

11

BERT NEIBORG'S LOG DUMP was at the edge of town. As Coswell and Blakemore drove up from their hotel, huge stacks of timber seemed to go on endlessly in the predawn light before they saw the entrance to the yard. In a large clearing, intense xenon arc lights reflected off a single-rotor helicopter and a white truck parked beside it. Two men were transferring boxes from the truck to the helicopter. One turned out to be the pilot; the other was Bert Neiborg.

Coswell saw that Jean Neiborg had come by her body shape honestly; her father carried at least fifty excess pounds on his large frame. He didn't lack strength, though, hoisting the heavier boxes that the skinny pilot avoided.

"Glad you're on time," he said. "Just about ready to take off. I'm Bert. This is Les."

Nods were all that could be exchanged as both men continued with their loading. When they finished, Bert drove the truck away from the copter and parked it beside the cruiser.

"Climb aboard, gentleman," the pilot said. He sized the two of them up, and added, "Heaviest behind me, if you don't mind."

"No doubt who that is," Coswell said.

As Blakemore took his seat, Coswell spoke softly to the pilot. "I have a bit of a weak stomach. Could you keep this thing as steady as possible?"

The pilot looked at him with some apprehension. "Barf bags are in the seat-back in front of you," he said. "Can't help bouncing around a bit up there."

The pilot took his seat, strapped in, and the minute Bert climbed aboard, flicked on the ignition. The engine roared and the rotor began to turn. When they reached an ear-splitting pitch, the pilot lifted off. Coswell's stomach lagged slightly behind.

The morning air, fortunately, was dead still and the pilot had no difficulty holding his craft steady. The country below began to take on colour as the sun rose — the rich green of alfalfa fields, then darker forest broken by large yellow patches of muskeg. But a peculiar purple dominated most of the wooded area, the result of dying pine trees attacked by a beetle that had spread across the province like wildfire.

Bert turned in his seat and shouted back. "Ugly, isn't it? Goes to show how much damage environmentalists can do. Could have nipped this in the bud when it first started if they'd just let up a bit on the red tape." Coswell had to agree. The little patches of logging were minuscule in comparison to the sea of purple.

"Turns black next," Bert said. "And when that happens, the wood's of no use to anyone. Even now it doesn't pay well. That's why I want to keep this operation going up top. Still some good fir there."

The flight provided Coswell with useful information beyond the ecology lesson: from above, he could see a road that extended from the village well up into the hills—an access route for Tom Porter and his horse trailer. He also noticed a newer road that had been pushed through into Bert's logging operation on the far side—yet another possible route for a killer.

The landing pad for the helicopter consisted of a crude platform of logs but it lacked nothing in sturdiness. The machine settled onto it without a quiver. The pilot turned the engine off and in a moment the rotor came to a halt. Two men were waiting for them.

Bert took command immediately. He got out, opened the cargo door, and pointed to the heaviest of the boxes. "Okay, you two. Get over here and pull this part off first. I want it taken up to that skidder site as fast as your hairy legs can carry it. No hurry with the rest of this." He looked around. "Where are those hippies, anyway? They're damn lucky I bring their stuff in on my helicopter time. They should be here."

"Don't know, boss," one of the men said. "Maybe they didn't want to freeze their asses off getting out of their sleeping bags so early."

"Well, just put it off to the side. Leave it up to them to come get it. Most of it's booze anyway."

Coswell's ears perked up. Were these the grow-op people Richard's friend had mentioned? "There are people staying overnight on the mountain?" he said.

"Crew of tree-planters," Bert replied. "They've been coming up a few years now. Scruffy lot and my men can't stand them. Tree-huggers for the most part, but they make damn good money."

"I've heard they work hard for it, though," Coswell said. "And it can't be much fun living in the bush. I presume they stay in tents."

"Yeah, but they love it. Real outdoorsy, commune-with-nature types. They're useful to us. People aren't so dead set against cutting down trees if they think they're being replaced with new ones. That's why I do them a few favours."

"I've heard a rumour they could be planting more than trees up here."

Bert frowned. "A grow-op, you mean? I don't see how they'd have the time to tend it. There's a truck that brings up boxes of seedlings every couple of weeks for them. Uses my road. One of these days I'll charge them a toll."

Blakemore joined them. "How do you know they plant the seedlings?" he asked. "Does anyone check?"

"Government inspectors do spot checks. If the job's not being done right, the company's out of business."

"Have you actually seen an inspector come in here?" Coswell asked.

Bert thought for a moment. "Now that you ask, no. And I haven't heard any mention of one by my men. They'd have noticed for sure. Government people use helicopters a lot and I've got the only pad in the neighbourhood."

"Have you or any of your men gone over and looked at some of the planting?"

"No. Like I said, there's no love lost between loggers and hippies."

He pondered that for a moment. "You know, that would be one helluva cover," he said. "Plant a seedling and a pot plant together. They don't call it 'weed' for nothing. It would leave the fir seedlings in the dust. Brilliant. You've got to hand it to them if that's what they're doing."

"I'd like to talk to them and any of your men who were working near the top of the Hobson's trail three days ago."

"That's well above any of my operations. Closest would be a couple of fallers, but they sure as hell wouldn't be walking up any higher than they had to. Christ, they carry at least fifty pounds of equipment each trip."

Coswell persisted. "I'd still like a word with them."

"Well, now's a good time. Everything's backed up because of that broken-down skidder. Let's head on up to the dining hall. Les and I haven't had breakfast yet and I know damn well you haven't. Anahim's just waking up."

Blakemore beamed.

Les said he'd join them later. He wanted to check something in the engine first. "She was running a bit too hot coming up," he said.

"Hall" was a peculiar designation for the two trailers arranged side by side, one serving as kitchen, the other the eating area. In the latter, three men sat around a table for eight, empty plates in front of them, drinking coffee and smoking cigarettes. They were in stocking feet, their spiked boots lined up just inside the door. Coswell estimated the temperature in the room to be in the thirties. The men were stripped to the waist except for light undershirts. The arrival of their boss appeared to have little impact; there was barely a nod from either man. Bert noted Coswell's surprise.

"Fallers," Bert said. "Most arrogant bastards in the bush."

Finally, a reaction: "You'd be nothing without us," one of them said.

Bert just grunted, then walked over to the passage connecting the two trailers and shouted. "Four more breakfasts, Rudy. Three up front and one coming later. I want the works too, and don't mess up the eggs. I like them looking at me."

They sat down at the table facing the fallers. Bert made the introductions. "Lars, Sven, and Bernie," he said. "Meet Inspector Coswell and Sergeant Blakemore." They actually shook hands.

"I've lied about your records," Bert said to them. "So you can relax."

A couple of the smiles looked a bit crooked.

Blakemore took over the small talk, at ease in this environment. "How's the mulie hunting up here?" he said.

"None of us hunt," Bernie replied. "Working in the bush is enough. When we're through, we head for civilization. Don't see many animals either. We make a lot of noise."

"Probably a good thing. Wouldn't want some buck-fevered hunter sending a round in your direction."

"What time do you usually start work in the morning?" Coswell said.

"When it's dry like it is now, we start cutting as soon as we can see. Bert here is a slave-driver. Has us going up with headlamps seven days a week."

"We're particularly interested in gunshots you might have heard early in the morning three days ago."

Bernie looked at the other two fallers. "See? I told you I heard shots, you deaf buggers." He turned to Coswell. "They told me I was imagining things."

"Can you tell us approximately what time that was?"

"I can tell you exactly. Woke me up, so I went for a piss. Three friggin' thirty in the morning—two hours before I had to get up. Wondered if the hippies were into a little middle-of-the-night pit-lamping. Tired of living on granola."

A warm feeling of success came over Coswell. They now had a precise time of death.

Breakfast arrived. Rudy looked the part of camp cook: short, round, sweating, and sporting a two-day growth of black beard. He wore a stain-covered apron and kept a well-chewed matchstick in his mouth. The plates of food he delivered, however, were glorious: eggs sunny side up, a pile of bacon, hash browns with tomato slices, and parsley placed decoratively on top.

"What's with the salad?" Bert said.

"Guests," Rudy answered.

Bert scraped the tomatoes and parsley off to the side of his plate.

They ate in silence, resuming conversation only when they'd pushed their plates away and refilled their coffee cups. Bernie appeared to be the talker of the group.

"We heard you were coming up here to investigate a murder," he said. "Is that what those shots were?"

"Almost assuredly," Coswell said.

"Who got murdered?"

"Two First Nations men. We think they were involved in the marijuana trade. We're considering a drug-related homicide."

"Marijuana? Ahh ... the hippies. That wouldn't surprise me one bit. The two that come down to pick up supplies look like they'd kill their own mother."

"How far up are they?" Blakemore asked.

"Takes us a half-hour to climb to where we're falling. I don't know exactly where they are, and they sure as hell haven't told any of us, but I think they're a fair bit higher and more to the south."

Coswell thought that over. He'd already decided that the fallers weren't suspects, but the tree-planters definitely were. Getting the jump on them would be difficult, though, and the thought of climbing up that mountain to where they were camped definitely didn't appeal to him.

Blakemore was of the same mind. "We'd like to pay them

a surprise visit, if you know what I mean," he said. "What do you think of coming down from above on horseback using that Hobson's trail?"

"From Hansen's property?" Bert said. "I hear you've done part of that already. Yes, it would give you an advantage, for sure. They've got to be set up on that south slope—ideal growing conditions. We'll fly over."

After breakfast, the fallers left with Bert, leaving Coswell and Blakemore to linger a bit longer over their coffees. Eventually they made their way back to the helicopter where Les, the pilot, was still tinkering with the engine.

"Nothing wrong, I hope," Coswell said.

"Nothing serious. Needs a new thermostat, I think, but there'll be no problem getting back. It's all downhill."

"We were hoping for a little tour slightly higher up, but not if you think there's any risk."

Les smiled. "The risks start ten feet off the ground in these machines, but don't worry. I'll get you back safely."

When it came to flying, the only time Coswell liked hearing the word "risk" was after the word "zero." Blakemore didn't help, either: "Yep," he said. "Copters don't glide. Straight down. Bang."

"You're a joy to be with," Coswell said.

They sat on the edge of the pad, dangled their legs, and looked around the camp. Three additional trailers, identical to the dining hall, were set slightly back from it. Clothes dried in the breeze, hanging on lines strung between trees. They could see Bert and two of the fallers below talking to a man beside a stack of impressive timber—logs with butts three feet across. Parked off to the side sat a crablike machine with huge tires and a grappling hook dangling from its maw. A rough road could be seen beyond that, beginning with the first of what were probably innumerable hairpin curves down to the valley below.

"You want to drive up to Hansen's when we get back, or wait 'til tomorrow morning?" Blakemore asked.

"We'll go today. Chief Ward's no doubt agitating in Vancouver and your men in Williams Lake want you back ASAP. We need to wrap this up quick."

"You think those hippies are the answer?"

"They were in cahoots with the Johnsons, supposedly. They have to know something. I'll bet their camp isn't that far away from the crime scene."

"I don't see them doing the killing," Blakemore said. "They know damn well how to get rid of bodies up here. Between the bears, the coyotes, and the ravens, three days would deal with a lot of flesh."

Les interrupted their deliberations. His attention had been drawn to something behind them. "Well, don't tell me," he said. "They finally showed up for their booze."

The Mounties quickly got to their feet. Two figures were walking down the trail from above, one twenty feet ahead of the other, both with backpacks. Suddenly, the first one stopped and stared in their direction. The other joined him. They huddled together for a moment before the first continued down the slope. The other set his pack down, pulled out a radio, and spoke into it.

As the first man neared, Coswell recalled the faller's description — "mother-killer." He would have fit in well with the denizens of Vancouver's downtown East side — scraggly beard, dirty bandana tied around his head, the ubiquitous mac and unwashed jeans. Fortunately his body odour stayed mostly upwind, but when he came to a halt, some wafted ahead, reminding Coswell of his Chinatown street people.

"Good morning, officers," the man said. "What brings two high-ranking Queen's men into these verdant hills? A sergeant and a full inspector, no less. We are truly honoured."

His language definitely wasn't street. University, more

likely, but Blakemore paid no notice. He pulled a notebook and pen out of his breast pocket.

"Investigating a double homicide," he said. "And you're on our people-of-interest list, so let's hear the spiel: name, history, and whereabouts in the last week."

The amused expression disappeared. "My name is Jason Radcliffe. I'm up here on a tree-planting contract with a small crew — four of us. We've haven't been off this hill in weeks and we definitely don't know anything about any homicide. Who got killed and why the interest in us?"

Blakemore didn't answer. Instead, his attention shifted to the second man, who had finally walked down the trail to join them. His age and appearance mirrored Jason's, but he had a furtive look about him and none of his partner's self-assurance.

"This is Larry, my number-one man," Jason said. "He's not a talker. Best you ask me all your questions."

Blakemore appeared ready to read the riot act to this impertinent kid, but Coswell interrupted. "That'll be fine," he said.

Jason looked as surprised as Blakemore, but promptly directed his partner to begin gathering their supplies. "Leave what you can't carry," he said, "and start back. I'll bring the rest."

Coswell knew that Blakemore didn't agree in the least with letting one of their suspects leave like that, with the opportunity to warn the others, but a plan had formed in his mind. He took over the questioning.

"Perhaps, Jason, you could start by giving the sergeant a list of your crew — names, addresses, and so forth. A visual of your ID will suffice. We can always contact you later if necessary."

Jason pulled out his wallet and handed it to Blakemore. "Okay," he said. "I've answered your questions. Now, before

I start giving any names, how about answering mine. Why are we 'persons of interest'?"

"The homicides took place in this vicinity," Coswell said. "You and your crew are the only ones around ... ergo, our interest. Now, if you'll give Sergeant Blakemore those names ... "

"Well, I can tell you none of us had anything to do with any killing."

"Maybe so, but your cooperation would be appreciated."

"I'm cooperating."

Blakemore took down the names as Jason reluctantly gave them to him.

"How far away from the top of Hobson's trail is your camp?" Coswell asked.

"Quite a bit below that and well off to the side. I'd say a kilometre or so."

"Shots were heard at three-thirty A M, four days ago. Did you hear those shots?"

"Three-thirty in the morning?" Jason said. "No way. Camp up here long enough and you learn to block out all the night sounds. The slightest wind starts those dead pines to dropping limbs and even whole trees come down. At three-thirty in the morning we're sound asleep."

"Did you see anyone coming or going on the trail the day before?"

"Not a soul. Pretty rare for anyone to come all the way up that trail at this time of the year. Few hunters, that's all. None recently."

He said that convincingly, but Coswell knew he was lying. If he could see hunters, the trail couldn't be that far from where they were working. And to miss men riding up on horses? Unlikely. Also, if they were in business with the Johnsons, not to meet with them would have been even more unlikely.

Larry, the quiet one, had loaded up his pack and was about

to head back up the trail when Jason called over to him. "Did you pick up the cigarettes?"

Larry nodded.

"Pull a pack out and throw it over," Jason said.

Larry obeyed, but the moment he had the carton stowed and the pack hoisted onto his shoulders, he set off at a pace just short of a trot. Jason smiled after him. "Bundle of nerves, that guy," he said. "But he's a good worker."

He calmly cracked open the package, pulled a cigarette out, and lit it with a butane lighter. He didn't speak again until he'd taken two long drags, sighing with each one.

"Ran out three days ago," he said. "Hell for a nicotine addict."

As though just remembering his manners, he held the package out to Blakemore and Coswell who both shook their heads.

"Yeah. I know," he said. "Bad habit, but there aren't many pleasures to be had up here."

"How often do you get out?" Coswell asked.

"Not often, once we start the job. Tree-planting's like that. Blitz the thing, then leave. A trip down to this camp is about as close to civilization as we get for weeks at a time."

"Must take a special breed."

"It does."

A few more deep pulls and the cigarette was finished. He flicked the butt into the dirt and ground it in with his heel. "Well," he said. "Unless you've got any more questions or you're going to tell me more about those homicides, I have to get back to camp."

"That'll do for now," Coswell said. "We'll send word up if we need to talk to you again. When will you finish your present contract?"

"Pretty well done now."

He started to shove what Larry had left him into his pack

—a case of beer and a twenty-six of tequila. "This is for a little celebration tonight," he said. "Beer with tequila shooters. That's living." He hoisted the pack onto his back and made ready to leave. "Nice talking to you, gentlemen," he said, and shouted over to Les who had returned to tinkering on his engine. "And goodbye to you too, Les, you antisocial old whirlybird jockey."

He merely laughed at Les' one-finger salute.

"You had a reason for all that, I'm sure," Blakemore said once the young man had disappeared into the forest.

"I did," Coswell replied. "You'll get your chance to grill the bastard when we drop in on him tomorrow. After the beer and tequila, he should be nicely softened up and that Larry will be a piece of cake."

"Gotcha," Blakemore said. He walked over to where Jason had ground out his cigarette. "Did you notice the brand he smokes?"

"Can't say I did," Coswell replied.

"Rothmans. Same as my dad smoked for years and same as the butts Richard and I found at the crime scene. Maybe a coincidence, but if somebody's DNA other than the Johnsons' turns up on those, a little comparison with this might be interesting."

He bent down, slid the squashed cigarette onto a piece of paper from his notebook, and then dropped it into one of his supply of Ziploc bags.

Coswell nodded his approval. "Good thinking," he said. "I'd also suggest that you get a search warrant faxed to the hotel which includes everything within a kilometre of their camp down to their jockstraps."

"No problem. A big pot bust in the offing? The judge will fall over himself writing it out. That's assuming I can find him on a Sunday."

✱✱✱
✱✱✱

Their wait for Bert Neiborg to return to the helicopter was a short one.

"Got it all solved?" he said, striding down from the dining hall. "I saw you talking to the chief hippie. Didn't see the handcuffs come out, though. Too bad."

Coswell smiled. "It's a little early for that, but we did make progress, and with a little help from Les here, we'll make even more."

"Good. I personally made one helluva lot of progress. Boys just radioed down. Skidder's fixed and we're movin' wood again. Hallelujah. And don't feel sorry for those fallers. They might work seven days straight when we need the cutting, but they sit on their asses a lot in between when we're hauling it out."

They all climbed into the helicopter and Les lifted off, gaining altitude quickly. Bert pointed out the route he wanted him to take. "Stay well up," he said, "and go by fast. Everyone keep their eyes peeled."

Blakemore spotted the camp first. "There it is," he shouted and pointed down.

"I got it," Les said and took a fix with the GPS mounted on his console before swinging away and dropping down to the valley.

"I'll plot that out for you on a topo map," Bert said. "I've got a stack of them in my yard office."

"Good," Blakemore said. "Give me a compass and a map anytime. Never got the hang of those GPS gadgets."

✸✸✸

They returned to the hotel where they found the clerk ensconced behind his desk. Wishing to keep their phone calls as private as possible, Coswell remained in the lobby while Blakemore went up to his room to call the judge in Williams Lake. Ten minutes later he came back.

"Done," he said to Coswell and then went over to the desk to speak to the clerk. "A confidential fax will be coming through in the next few minutes," he said. "I'll deal with it. You stay put."

"Yes sir."

He came back and sat down beside Coswell. "My kind of judge," he said softly. "Has a stack of warrants at home and his own fax machine."

Five minutes later, the phone rang, the fax machine squealed, and the precious warrant came spewing out. Blakemore got up, pulled it off the rack, and read it over.

"Yep. Word for word, just like I told him."

Coswell, his stomach not yet settled from his helicopter ride, had no interest in stopping at the bar for a coffee break.

"We're off," he said. "Time for a little cruise."

They were halfway to their vehicle before Coswell defined his "little cruise." "We'll start with a visit to Chief Isaac. He had to know what his sons were up to. Richard told us the old man didn't go out much. People came to him."

"Customers, maybe?" Blakemore said.

"Maybe ... or associates."

"Yeah, one of whom might have done in his sons. Surely we'll get some cooperation this time."

"I hope so," Coswell said. "Then I want to pick Richard up. We'll need his help tomorrow with the horses and finding our way. I can't say I have a lot of faith in a map and a compass, especially since I don't think you *have* a compass."

"Aren't we going to conscript Hansen again?"

"No. All we need is the loan of his horses. I want to ride up to that cabin at the top of Hobson's trail this afternoon and stay overnight. That way we'll really have the drop on our tree-planters in the morning. Catch them still in their sleeping bags."

"We should have brought our riding clothes."

"No. We'll go in uniform. Adds to the effect."

✶✶✶

Coswell pulled to a stop at the edge of the clearing on Chief Isaac's property. Three or four pickups and a couple of '70s clunker sedans were parked in front of the house.

"Looks like the chief's holding court again," Blakemore said. "Probably not a good time to disturb him."

"On the contrary. This is a perfect time," Coswell said, and promptly started up again. He double-parked beside a car directly in front of the house, got out and slammed the cruiser's door. Momentarily, a man stepped out onto the porch and when he saw them, turned and called inside: "Cops."

Four more men appeared and lined up shoulder-to-shoulder facing the Mounties — arms crossed, silent, hostile. Coswell recognized them all as part of the contingent of male elders at his school talk.

"Good day, gentlemen," Coswell said. "Chief in?"

"Hiss greevin'. Gohway."

"I understand, but I'm sure he'll want to talk to us. We have information about his sons' killers."

He turned to Blakemore, who hadn't moved from the cruiser. "Come along, Sergeant," he said. "We have news to deliver."

Blakemore got out and came over, making a show of adjusting his pistol holster. When they were side by side, Coswell stepped forward. "Excuse me, my good man," he told the elder blocking the door. "We mustn't keep your chief waiting."

Confusion reigned just long enough for Coswell to gently slip past him. Blakemore followed with the finesse of his football days, using his shoulders to bounce aside the two men standing in his way.

The smell of tobacco smoke greeted them again — fresh

this time. The chairs in front of the woodstove were turned around. Chief Isaac sat in the La-Z-Boy. On either side of him were two men of similar vintage. Wooden chairs and a couple of benches were arranged in a semicircle in front of them. Six men sat there, two of them smoking pipes. The four men who'd been out front filed in quickly and remained standing.

Isaac fixed his gaze on Coswell with a look of hatred twice as intense as that of his confrères.

"We've come to offer our condolences for your loss, Chief Isaac," Coswell said. "And to inform you of our investigations to date."

The look didn't soften.

"We know now that your sons were heavily involved in the marijuana trade — a dangerous criminal activity. To put it bluntly, we think your boys pissed off someone in the business and were killed for it."

Isaac almost spat out his response: "White man kilt dem."

Coswell sighed. He couldn't help but think that the old man secretly enjoyed fuelling his hatred and for some sick reason didn't care who killed his sons. But on the off-chance that someone in the room might listen to reason, he proceeded with his attempt to head off any vigilante action the group might be planning. He walked right up to the chief and turned around, effectively blocking everyone's view of the old man, and spoke directly to the men before him.

"It could have been a white man who killed them," he said. "But it might not have been, and since no one's owned up to it, a thorough investigation covering all possibilities is necessary. That is what we are doing. Now, if any of you have knowledge of the illicit activities that have gone on here, I can tell you that withholding such information will come back to haunt you down the line. Sergeant Blakemore and I are close, we believe, to solving this case, and when we do, I promise you that anyone not cooperating will feel the wrath of the courts."

With that, he walked straight ahead, his jaw clenched, and disappeared out the door. Blakemore followed behind.

As they drove away, Coswell smiled. "That'll rattle the old bastards' cages."

***

Richard and his grandmother were just returning from church when Coswell and Blakemore drove in. She insisted they stay for lunch and got no argument. Coswell was glad, too, for the opportunity to quiz her about the meeting at Chief Isaac's place. He related to her what had gone on.

"Tink der warrioss, dum buggerss. Whachit doh. Dey still got teet."

"She's right," Richard said. "I remember an incident when I was still in high school. A gang of bikers rolled into town and started to raise hell. They ended up in the Anahim bar. Left their machines nicely lined up in front. Chief Isaac and his group arrived in pickups, armed to the teeth. They pulled up beside the motorcycles and shot all the tires out. When the bikers came out, they must have thought time had rolled back two hundred years, looking down the barrels of Indian rifles."

"What did they do?" Blakemore asked.

"Headed out of town on foot and presumably hitchhiked back to Williams Lake. They sent a big flat-deck truck a day later to pick up their bikes. We never saw them again."

"That's a sobering story," Coswell said. "But I think I've given them enough food for thought to prevent that kind of coordinated action."

Gramma didn't respond, causing a twinge of doubt to pass through Coswell's mind.

***

Hansen's big Dodge was gone when they arrived at the ranch. Garret and the two First Nations hands, Andy and Verne, were unloading bales of hay from a wagon in front of the stable. Coswell parked the cruiser at the house and walked over with Blakemore to where the men were working. Richard went inside.

"Boss took Bonny to the airport," Garret said between bales. "Don't expect him back 'til tomorrow. Said he had some business to tend to while he was there."

"I guess that leaves you in charge," Coswell said. "Could that include loaning us your excellent horses once more? We'd like to go back this afternoon to where the Johnsons were found."

"Bit late in the day for that, isn't it?"

"We'll stay overnight at the cabin up top. Our game warden friends should still be there."

Garret pulled his gloves off and tilted his hat back. "Richard going with you?"

"Yes."

"Then I guess it'll be okay. The horses could use the exercise. Not much for them to do these days but stand in the pasture and eat."

Coswell sent Blakemore to extract Richard from the house while he followed Garret into the stable. "Is this a slow time of the year in the cattle business?" Coswell asked.

"Slow all year round now. Too many tofu eaters."

The stable had eight stalls but only one was occupied. Coswell recognized Garret's horse.

"This guy gets exercised ... by me," Garret said. "Cursed ATVs are taking over at a lot of ranches. Glad the boss hates them as much as I do."

He saddled the horse and led him out to the yard just as Richard and Blakemore came over from the house. Coswell noticed that Richard seemed unhappy about something but attributed it to being dragged away from his love so soon.

Garret swung himself up into the saddle and called to the

older of the two hands. "I'll round them up, Andy. You get ready to grab them at the gate."

Blakemore made a plea before Garret rode off: "Could you bring me a skinnier one this time?"

✳✳✳

It took a while to corral the three chosen horses and get them ready to ride. Blakemore and Coswell did no more than hold onto the halters while Garret and Andy put on the bridles and saddles. Richard did his own saddling up.

"You'd better go a little faster this trip," Garret warned, "or you'll be climbing that trail in the dark. I put a couple of flashlights in the saddlebags for you, just in case."

No way did Coswell wish to ride a horse up a steep trail by flashlight.

"You lead us, Richard," he said. "And as the expression goes — don't spare the horses. We'll keep up."

Richard merely nodded, and Coswell noted a worried frown that probably had nothing to do with riding in the dark. He'd question him later about it.

Blakemore's athleticism kicked in. In just a few hundred metres, he was riding like a veteran, becoming as one with Rusty, Garret's choice for his mount. They made it to the cabin in just under three hours.

Frank Crawford, the wardens' crew chief, greeted them at the door. "Hope you're not coming up after more bodies," he said. "We're all packed up and ready to move out at dawn tomorrow."

"Bodies, yes," Coswell replied. "But live ones this time." He related the events surrounding the tree-planters.

"Damn," Frank said. "Right under our noses. But they're smart, eh? No one hunts that slope, so we had no reason to go there."

Coswell asked to use the satellite phone again.

"Help yourself," Frank said. "Government pays the bill."

"You use it first," Coswell said to Blakemore. "See if the fog's lifted in Williams Lake and if it has, get a copter up here with a couple of your men to deal with the tree-planters and their grow-op. If not, have them boot it to Nimpo and get flown up to that Itcha Lake where the hunters were camped."

Blakemore received good news when he phoned: the fog had lifted and the necessary helicopter with two Mounties would arrive in a couple of hours.

"Got a quickie on the autopsy report too," Blakemore said. ".38 slug through the nose in one of them, took his brain stem right out. The other got it in the back; bullet went through the lungs and heart. Few powder burns on the nose guy."

"Shot at close range," Coswell said. "Interesting."

His turn came next. He got Blakemore's list of the tree-planters' names and called his corporal in Vancouver.

"Find out as much as you can for me on those today," he told him. "I'll have a lot more information for you later when we get them to Williams Lake. I also want you to delve further into that Garret fellow from last time. If he turns out to be an American, run his name across the border. The file might date back thirty or forty years, but concentrate on Chicago and maybe juvenile records."

"Will do," the corporal said. "What time should I send the fax?"

"Five this afternoon."

Pause.

"I hate to bug you," the corporal said.

"I know, I know. It's Ward, right? Okay, put me through."

Inspector Ward came on the line almost immediately. "All right," he said. "Let's hear it."

Coswell gave him a full report, ending with, "I think we're getting close."

"You've been gone a week," Ward said. "I'll give you three more days, but that's it."

"Yes, sir."

Click.

He looked at Blakemore. "Come Friday, you may be on your own."

Richard came in from tending the horses.

"You're just in time for our last-night party," Frank announced. "It's a tradition."

Two bottles of red wine, cheeses, cold cuts, and a monstrous loaf of sourdough bread appeared on the table. Glasses were handed out. No one commented when Richard asked for juice to be poured into his.

Toasts all around and when the bottles were empty and the stories told, lights went out at ten-thirty.

As Coswell drifted off in his bunk, he continued to worry about Richard, who had been almost mute for the entire evening and looked as though his mind were a long way off. Something had happened with Maggie inside the Hansens' house. He was sure of it.

12

AT FIVE AM AN ALARM WENT OFF, but only two men got up right away: Frank and Richard. Frank lit the gas lamps and got the fire started. Richard went outside to see to the horses. With great reluctance, Coswell was next to crawl out of his warm bed. He wanted to speak to Richard privately and wouldn't have a better opportunity.

He dressed quickly and picked up one of the several flashlights on a shelf beside the front door before stepping outside into the darkness. He could see Richard's light flashing where they'd tethered the horses.

He was putting a feedbag on Rusty when Coswell walked over to him.

"Oats," Richard said. "Recharges their batteries faster than hay."

"Good, and I hope Frank also charges us up with something this morning before we head down that trail."

"I'm sure he will," Richard said, his voice flat.

Still in a funk. Time to dispel it. "What happened back at the house, Richard? And don't tell me 'nothing' because it's pretty damned obvious something did."

Richard took a deep breath. "It's so sad," he said. "Drugs destroy the nicest people. Maggie turned into a different person yesterday, like a coyote cornered by dogs. She said the methadone dose Hansen gave her before he left hadn't done a thing."

The story was one Coswell found only too familiar. True addicts were manipulative devils who would go to any length to satisfy their needs. To Maggie, Richard had merely become someone to use.

"She wanted me to speak to Garret. Apparently he knows where the drug is kept, but he refused to get her a second dose."

"But you knew better and didn't speak to him."

"Yes," he said sadly. "I know better and I didn't speak to him."

"She's had a lot of stress in her life lately," Coswell said. "The death of her mentor, Mrs. Hansen, Brent's murder, and probably worst of all, getting left with Sam Hansen and all his hangups. Maybe if she moves to another facility, she'll have a chance."

"Maybe," Richard said, with little enthusiasm.

***

They rode out before the wardens left. Frank wanted to do a

thorough cleanup first, and insisted they didn't need help. Coswell thanked him profusely for all that he'd done.

"Think nothing of it," Frank said. "Lawmen have to stick together."

"If you ever need a ticket fixed anywhere south of Quesnel," Blakemore said, "just let me know."

Richard led the way again. He'd studied Bert Neiborg's map carefully and didn't foresee any difficulty finding the tree-planters' camp.

"I'm getting a good picture of the trails. My memory's better than I thought."

"Enjoy it," Blakemore said. "Memory rot starts sooner than you think."

They rode slowly at first because of the steepness of the trail and the poor early morning light; the rising sun was still blocked out by the fir trees. But when they reached the point of traverse to the south, their pace quickened.

Suddenly, Richard reined in his horse and held up his hand. Coswell and Blakemore did likewise and listened. The sound of chainsaws drifted up from below, but much closer, two men were arguing—loudly.

They dismounted and tied their horses to the nearest tree. Coswell led this time and moved toward the voices, making as little noise as possible.

"We should have buggered off last night," one of the arguers said.

"You worry too much," the other replied. "This morning's soon enough. Haven't seen that copter again, have you?"

"I don't like it. The sooner we're out of here, the better."

Coswell stopped at the last bit of cover before the camp. Two men were squatting beside a small fire with their backs to him, warming their hands; behind them was a large white canvas tent with a chimney protruding from the top. Off to either side of it were three small dome tents. Smoke rose from the chimney. As they watched, the flap of the big tent flew open and a young woman stuck her head out.

"Breakfast's ready," she shouted.

The two at the campfire rose and went inside.

"Perfect," Coswell whispered. "We've got them all in one place. Let's give them a morning surprise." He turned to Blakemore. "Pull out your sidearm and stand beside me. Have it pointed right at them when they come out. Richard, you stand more to the side where they can just see you."

They got into position five metres in front of the tent.

"Police!" Coswell shouted. "We have you surrounded. Come out with your hands up."

It was corny, but effective. After a few religious invocations and terms related to bodily functions, the crew emerged — three males and a female. Jason Radcliffe, the talkative one from the helicopter pad meeting, came out first and Larry, the quiet one, last. None put their hands up until they saw Blakemore, and then all immediately obeyed.

"Frisk them," Coswell said.

Richard moved forward and patted them all down, being slightly less efficient with the woman. "They're clean," he said.

"All right," Coswell said. "You can put your hands down."

Blakemore holstered his pistol but left the flap undone. That was the signal for Jason to start talking.

"What's the meaning of this Nazi manoeuvre?" he said. "We've done nothing to warrant it. We're simple tree-planters, for Christ's sake. You have no right ...."

Coswell calmly pulled the warrant from his breast pocket and handed to him. It took just three seconds for the balloon to pop.

"We're busted," he said, looking up from the paper.

"That's certainly true," Coswell said. "But a much more serious charge than trafficking in marijuana may be in the offing … murder."

Jason paled, and a dark wet patch began to form at the crotch of the woman's jeans.

"Murder!" he said. "Us? You've got to be kidding."

"Not in the least," Coswell said. "Two of your accomplices, Art and Bill Johnson, were shot to death on this very hill, not far from here."

"Oh my God. We just met with them three days ago. They were going up high to hunt for caribou."

Coswell continued to press. "Did the meeting not go well? The Johnsons want a bigger cut?"

"No. Nothing like that. We just rescheduled delivery dates. Everyone was happy."

"You never went to their camp?"

"No. Never."

"Okay then, here's what we're going to do. I want Larry to go along with the constable and give him a tour of your planting site. Meanwhile, I'm going to have a look around your camp, and while I'm doing that, I want all firearms produced, posthaste."

"We just have bear-bangers," Jason said.

"Fine, but there will be more officers coming down here shortly so if you've forgotten about any weapons you've left lying around, now's the time to remember."

No one moved.

"All right then. One at a time, we'll check out your tents. You first, young lady." Blakemore found a comfortable log to sit on and watched with some amusement as the damp woman led Coswell to the farthest of the domed tents. Coswell emerged alone after just a few minutes, carrying two pencil-like objects. He repeated the process with the two men. Jason and the woman apparently shared a single tent. By the time he'd finished inspecting the large cook tent, the woman reappeared, wearing dry jeans.

"Okay," Coswell said. "Now go ahead and finish your breakfast. You have a long day ahead. It'll start with a march to the top of Hobson's trail, taking whatever you think you can carry. Secure the rest. It may be a while before you can retrieve it."

Richard reappeared with Larry ten minutes later and Coswell ran him through a tent check before letting him join the others.

Blakemore picked up one of the bear-bangers Coswell had confiscated and examined it. "I've heard about these things," he said, "but I've never seen one in action."

"Don't fiddle," Coswell said and took it from him.

***
***

They were quite a spectacle, returning to Hobson's trail and then proceeding up it to the cabin: three men on horseback with four pack-laden hikers between them. Coswell led the procession. Blakemore and Richard took up the rear, the latter dismounting frequently to mark the trail with fluorescent surveyor's tape borrowed from the wardens.

The helicopter had already arrived when they got to the top and three RCMP officers were waiting.

"I hope you brought all the right stuff," Blakemore said to them. "There's a big grow operation down there that needs photographing and a lot of weed-pulling to get done."

One of the officers grinned. "We've had some experience, Sarge. This won't be our first."

After a short discussion with Coswell, it was decided that Blakemore would fly out right away with Jason and his crew to Williams Lake.

"We get charged for every hour this thing's away from base," Blakemore said, "so we'll save a bit of money for the taxpayers. I'll get dropped off at the village when it's time to come back here to get the weed-pickers."

The three Williams Lake Mounties headed off down the trail, carrying shovels, mattocks and their camera equipment.

"We need to lead these horses a good ways away," Richard said. "The helicopter will really spook them."

He was right. Even fifty metres away, the horses reared and snorted as the copter lifted off in a cloud of dust. Richard managed to handle both his horse and Rusty. Coswell's horse, however, almost pulled him off his feet despite his death grip on the reins.

When all calmed down, they watched the copter sweep east. After it finally disappeared over the horizon, they mounted up again and started the long ride back to the Hansen Ranch. They rode slowly because of the danger of slipping downhill; with plenty of daylight left, there was no need to hurry. But as they neared the ranch, the horses began to speed up on their own.

"They sense food and they can't wait to get the load off their backs," Richard said. "Let's run them."

It was exhilarating to gallop across the last of the pastures before the ranch buildings. Rusty, without Blakemore up, strained to go ahead. Coswell gave out an undignified whoop. He expected that all the noise they were making would bring Garret out, but when they pulled up in front of the stables, the whole ranch seemed deserted, and still no sign of Hansen's truck.

"Something's happened," Richard said, sliding off his horse. "It's too quiet."

He let the reins of the horses fall to the ground and walked swiftly to the house.

Coswell, taken aback by Richard's haste, waited a few minutes, but when Richard failed to reappear, led the horses into the stable and turned them loose. Each entered a stall and began munching on hay piled in the mangers. Coswell turned and headed over to the house.

***

Richard had left the front door wide open. He went inside and saw no one in the kitchen. A silence hung in the air.

"Richard?" he called. "Where are you?"

A barely audible response: "Upstairs. In the den."

The sight that greeted him when he went into the room reminded Coswell of a scene from a silent movie: Maggie, dressed only in a flannel nightgown, lolled back in one of the leather chairs, feet bare, eyes closed, barely breathing. Richard knelt alongside the chair, holding her hand. An empty shotglass and a half-empty container of red liquid sat on the coffee table in front of them.

"She's overdosed," Richard said.

Coswell looked across at the rolltop desk. A single drawer was pulled out, a key stuck in its lock. He walked over to the comatose woman and lifted one eyelid. She reacted with a faint moan. He noted the severely constricted pupil.

"Out cold," Coswell said. "No doubt why, but where the hell is Garret?"

The look on Richard's face reflected such concern that Coswell took pity on him. "You stay with her," he said. "I'll go look for him."

As he descended the stairs, he knew the reason for Richard's concern. A desperate drug addict and a man withholding the cure were not a good combination.

Garret had to be somewhere nearby; he could see his horse grazing in the pasture. Would Garret leave the ranch with only Maggie at home? Not a chance. He was probably napping in his cabin, Coswell concluded, although the man had to be deaf not to have been wakened by the noise that he and Richard made when they rode in.

He walked around the corral to the cabin. No smoke rose from the chimney and the stillness seemed unnatural. He paused at the door. A feeling of foreboding came over him. He knocked and waited. No answer. Curtains were pulled across the windows, blocking any view inside. The latch consisted of a simple lever apparatus. He pulled a pen from his pocket and lifted the lever. The door opened easily with a gentle push from his knee.

The interior smelled of leather and tobacco. The heavy curtains did a good job blocking the light, but he could make out a small kitchen to his left with a tiny table and two wooden chairs set beside one of the windows. Ahead and to his right he could see a sitting area with a single big-armed chair and an upholstered footstool, both well worn. Beside it sat a wooden table stacked with magazines and an empty ashtray. The walls were devoid of decorative touches other than a couple of calendars with pictures of big-breasted nudes and a gun rack holding Garret's 30.30, a double-barreled shotgun and a single-shot .22. In one corner, hung on a series of hooks, were chaps, two hats, and a couple of denim jackets, one lined with sheepskin. On the floor below, footwear of various types were lined up — two pairs of cowboy boots, one well-polished, the other scuffed, heavy rubber boots stained with manure, and an incongruous pair of Nike runners.

He looked into the dimness at the back of the room. A short corridor led to a rear exit. On either side were doors, one shut and the other, a pocket door, pulled back. He moved toward them. Through the open door he saw a small bathroom with a sink, toilet, and shower. Towels hung neatly on a rack by the sink, save for one slung over the shower door. A wicker basket with a lid sat in the corner in front of the toilet. On it, a stack of magazines. Coswell could just make out the word *Hustler* on the top one.

He turned and regarded the other door. This one had a knob. He searched in his pockets and found a piece of

Kleenex, which he draped over the knob before carefully turning it with two fingers. A push with his elbow opened it.

He had entered enough crime scenes not to be shocked. In fact, this one was downright peaceful. If the bullethole just in front of Garret's ear could be ignored, one would think he was asleep in his bed. The covers were pulled up around his shoulders and his head rested nicely on the pillow, eyes closed. The only blood visible was a matted clot in his sideburn and a tiny trickle that had just reached the pillow. He lifted the head gently. No blood underneath. Small calibre, Coswell reckoned, not powerful enough to create an exit wound. Another .38?

He looked around the room. He saw no signs of struggle: clothes were neatly folded over a chair, and the drawers of a small nearby dresser were shut tight. A wallet, keys, comb, and a small penknife lay scattered on top of it. A double-shelf book cabinet with magazines stacked inside it served as a bedside table. A lamp and another ashtray, this one containing two cigarette butts, sat atop it alongside a glass with the residue of a brown liquid in the bottom. Coswell sniffed it—Scotch.

He looked down at the magazines. Hustler again. How a man of Garret's age could still summon such interest in sex perplexed Coswell.

All signs pointed to a man going about a bedtime routine without any concern for what was about to happen to him. But something had happened, and now Coswell found himself with yet another murder on his hands. This time, however, the chief suspect was a lot closer. Maggie would come out of her drug haze soon and when she did, the questions would fly.

***

When Coswell returned to the house, he decided to phone Williams Lake before he went upstairs to tell Richard what had happened ... give him a little more time with his love. Blakemore was still at the station when he called.

"You just caught me," he said. "The boys are finished up on the mountain and they want to come home. I'm about to drive over to the pad."

"Well, hold off a bit," Coswell said. "You're going to have another passenger—Doc Basra. I hope he's recovered, because he's got another job to do."

He related what had happened.

"Good God!" Blakemore said. "I don't mind being busy in my new post, but this is ridiculous. Three bodies a week. Keep that up and we'll depopulate the whole Cariboo."

"We're not the depopulaters," Coswell said. "But we are obliged to put an end to it. Now, aside from getting your coroner moving, I want you to check on Sam Hansen's whereabouts. According to Garret, he planned to stay over in Williams Lake last night after doing some business there, so check out the motels. If you can find the man, get him to account for every hour since he left the ranch."

"You don't think *he* could have shot Garret, do you?"

"Anything's possible. Maybe Garret knew he killed the Johnsons and needed shutting up. Maybe a little blackmail was involved, I don't know. But we have to keep our minds open."

"Well, one murder's solved anyway," Blakemore said. "The blood on the tire-iron in the Johnsons' pickup matched Brent Hansen's and the fingerprints belonged to brother Art. With that and the kid's statement, we can close those books, at least."

"No argument there, but keep the hippies in sight. The Johnson murders are still very much on the books."

"No problem. The judge is delighted to be able to preside over such a nice drug bust."

***
***

Maggie's eyelids were flickering when Coswell went up to the den, but other than that, she appeared to be still out cold. Richard had moved her over to the chesterfield and was sitting in a chair across from her.

"It can take four or five hours for methadone to wear off," Richard said. "Judging from her pupils and her respirations, I'd say she either took one huge dose or she's been reinforcing it."

Suddenly, he realized the significance of Coswell being alone. "Where's Garret?" he said. "How could he have let this happen?"

"Garret's dead, Richard. Shot in his cabin while he slept."

Realization came quickly this time. Both men looked down at the drugged woman. "I don't believe it," Richard said.

"I'm sorry," Coswell said. "But drug addicts turn into animals when they believe they're on the verge of withdrawal, especially if they've been through that hell before. She probably got her morning dose earlier than usual yesterday and felt it wearing off. Not knowing when Hansen would return today probably tipped her over the edge."

Richard looked totally deflated. He knew the inspector probably had it right.

"Stay with her," Coswell said. "But if she comes to, please don't question her without me around ... promise?"

"I promise, but what are you going to do?"

"I've already called Blakemore. He's flying in with the coroner shortly. Meanwhile, I want to take the opportunity to look around the house before Hansen gets back."

***

The den was at the top of the stairs in the middle of a U-shaped balustraded landing. Coswell began his inspection by walking down the corridor to the right. The first door he came to opened into a large bathroom complete with an old-fashioned iron tub. All the shelving was exposed except for a mirrored medicine cabinet. A quick check inside revealed nothing more ominous than a big bottle of ibuprofen tablets.

From the bathroom, a door led directly into the master bedroom. He noted the wife's touch again: a king-size bed done up hotel-style with a charcoal grey duvet and a mass of decorative pillows had been stacked up against the headboard, the biggest antique armoire that Coswell had ever seen took up one entire wall, frilly curtains pulled back from the double window, let the light stream in. Old World landscapes hung on the wall opposite, and an ornate dressing table sat beside it. Everything neat and tidy. Maggie undoubtedly kept it that way. It took Coswell less than five minutes to find absolutely nothing.

He walked around to the other end of the landing and found two smaller rooms. The one closest to the den turned out to be Bonny's. It too was neatly made up. He thought at first that it was Brent's room with a bed minus a headboard and made from heavy wood beams. Too spartan for a girl, he thought, until he noticed the pink floppy slippers peeking out from under it. A patchwork quilt, flannel sheets turned back, and a lumpy-looking pillow made up the bedding.

The window curtains were some gauzy material that would have blocked almost none of the morning light. Pictures adorned the walls, all of them featuring horses, cowboy scenes, and wild animals. Just a single lamp on the bedside table — no books or magazines. Odd, Coswell thought, but perhaps she did her reading elsewhere in the house.

He opened her wardrobe: jackets, a few dresses, blouses, skirts, jeans, and more formal slacks. The floor was almost covered with shoes: everything from expensive-looking cowboy boots and evening pumps to runners and sandals. He noted with amusement a pair of English riding boots, badly in need of cleaning and a good polish. Maggie obviously drew the line at cleaning boots.

A single dresser drawer unit contained underwear, an assortment of scarves, stockings, sweaters, and a box of tampons. He felt mildly guilty rummaging through her things but he had to be thorough. Again finding nothing of note, he left, closing the door firmly behind him.

The last room had obviously been Brent's. Rodeo posters covered the walls and trophies were lined up on almost every shelf. The clothing in the closet and dresser drawers consisted of jeans, western shirts, and men's underwear. Riding boots and a couple of well-worn cowboy hats lay on the closet floor. A spider had set up residence in one of the boots, suggesting that Brent's visits home were infrequent.

Where did Maggie stay? That came next.

He walked quickly past the den and down the stairs. The thought of Sam Hansen driving up and catching him poking around hurried him along. He found her room at the very back of the house, across the hall from a laundry-service area and another small bathroom. The door to her room had been left slightly ajar. He gave it a push with his foot and looked in.

The entire room looked dishevelled. The covers hung off the end of the bed as though the sleeper had been too warm and kicked them off. Two pillows lay on the floor, one obviously stepped on. He walked closer. Clothing had been piled beside the bed—jeans, a shirt, bra, socks, shoes, and in the corner, a pair of panties crumpled up in a ball. But when he looked at the bottom sheet, still in place on the bed, the whole story became apparent. Coswell had seen plenty of semen stains in his day. Maggie had entertained a visitor.

He searched everywhere for a gun—the closet, drawers, under the bed, every possible hiding place—nothing. He went into the bathroom. Toilet roll almost used up, the end hanging down to the floor. A bath towel carelessly thrown in a corner. Washcloth in the sink. Nothing besides woman things in the medicine cabinet, not even an aspirin. No birth control pills.

He stood for a moment, letting his pulse slow. What had happened? He thought he knew. Maggie needed that key to her methadone in the worst way. What did she have to offer Garret to get it? Pretty damned obvious. But why kill him? As an ex-Vancouver street worker, she wasn't likely a virgin avenging her lost maidenhood.

But would Garret let her keep the key? Hardly. Hansen would surely have raised hell when he found out. Did he put it in his pocket and take it to his cabin?

Not likely either. He'd have put the key back where Hansen normally kept it and he wouldn't have let Maggie see him doing so.

Too many unanswered questions, but it looked bad for Maggie.

★★★
★★★

He'd barely stepped back into the hall when he heard the Dodge diesel pull up in front of the house and park behind the cruiser. He hurried to intercept Hansen on the front porch.

"Get Bonny off okay?" Coswell said.

"Yes, but what's happened here? I didn't expect to see a police vehicle waiting for me."

"Not waiting for you. I'm afraid there's been another killing ... Garret."

Hansen's legs almost gave way. He grabbed onto a railing to steady himself.

"Better sit down," Coswell said.

Hansen slumped into the nearest deckchair. Coswell pulled another over and sat facing him.

"He was shot in his sleep. Never knew what hit him. We've called the coroner and he'll be here very soon. Blakemore's arranged to fly him in by helicopter from Williams Lake."

"When? Who?" Hansen remained stunned.

"Late last night or in the early hours this morning. We don't know who, but I'm afraid Maggie is our prime suspect."

Rage replaced shock. "That drugged-out Indian bitch," he said. "I just knew something like this was bound to happen. She'd shoot her own mother to get a fix. Poor Garret. I should have given him more warning. He doesn't know drug addicts from panhandlers."

"She got into the methadone supply," Coswell said. "I don't know how, but she's upstairs right now in the den, almost comatose. Richard's with her."

"She needs another Indian, all right. No one else would have any sympathy for her."

"Except your wife," Coswell said softly.

Hansen glared at him. "I want her out of my house right now. Throw her in your cruiser and take her to a lock-up. Let her wake up there. She should feel right at home."

Harsh as that statement was, it reminded Coswell that he needed to obtain Maggie's file from social services. Meanwhile, he had to impose some rules on Hansen.

"We will deal with Maggie," he said. "But right now, your house and Garret's cabin are part of a murder scene. Until the coroner clears everything, I'm afraid they're off limits."

"I can't go in my own house? You've got to be joking."

"Please, Sam," Coswell said. "Don't make this any harder than it already is."

Hansen's anger eased. "The world really is a piece of shit," he said. He looked at Coswell, depression beginning to take over. "Is it okay if I take my horse out? I need some fresh air."

"I have no objection to that," Coswell said. "Maybe I can help you round him up."

"No need. He'll come to a nosebag of oats."

Coswell watched as Hansen disappeared for a few minutes

inside the stable and then emerged with a saddle over his shoulder, a bridle and nosebag in his hand. He walked to the pasture, opened the gate, and went in. A few shakes of the bag and clicks with his tongue brought the Arab running. In no time, the rancher had the horse saddled and ready to go. He mounted up and set off at a gallop.

But another animal drew Coswell's attention. Spook, Brent's unrideable quarter horse, had been agitated by the departure of his companion and galloped along the fence parallel to Hansen and the Arab, snorting and shaking his head. Something about that animal disturbed Coswell, but he couldn't put his finger on it.

He went back inside the house to check on Richard and Maggie. She hadn't moved. Richard was pacing the floor.

"How did you get him to leave?" he asked when Coswell came into the den.

"More or less ordered him to, but he didn't offer much resistance."

"I'm amazed. Didn't you tell him about Maggie?"

Maggie stirred at the sound of her name. Richard went over to her and gently shook her shoulder. She opened her eyes and looked at him. Slowly her expression changed from sleepy innocence to terror. She tried to sit up but fell back on the couch and closed her eyes.

"Maggie. It's Richard. Please try to wake up."

No response, but this time they both knew she was faking. Maggie did not wish to face the real world. Coswell took over. He sat on the arm of the couch and looked down at her.

"Maggie. You can lie there and pretend, or you can sit up and answer my questions. You'll have to do that eventually and the setting may not be so pleasant. A man has been shot and you are the prime suspect."

Her eyes flew open. Coswell noted her methadone-constricted pupils dilating as her fear grew. She sat up, still woozy, struggling to comprehend.

"Who was shot?" she asked, her words slurred.

"I think you know," Coswell said.

She looked frantically over at Richard, who had put on his policeman's face and said nothing.

"I don't," she said, appearing genuinely confused.

Coswell waited.

"Mr. Hansen?" she said.

That set him back. She'd essentially just been abused by Garret and yet his wasn't the first name that came to her. But, he reasoned, the foreman probably moved out of her mind the minute she got what she wanted, a scenario that most surely played out many times before in her drug-besotted life.

"No ... Garret," Coswell said. "Shot in his bed last night or early this morning."

She was quickly regaining full consciousness. "Who did it?" she said, and then seeing the look in their eyes, suddenly realized her predicament. She began to talk, faster and faster. A child caught in a misdeed.

"Me? No. I didn't do it. Bonny gave me my dose way too early yesterday morning. It wore off right after supper. I couldn't take it any more last night so I went out to Garret's cabin. He knew where the key to the methadone was kept. Mrs. Hansen made sure everyone knew in case she wasn't around to give it to me and that happened a lot when she got sick. I pleaded with him to give me some and we made a deal."

"What deal did you make?" Richard asked.

She hung her head. "It was nothing," she said, and Richard knew.

"And then what happened?" Coswell said

"After we finished in my room, he said he'd changed his mind about giving me the meth. Said I didn't satisfy him at all. I don't know what he expected, he's old, but I said I'd try harder next time. First, he just laughed, but then he said okay.

We went upstairs to the den. I waited there while he got the key. When he came back, he opened the desk and poured me a dose."

"And then presumably locked everything back up again," Coswell said. "But how did the key end up where it is now? Surely he didn't leave it there."

She looked up at him with pleading eyes. "I don't know … honest. I fell asleep after I got the dose and when I woke up, it was there in the lock."

"And you couldn't help yourself," Coswell said.

She hung her head again. "It's my weakness," she said. "What Garret gave me was wearing off and I didn't know when Mr. Hansen would be coming back. I just took it … extra, 'cause I knew Garret wouldn't give me anymore."

Richard walked out of the room. Maggie followed him with her gaze, and then turned back to Coswell, tears in her eyes. "I didn't kill anybody," she sobbed.

Coswell went into the bathroom and brought out a box of Kleenex. She pulled out a handful and blew her nose.

"Garret must have made you very mad," he said, "threatening to break his deal like that."

"No," she said. "Every time I get mad at men, I get hurt. I don't do it anymore."

In that moment, Coswell was certain the girl hadn't killed Garret. All logic pointed to her, but his instinct didn't. He sat down on the couch beside her and took her hand.

"Maggie. I believe you, but I'm afraid I might be the only one, and I have a job to do."

The tears welled up again. "You're going to put me in jail?"

"I'll try hard not to, but it's going to take a lot of talking," he said. "And one thing's for certain: you must leave here."

The sound of a helicopter, at first faint, then louder, announced that Blakemore and the coroner had arrived. Coswell debated what to do. He decided to get her moving.

"Okay, Maggie. We're going to take you to your room so you can get ready to go. Up you get."

He took her arm and pulled her to a standing position. She sagged for a brief second but quickly recovered and allowed herself to be led out of the room. By the time they'd reached the bottom of the stairs, she could move on her own.

"I'm okay now," she said. "I'll pack my stuff like you said. I don't need help."

She went into her room and started to close the door. Coswell held it open.

"Sorry," he said. "I've got to be here and don't be embarrassed. I was through here earlier this morning."

She didn't argue, but the stains in her bed obviously had embarrassed her. She quickly pulled the sheet over them. Coswell didn't stop her. She picked up the jeans, bra, shirt, and socks off the floor and laid them out on the bed. He saw her glance over at the panties crumpled in the corner and turned his head as she snatched them up.

"You going to stand there while I dress?" she said.

"I'll turn my back. Let me know when it's safe to look."

He almost smiled at her modesty, but the expression on her face didn't invite it. She dressed quickly and gave him the okay to turn around.

"I'll pack now," she said.

He watched her pull out a backpack and start filling it with clothing—a single pair of jeans, two shirts, socks, and a sweater. He noticed she left numerous items behind in the wardrobe and the dresser.

"You can take more," he said. "We'll find some bags for you to put it in."

"None of that's mine," she said. "Mrs. Hansen bought it. I'll just take my own things."

He let her go into the bathroom. "You can close the door if you like," he said.

She did. He heard the sound of urination, the rattle of a toilet paper roll, water flushing, a tap running, hands being washed, a cupboard opening, the tap running again, teeth being brushed. At last, the door opened. She carried only her toothbrush, toothpaste, and a bottle of shampoo. Coswell was going to tell her she could take a shower, but she brushed past him, went back into her room, put the bathroom items into her backpack, and zipped it shut.

"I'm ready," she said, one hand on the pack. "Where am I going?"

In truth, he didn't know. "Sergeant Blakemore will make the arrangements," he said. "Meanwhile, the sitting room is probably the best place for you to wait."

"Okay," she said and followed him down the hallway.

He'd barely gotten her settled in the sitting room when he heard the helicopter take off. A few minutes later, Blakemore pounded onto the porch and came through the front door. Coswell intercepted him as he was about to climb the stairs to the den.

"Maggie's in the sitting room," he said. "Let's go into the kitchen for a minute."

Blakemore followed him. "You got her cuffed to something?" he said.

Coswell looked out the kitchen window. Richard and Dr. Basra, a diminutive dark-skinned man, were rounding the corner by the stables on their way to Garret's cabin. Richard carried two large suitcases, the doctor a small medical bag.

Coswell turned back to face Blakemore. "She didn't kill Garret," he said.

Blakemore's eyes widened. "What? Then who the hell did, and how the hell do you know?"

"I can't answer that."

Blakemore just stared at him for a moment. "You're going to have to come up with something better than that. The conversation I just had with Richard has left no doubt in my mind, I can tell you."

"I know, I know. But I've got a gut feeling. The girl's innocent."

"Well, as long as you're so logical, I guess I can't argue."

Coswell winced at the sarcasm.

"But," Blakemore went on, "the way I see it, unless the lawyer's proverbial 'unknown third person' sneaked out of the bush and shot poor Garret, there's enough circumstantial evidence to convict her. Motive for sure, opportunity, nobody around for kilometres, plus a bloody arsenal to choose from."

"I didn't find a murder weapon."

"You mean you didn't find her holding one, still smoking. She'd have disposed of it somewhere and probably not far off. A proper search will turn it up."

Coswell could argue no further. A hunch made for a weak argument.

"I don't always agree with by-the-book," Blakemore said. "But I see no other reasonable option here. Therefore, I'm going to charge her with Garret's murder and take her into custody. Let the courts decide if she's innocent."

Coswell understood. Lessening the caseload by one, especially a murder, gave relief and even status to an officer in charge. A fledgling sergeant, new at his post, needed positive results like that.

"I've told the helicopter pilot to bring my three men directly here instead of flying them back to Williams Lake," Blakemore said. "They can do a lot of the legwork and then escort Maggie to the holding cell at the station."

"That's all well and good," Coswell said. "But, Maggie aside, you seem to have forgotten the Johnson murders."

"We have the hippies in custody. That'll do until something better turns up. Time for you and me to return to base."

Blakemore's sudden burst of man-in-command self-confidence annoyed Coswell, but he didn't object. Instead, he decided to make use of a more sympathetic colleague. "Well. If that's the way it's to be, go to it," he said. "I'm going to see what the coroner and Richard are up to."

"Wait a minute," Blakemore said. "I need someone to witness my reading her rights to her."

"Your men will be here momentarily. Use one of them. They'll be more accessible to the courts when you need them. I'll be back in Vancouver. Meanwhile, you'd better go sit with her in case she jumps on a horse and rides into the sunset."

With that, he turned on his heel and vanished out the front door. Blakemore headed for the sitting room.

✳✳✳
✳✳✳

On the way to Garret's cabin, Coswell looked across the fields but saw no sign of Sam Hansen. Strange. The man must have heard the helicopter land and then take off from his front yard. It had probably flown right over his head, and yet he hadn't ridden back. Why? Was he simply waiting for everyone to leave? Did he think all would magically return to normal? Something wasn't right there and Coswell felt his antennae twitching.

Dr. Basra was already packing up when Coswell walked in and introduced himself. Basra stripped off his rubber gloves and shook hands.

"Finished so soon?" Coswell asked.

"Yes. An assistant makes the job much easier. Thank you, Richard."

"Thank you," Richard said. "At university, all we get to do is observe professionals, not work with them."

"Well," Coswell said. "What did you two learned men find?"

"Death by gunshot wound to the right temple," Dr. Basra said. "Small caliber. A .38, I'd say. Seems to be a run on those lately. No sign of trauma elsewhere. Estimated time of death: three AM, plus or minus. I'll have a more exact figure for you when I can get the body to the morgue. How soon can that be done?"

"The minute the helicopter returns," Coswell said, "which should be momentarily. It didn't have far to go."

He was right. They'd barely made it halfway to the house when the copter appeared over the treeline. It swept in and landed once more between the parked vehicles and the corral. When the blades had come to a complete stop, the pilot got out and opened the passenger door for the three Mounties.

Coswell immediately directed them to assist Dr. Basra in moving Garret's body. Richard turned to go with them.

"Hang on, Richard," Coswell said. "I'd like you to come with me. You might as well add to your learning by witnessing a sometimes unpleasant task."

***

The scene in the sitting room would have been almost comical had the situation been different. Blakemore was pacing the floor, while Maggie sat stiffly upright on the chesterfield, clutching the backpack on her lap like a child receiving a reprimand for some mischief.

"It's about time," Blakemore said. "Richard, you'll do as a witness."

He walked over to Maggie and stood in front of her. He pulled out his wallet and selected a card. Holding it at arm's length in the dull light, he began to read.

"Margaret Peron. You are under arrest for the murder of Garret Parker. Do you understand?"

She bowed her head and gave a barely perceptible nod.

"Would you please say yes, if you agree."

"Yes," she said in a flat voice.

Blakemore continued, tilting the card to gather more light.

"You have the right to retain and instruct counsel without delay. We will provide you with a toll-free telephone lawyer referral service if you do not have your own lawyer. Anything you say can be used in court as evidence. Do you understand?"

"Yes," she said, unprompted.

"Would you like to speak to a lawyer?"

He tucked the card away and returned the wallet to his hip pocket. She turned to Richard, confused. Richard, in turn, looked at Coswell.

"Did you interrogate her before we came in?" Coswell said to Blakemore.

"No use. I didn't have a witness ... remember?"

Coswell walked over and sat beside Maggie.

"Here's what's going to happen," he said. "Sergeant Blakemore or one of his men will take you in the helicopter to Williams Lake, where you'll be put in a cell."

Her eyes widened.

"But don't be too upset. A lawyer will be found for you quickly and a bail hearing will be arranged."

He knew that bail was a faint hope, even if she could find someone to put it up. But hearing the possibility appeared to give her confidence. "Bonny Hansen's my lawyer. She'll help me."

He'd momentarily forgotten Hansen's lawyer daughter. Bail suddenly became more of a possibility. "Of course," he said. "You can phone from here. I'll get her on the line for you."

"Jeez," Blakemore hissed. "Whose side are you on?"

"Justice," Coswell replied, "and the rights of the accused. You just read them ... remember?"

"All right then. She's all yours for the time being. I'm going outside so I can put my men to work collecting evidence."

Coswell smiled as Blakemore stomped out of the room. "Pissed him off, did I?"

He caught a little smile from Richard.

"You two stay put," he said. "I see there's no phone in this room, but there is one in the kitchen. I'll phone Bonny from there and give you a shout when I've got her."

***

The kitchen phone was a wall-mounted relic with an actual dial. A phone list was tacked up beside it with two numbers under Bonny's name. He dialed the first one and got a recorded message. He recognized the law firm: Hewlett, Morris, Cawston, a veritable department store of legal counsel. He ignored all the options and waited for a voice to come on. He identified himself and asked to speak to Bonny Hansen.

"I'm afraid Ms. Hansen is away from Vancouver, Inspector," the operator said. "She didn't give us a definite day she'd be back. Her brother died unexpectedly. May I direct you to someone else?"

He was about to ask for Bonny's residential phone number but decided he'd simply dial the second one on the list and spare the woman the agony of deciding whether to give out personal information to a stranger calling himself an RCMP inspector.

The second number got her residence, but again, a recording: "I'm sorry I can't speak with you right now, but please leave a message after the beep."

She didn't say her name, but he recognized Bonny's voice. He spoke quickly, outlining the situation and the urgency. As he hung up, a question occurred to him: why hadn't Bonny checked in with her office? Brent's funeral was over and she'd flown back to Vancouver.

But there could have been any one of a dozen reasons. Maybe she just wanted a day or two to herself. God knows he'd used the "out of town" excuse himself a few times. Otherwise he'd be on call 24/7.

On his way to the sitting room from the kitchen, he almost collided with Blakemore bursting in through the front door. "Basra wants to get back to Williams Lake with the body right away," he said. "I want Maggie to go with him. I hate to spare a man, but the sooner she's locked up, the better. One less worry."

When they went into the sitting room, they found Richard beside Maggie on the chesterfield. It may have been proper procedure, but Coswell hoped Blakemore wouldn't insist on handcuffing her. The fear returned to her eyes when she saw the stern look on Blakemore's face.

"Bonny wasn't in, Maggie," Coswell said, "but I left her a message explaining everything. Don't worry. You can call her when you get to Williams Lake."

Blakemore cut off further reassurance. "Time to go," he said. "Your transport's waiting outside."

Richard reached for her backpack, but she hugged it even tighter and got up to leave. Blakemore put his hand on her shoulder and guided her out. She flinched when he first touched her, but then submitted.

Coswell had difficulty maintaining his policeman's mindset. Blakemore was doing everything by the book and he had no right to interfere, but Richard's pained expression and the pathetic sight of the girl being led to jail set his mind awhirl.

When they reached the helicopter, they found Dr. Basra and one of the three Mounties waiting for them; the pilot was already in the cockpit checking his gauges and Garret's corpse was in a body bag, visible through the open door. Blakemore helped Maggie board. The pilot instructed her to stow her pack in the back and fasten her seatbelt. As soon as she'd obeyed, Blakemore spoke to the Mountie he'd assigned to accompany her.

"Cuff her," he said, "before you take off. I don't want any hysterical scenes causing a problem. Hands in front okay, but keep an eye on her." And then, with a quick glance at Richard, he strode off in the direction of Garret's cabin.

The Mountie climbed up and took the seat beside Maggie. Dr. Basra sat in the co-pilot's seat. The moment all doors were shut, the pilot fired the engine up, the rotor began to turn, and in seconds, the copter lifted off in a cloud of dust. They watched in silence as the remarkable machine swung away to the east. When it had flown out of sight, Coswell put his hand on the young man's shoulder.

"Don't worry too much," he said. "She'll be well looked after where she's going, and getting away from here right now might be a good thing. We can concentrate on finding out who really did kill Garret."

Richard looked at him. "You don't think she did it?"

"No, I don't."

Hope flared, then died in Richard's eyes. "I don't see how it could have been anyone else," he said.

"What happened to that wonderful deductive reasoning of yours? There are a number of other possibilities."

"Like what?"

"First, it could be a revenge killing by Chief Isaac or his cronies. They've already convicted Hansen and it wouldn't be too big an assumption to think that Garret was an accomplice. Get the underling first, scare the shit out of the other."

Richard brightened. "What else?" he said.

"Maybe Garret in some of his back-country rides got intimate with the hippies and their drug ring. He might have been around when the order came in to eliminate the Johnsons and was dumb enough to try a little blackmail. Drug lords tend to deal harshly with threats like that."

"I don't think Garret would be that dumb," Richard said, "but if he did know the identity of the killer, and that someone had assets worth tapping into, Sam Hansen comes out as the likeliest candidate, hands down."

"Now you're thinking. All we have to do is find out which possibility is the right one. Now you go help Blakemore and his men. I have to make a call."

***

Corporal James, Coswell's gift from "M" Division, transferred from the Yukon a mere two months previous and had brightened the inspector's life like no one before him.

"I'm not one hundred per cent sure of his persuasion," Chief Ward had said, "So I'm assigning him to you, seeing as you're experienced with that ilk."

The corporal answered the call on the first ring, recognizing the 123 area code on the call display.

"Happy Monday, Inspector," James said. "Good to hear from you."

"Happy Mondays come only as part of a long weekend," Coswell said, "but you'll be pleased to know that I'll be back in the office tomorrow. I want you to set up an appointment for me."

"With Inspector Ward?"

Coswell could almost see James' grin over the phone. "Very funny. No, I want you to track down the social worker who dealt with Maggie Peron, formerly of Hobbema, Alberta, and now of the Williams Lake hoosegow."

"Right, sir. Anyone else?"

"Not right now, but let's hear what you found out about the tree-planters and Garret Parker."

A rustle of paper. "Your tree people appear to be fine young citizens, save one who got caught with a tad more weed than he could smoke—name, Larry Kincaid. Did his time and no further problems. They all went to university; one is still attending and three have already graduated, Larry included. No guns registered to any of them."

"Good work. And Garret?"

"Much more interesting. Americans are amazingly generous with their juvenile records. Your boy Garret was a busy young lad—graduated from shoplifting and stealing hubcaps to one count of armed robbery at age sixteen. Graced the juvenile pen for a while—long enough to get smarter, I guess. No convictions after that. Nothing on the adult blotter. Left Chicago for points west, according to the probation records."

"Drugs?"

"No. Drugs weren't the style in those days. They were more into intimidation."

"Weapons charges? A .38 in particular."

"A gun was used in the armed robbery but I don't see any note of the calibre. Not likely they'd let him keep it."

"He knew the source, though. Getting another wouldn't be a problem."

More rustling of paper.

"One last item here. Our forensic people received a package from Williams Lake containing DNA samples from the dead men along with some cigarette butts and two slugs."

"And?" Coswell said impatiently.

"The DNA analysis hasn't been done yet, but I pressed them. Results will be available tomorrow. The slugs were easy. Same gun: a .38, but no ordinary Saturday night special. Constable Ralph almost had an orgasm over the whole thing. Said they were fired from a Colt New Service revolver, possibly as old as 1905. A real antique."

"This is antique country," Coswell said. "I'm not surprised, but it's good to know exactly what we're looking for."

The age of the gun didn't help a lot. It could have been lifted from a collection or someone's dusty attic. The results of the DNA analysis would come soon enough, from Coswell's point of view. The tree-planters weren't going anywhere.

"And to show you just how efficient I am," James went on, "I have a Margaret Peron up on my screen as we speak.

"You're a true prince," Coswell said.

"From someone else I'd be thrilled, but I detect a note of sarcasm." He gave a theatrical sigh. "Oh well. Here it is. First entry: a 'living off the avails' charge ten months ago and a second two months later. Age: eighteen. No jail time. Paid her fines with the profits, I guess. Address, a basement suite on Keefer. Registered with the safe injection site on Gore. Social Services assigned through the courts after the second charge. Next part's a bit fuzzy but there is a name: Elizabeth Faulkner, case worker. I'll get on that."

"Good. Now just one more thing."

"The Vicinage, sir? For seven o'clock? Party of one?"

"Do you have my dining habits in your computer too, you cheeky bugger?"

"Just part of the service, sir."

"All right. Do it, but make it for two. We'll have a working dinner. It'll likely be late afternoon when I get there, so a pickup at the airport would be appreciated. But for Christ's sake, don't bring a company car. And ditch the uniform."

"I might be from the Yukon," James said, feigning hurt, "but we know enough to wear our best mukluks when dining out, even if it's just a seal flipper meal at an igloo."

"Don't give me that hick bullshit. I know for a fact you were born and raised in Ottawa."

"Ah, no secrets from Big Brother, the Force ... well, maybe a little one."

"Keep it little," Coswell said, "if you want to make sergeant someday."

***

Coswell had barely hung up the receiver when the phone rang, startling him. It was Bonny Hansen.

"I've just gotten your message," she said, "and I have two quick questions for you. Where is Maggie? And has she given

215

a statement to anyone?"

"She's on her way by helicopter to the Williams Lake jail. I expect she'll arrive there within the hour. She's spoken only to me about Garret's murder. Claims total innocence. No official statement's been taken."

"Good. She's not to say a word without me present. That's an official request, by the way, which I expect to be passed on. There's a flight out of here at five PM. I can just make it if I leave right away. Bye."

Coswell stood with the receiver in his hand, dumbfounded. Not a word about poor Garret or even her father. She'd switched fully into lawyer mode.

He hung up again and looked out the kitchen window. Blakemore, Richard, and the two Williams Lake Mounties were on their way to the house. Blakemore carried a camera. One of his officers toted a suitcase.

Blakemore came in first and began giving orders. "Okay," he said, "We'll start with the den upstairs." He spotted Coswell standing in the kitchen. "Are you going to help?"

"I've made the rounds already," Coswell replied, "and aside from some fingerprint collecting and analysis of the methadone, I don't think you'll have much to do upstairs. Maggie's room, however, is just down this hall. I'd suggest taking some samples from the semen on the bedsheets for DNA and the usual fingerprint dusting."

"How hard did you look for the murder weapon?"

"I checked all of the rooms and the gun cabinet. I'll let you do the outside garbage containers."

"What are you going to do?"

"Have a look for Sam Hansen. I want to talk to him before I go back to Vancouver, which reminds me. You've ordered that helicopter back, haven't you?"

"Of course," Blakemore said. "Getting an inspector back to base is worth a thousand dollars of flying time, eh? Especially when I can go along and bill the trip to Vancouver 'E' Division. Keeps my budget healthy."

Blakemore's newfound authority continued to annoy Coswell, but he chose not to show him up in front of his men. Besides, finding Hansen took priority at the moment.

"I need Richard for a few minutes to get a horse ready," he said, "and then you can have him back."

"Go ahead, but I do want him back," Blakemore said. "He's been a great help."

Coswell didn't miss the implication, but he ignored it. Richard would be looking for evidence to corroborate Maggie's story, not refute it.

"Listen for the helicopter," Blakemore was telling him. "When you hear it, come back. The Vancouver bean-counters might balk at paying for idling time and the company charges by the hour, in the air or on the ground. Besides, I want to be the one to take Maggie's statement in Williams Lake and the sooner the better."

Coswell decided not to mention Bonny's phone call. Blakemore would find out soon enough.

***

Richard had saddled Rusty for him, and she cantered along with the efficiency typical of her breed, a pace Coswell knew she could hold all day. He let himself relax as the ground slid past beneath him. He hoped that Hansen hadn't gone far. An hour was probably all the time he'd have before the helicopter returned. If Hansen had ridden all the way to the cabin at the top of Hobson's trail, planning to spend the night there, he'd be out of reach.

But he hadn't. Coswell saw a flash of white ahead and then Hansen, mounted on his Arab, coming towards him at a slow walk. He pulled Rusty to a halt and waited.

"I thought you'd be gone on that cursed helicopter,"

Hansen said when he drew close. "Don't tell me they're still ransacking my house."

"They'll be leaving soon."

"And you've ridden out, concerned about my welfare. How nice."

Coswell felt a little ridiculous doing an interview sitting on a horse, but Hansen showed no sign that he planned to dismount, leaving him no choice.

"I must return to Vancouver tomorrow," he said, "but I wanted to have a word with you before I left."

"About what?" Hansen said, "You have Garret's murderer and I've answered all your questions about the Johnsons."

"I'm not convinced that Maggie did kill Garret."

"Hasn't she been charged?"

"Yes, but Sergeant Blakemore did that, not me. I'm ... let us say, looking into other possibilities. What time did you check out of your Williams Lake lodging this morning? Breakfast anywhere?"

"I stayed at the Clearwater Hotel. Did the checkout last night because I planned to leave very early before the office opened up in the morning, and, no, I didn't have breakfast. I made a coffee in my room and took it with me." He frowned. "Surely you don't suspect me of killing Garret. He's been with me for years."

"Maybe he was worried about the ranch going broke," Coswell said, "and thought he'd get a little cash stake to tide him over."

"You think he was blackmailing me?" Hansen smiled. "Don't tell me," he said. "Let me guess."

He put his finger over his lips and looked skyward.

"I'm responsible for the Johnsons' death, Garret knew it, and threatened to go to the authorities. Right?"

He looked mockingly back at Coswell. "Well, la-de-da. You'll have one helluva time proving that. First of all, because

I wasn't responsible for the killings, and second, I wasn't being blackmailed. But I can understand your reasoning. You've solved only one case with Maggie, but if you substituted me, you'd have the answer for everything. One size fits all, eh?"

Coswell returned his gaze. "It has been my experience that cases like these most often are linked. One merely has to find the link. You were a reasonable start."

Hansen gave a shrug. "I suppose. But you'll have to look elsewhere. Now let's get back to the house. I have a ranch to run and I need to find a replacement for Garret ... and Maggie."

If Hansen felt any sentiment towards Garret, it appeared to have been pushed aside. But Coswell had to concede that you probably needed to be hard if you wanted to keep your head above water in the cattle business. Nevertheless, a check with the Clearwater Hotel was definitely in order. He wheeled Rusty around and followed Hansen back to the stable.

COSWELL AND BLAKEMORE were the sole passengers in the helicopter flight back to Williams Lake. The two constables were assigned to drive back in the cruiser after dropping Richard off in the village. Coswell took the young man aside while Blakemore loaded the suitcases.

"You'll be on the payroll until you return to university," he told him, "which means I want you to keep digging. No way did the tree-planters kill the Johnsons. Work on that mechanic, Tom Porter, some more."

"What about Maggie?" Richard said.

"We'll have to let that play out for the time being, but a visit or two from you wouldn't be out of order ... if you can get by Bonny Hansen. She's taken on Maggie's case."

"I'll get by her. She wasn't that big of a sister."

"Good luck."

He turned and saw Blakemore about to climb into the front seat of the helicopter.

"Hold on," he said. "Unless you want me to barf on the back of your neck, that's where I want to sit. Less motion up there and I see the horizon better."

No argument. Blakemore got in the back.

***

A Constable Fraser had driven over to the helipad from the Williams Lake station to pick them up and broke the bad news to Blakemore.

"Her lawyer just rolled in," he said. "And guess who it is?"

"Oh, shit," Blakemore said. "Bonny Hansen. Why didn't you stall Maggie Peron's phone call 'til I got back? It wouldn't have bent her precious rights that much."

"We did stall her. The Hansen woman literally dropped out of the sky."

"Who ... ?"

"Matters not," Coswell said, "and it's really for the better. Makes for a nice neat case when interviews are done with a lawyer present. Judges like that."

"And so do the defence lawyers," Blakemore said. "Nothing like some good coaching beforehand. Cook up a good story."

"How cynical. Surely you haven't lost faith in the wheels of justice."

"Too many flat tires, and that Bonny Hansen's going to be one giant puncture, I just know it."

"Well, you still have the tree-planters in custody. Perhaps your interrogation skills with them will get us closer to a solution to the Johnson case."

"They got a lawyer too," Fraser said. "Almost as soon as we locked the cell doors."

"Double shit," Blakemore said.

When they arrived at the station, Coswell swiftly dodged any involvement with either lawyer—defence or prosecution. "I'd like to go directly to the airport," he said. "Standby might be the quickest way to get me back to Vancouver. Could you give me a lift, Constable?" Blakemore grumbled but gave his okay.

They'd barely backed out of the station parking lot when Coswell arranged a stopover. "The Clearwater Hotel, Constable," he said. "Do you know it?"

"Intimately. The bar there's a popular watering hole. Two officers and a cruiser park out front from sundown on. Fights, drunk and disorderly, wife beatings—enough to keep them busy all night." He glanced at Coswell. "Why the interest?"

"A hunch I'd like to check out." No elaboration.

The constable proceeded to drive five blocks, turn right, and pull up in front of a building that looked a hundred years old. It reminded Coswell of a larger version of the Anahim Hotel, painted a Canadian Railway maroon. It lacked only the swinging doors to make it a perfect oater movie set.

"Doesn't look too upscale," he said.

The constable laughed. "That's for sure. But it's a landmark and a favourite for ranching types and loggers. Unfortunately, the Injun warriors like it too which makes for a frequent battleground."

Odd that Hansen would stay in such a rowdy place, Coswell thought. He told the constable to wait in the cruiser. "I'll just be a minute," he said. "If you hear gunfire, though, come running."

"That may not be as far-fetched as you think," Constable Fraser replied.

★★★

The foyer of the hotel was a mixture of old and new. A bank of recently added machines dispensed everything from cigarettes to disposable razors. Two enormous ferns cascaded from pots set on wooden stands, and in one corner, a split-leafed philodendron reached for the south-facing front windows. A single set of stairs led upwards. No elevator. The check-in desk was a handsome old dark mahogany structure with a traditional slotted rack for keys hanging behind it. A bell with a sign reading RING FOR SERVICE sat beside a modern multi-line telephone. Coswell gave the bell two swift jolts with the heel of his hand and waited. Nothing.

He was about to ring again when he heard someone running down the stairs and a young man appeared, quite out of breath. The man did a double-take when he saw Coswell's uniform.

"What now?" he said. "Isn't it a bit early for the horsemen to be about?"

Coswell would have sworn that one of the tree planters had gotten loose. The man could have been Jason's brother: same eyes, same insolent manner and a two-day growth of whiskers.

"What is your name?" Coswell said. The term "horsemen" implied more than a little familiarity with the Force.

"Bob."

"Bob who?" The man's attitude was getting annoying.

"Robert Patterson, formerly of Vancouver and now a legitimate resident of this fair city."

"What did you do during your illegitimate years?"

"Couple of possession charges. Nothing serious."

Coswell smiled at Patterson's apparent assumption that his criminal past stuck out like a sore thumb.

"Actually, Bob," he said. "I'm not the least bit interested in you unless you're related to a tree-planter named Jason Radcliffe."

"Never heard of him."

So much for physical similarities, and Coswell wondered

if he had reached the age where all young people begin to look alike.

"I want to know if a Sam Hansen checked in here this past weekend."

"The Marlboro man? Yes, he certainly did. Yesterday evening. I almost asked him if he'd done some commercial work. I swear I've seen him on TV."

He pulled out the register, flipped to the last page, and spun it around for Coswell to read.

"Checked in and checked out all at once. Said he was heading home real early today."

"Anyone see him leave? The night clerk?"

Bob laughed. "This is the night clerk," he said and pulled out a sign from behind the desk informing any latecomer that the office was closed from one AM 'til seven AM. An addendum offered up the name of another hotel with twenty-four-hour service.

"The truth of the matter," Bob said, "is that we only keep hotel rooms to qualify for the liquor license. We don't get many guests. The bar supports the place."

Coswell now had an explanation for Hansen's choice of lodgings. It provided the perfect alibi: check in, slip out unobserved in the wee hours of the morning, boot it along the highway back to the ranch, shoot Garret, and hole up along a side road somewhere until it was safe to show his face. Even if someone saw him parked there, he could claim that road fatigue had forced him to stop for a short sleep.

Garret's death had changed the whole focus of the investigation in Coswell's mind, assuming that Maggie truly hadn't shot him. He was sure now that the answers to all the murders could be found at the Hansen ranch, and that looking anywhere else would be a waste of time, despite his directing Richard to check out Tom Porter again.

But where would he find the answers? Forensics maybe,

although that was running out. Something from Blakemore's search? The coroner's findings? A few hoofprints? But even if those had been made by Hansen's Arab, it didn't prove he was the rider—Garret and even Maggie had access to the animal. But Sam Hansen still ranked highest on his list of suspects. Everything fit: motive, opportunity, and capability. Pinning the murders on him, however, would be a daunting task. He returned to the cruiser discouraged.

"Time to go home, Inspector?" Constable Fraser said, seeing his downcast expression.

"Yes," Coswell said. "There's nothing more for me here."

✱✱✱

His mood didn't improve on the flight to Vancouver, which ended with bumpy air over the north shore mountains during the descent. Corporal James was waiting for him at the South Terminal.

"You look the picture of health, Inspector. That clean country air, I presume."

Negativity and Corporal James were simply incompatible.

"I look like a piece of shit and feel even worse," Coswell said.

"Well, that will just vanish in ever so few minutes. Your chariot awaits, sir. Let us hie to the Vicinage."

That was all it took to elevate Coswell's mood. He even let James drive.

✱✱✱

A sizable dinner crowd had gathered at Pope's Vicinage despite the blustery, wet Monday evening outside. Coswell's regular table had a reserved sign neatly placed on it. James drank it all in.

"Oh, look at all the beautiful people. I feel so out of place."

"Don't. I've dropped so much of my salary here since it first opened, they should have rolled out the red carpet for us."

They came close to doing just that. Nicole, their gorgeous hostess for the evening, led them to the reserved table. "We missed you last week, Inspector," she said. "Mr. Pope's off tonight but he left special instructions for Chef Andrea: a dinner treat for you and a special wine to go with it."

"See if she'll make that times two," Coswell said. "My partner here needs a treat."

"Of course. There was some confusion about the reservation."

No doubt. Coswell always ate alone.

"Meet James, Nicole," he said.

James batted his eyelids at her. "I'm oh so charmed to meet you," he said, giving her his limpest handshake.

Nicole maintained her composure. Coswell quickly cleared up any misconception. "We're not a number," he said. "James is a cop."

She gave them a big smile and went to fetch the wine.

"Spoilsport," James said.

★★★
★★★

Although Coswell had labeled their evening a working dinner, neither man engaged in any shop talk while dish after magnificent dish was set before them: butter potato soup, grilled sloping hill Berkshire pork, and for dessert, a chilled lime cheesecake with sour cherries. The wine proved to be the biggest treat: a 2005 Grgich Hills Chardonnay which complemented all three courses.

"I don't know how the man lays his hands on this stuff," Coswell said. "It's like gold. San Francisco restaurants alone must offer to buy every bottle. A little Vancouver restaurant like Iain Pope's shouldn't stand a chance."

"It would be rude of me to ask what the bottle costs, wouldn't it?" James said.

"Yes it would."

Nicole brought coffees and complimentary snifters of cognac.

"You can have mine," James said when Nicole moved off to serve other patrons. "I feel a little buzz from the wine despite all that food, and blowing an .08-plus on the breathalyzer wouldn't do my record any good."

"Wise man," Coswell said. "Now let's get down to business. Whenever a case has me stumped, I often find it useful to get an outside opinion. Sometimes the trees get in the way of seeing the forest."

For the next five minutes he related to James every detail of the Chilcotin killings that he could remember, as well as his current thinking regarding his choice for the guilty party.

"So you can see that Sam Hansen is by far the likeliest candidate."

James thought the matter over for a few minutes before delivering his summation. "If the slug the coroner digs out of Garret's head matches those from the Johnson brothers, then I agree: the crimes are linked. If not, then your Maggie comes to the fore again in Garret's death, and you are out to lunch on the Johnsons. Of course, it sounds as though they had enemies everywhere, not just the Hansen ranch."

"True, true, but I'll give you ten-to-one odds the slugs match."

"Then we have an Agatha Christie-type whodunit with all the suspects in one house. There is one person in that house, though, that you've only given passing mention to — Bonny Hansen. Has she been ruled out? Having her brother killed by those two natives must have made her a little bit mad at least."

A twinge. She could ride, too. It would have been easy for her to slip out after everyone had gone to bed. But she was long gone at the time of Garret's death. Or was she? He cursed himself for not checking whether she did fly out that evening.

"Still on my list, of course," Coswell lied, "but a very long shot. No pun intended."

He signaled to Nicole. "L'addition, s'il vous plaît," he said. She smiled and went over to the cashier.

"Nicole's from Trois Rivières," Coswell said. "She likes to hear her first language every so often."

"Indeed," James said. "I should have spoken to her, then. I spent twelve years in French Immersion when I grew up in Ottawa. Your accent, by the way, is awful and no one in French Canada says l'addition. The word for 'bill' is la facture."

Coswell couldn't contain a laugh. "James, if you don't learn a little diplomacy with your superiors, those sergeant's stripes are not in your future."

"Oh, darn. But I did line up your social worker, Elizabeth Faulkner. You have an appointment to see her at eight tomorrow morning in her office on Gore. Not the nicest of locations, but she insisted."

"Don't tell me. The safe injection site."

"Yep. Her office is in the back. You might want me to go with you. I'll sign out a Taser."

"No need. My condo's just a couple of blocks from there. I'll walk."

James looked truly shocked. An RCMP inspector choosing to live next to Vancouver's most notorious district? Incomprehensible.

"When I'm done," Coswell went on, "I'll have you pick me up. But get an unmarked car, and leave your hat off."

Nicole arrived with the bill. Coswell gave her his plastic.

"She's quite lovely," James said, watching her descend the stairs to the main floor. Seeing Coswell's raised eyebrow, he added, "If you like that sort of thing."

***

Coswell woke early as usual and finished his morning preparations, happy to be donning his baggy Dockers, sweatshirt, and windbreaker. His abhorrence of wearing a uniform reached a peak when the damned flak vests became mandatory.

After activating the alarm system, he went out the front door of his three-storey, gentrified Chinatown residence at five minutes to seven. A long flight of stairs led from his porch to street level. Sitting on the bottom step were two scruffy characters sorting out their early-morning scavenging finds. Parked on the sidewalk were two shopping carts, the contents threatening to spill onto the concrete.

"Morning, folks," Coswell said, tripping down the stairs. "Good haul today?"

They looked up at him. One, a woman of undistinguishable age, gave him an uninhibited smile that displayed a mouthful of tobacco-stained teeth. "Pretty good, Inspector," she said. "Could still use some spare change, though."

He reached into his pocket and pulled out a couple of toonies. She reached out a filthy hand and took them. "Thanks," she said. "You're a peach."

Regulars. They showed up a couple of times a week, always on weekdays. The woman, Sally, explained once that they avoided the downtown eastside during the weekends. "Too many loonies and drunks," she'd said. She stood up and gave her partner a boot. "Out of the way. Inspector's got to go catch crooks."

The man rose painfully. He was younger than Sally and unbelievably ugly. His face, obviously altered by numerous encounters with superior opponents, was further marred by acne. They both gave off what could only be described as an earthy odour, although his resembled something closer to a manure pile.

Coswell slipped by them, dodged the shopping carts, and

began walking up Jackson Avenue. Across the street stretched a massive low rental housing development, landscaped in front by a dense ground cover. A well-dressed young man with a pager clipped to his belt was searching for something, his body bent over a section of greenery near a sprinkler-head. A black Miata idled at the curb. Coswell kept his eyes straight ahead and continued walking, memorizing the license plate number. The narc boys probably already knew about the drug drop, but a little interdepartmental tipping always paid off down the line.

Before turning left, he stopped for a moment at Keefer Street and looked across at the Strathcona Elementary schoolyard. On the basketball court, a dozen elderly Chinese men and women were going through the beautiful slow movements of Tai Chi, two of them wielding swords. A motorized cart buzzed up and down the yard in a grid pattern. Periodically it halted and a gloved worker got out, picking up needles and depositing them in a container mounted on the back of the cart. In an hour or so, the students would arrive and the air would be filled by shouts and jabbers, mostly in foreign tongues.

As he neared the corner of Keefer and Gore, the produce stalls came into view. Already trucks were being unloaded and their contents stacked in attractive displays. Cigarettes dangled from the mouths of most of the men and a few of the older women. There was little banter, everyone seemingly in a great hurry to meet a deadline. But Coswell had no interest in produce. He'd delayed his breakfast by half an hour and his stomach rumbled. Phil's Diner, open at seven, lay ahead.

Phil, born Ming Wong, emigrated from Canton to Vancouver forty years ago with his young family and had accumulated enough money to be accepted into Canada as a desirable addition to the country's tax base. He wanted to start up a restaurant but decided immediately that competing with the numerous Asian eateries in the area would be a bad venture. Instead, he specialized in North American soul food — bacon and eggs, hamburgers, milkshakes, BLTs. Seating in his restaurant consisted mainly of booths, but a row of padded stools along the counter added another dozen places. He reasoned that when it came time to eat, most tourists wanted cheap and familiar fare in equally familiar surroundings. His chief clientele, however, were street people and working stiffs who couldn't afford to live elsewhere in the city. It made for an eclectic mix. Phil and Coswell were on a first-name basis — Coswell had pointed out to Phil that the presence of an "inspector" would not be good for business.

"Morning, Mr. Mark," Phil said, his Cantonese accent strong. "Not see you long time."

"Work, work, work," Coswell said. "No time to eat."

In truth, he'd been patronizing the Old Dutch Pancake House near headquarters on Kingsway and had gotten into the habit of starting the day with a healthy dose of sugar. Also, Phil had never learned to make a decent cup of coffee and green tea simply didn't do it first thing in the morning.

"Ah, I see you get skinny," Phil said.

"Yeah, right," Coswell said feeling the snugness of his belt. "Okay. Let's fatten me up a bit this morning. I want the classic breakfast with sausages, white toast, and be generous with the hash browns."

"Good choice," Phil said, flipping over the downturned mug in front of Coswell and filling it up before he scurried off to the kitchen. The trite phrase was new since the inspector's last visit and he hoped Phil would soon forget it.

He took a sip of the coffee, black being his preference. Dreadful as usual. He decided to experiment with two of the dairy creamers and a teaspoon of sugar. Another sip told him he'd made it even worse.

The regulars began to straggle in, most of them grizzled

street people just finishing their early-morning scrounging. He looked for Sally and her partner but they didn't show. A young native girl came in, eyes still glazed from lack of sleep or drugs or both. She was dressed in ridiculous high heel pumps, a man's pajama top, and nothing else. The top, which she had neglected to button all the way to the bottom, revealed a clump of pubic hair. Phil came charging out from the kitchen.

"Vicki! You go dress, then come back."

"Aw, Phil. Couldn't I just sit in a corner booth and have a coffee? I won't bother anyone and I don't feel so good."

Phil stood for a moment, hands on his hips, and glared at her.

"Oh, let her stay," Coswell said. "I'm sure you've got something in the back she can use as a skirt. Put it on my bill."

The girl slowly turned her eyes to his booth and, with some effort, focused on him. "Can I sit with you?"

"Why not?"

Phil almost choked, but Coswell persisted.

"Bring my guest coffee and some breakfast ... and that skirt," he said, and, fearing for Phil's blood pressure, added, "I think Vicki might supply me with some information."

That defused the situation. Phil still did not look happy, but he dropped his arms and went back to the kitchen. Vicki hobbled over to the booth and slid in opposite Coswell, bumping her hip sharply on the edge of the table in the process.

"Shit!" she said. "Another bruise. I'm going to look like a goddamned Holstein."

"Oh. Are you from the country? Not many city girls know what a Holstein is."

"Yeah. I know cows all right. First job I got was shovelling their shit for a white guy. Hired kids from the reserve under the table. Paid us bugger-all, but we got free milk and stuff."

"Where was that?"

She stared intently at his coffee. "If you're not drinking that, I'd sure like it. I don't want to bug Phil."

He pushed the coffee across the table to her. She took the mug in both hands and quickly drained it.

"I don't suppose you smoke?" she said.

"Sorry."

"That's okay."

Silence for a moment.

"What was it you asked me?" she said.

"Where are you from?"

"Barrière. Know where that is?"

"I sure do. It's on the Yellowhead Highway north of Kamloops. Part of the 2003 forest fire disasters. My folks in Kelowna lost some buildings that summer when the fires hit there."

"I'll bet they got compensated real quick, though. Government forgot about Barrière. Indians and broke loggers didn't interest them."

More racial anger, unfortunately justified.

Phil appeared at the door of the kitchen, looking like a circus performer balancing plates, seemingly determined to deliver everything in one trip. Vicki quickly shoved her empty cup back in front of Coswell and turned over a clean one for herself.

After deftly sliding the plates onto the table — identical breakfasts — Phil went back and got the coffee pot. Returning to their table, he refilled Coswell's cup and then poured Vicki's.

"Thanks," Coswell said. "We've got everything now except the skirt."

Grumbling, Phil whipped off his apron and handed it to her. "Keep it," he said.

"You're a generous man, Phil," Coswell said. "God will reward your kindness."

"I'm Buddhist."

With that, he left and made the rounds topping up coffees. Vicki switched cups again. "Don't want to poison you," she said. With a combination of wiggles and grunts, she manoeuvred the apron around her and managed to tie it on securely. "There," she said. "I'm decent. Let's eat."

She rolled up the sleeves of her oversized pajamas and attacked the food on her plate. Coswell noted her skinny arms. Eating was obviously not a high priority in her life, but he also observed that she had no needle tracks.

"Have you lived down here for long?" he asked.

"Couple of years. Long enough to get stuck."

"Stuck?"

"Money stuck," she said. "I got a weakness."

He waited while she shoveled in another forkful of egg.

"I like my wine too much."

Coswell cringed at the thought of how much plonk the girl would have had to drink to use up all her financial resources. "Do you get help from Welfare Services?" he said.

"Yeah, but it ain't much and they push counseling. Counseling's okay but it takes time and you got to show up sober. Makes it hard to earn a little money on the side and hang out with my friends."

"I understand there's a good social worker assigned down here," Coswell said. "Elizabeth Faulkner."

"Lizzie the Lez?" she said. "Yeah. Handles all us Indian maidens." She put her fork down and peered at him. "You a government spy or something? Lizzie's okay. Does a good job."

"No, I'm no spy, but I have an appointment to see her this morning on another matter."

She continued to eye him. "You're a cop ... right?" A flash of fear. "Vice?"

He laughed. "No, and don't worry. Your secrets are safe with me."

"Did that 'no' mean you're not a cop or not vice?"

The girl was not as dumb as she looked. "RCMP — homicide, not vice," he said. "I'm presently working a case up north that involves a First Nations girl who I believe has been wrongfully accused. Your help would be appreciated."

She picked up her fork and began eating again, pausing briefly to gulp down some coffee. "What help?"

"The girl's name is Margaret Peron and she used to live in this area. Did you know her?"

"Maggie? The princess from Hobbema? Yeah, I knew her. Full blood, like me, not half-breed trash that call themselves Indian, which is most of what you see down here."

"What can you tell me about her?"

"Never fit in well with the rest of us. She showed up about a year ago, kind of snooty, which is normal for those Samson Cree. Oil money, smart lawyers on their payroll. Don't know why any of them ever leave the reserve. I'm Simpcw, Salish. We've been poor as shit forever."

She warmed to her subject.

"Also, Samson women are born beautiful. Look at me — head like a pumpkin and if I ate more I'd look like a walrus. Maggie could have been a model, but she had a weakness, too ... the big H. When she couldn't hook enough bread to feed her habit, she turned into a spittin' cougar caught up a tree, clawing at everything."

"She became violent?" Coswell said.

"You got it. Raked a couple of her johns which put her on the pimps' blacklist. But her good looks kept her in business 'til something happened with the cops and she got shipped out of town by Lizzie. Must have been something real bad, 'cause everybody said Lizzie had a thing for Maggie."

Coswell looked at his watch. Time to go.

"I'll pay for everything at the till," he said. "You stay and finish. Phil will bring you more coffee." He opened his wallet, pulled out a fifty-dollar bill, and handed it to her. "You've been a real help, Vicki," he said. "Why don't you take the day off and do one of those counseling sessions?"

She looked up at him as he rose from his seat and the light in her eyes seemed to go out again. Giving her the money was probably a mistake.

"Thanks," she said.

14

VANCOUVER'S ONLY SAFE INJECTION SITE, hailed by public health workers and supported by government, maintained a low profile to reduce the wrath of the powerful Christian anti-drug abuse lobby. Nowhere was it advertised. Instead, one found the place, tucked in the ground floor of an old wooden office building, by word of mouth. The police cooperated by keeping away, despite the temptation to interview its users, a consideration the staff and the clients both appreciated.

Coswell made his way through the crowd exiting the soup kitchen half a block from the site. No one paid him any attention, including the two beat cops observing the exodus. He walked quickly until he spotted the plain, solid steel door with the address bolted on a sign above.

The place seemed deserted when he first entered. It had a tiny, spotlessly clean waiting room containing six chairs, a glass table with neatly stacked magazines, and a single coat rack. The only adornment on the walls was a large printed list of dos and don'ts; the remainder of the space consisted of a partitioned-off reception area that reminded Coswell of a tollbooth. A security camera mounted on the ceiling looked down on him.

Momentarily, a woman dressed in hospital greens, a stethoscope draped over her neck, entered through a door in the back, adjacent to the reception area. She did not wear a nametag, nor did she identify herself. Her dress, however, indicated she was a nurse or perhaps a doctor. Nurse, Coswell decided. A doctor would have identified herself as such.

"Inspector Coswell," she said. "Elizabeth is expecting you. Come this way."

Disappointed that his identity was so obvious, despite his civilian garb, he crossed the room and followed her down a short corridor. A door to his left revealed a long, brilliantly lit counter with three chairs in front and a huge continuous mirror behind. Injection paraphernalia in steel trays marked each individual space. A single video monitor hung down from the ceiling, giving a panoramic view of the waiting area. No clients had arrived as yet. Coswell wondered at the mirror, but figured it was all part of the psychology — a way to confront clients with the sight of themselves shooting up.

There were two doors to the right; the first was open, revealing a staff lounge. Two coffee cups and an open newspaper sat on a large table. The second door, at the very end of the corridor, was closed and unmarked. The nurse gave it a rap.

"Here's your man, Liz," she said. "Right on time."

The door opened. A small wisp of a woman appeared, dark hair pulled back in a bun, badly in need of a colour rinse. She gave him a fleeting smile and then replaced it with an expression of chronic consternation that suggested a burden of cares weighing on her thin shoulders. She offered her hand in an unfeeling handshake.

"I'm pleased to meet you, Inspector," she said. "Come in and have a seat."

The nurse left, pulling the door shut behind her.

The room wasn't much larger than a walk-in closet. A

small, open desk took up most of the space. On it sat a huge, outdated computer monitor and an economy-size box of Kleenex. The computer tower hummed away beneath the desk, leaving scant room for Elizabeth's spindly legs. She wore a shapeless black jumper and unflattering, brown-spotted pedal-pushers. Her shoes were stark white Reebok walkers. The outfit's only virtue, so far as Coswell could imagine, was that it blended in perfectly with the bizarre dress worn by many of the female street people. She had a peculiar habit of never meeting his gaze, even when she spoke to him.

"Corporal James told me that you were looking for information on Maggie Peron," she said. "He wouldn't say why. Is she in some sort of trouble?"

"She's been charged with murder."

The woman recoiled at the news. Her eyes flew wide open and for once she looked right into his. "Nooo," she said. Tears welled up.

"If it's any consolation to you," Coswell said, "I think she's innocent. That's why I'm here. To find out more about her."

She reached for a Kleenex and wiped away the tears. "Excuse me," she said. "One shouldn't get attached to one's clients, especially down here. But Maggie was sort of special." She sniffed. "I feel so guilty."

"Guilty? My goodness. I'm told that you were responsible for getting her out of this environment and under Anne Hansen's care at their ranch in the Cariboo."

She sighed. "Yes. I did facilitate that. Made up a little anyway for the court mess I got her into."

Coswell's ears perked up. "Her record lists only two charges for prostitution," he said. "Did I miss something?"

She gazed at the blank computer screen, her mind apparently adrift. "Maggie came in to see me one day in a terrible state. She'd been badly beaten by two men who'd hired her services in their hotel room. Two native men, to make the whole affair worse. I guess I snapped. Sometimes it's all too much."

More welling of tears.

"I insisted she report the two men. One of the policewomen assigned to this district is a good friend of mine and I got her to convince Maggie to lay charges. The men were apprehended at their hotel and put in a lineup. I went with Maggie when she pointed them out."

Another lapse as she conjured up the scene and then abruptly switched her train of thought. "Who is she accused of murdering? Surely not anyone looking after her."

"The ranch foreman." Coswell said, "And under rather unsavoury circumstances. But tell me more about the court incident."

"Oh. We went to court, all right, and had our ears pinned back. Those two evil creatures obviously had money. They hired a first-class lawyer. We got a junior prosecutor who was just putting in time waiting to get into a big private law firm." She paused. "It's all so ironic. The two men gave their address as Anahim Lake, not far from the Hansen ranch, and the prosecutor was Bonny Hansen, Anne Hansen's daughter."

Bonny Hansen? Two Indians from Anahim Lake? Coswell's mind buzzed and he listened intently as she continued.

"Ms Hansen botched the case entirely, in my opinion, but she completely snowed Maggie with excuses and offered up her mother's program in the process. Maggie thought she was wonderful and I didn't tell her otherwise. The Hansen ranch, I thought, might be the answer for Maggie and so I ran with the offer. It appears I made another mistake."

"No. You made the right decision getting the girl out of Vancouver and into a controlled environment, a chance she wouldn't have gotten otherwise. There's no predicting bad luck and that's what got Maggie into her present mess, not anything you did."

"Please keep me informed," she said.

"I promise, and thank you for your help."

She remained seated behind her desk when Coswell got up to leave, her face suddenly aged with defeat. He wanted to say something that might cheer her a bit, but nothing came to him. He walked down the corridor to the waiting room. No one was there. He turned to the camera and waved, mouthing "Thank you."

***
***

Back on the street, he saw Corporal James parked in a fifteen-minute loading zone directly across from the safe injection site. Even without a hat and driving an unmarked vehicle, he was unmistakably a cop. There wasn't a soul within fifty metres of him.

"You sure know how to clean up the neighbourhood," Coswell said, climbing into the passenger's seat after a quick jay-walk. "You'd never make it in the narc squad."

"I'd never want to ... at least not undercover. Unwashed hair, dirty clothes, and all that macho stuff—ugh."

"You'll go far, James," Coswell said. "With that attitude, you'll be my boss in no time. I see a brass plate and superintendent in your future."

"Do you really think so?"

"I guarantee it, but meanwhile you're my driver, so get this pig in motion. We're going to the courthouse. I want to look up a trial proceedings."

Coswell found it hard to believe that Bonny Hansen would ever be incompetent, no matter what her position in the courts. Something didn't add up.

"Right, sir," James said. "But I'm bound at this point to remind you to check in with Chief Inspector Ward at your earliest convenience this morning. 'Earliest convenience' being his exact words, although I detected a touch of malice in his voice."

"I read you. Your duty's done. Now get me to the court-house," Coswell growled.

"Just the messenger, sir. Just the messenger."

✱✱✱

Coswell had never been to the courthouse library. On the rare occasion when he wanted a transcript of a trial, he had it sent over to his office at RCMP headquarters. Today, however, he wanted as much information tucked under his belt as he could muster before his fateful meeting with Ward.

It looked like any other library: law students with their laptops and books spread out on almost every table. Coswell went to the main desk and gave the details of what he wanted to the librarian, an older woman who looked the part: white hair, no makeup, and a motherly personality. She had no difficulty with the computer in front of her, however, and in seconds she had Maggie's day in court up on the screen.

"We have an audio of this one, Inspector," she said. "I'll get it for you."

Coswell was delighted. He'd noted the disappearance of the peculiar transcribing machine in the courtroom and its replacement by audio recording devices. It was a change for the better, in his opinion, even if it meant another skill going the way of the dodo. The spoken word expressed so much more than bare words on a page.

The librarian cleared a carrel for him, suggesting to the male student parked there that a short break would do him good. Coswell's casual dress didn't impress him, but the librarian's voice did. He relinquished his seat.

Coswell put on the headset, plugged it into the machine, pushed play, and began to listen. One sentence in and his heart skipped a beat: "Case twelve, Regina versus William and Arthur Johnson ...."

It all played out: an argument over services to be rendered, a fight, and an injured party. Bonny's presentation was almost amateurish. She expounded on the plight of the poor natives in the downtown eastside, struggling to survive, and presented Maggie as an innocent young girl taken advantage of by the evil Johnsons. Their lawyer shot her argument down without even breathing hard. Maggie, he said, was a confirmed drug addict and practiced hooker who had physically injured some of her clients—including the Johnsons. At that point, he had Art Johnson display the scratches Maggie had inflicted on his face.

He switched off the machine, not bothering to listen to it all. A wave of depression swept over him. Maggie could have done all the killings. She had the temperament, the motive, and the skill to carry them out. After fifteen years of dealing with dozens of homicides, had he been fooled by the girl? Had he been as smitten by her as Richard?

Blakemore certainly hadn't been taken in, and Coswell was duty bound to pass on this latest revelation. But a question still nagged. Why had Bonny done such a shoddy job at the Johnsons' trial? He hadn't the slightest idea.

***

Coswell's session with Chief Inspector Ward turned out to be more benign than he expected. A summary of the events appeared to satisfy the old warhorse.

"Good," Ward said. "Sergeant Blakemore seems to have all he needs to proceed to a conclusion. Fortunately, the homicide unit's been relatively quiet while you've been away but Corporal James tells me there's rumour of a gang war in the offing. I want you to jump into that with both feet as of right now."

"Yes sir."

The prospect of dealing with gang killings should have been enough to divert Coswell, but it wasn't. The Maggie business stuck in his mind. He phoned Blakemore. The sergeant's reaction to the courthouse tape came as a surprise.

"Just great," Blakemore said. "Meanwhile, the shit's really hitting the fan up here."

"Now what?"

"Maggie has suddenly become a martyr up here. Chief Isaac and his cronies, including that bastard Daniels, are accusing us of railroading the woman. They say we're using an Indian as a scapegoat again, so to speak. If I add that Maggie may be responsible for Garret's murder and the Johnson killings, they'll explode."

"So? Our job's to solve the case and hand it over to the prosecutors. Nothing personal." He almost blushed at his last statement.

"Easy for you to say, down there in good old safe Vancouver. If you could see the war parties descending on this town, you'd think different. I'll bet Willy's Pond hasn't had that many pickups roaring up and down the main street since last New Year's Eve. I'm telling you, there's going to be a riot."

"Hasn't Bonny Hansen managed to arrange bail? Get Maggie out of town, maybe back to the ranch? That should defuse matters. She could guarantee recognizance."

"If I add the Johnson killings, she sure as hell won't. Not only is it multiple murders, but the Johnsons will be murder one. No chance of bail."

"Then hold off mentioning it to anyone. We haven't even begun to work on that angle anyway."

"Okay, but can you hurry it up from your end? All the forensic stuff's been sent to Vancouver. The tree-planters are hanging around waiting for trial on the pot charges, but that'll be over soon. Maggie's bail hearing is this afternoon, by the way."

"Let me know what happens. In the meantime, I'll push our forensic guys." And then he suddenly remembered. "Oh, and I want you to tidy up a loose end. Check with your local airline people and confirm that Bonny Hansen got on that Sunday flight to Vancouver."

"What?"

"Bye for now," Coswell said, hanging up before Blakemore could say another word.

***

Corporal James was not happy when Coswell told him their next stop would be the forensics lab.

"Did Chief Ward mention the gangland threat?" he said. "I have a considerable file for you to peruse."

"They haven't started shooting yet and I'm sure you'll tell me before they do."

"It could be soon," James said, a slight quaver in his voice.

"Duly noted. Now away you go. We'll start with your ballistics expert. He's key."

***

Constable Ralph Gransden languished at the bottom of the ballistics hierarchy, but only because of his lack of seniority. His knowledge was second to none and James had discovered this fact himself—another plus for the corporal, in Coswell's book. The sergeant in charge came out from his office when he saw them enter.

"Good to see you again, Inspector Coswell," he said. "I've assigned your slugs to young Gransden over there, but I haven't had a chance to check him out."

"No problem," Coswell said. "We'll speak to him directly. I'm sure you're busy with other matters."

For a moment, it appeared the sergeant would object, but he merely nodded and returned to his office.

Constable Gransden was indeed young—barely out of his teens, Coswell figured. He spoke with a stutter, exacerbated, no doubt, by having to report to a senior homicide inspector.

"I've done the comparison, sir, but I really should have Sergeant—"

"Oh, spit it out, Ralph," James said. "He doesn't bite ... often."

Coswell frowned. "Match or no?"

Ralph gulped. "It's a match, sir. The same .38 pistol killed all three men."

"You're sure," Coswell said.

"I'm positive."

***

In contrast to the tiny, windowless space in the basement given to ballistics, the rest of the forensic staff enjoyed bright, airy surroundings and banks of sophisticated laboratory equipment befitting their role in modern criminal investigation. Marie D'Allarde, a short, bespectacled bowling ball of a woman in her forties, was a civilian on contract serving as chief. She had an MD from McGill and a Ph.D. in forensic science from George Washington University. A mere RCMP inspector held no great sway with her.

"Ah, the biblical Mark," she said, exaggerating the "ar" and coughing out the "k." "You should have it changed to the French, Marc with a 'c.' So much sexier. But then of course, you have Coswell. I don't think anything can be done about that."

He liked her and enjoyed their repartee, an invariable part of every visit to the lab. "Marie," he said. "I'm a little nervous about your thinking of sex when you have all this forensic material to keep you busy."

"I'm French. I can't help it."

She led them into her office, a space as organized as her laboratory: utilitarian chairs, an L-shaped desk almost entirely taken up by computer equipment, and not a paper in sight. Also of note was the absence of a conventional telephone. Marie communicated solely by means of a multitasking cellular device. A single picture decorated the only wall that wasn't glass: a huge microphotograph of a DNA molecule. She saw James looking at it.

"It's mine," she said. "Cute, wouldn't you say?"

James didn't know what to say.

She sat down at her desk and grabbed the cordless mouse. "All right, then," she said. "Set your maximal glutes on a chair and let's get down to business. I'll give you the results we've gleaned from your crime scenes collection."

They sat.

"First, the horse thing," she said. "Why you sent those casts down to us is beyond me. Any local cowboy could have told you they were all from two horses, save one — and that one was missing a shoe. The labels on the casts identified the two shod horses as belonging to the victims. I presume they were tethered together somewhere."

"They were," Coswell said. "Close to the tent."

"Ah. The tent. The lab stank of smoke for days from that damn thing and it revealed nothing but fingerprints and DNA matching the deceased. Ditto the cigarette butts."

So much for linking Jason the tree-planter to the scene.

"A couple of the swabs had no DNA, period, but the semen sample from the ranch scene contained two sets — the deceased Garret's and an unknown who was later identified from a sample labelled 'Maggie.'"

"She's the accused killer," Coswell said. "Blakemore got samples from a cup."

"Which contained methadone, if you don't know already. We did a freebie for you."

"Fingerprints?"

"Yes. A ton of those. Here's the list."

She handed him a large printout. He looked it over: Garret, Maggie, Sam, and Bonny Hansen. "No unknowns?"

"None. What you see is what we were sent."

He looked again. The prints were found on expected places: chair arms, glasses, tables. The latch on Garret's cabin door showed only the foreman's. The print on the cabinet key belonged to Maggie.

"Anything else on the key?" he said. "There should have been a set of Garret's under Maggie's."

"Sergeant Blakemore obviously thought the same. He added a note to the specimen asking that we examine it with that in mind but we found only Maggie's. Two beautiful prints, by the way—thumb and forefinger."

He handed the sheet back to her.

"Well, that's it," she said. "Not much help, I think."

"On the contrary. It helps rule out a number of possibilities."

The tree-planters were virtually out of the running, a killer from anywhere but the ranch seemed unlikely, and Maggie now led the list of suspects by a bunch. Sam Hansen had dropped to a poor second. The shoeless horse was interesting, though. He'd suggest Blakemore check it out.

They left the lab and returned to their vehicle. James was happy when Coswell told him to drive to headquarters.

"Okay, James," he said. "Let's tackle that gang menace of yours."

✱✱✱

The afternoon went by peacefully: a review of the files on Vancouver gangs, lunch, more review, then a call to the city police liaison officer assigned to the problem. Coswell had almost pushed the Cariboo from his mind when Jane, Inspector Ward's secretary, rushed into his office.

"Robert Gillings is on the phone for you," she said.

It was almost quitting time and the Attorney General wanted to speak to him? Coswell picked up the phone, his pulse quickening.

"Inspector. Nice to hear your voice again," Gillings said. "We haven't spoken since that West End murders affair."

Coswell waited for the shoe to drop. He and the Attorney General didn't exactly call each other up for weekly chitchats.

"I understand that you've just returned from a murder investigation in the Cariboo," Gillings said.

"Yes, but I left that in good hands. Corporal Blakemore —who's now sergeant, by the way—runs the detachment up there. You'll remember he was our undercover man in those gay murder cases."

"Not really, but his name has certainly reached my ears this afternoon."

Uh-oh. What had Blakemore done this time?

"There's been, for want of a better term, a riot at the Williams Lake courthouse during what should have been a routine bail hearing for a First Nations woman accused of murder. The place was jammed with First Nations people. The few that weren't inside virtually barred entry to anyone else. Your Sergeant Blakemore tried to maintain order, but his methods, according to reports, were somewhat crude and hence ineffectual."

No surprise there. Physical force would have been Blakemore's knee-jerk reaction.

"Judge Wilkinson, the presiding jurist, phoned me, highly agitated. He literally fled the building from a back exit and barricaded himself in his home. Your sergeant arranged for protection, but the judge plans to leave town as soon as possible and will not return 'til the trial's over."

Coswell knew what was coming and his heart sank.

"How ironclad is the case against this woman?" Gillings said. "Her lawyer submitted a not guilty plea."

"Everything is solid. But we still need a murder weapon and a witness, I guess."

"You guess? What exactly does that mean?"

"I don't think the girl's guilty."

Pause.

"A hunch, eh?" Gillings said. "Well, your hunches have considerable credibility, as I recall. Okay. Here's the plan."

Coswell's dread deepened.

"I want you to get back up there immediately and solve this thing. I've cleared it with Chief Inspector Ward. He wasn't happy, but I convinced him you could be spared for a few days."

A few days to solve a case that had brought him to a complete halt. Wonderful.

"Meanwhile, I'll arrange for the actual trial to take place in Quesnel. I know it's not a long ways away, but the man there, Justice McLeod, is made of sterner stuff."

"He'll have to be," Coswell said. "It looks as though a couple more murders might be added to this girl's count—two local natives."

He related the recent events.

"Good God!" Gillings said. "What a mess."

No argument from Coswell.

"Then tie it all up tighter than a drum," Gillings said. "I don't want one shred of doubt in anyone's mind—First Nations or otherwise. That will solve the whole problem. No one can deny that murderers need to be punished … in any society."

Coswell barely heard the rest. His mind whirled. If his hunch didn't turn into fact soon, the mess, as Gillings so correctly termed it, could quickly turn into chaos.

HE MADE THE FIVE O'CLOCK FLIGHT from Vancouver only because of a weather delay and Corporal James' liberal use of the cruiser's siren to get him to the airport before the plane left. Once he was aboard, he regretted taking the Attorney General's advice to return to the Cariboo "immediately" so literally. The flight was an awful combination of lightning, driving rain, and fearsome turbulence. He spent most of it with his face stuffed in a barf bag, his only consolation being that he wasn't the only one suffering. His seatmate, a young logger, joined him in a symphony of heaves.

Blakemore's nattering, when he picked him up at the Williams Lake airport, didn't help.

"We've got to find the murder weapon," Blakemore said. "But where do we look? This country's a huge haystack." He thought for a moment. "I've got an idea. Let's use the 'good cop, bad cop' technique with Maggie. I've pretty well done the bad, but now that you're here, you could be the good guy. Reason with her. Tell her she'll get off a lot lighter if she cooperates and lets us know where she hid the gun."

"Bonny Hansen won't let that happen," Coswell said.

"What, then? Send every available man out in the bush with metal detectors? That could take forever. And a one-shoed horse? Big help that'll be."

"Worth a look at the Hansens', though, and I'd like one more walk around the ranch. Maybe something will come to me, but right now I need my stomach settled — at a bar. For once, a beer sounds like the best cure. And maybe a small hamburger."

"Okay. There's a bar in the hotel I've got you booked into, but right after you eat, I think we should talk to Maggie. Maybe if we spring the fact that she's a suspect in the Johnson killings we'll get a reaction."

"No doubt, but you set it up with Bonny while I eat. I'm too woozy to think at the moment."

"Okay. And, by the way, Bonny did get on that flight to Vancouver. The airline, luckily, saves their passenger lists for a month. B. Hansen got ticked off as boarding."

***
***

Coswell waited in the jail's single interview room while Blakemore collected Maggie from her cell. Bonny, who had arrived earlier to prepare her client, came with her. She marched into the room with typical lawyer's bravado.

"I trust this won't take long," she said. "Tomorrow, after I've filed an appeal to get another bail hearing for Maggie, I plan to drive up to the ranch. I spoke with my father on the phone when I flew in yesterday. He's very upset about Garret's death, and doubly so because I understand that you, Inspector Coswell, consider him a suspect."

"That's true," Coswell said, glancing at Maggie.

"Well, your suspicions are absurd. Father and Garret have been friends for years. But enough of that. Let's get to Maggie's case — another error by your illustrious force. Circumstantial evidence at its flimsiest."

"Bullshit, counselor," Blakemore said. "You know damn well our 'circumstantial' evidence is solid, and guilty verdicts have been given in this country for a lot less. You'd better get a little more real with your client. Cooperation means a lighter sentence."

"I don't need you to tell me how to practice law, Sergeant," she said.

"Now, now," Coswell said in his best grandfatherly tone. "Bickering isn't going to help Maggie here. Let's try to work out something, shall we?"

Bonny gave him a glare that said he wasn't fooling her one bit. A flash of hope, however, appeared in Maggie's eyes. He turned to her.

"If you are innocent in all this, Maggie, you will have to help us. Sergeant Blakemore's right. It doesn't look good for you right now."

Fear replaced the look of hope. "Anything," she said.

"Let me be the judge of that, Maggie," Bonny said. "They're just trying to set you up. I'm the only one truly concerned about your welfare so don't say anything without my okay."

Maggie bowed her head and nodded slightly.

"I've just returned from Vancouver," Coswell said, "where I had a very interesting meeting with Elizabeth Faulkner, Maggie's former social worker."

Bonny almost flinched, only too aware of the implications. Coswell caught it.

"The Johnson brothers hurt you very badly, Maggie," he said softly, "and they got away with it. That must have made you angry."

Bonny gave a harsh laugh. "Whoa," she said. "Are you doing the same to her as you did to my father? One suspect to fit the whole bill?"

"Don't answer that," she told Maggie. "They've got nothing to make a charge or they would have done so."

"But we're working on it," Blakemore said, "and getting a lot closer." He leaned over and put his face inches away from Maggie's. "Think about it."

"Back off, Sergeant," Bonny said. "Now, unless you have specific questions, I see no point continuing here."

Blakemore looked at Coswell, who shook his head. Bonny immediately rose and headed for the door. Maggie followed with one brief pleading look back at Coswell. He tried to return the look with one as beneficent as he could muster.

"Ten minutes with that girl, alone, would have done the trick, I'll bet," Blakemore said when they'd gone. "I think she was on the verge of confessing."

"Or reiterating that she didn't do any of the killings. But don't worry. Next questioning session, you can get tougher. Let Bonny think she has the upper hand for the moment. And you're right, we need to get moving on this."

"You up to riding the helicopter this time?" Blakemore

said. "Saves you a lot of driving time, and it'll be safer. I won't be with you to spot for moose and cows."

"All right. Two good reasons, I have to agree. Now, have you had any contact with Richard since I left?"

"No."

"I've been thinking. Let's put Maggie aside for a moment and consider that someone else killed Garret. Who, why, and how?"

"Well, we sure as hell know how," Blakemore said. "A .38 slug in the head from the same gun that killed the Johnsons and I doubt that the killer is lending it around."

"Good point. That does tend to rule out an act of retribution by the dead men's brethren. That leaves us with the logical suggestion that Garret knew the identity of the Johnsons assassin and needed to be silenced. But how would Garret know?"

"Search me. Probably because he saw whoever it was ride out or return on the night of the shooting," he said.

"Someone from the house?"

"Presumably. But that someone could still have been Maggie."

Coswell shook his head. "Garret's cabin is sheltered in the trees a good ways from the stable and the pasture. Unless he had insomnia and decided to go out for a walk in the dark, the chance of him seeing or hearing anyone from the house coming or going would be pretty close to nil."

"Possible, though," Blakemore said. "Maybe he got up for a smoke or something."

"Outside in the cold air?"

"What, then?" Blakemore said, losing his patience. "I give up."

"Think," Coswell said. "What if he accompanied the killer to the Johnsons' campsite?"

"Hansen again, eh? You've really got it in for him."

"A hunch, I admit."

"Hunches don't convict," Blakemore said. "Maggie's more real."

"All right then. I'll fly to Anahim, call Richard, and have him drive me up to the ranch. He can look for the shoeless horse while I question Hansen."

"I'll arrange to get you a lift on a logging helicopter going up to Anahim. They leave awfully early in the morning though."

"The earlier, the better," Coswell said. "I'd like to be at the ranch well in advance of Bonny. I doubt that she'll clear the court bureaucracy with her appeal much before noon, and with a three-hour drive ahead of her, that'll give me plenty of time to investigate."

Blakemore made a call to the helicopter company and got Coswell on a seven AM flight out. "You'd better be there at least half an hour before," Blakemore said. "This flight's a freebie courtesy of Bert Neiborg. Normally it flies straight to the logging show up in the hills."

"No problem, but perhaps you could have the graveyard duty officer drive me to the helipad."

"I'll leave the order. Now what do you want to do? Go back to your hotel?"

"No. First, let's go over to the bar at the Clearwater. I want to get a feeling for this so-called Native uprising first-hand."

"If I go with you, you'll get a feeling all right, and it might be a painful one. I'm at the top of their shit list right now, along with Judge Wilkinson. He's the poor devil who denied Maggie's bail."

"I'll keep my back to the wall," Coswell said.

"We'll be cozy then, because that's exactly where I'll be," Blakemore said.

***
***

There wasn't a parking space to be had for a block around the Clearwater, not even in front of the fire hydrant adjacent to the lobby entrance. He pulled the cruiser alongside the pickup truck parked there.

"You take the wheel," he instructed Coswell, "and pull in when this heap departs."

He got out and went inside. A few minutes later, two men emerged from the bar, walked over to the truck, and got in. Coswell backed the cruiser just far enough to allow their vehicle to pull out and when it left, quickly took its place.

***

The din that greeted him when he swung open the door to the bar, almost made him recoil. Standing room only appeared to be the order of the evening. Smoke filled the air to the point that he could barely see into the back recesses where he expected Blakemore to be. Finally he saw him, all by himself at a table for four.

"How did you manage this?" Coswell said. He slid into a chair beside him and then turned it to face the centre of the room.

"Our illegal parker and his friends had this table," Blakemore said. "For some reason, they all got up and left when I gave them the good news. Two went out the door and the rest are mingling in the crowd somewhere. I doubt if anyone will join us. Something about the uniform, I guess."

But they were joined. A familiar figure appeared at their table — Chief Daniels. "Saw you come in," he said, pulling up a chair.

"Have a seat," Blakemore said.

Daniels ignored him and directed his attention to Coswell. "Surprised to see you in town, Inspector," he said. "I'd heard you were long gone to the Big Smoke."

"Vancouver? Yes, I suppose you could call it that if you

consider the smog. How are things in the village? You're a ways from home yourself."

"Came with the rest of the Tsanshmi contingent to stop another Indian from getting hung by white man's justice."

Blakemore jerked forward, but before he could speak, Coswell cut him off. "I must say that I am surprised at you, Chief Daniels. A lawman joining such a cause? Surely you don't believe we're still living in the nineteenth century. The case against the girl is based solely on factual evidence, not her racial background."

As he spoke, Coswell scanned the bar in a vain attempt to spot the Tsanshmi group, looking specifically for Chief Isaac. It seemed out of character for Daniels to be leading the protest. Maintaining the status quo was more his style.

"The white man's attitude hasn't changed much since the 1800s," Daniels said. "He only stops his bullying when we make a big noise and even then, it's just for a little while. Indians will always be an easy target for your lawmen. Just look at who's packed in the jails across this country right now — I can tell you they ain't white guys."

Blakemore couldn't contain himself. "They're in jail because they broke the goddamned law," he fumed. "Like you and the rabble who disrupted the court proceedings yesterday. Judge Wilkinson should have charged the bunch of you with contempt."

"He didn't, though, did he?" Daniels said. "Amazing what a little coordinated action will do."

"Bullshit. You're just lucky you got a soft judge. And why are you doing this anyway? Maggie's prairie native. It has nothing to do with local tribes."

Daniels leaned back in his chair, enjoying what he perceived as the upper hand. "If we had some white woman from Ontario locked up, waiting to be tried by our tribal council, how do you think your people would react? Look what happened with Brent Hansen—taken right out of our hands."

"Because you were incapable of doing a proper investigation," Blakemore said.

"And what great investigation have you done to lay a charge on this girl? She hasn't caused any trouble that I know of as long as she's been here."

Coswell cut in before Blakemore's ire reached the boiling point. "We're not at liberty to discuss that," he said.

"Fellow lawman, eh?" Daniels countered. He got up from his chair. "See you in court," he said.

Coswell watched as the tribal policeman made his way through the crowd, eventually joining a group of men sitting at two tables pushed together, covered with glasses of beer. He could barely make them out, but one he recognized—a Tsanshmi elder who had been sitting at Chief Isaac's right hand when the suspect vigilante meeting took place.

"Daniels is an asshole," Blakemore said. "He's no better than those hippie bastards who love seeing themselves on TV protesting on the courthouse steps in Vancouver."

"Interesting comparison," Coswell said. "Both advocating a cause."

"Shit-disturbers. They'd protest mother's milk just to make a noise and be seen."

"Bitter, bitter."

Blakemore grunted. "I need a beer," he said. "Wash the bad taste out of my mouth. Order me a pint of Okanagan Lager, would you? I've got to take a leak."

Coswell contemplated Blakemore's apparent disregard for the fact that he was still in uniform. *A healthy attitude,* he thought. A similar situation in Vancouver just wouldn't have happened—a uniformed Mountie seen drinking on duty.

"Whatcha doin' here, cop luver?"

The man's stink—a sour mixture of beer, stale tobacco, and body odour—caught Coswell's attention even before he saw who was speaking. "Pardon me?" he said, regretting momentarily that he had decided to leave his uniform where it usually lived—in a drawer at his Chinatown condo.

"Chickunshit."

Coswell caught Daniels looking his way with a smirk on his face. "And a good evening to you, too," Coswell said to his drunken harasser.

"Smaht alick. I shud knock yer teet out."

The man looked about sixty. Native, white hair, greasy face, cowboy garb. He swayed unsteadily on his feet. Coswell debated whether to call a staff person over or simply dodge whatever might be coming.

A barman solved his quandary. A wiry, biker-looking individual with tattoos on his tattoos rushed over. "Are we having a spot of trouble here?" he said in a tough London accent.

Coswell's tormentor appeared to sober slightly. One look at the barman's face did the trick. He staggered off, bouncing from patron to patron, many of whom gave him a shove to help him on his way.

"Thank you," Coswell said. "It appears my partner and I are in the minority here tonight."

"That you are, mate, that you are. In fact, you might consider cutting your visit a bit short. The natives are a wee restless tonight, as the story goes. Give them another hour and I might think about fleeing myself. Tipping a white man is against their religion, so sticking around and risking trouble isn't worth the lousy salary I'm paid. Let the boss run the place."

Blakemore returned to the table, having missed the whole exchange. "Now that's rare service," he said to the barman. "You're not supposed to come out from behind that bar, Solly, but since you're here, we'll have two pints of Okanagan Lager."

Solly grinned. "And I didn't think a man of your rank would come inside," he said. "We usually meet in court."

"Solly occasionally becomes engaged in fisticuffs," Blakemore explained, "and we have to remind him that as an ex-prizefighter, he mustn't do that outside the ring."

Solly returned to the bar, snapping his fingers en route to a waitress on the other side of the room. By the time she'd made her way in response to his summons, he'd poured two pints of beer and placed them on a tray along with a bowl of peanuts. She delivered it immediately.

"You tip her," Coswell said, "I'll cover the barman. Between him and Daniels, I've got a pretty clear picture of the native situation."

16

THE STORM THAT PLAGUED COSWELL on his flight from Vancouver had blown over, making the helicopter ride to Anahim smooth and spectacular. They passed over huge tracts of ranchlands, forests, and, just before Anahim, the Itcha Mountains rising to the north. They landed at Bert Neiborg's log dump. Richard was waiting there in the tribal police cruiser.

"How did you manage to get this?" Coswell said when he got into the vehicle.

"Daniels conscripted me," he said. "Told me that, as an auxiliary Mountie, I was duty bound to keep the peace here while he was away on urgent business. Left me the company car."

Coswell grinned. "Pretty easy assignment, I'd say," he said. "The rabble-rousers are all back at Williams Lake. But tell me, what got this protest going? Daniels?"

"Only after Chief Isaac's faithful paid him a visit at the

station. I saw their trucks parked out front when I dropped Gramma off at her friend's place in the village."

"I still don't understand why they're making such a fuss over someone who's not remotely connected to the local bands."

"Hatred," Richard replied. "And Chief Isaac's has doubled with his two sons getting murdered. He's beating that old Chilcotin War drum as hard as he can. Any Indian martyr will do, including Maggie." Pause. "How's she doing, by the way?"

"As well as can be expected," Coswell said. "Better now, I'm sure, since Bonny Hansen's flown up to take over her defence."

Richard didn't say anything until they'd gotten into the cruiser and began the drive into town. "You know, it's ironic," he said, "Bonny defending an Indian. She did have some of her father's prejudice when she went to school here. A big Tsanshmi girl, Bertha Windsor, and her gang used to beat Bonny up in elementary school. Brother Brent took a few of those beatings for her, which just made things worse. Bonny got back at her, though, in high school. Blackballed Bertha socially to the point that she dropped out and eventually disappeared. Became another Vancouver derelict, no doubt."

Coswell frowned. Why, then, did Bonny jump in so quickly when she heard about Maggie's predicament? It was unlikely that her prestigious Vancouver law firm would be eager to take on such a case; plus, Bonny had little time to form any real relationship with the girl. Maggie had been at the ranch for less than a year. Was her ego still suffering from the bungled Johnson abuse trial? Strange.

They stopped off at the Anahim hotel. Coswell had managed to down a Tim Hortons coffee and donut before his flight out of Williams Lake but needed more sustenance for the day to come.

While he ate, Richard gave his report. "I asked around about Tom Porter," he said, "but I didn't get much. Nobody saw or heard a horse trailer coming or going on that road behind the village around the time the Johnsons were found."

"Did you find out what time he got back from Williams Lake after he delivered the burned-out cruiser?" Coswell asked.

"Thursday, noon. People were bitching about the pumps being shut down 'til then."

"Enough time to ambush the Johnsons," Coswell said. "But I have to admit that a 350 Dodge diesel pulling a horse trailer makes a lot of noise. Someone in the village would have heard it."

This dropped Tom Porter well down the suspect list and so far no other locals' names had come up as possibilities. Sam Hansen, however, remained on the list, along with Maggie, of course. The answer had to be at the ranch. But where to look?

***

This time, Sam Hansen received them with almost total indifference.

"Look around all you want," he said. "But keep out of Helga's way. She's my new housekeeper and I'm damn lucky to get her. Good German stock. I'll be in the den."

He left them standing in the front hallway. Coswell could hear a washing machine chugging away at the end of the hall opposite Maggie's room. As soon as Hansen disappeared up the stairs to his den, Coswell gave orders.

"Richard, you hightail it out to the stable and the pasture. See if you can find a horse that's missing its shoe. I've got to get moving in here before that cleaning lady wipes up any more evidence."

Too late. Helga had stripped the bed, removed anything lying on the floor, and was in the process of vacuuming. When she saw him standing in the doorway, she stopped and turned the machine off. "Good German stock" described her well. Her blonde hair was streaked with white and tucked under a tightly wrapped turban. She wore a long-sleeved floor-length dress that accentuated her size, and she possessed a round face that could have been jolly, but currently was not. She looked at Coswell with annoyance and suspicion.

"Who might you be?" she said, her accent slight. She had obviously left Germany awhile ago.

"I'm Inspector Coswell," he said. "RCMP."

"You look more like my brother, the butcher," she said. "Why are you here? Mr. Hansen did not tell me about RCMP."

He didn't bother to explain. Searching the room would have been a waste of time. She had even emptied the dresser drawers and the closet. "Where did you put everything?" he said.

"In the laundry. Mr. Hansen said throw everything away, but that is a waste. I will wash all but the bedsheets. Those I will throw away, but the rest I will give to the Salvation Army."

"Did you find anything else in your cleaning?" he said.

She fixed him with a withering look. "Like what? Money? Jewellery?"

He felt foolish. A gun she would have mentioned. "Oh, anything unusual," he said lamely.

"No."

Questions over, she switched on the vacuum and got on with her chores. Coswell took a half-hearted look around the bathroom. Nothing in the toilet tank. No ceiling vents to check, even in the shower; the window to the outside served as the only source of ventilation.

He peeked into the laundry room. The washer and the dryer were both running; on the former sat a hamper with a few items in it. A black garbage bag lay slumped in a corner. Coswell went in and opened it: inside, he found only the sheets and pillowcases. He turned to leave, but something in the hamper caught his eye — a pair of fawn-coloured riding breeches. Curious, he lifted them up. They were obviously expensive: beautiful stretch material, brass buttons on the cuffs, soft suede on the outside of the crotch and padding of similar material inside. They definitely needed washing. The inner thigh areas were badly stained with a whitish substance. He took them across to the bedroom.

"Where did you find these?" he shouted above the noise of the vacuum.

Helga, looking even more annoyed this time, turned the machine off. "With all the dirty laundry, of course," she said. "They should be dry-cleaned, but whoever pitched them there obviously didn't care."

He inspected them more closely. Caught in one of the brass buttons on the right leg, was a single, long, coal-black hair. Maggie's? No one else on the ranch had hair that colour, but it was hard to imagine her riding in anything but jeans. He decided that they belonged to Bonny, but why would Maggie be using them? He couldn't think of why, but he'd learned long ago not to ignore things that he couldn't explain.

"I'll need to keep these for a bit," he said, and before Helga could say anything, "But don't worry, I'll let Mr. Hansen know I have them." Satisfied with his assurance, she went back to her work.

Coswell had no intention of telling Hansen anything. He quickly returned to the cruiser and tucked the breeches in the back, being careful not to dislodge the black hair. That done, he went to find Richard.

He saw him walking back from the pasture, carrying a feedbag. The horses were lined up at the railing watching him. Spook stood cautiously just behind the others.

"Couldn't get near Brent's horse," Richard said, "but I checked the others. Shoes on all of them, including Garret's bay and Hansen's Arab. But Sam had lots of time to replace any missing after we left."

"Or had Garret do it," Coswell said. "And maybe that's how he knew Hansen had ridden out on the night of the murders."

But all of this talk was just speculation, and no hard evidence appeared forthcoming. Coswell knew they'd made very little progress. He thought another interview with Hansen might make the man slip up somehow, but in truth, he couldn't think of a line of questioning that would achieve that end.

"Time to regroup, Richard," he said. "Do you suppose your grandmother would put the kettle on for us?"

"She'd love to, and I'm starting to catch your and Sergeant Blakemore's eating habits. She's making scones today — blackberry, I think."

"Wonderful. Then let's be off."

"Are you going to let Sam know we're leaving?"

"Why bother?"

***
***

Gramma served not only blackberry scones, fresh from the oven, but also goat cheese mixed with butter to smear on them, a heavenly combination.

She went outside again for her smoke, but returned shortly. By then, Coswell had consumed three of the scones to Richard's two.

"What pigs we are," Coswell said.

Her eyes twinkled. "No. Eat 'em up," she said. "Dey mak me fat."

Coswell laughed, feeling his paunch straining against his belt.

She poured them more tea from the pot and refilled her own before sitting down to join them. "Wherss da big guy?"

"Sergeant Blakemore's looking after things in Williams Lake," he said. "I'm here on my own."

"Gett da 'obbema gurl off?"

Richard had obviously filled her in on his and Blakemore's divergent views of Maggie's innocence. She doubtlessly also knew how eager Daniels and his cohorts were to come to her rescue. Like any woman, she wanted to know the latest gossip.

"I'm trying," Coswell said. "But so far we haven't found much that will help her. Bonny Hansen seems to be her only hope. Get reasonable doubt established with a jury."

"Tuff gurl, dat Bonny," she said. "Knowss how to fight durty."

"Richard told me about her run-in with the Tsanshmi girl in high school."

"Yess. Like her pa, not her mum. Her mum cums from Mounties lik you. Her dad and hiss dad before."

"Goodness," Coswell exclaimed. "The grandfather must have been North West Mounted Police."

"Yep. Saw his pitcher at ta moozeum. Teacher tuk us. Big mustash, funny belt 'cross hiss chest."

Coswell smiled. A young girl's memory. He recalled the many photos he'd seen in the Regina RCMP museum. Most young people would have been impressed with the traditional hat, not the Sam Browne belt. The mustache, though, would have caught her attention. Hair sprouting from a man's lip. No Indian would have anything like that. He wondered why she didn't mention the sidearm. That, too, would have drawn a child's eyes.

"And a pistol stuck on that belt?" he said.

"Yess. Dat too."

The words barely left his mouth when insight struck: Constable Ralph's ballistics results — a .38 Colt New Service revolver — the gun issued to the Royal North West Mounted

Police. Could the grandfather's pistol have passed down to Sam Hansen's wife and been available to Sam? Ann Hansen could have tucked it away somewhere as an heirloom. But if it was the murder weapon, how did it surface and where was it now?

"Which museum was that?" he asked.

"Kamloops. Big trip fer us."

"I've seen it too," Richard said. "Brent liked to stop off there whenever we went down for rodeos. They have a nice display of RCMP history, a lot of it donated by Mrs. Hansen's family."

"Any pistols in the display?"

Richard looked at him quizzically. "Yes. Brent's mom gave all her father's RCMP things to the museum when he died, including his gun. I remember that was a sore point with Brent. He thought it should have been saved for him."

"Any others? The grandfather's?"

"No, just his hat and tunic along with that picture Gramma mentioned, but why do you ask?"

Coswell regretted that he'd neglected to fill Richard in on the ballistic results from the murder weapon, but he didn't want to discuss it in front of his grandmother.

"Just curious," he said. "I have an interest in those old weapons."

It was a feeble answer and he could see that Richard didn't buy it, but chose to say nothing.

Coswell felt a glow of satisfaction as his so-called hunch suddenly became more plausible. Sam Hansen had just moved back to the top of his list of suspects, where he belonged. Maggie simply did not have motive enough to do all the killings. The Johnsons were merely bad tricks — and they likely weren't her first. And murder Garret, a potential drug supplier, in cold blood? It was time for another chat with Sam.

On the drive to the ranch, Richard didn't voice any great enthusiasm for Coswell's new theory.

"Mrs. Hansen hated guns," he said. "I doubt if she would have kept any around even if she did inherit them."

"But maybe Sam intervened somehow and got hold of it."

"Possible, but how are you going to find that out? He's not likely to tell you and if he did get the gun, why didn't he register it along with his other firearms?"

Good question. It took Coswell a moment to think up a rational explanation.

"His wife probably nagged him into registering his guns in the first place. I doubt if many ranchers around here bothered. She might have filled out the forms for him and he didn't want to admit he had her grandfather's pistol."

"Hmmm," Richard said.

Coswell sighed. "'Hmmm' is right, but at the moment all I can do is clutch at every straw."

"Do you have a job for me to do while you're talking to Sam?"

"Nothing specific, but a walk-around with your forensic eyes peeled might turn up something. Hansen said to help ourselves, so let's do it."

Helga, the new housekeeper, answered the door when Coswell knocked and directed him upstairs to the den. When he reached the top of the stairs, he could hear Hansen talking angrily on the phone.

"It's just too much, Bonny. I know she was your mother's pet, but goddammit, she sure as hell is no pet now. The girl killed Garret, for Christ's sake. Leave her in jail where she belongs."

Hansen was seated at his desk. When he saw Coswell standing at the door, he held up one hand, still holding the phone to his ear with the other. After a minute of listening, his shoulders sagged.

"All right then, but you keep her away from me and you'd better bring a good supply of that methadone crap. I don't want her cutting our throats if she's worried about running low."

He hung up and stared at the phone for a few seconds. "The things I do for that girl of mine," he muttered. Then, looking up at Coswell, he said, "And what do you want?"

"May I come in?"

"Why not?" Hansen said. "I seem to be at everyone's service today."

He got up from his desk, walked over to the liquor cabinet, and poured himself a Scotch. "It's early," he said. "But I need to brace myself." He took a good swallow and then went over and sat down on one of the leather chairs, signaling Coswell to do the same. "All right," he said. "Let's have it."

Coswell took a seat facing him. "I didn't mean to eavesdrop, but did I hear correctly? Bonny is bringing Maggie here? Her bail appeal must have been granted."

"You heard correct. They're on the way. Nice of her to phone on her cell and let me know. Now what is it you want from me?"

It took Coswell a moment to get his mind off of what he'd just heard. Finally, he focused on Hansen. "Did Garret have any life outside the ranch? Friends, acquaintances, clubs?"

"Not that I was aware of. Seemed content to spend all his time here. He went into town, of course, for supplies, and now and then to Williams Lake. I think he went down to Vancouver a few times, but nothing regular."

"Anyone you can think of that he might have rubbed the wrong way?"

"No one ... other than by association with me. The entire Indian nation probably hated his guts. We shared a disdain for the lazy buggers."

The man's bigotry was beginning to cloud Coswell's thinking. He changed the subject. "I understand that your wife comes from a long line of RCMP officers."

"Yes. But what does that have to do with anything?"

Coswell ignored the question. "Her father, her father's father, and her son were all officers." he said. "Quite a history. I can see why Brent would have been inspired. Did any of the family heirlooms come his way? An old service pistol for instance?"

Hansen laughed. "That's rich. You're looking for a murder weapon from the ancient past? Well, you're definitely barking up the wrong tree there. My wife had a particular aversion to pistols. Her father shot a bank robber in Quesnel with one when she was a girl. Newspaper photographer caught it all — robber dead in the dust and her father standing over him with his sidearm drawn. Made her sick, she said. Her dear old daddy blasting away a fellow human being."

"I can understand that," Coswell said.

Hansen grunted. "I can't," he said. "Personally, I'd be proud as hell if he were my dad. Would have given me all kinds of bragging rights at school. But girls are girls, I guess. Anyway, no gun. Sorry to disappoint you."

Coswell persisted. "Do you know what became of the service pistol your wife's grandfather had? It's a valuable antique and Richard told me it wasn't in the museum. I presume it stayed in the family?"

"Don't know," he said with a shrug. "I thought it was in the museum. Anne's family started donating that Mountie paraphernalia way back when the museum first opened. When her dad died, she persuaded her mother to donate all his stuff, probably because Brent showed an interest in it. I remember her bringing the bundle here right after the funeral and then getting Garret to drive it down to Kamloops."

Garret again. Coswell felt his brain take a right turn, now more confused than ever. Hansen detected the shift. "You look a little at sea, Inspector," he said. "Your theory shaken a bit?"

Coswell rose from his chair.

"Going so soon?" Hansen said.

"Yes. Thank you for your time."

Hansen smiled and held up his glass in a mocking salute.

***
***

Coswell guessed correctly that Richard would be concentrating on Garret's cabin in his search for clues. He found him sitting on a chair, gazing at the dead foreman's bed.

"Using my visualization technique, are you?" Coswell said.

Richard turned and gave him a tired smile.

"No," he said. "Just taking a break."

Coswell glanced around the room. Aside from fingerprint dusting all over the place, and the absence of a corpse, nothing appeared to have changed from when he saw it last. But something had sent Richard's mood down. He followed his gaze to the bed and then to the floor beside it where a large patch of dusting powder had been sprayed. He got down on his hands and knees and inspected the spot. The vague outline of a footprint could just be made out.

"What's this?" he said. "Certainly not a bootprint. Looks more like a bare foot and it's exactly where I'd expect the killer to have stood."

"Sergeant Blakemore thought it was Garret getting into bed."

Coswell's interest perked up even more. Richard had offered that explanation a little too quickly. And then he remembered: Maggie had been barefoot when they found her in the den.

"Someone else here that night has feet that size, Richard," he said. "Did Blakemore take swabs for DNA from this?"

"Yes, he did."

The glum expression on Richard's face prompted Coswell to give him some hope. "I don't remember anything about DNA from a footprint when I was at the forensics lab in Vancouver, but it may have slipped by me. I'll check."

***

Despite Richard's renewed interest in hanging around at the ranch, Coswell insisted they go back to the village.

"With Maggie getting bail, now," Coswell said, "the Tsanshmi protest will be put in abeyance for a while. They'll be coming home and your Chief Daniels will want his vehicle back. I'd also like to have a word with him. If they react like that to a bail hearing, what are they going to do at an actual trial? We owe it to Sergeant Blakemore to find out so he can prepare his troops."

Richard was about to get into the driver's side of the cruiser when he noticed the breeches in the back. "What are those?"

"Good thing you saw them. I damn near forgot and I need to put them back where they came from before Bonny gets here."

He opened the back door and carefully spread the breeches out on the back seat, making certain the black hair was visible. "These little cameras are a godsend," he said, pulling a compact Olympus digital from his jacket pocket. "Saves a lot of report writing. One picture, and there it is. My corporal in Vancouver suggested I bring it this time. Smart man."

Richard watched as Coswell took a number of shots with varying magnification. Once he was done, he stepped back to let Richard inspect his find.

"What do you see?" he asked.

"A dirty pair of women's riding pants. I remember Bonny

had a pair like that 'til her father laughed her out of them."

"Look closer."

Richard looked.

"Horsehair. And the stain's from its sweat. Hard to figure how that happened, unless she rode bareback, and I'll bet Bonny hasn't done that since she was a kid. And wearing ritzy breeches? Odd."

"Why not a human hair?" Coswell asked.

Richard looked more closely. "Nope. Too coarse. Came from a horse's mane or maybe broken off from its tail."

"I haven't seen a black horse here," Coswell said, "other than that Spook animal of Brent's, which no one, supposedly, could ride except him. But do you think Bonny could?"

"No way. That's a one-man horse. Brent raised him from a colt. He'd be furious if anyone even tried to ride him. Garret made that mistake once. Got thrown and cracked a rib, which was surprising since he did most of the bronc-busting on the ranch. I remember Brent wouldn't speak to him for days after and they were real close. He'd have had a fit if Bonny even suggested she wanted to ride him."

He thought for a moment. "I guess I was the only one he ever allowed up and that wasn't 'til just before he went off for basic training. You heard Garret describe how that turned out. Nope, nobody's ever going to break that horse."

In Coswell's mind, however, there was one other person with considerable riding skill and perhaps a way with horses that might have been able to handle the animal — Maggie. Richard, he sensed, had the same thought.

He gathered up the riding pants and returned to the house. Olga met him at the door to the laundry room. After extracting the black hair and placing it in a tissue, he handed her the breeches.

"I'm returning these to you," he said, tucking the tissue into his jacket pocket. "I think they belong to Mr. Hansen's daughter, not the girl who was staying downstairs here. But they're both coming to the ranch this afternoon so you can find out whose they are."

"Mr. Hansen did not tell me —"

Coswell cut her off. "Toodle-oo," he said. He turned and headed for the front door, leaving her with her mouth agape.

DANIELS HADN'T RETURNED to the tribal office when they stopped in at the village.

"On to the lovely Anahim Hotel, then, Richard," Coswell said. "I'll book in while you check out the bar. Maybe you can find out when Daniels and company are expected back." He also planned to make a call to the forensics lab in Vancouver without Richard overhearing.

Gerald, the desk clerk who had booked him and Blakemore in originally, was on duty. "Good to see you back again, Inspector," he said. "It's been pretty dead around here without you." He handed Coswell the registration card. "Oh, and there's a message for you already. Sergeant Blakemore wants you to call him."

"Thank you. I'll do that from my room. But first, I have an item I'd like sent to Vancouver by the quickest means possible."

"Greyhound bus is the fastest. Should be coming through from Bella Coola any minute now and it stops here. I know the driver well. He'll look after it."

Coswell asked for an envelope, wrote the RCMP headquarters address on it as well as Corporal James' phone number, slipped the tissue with the hair inside and handed it over.

"Much appreciated," Coswell said. "Now, if the same room is available as last time, I'd like to settle in."

Gerald laughed. "Everything's available, including the bridal suite."

"I'll save that for next time," Coswell said.

***

Corporal James, as usual, had all the information Coswell needed at his fingertips — or, more specifically, on his computer screen.

"The footprint by the bedside in the deceased's cabin?" Pause. "Yes. Here it is. Not a bare foot — no whorls and no DNA."

Coswell wasn't surprised. The idea of Maggie trotting over to Garret's cabin in her bare feet after dosing up on methadone was a stretch, but he had to be sure. The print, then, like everything else, merely added to the mystery.

"Okay," he said. "Now I'm sending a hair down to you by bus. I need you to pick it up at the depot and have it analyzed. If it's human, then get a DNA analysis done."

"My, my. Down to splitting hairs, are we? Things not proceeding too well?"

"Let's just say the investigation is still ongoing."

"Right, sir. I'll pass that along to Chief Ward, should he ask."

"You do that."

He returned Blakemore's call next, and to his relief, the officer who answered the phone said the sergeant was temporarily unavailable. One fewer distraction.

He left his room and went down to the bar. It was almost deserted, except for Richard sitting at a table with Allen, the young man with the pot-smoking kid sister. Richard introduced them. Coswell shook hands and sat down.

"Allen's great-uncle needed a ride to Chief Isaac's big pep rally," Richard said, "so he stayed while it went on. The Chief really got them riled up, but best he tells you the story himself."

Allen looked slightly uncomfortable but he related the affair, avoiding eye contact in the process. "I've been to a few of these," he said. "My uncle's tried hard to get me into the club; wants me to carry on the old traditions and all that bullshit. This one started with the usual chanting and worship of that old dead chief Klatsassin."

"Sounds like a Presbyterian church service," Coswell said.

Allen laughed. "Good comparison. Get them in the mood for some preaching. And preaching is what that old Isaac did. Started off by saying that the Hobbema girl was being raped by the white man Garret and she fought him off."

"That's totally untrue, as I'm sure Richard told you, and shooting him is pretty rough fighting," Coswell said. "How did they swallow that?"

"Hook, line, and sinker," Allen said, "even though he didn't say where he'd gotten the information. He made sure he was sitting under Klatsassin's picture when he came out with it, so I suppose the audience figured word came from above."

"Or from Daniels," Richard said, "with a little poetic license."

"Daniels wasn't there," Allen said, "but Isaac suggested someone inform him after the meeting and I'm sure that got done. The whole thing turned into quite a mob scene. I was glad to get away when it ended. Never said a word to my uncle on the drive back home. Didn't have to. He went on nonstop the whole way, talking about Indian persecution, white man's justice, and all that crap."

"You've got to admire Isaac's tactics, though," Coswell said. "Get the falsehood accepted right off the bat, fan the emotions, and soon he's won whatever game he's playing."

"Carrying on Klatsassin's war against the white man, I guess," Allen said.

Richard shook his head. "And so sad, really. I believe in

standing up for our rights, but using hatred will just keep us stuck on the reserves."

"I agree," Coswell said. "But his ilk will die out soon and your generation will take over. Keep your heads up—that day will come."

Both young men nodded.

"Meanwhile, Allen," Coswell went on, "we'd appreciate your keeping an ear cocked for word of any action planned for the trial itself. It's been moved to Quesnel, which, unfortunately, is not far enough away."

"Quesnel!" Richard said. "That's brilliant. The site of Klatsassin's hanging in 1864. Are they resurrecting another Matthew Begbie to preside?"

"Oh, dear," Coswell said. "I don't think our attorney general is up on his B.C. history. I'm sure he never thought of that when he moved the trial."

"You'd better let him know," Allen said. "Isaac would like nothing better than another Chilcotin battle at the very place his revered ancestor died with the white man's rope around his neck."

And Blakemore would have another riot on his hands. Likely a worse one.

Concerned that the protesters might soon be returning from Williams Lake looking to ease their parched throats at the bar, Coswell excused himself.

"Probably not a good idea for you to be seen with me, Allen," he said, "but you can stay, Richard. I have to make a phone call or two. I'll give you a wave when it's time to go back to the village."

He had barely stepped into the lobby when Gerald, the desk clerk, spotted him. "Sergeant Blakemore phoned again and wants you to call him immediately," he said. "Would you like me to dial him for you?"

"Thank you, but put it through to my room will you and

give me a few minutes? I'd like to have a quick whiz first."

In truth, Coswell wanted privacy, suspecting that the clerk would try to ease the boredom of his job by listening in through the switchboard. Next time he'd get Richard to sit in the lobby.

He picked up the phone on the second ring. "Thank you, Gerald," he said immediately. "I've got it."

Blakemore understood. Neither spoke. A moment later, they heard a click. Gerald also got the hint.

"I know about Bonny bringing Maggie to the ranch," Coswell said. "I was with Sam Hansen when she called. Anything else?"

"Yes. The bail judge gave a proviso. One of us has to check on Maggie daily. He felt she could be a flight risk and didn't want her to have a big headstart. I said you'd do it. I hope you don't mind."

"Not a bit. Gives me an excuse to keep tabs on them all."

"Have you found out anything new?"

Coswell decided not to tell him about the breeches. Maggie was in deep enough trouble already. "Not really," he said.

Blakemore sighed. "I hate to say this, but it would almost be better if Maggie got off. That would quiet the natives down and dead Garret is probably enough blood to satisfy their revenge over the Johnson boys killing. Could be declared a draw."

"This isn't a football game," Coswell said. "Our job is to catch killers, no matter who they are."

"I know, I know. Just a random thought, but be sure to keep me in the loop. Anything you can find out will be appreciated for sure."

"I will, but there is something I want you to do. Don't let a soul know about that shift of trial venue to Quesnel. We need as much time between riots as possible."

"I've already done that," Blakemore said. "Spoke personally

to the judge there and it didn't take much convincing. He may not be as brave as your Attorney General Gillings thinks."

Coswell hung up after assuring Blakemore he would contact him daily. He contemplated a phone call to Gillings, but decided it could wait a few days.

He went back to the lobby and was about to open the door to the bar when he saw Tom Porter across the street screwing the gas cap back on a pickup parked at his pumps. On impulse, he decided to have another session with the garage owner. He quickly retraced his steps and went out the front door just as the driver handed the garage owner some bills and pulled away. Coswell called over. Porter turned and waited for him to cross the street.

"Thought you'd be long gone to Vancouver by now, Inspector," he said. "I hear you caught at least one killer."

"*Alleged* killer," Coswell said. "Nothing's been proven yet."

"That's good. Word around here is you've got the wrong person."

"It's the word around here that continues to interest me. I'd appreciate another chat with you, if you don't mind."

Tom shrugged. "Why not?" he said. "Quittin' time's a ways off yet."

Coswell got the grandfather's chair again; Tom took the piano stool. "What can I tell you?" he said.

"Sam Hansen's foreman, Garret. Where did he stand with the locals?"

"To get himself killed? No more than any other of the white cowboys around here. Actually less, I'd say, mainly because he was a loner. Hardly ever saw him in the Anahim Hotel."

"No friends or acquaintances? That seems odd. He's lived here a long time."

"Odd — that's a good word for him, all right," Tom said. "Been that way ever since I can remember. Brent Hansen,

I guess, was the only person he showed any interest in. Went to all his rodeos."

It occurred to Coswell that Tom was about the same age as Brent and Bonny Hansen. "The schoolyard is a great place for information," he said. "Kids don't hold back when it comes to spreading gossip. Anything about Garret?"

Tom laughed. "Bonny Hansen. She wound a few yarns around him. Said he killed a man in the States and ran up here to keep from getting the electric chair. Told us her grandfather took him in so he'd have a hand who'd do whatever anyone in the family ordered — the implication being that he'd kill anyone who hassled a Hansen, herself included. Garret sure as hell looked the part, so she had plenty of believers."

"You?"

"Nah. Bonny had a big mouth. Told lots of lies."

"About Bertha?"

Tom looked at him sharply. "Bertha didn't buy any of that bullshit either. She and me are cousins. But Bonny didn't need Garret to beat up on Bertha. She did it all herself. Took her a while but she damn near caused Bertha to commit suicide. Her and that Neiborg buddy of hers."

"Jean Neiborg? I'm surprised. I've met her. She seems like an all right person."

"Maybe now, but back then I wouldn't turn my back on her any more than I would on Bonny Hansen. They were thick as thieves."

Coswell hesitated before asking his next question. They had managed to keep the details of both murders quiet so far, but time now was against them. He decided to take a chance.

"Our investigation is centring around a gun," he said. "An antique .38 revolver. Did you ever hear of such a weapon around here? During your schooldays or otherwise?"

"No. This is rifle country. Pistols are useless, but I guess some of those old cowboys had them in the days when it was fashionable to wear a sidearm."

He paused for a moment, seemingly just getting the drift of Coswell's question.

"But I'll guarantee you won't find one in any Indian family, mine included, and I'll bet the same goes for that Hobbema girl. If she shot Garret with a pistol, it was probably his own. According to rumours, she needed to grab something to defend herself."

Tom had obviously received Chief Isaac's message, and if young men like him believed it, keeping order would be an even more formidable task. Decrepit old men were one thing; young, vigourous hotheads were quite another. Coswell wondered if he should reconsider his phone call to Attorney General Gillings.

"You could very well be right, Tom," he said, getting up from the chair, "and if you hear anything else you think might help us clear her, let me know. I'm staying at the Anahim Hotel. Thanks for your time."

Tom merely nodded and remained seated on his stool, watching as the inspector headed back across the street. Pickups were rolling in from the highway and pulling up in front of the hotel. The protesters were returning. Fortunately, it wasn't necessary for Coswell to go back to the bar. Richard was sitting at the wheel of the tribal cruiser waiting for him. Coswell made a beeline for it and got in. Richard fired up the engine and quickly drove off.

"I've got to return this thing to Daniels," he said. "He'll be back at the station now."

"Good," Coswell said. "Time for another talk with him."

***

The arrogance Daniels had shown in the Clearwater bar continued when they got to the tribal office. He leaned back in his chair with his feet up on the desk and his hands clasped behind his neck.

"Well, well," he said when they entered. "Looks like I had two for the price of one looking after law and order in my absence. Anything happen I should know about?"

Coswell pulled over a chair and sat down. Richard dropped the keys to the cruiser on the desk and remained standing. "Nothing," he said. "It's been quiet."

"Probably because all the troublemakers went with you to Williams Lake," Coswell replied.

"Troublemakers? Sounds like old Matthew Begbie, the hanging judge. How long ago was that, you said? One hundred and fifty years?"

The man's insolence infuriated Coswell but he held himself in check. Losing his temper would accomplish nothing. "All right," he said. "But now I have a question for you. Where did this notion that Maggie Peron was being raped by Sam Hansen's foreman come from? It's totally untrue."

"She's a young, good-lookin' Injun maiden, and there was nobody close by to hear her complain. It'd be a big temptation for old Garret, who, it's said, liked a bit of dark meat now and then, especially young ones."

"Who said?"

"It's common knowledge around the Clearwater Hotel. He'd keep his eye out for one who was liquored up and invite her to his room. Word gets around."

"Well, that wasn't the case with Maggie and I want you to dispel that rumour before there's any more trouble at the courthouse."

Daniels looked at him through half-closed eyes. "Your orders don't mean bugger-all in my territory," he said. "Now I'll ask you to leave. I've got a lot of work to catch up on, and you, Richard, might as well go with him. I've heard your report ... bye."

Coswell remained seated for a few seconds, willing his

blood pressure to stop rising. Finally, he stood up and faced Daniels. "You'd better sit tight in your little kingdom," he said, "because the minute you set one foot outside it, you're in my territory. And I can tell you, even the slightest indiscretion will land you in a barrel of shit, which I personally will have filled and waiting for you."

Before he turned and led Richard outside, he thought he saw the slightest flicker of apprehension in Daniels' eyes.

Richard couldn't contain a large grin as he closed the office door behind him. "I wonder why he didn't offer to drive us to my Gramma's?" he said. "Now we have to hoof it."

Coswell chuckled. "I've got enough adrenalin in my veins to *fly* to your Gramma's, I think. Let's get going. I want to go back to the Hansen ranch. Maggie is not going to be a welcome guest, and I need to assess the situation."

"I don't think we'll be too welcome either," Richard said. "Bonny was smart to get Maggie far away from investigating officers, but us being around will throw the proverbial wrench into her scheme."

"Indeed, and investigate we will."

Coswell's adrenalin wore off quickly and by the time they made it to Gramma's and the pickup, he was wheezing badly. "Damn pollen," he gasped. "Gets me every time."

Richard chose not to point out that the pollen count in the late fall was very low. He left Coswell to catch his breath and ducked into the house to let his grandmother know where he'd be with the pickup.

✸✸✸
✸✸✸

Coswell was mildly surprised to see Bonny's rental car parked behind her father's Dodge when they pulled into the yard. He'd figured that the paperwork involved before Maggie could be released would have taken some time, delaying their arrival until evening at the earliest.

Helga answered Coswell's knock at the door. "Nobody's here," she said. "Mr. Hansen's ridden off with the new foreman and the two ladies are in the cabin, which I had to get cleaned up in a big hurry."

Another unhappy person on the ranch. Coswell could already feel the tension.

Since Helga made no move to invite them inside, he decided they would wait on the porch. Each took a chair and faced Garret's cabin.

Bonny spotted the cruiser the second she stepped outside the cabin door. She turned to say something to Maggie, then marched to the house with long, determined strides, an incongruous figure in her trim business suit and leather pumps. She came to an abrupt halt in front of them and crossed her arms.

"What are you two doing here?" she asked. "Can't you at least let us settle in before you come snooping around?"

Richard got to his feet. Coswell remained seated.

"Nice to see you again, Bonny," Coswell said. "We're not snooping. We've been told to keep an eye on Maggie. A term imposed at her bail appeal, I understand."

"I don't think the judge's intention was for you to do that on a twenty-four-hour basis."

"I hadn't intended to, but I must say that cabin doesn't look terribly secure, unless you plan to lock her in there."

"Don't be ridiculous. Maggie's no flight risk. Where would she go? Besides, she needs her daily methadone."

"Not so ridiculous. A thumb and a little leg, and she could get as far as Prince George or even Vancouver in no time and find a lot better stuff than methadone."

She uncrossed her arms and took a deep breath. "Have a little heart," she said. "My father just laid down the law to me. Maggie's not to come within fifty yards of the house and I'm not to stay with her. 'Deranged addict,' he called her. 'Might do you in like she did Garret.'"

She stepped up onto the porch, pulled over a chair, and sat down. "What kind of deal can we make here?" she said. "The trial's set for next week in Quesnel."

"Next week! That's got to be an all-time provincial record," Coswell said.

"The judge wants it done and over with as quickly as possible and I agree. Delaying will just create more chaos."

"But the chaos is to your advantage, I notice. Had a big effect on proceedings in Williams Lake."

She ignored his remark. Instead, she leaned back and regarded him with a calculating stare. "Off the record," she said. "Do you think she'll be convicted? I have to admit that the prosecution has a strong case, seeing as Maggie and Garret were the only two here at the time of the murder. I plan to use the 'unknown third party' defence, but Maggie has been a bit resistant to some helpful coaching."

Coswell weighed his response carefully. There was no such thing as "off the record" when talking to a lawyer. "Depends on the jury, of course. The judge would be a fool not to include some First Nations members who, no matter how impartial they claim to be, will favour Maggie's version of events. Also, she had no clear motive and we haven't found the murder weapon. In a fair-minded jury, that should instill a little doubt at least."

Bonny sat pensively for a moment before speaking again. "Thank you for that. Now let's settle this surveillance problem."

"Let me speak to Maggie in private," Coswell said. "If she has any thoughts of fleeing, I think I can erase them more effectively than you, and I can take the responsibility. How does that suit you?"

"Fine. It seems ridiculous to lock the door and nail the windows shut."

"And," Coswell said, "a visit from Richard after that might help lift her spirits a touch."

He could almost hear Richard's heart thump.

"Whatever," Bonny said. "Now I'm going to go inside and pour myself a big Scotch before dear old Dad comes storming back. Feel free to join me when you're finished. We can share the Scotch and Daddy's vitriol."

"I might do that."

***
***

When Coswell entered the cabin, Maggie was sitting on Garret's bed like a prisoner waiting to be led to the scaffold. Her eyes were devoid of any spirit. He walked over and sat down beside her. She didn't move.

"You're going to be all right, Maggie," he said.

"I don't think so. Bonny told me everyone's saying I did it."

That surprised him. Defence lawyers typically keep up a positive front right up until moment the gallows trapdoor springs open.

"Not everybody," Coswell said.

She looked him in the eye. "You?"

He held her gaze. "Did you kill Garret?" he said.

Her eyes filled with tears, but she continued to look at him. "No," she said. "I didn't." With the last two words, her voice rose to a wail and she began to cry.

Coswell struggled to remain objective. If she were lying, he'd just witnessed the best acting he'd ever seen and he'd seen plenty over his years in the Force. He knew he shouldn't take sides, but his resistance melted.

"I believe you," he said.

She sniffed and used her shirtsleeve to wipe away her tears. "What should I do?" she said. "Bonny told me sometimes it's better to throw yourself on the mercy of the court—tell them I can't help myself when I'm stoned." She sniffed again. "I'm sure Bonny thinks I killed Garret, and I guess I can't blame her. The evidence is real strong against me."

Coswell tried to wrap his head around what he'd just heard. Bonny giving up so easily? It was totally out of character, unless Maggie's social worker in Vancouver had been right. Maybe Bonny was lazy and incompetent, at least in criminal cases. He'd forgotten to check what branch of law she practiced in the august firm of Hewlett, Morris, and Cawston.

"It's not that strong," he said, "and Richard and I are looking hard for the real killer."

"Richard?"

"Yes, and he'll be in to talk to you when I leave. I want you to think hard about all that's happened, especially about the Johnson brothers. Did you hear anything the night before we rode out to find them? Try to remember every conversation you overheard between Mr. Hansen and Garret and even Bonny. Any comment about getting back at the brothers for killing Brent."

She shook her head. "Mr. Hansen was very angry and Garret, too, but I didn't hear any plans."

"Talk it over with Richard. Something may come to you."

He got up to leave. She reached for his arm and squeezed. "Thank you," she said.

He left the cabin door open and waved to Richard, still standing on the porch. They met halfway.

"Some sympathy's okay," Coswell said, "but don't forget you're on duty. Her memory may be better when she talks to you. Go for it."

***

Bonny was in the den, feet up on a hassock, a glass of Scotch in her hand, her business suit replaced by an elegant satin dressing gown left generously open at the top, revealing nicely curved breasts. The picture's only jarring element were her well-worn slippers — the floppy pink things Coswell had seen under her bed.

"Good. I need some company," she told him. "Come in and take a load off your feet." She raised her glass to him. "Is it near enough the end of your workday to join me in a libation? I'd get it for you, but I'm too comfortable to move."

"No thank you, but I will keep you company for a bit."

He sat opposite her, sinking down into the delicious leather armchair. An aperitif of white wine would have suited him, but he decided to stick to business.

"What's the word on Maggie?" she asked.

"I'm satisfied that she isn't a significant flight risk, but I am under orders, so daily visits will be necessary."

"Well, one person at least will be happy about that—father. He'll be glad you're keeping an eye on the bloodthirsty killer."

"Do you expect him back soon?"

"God knows. He told me he was riding out with Andy, our part-time hand. He's moved up to fill Garret's place. They're doing some sort of inspection, he said, but I think it was just to avoid Maggie. He did tell Helga, the new housekeeper, he'd be back for supper. I'd guess not for a couple of hours, though."

As she spoke, she crossed and uncrossed her legs, causing the robe to slip off her knees and expose a considerable amount of inner thigh. Coswell tried to ignore the view by focusing on the soles of her slippers, but it was difficult.

"My Vancouver sources tell me you're a man of intuition," she said, "and your success in solving cases is often a result of that. I'd be interested to know if you've had similar thoughts with the deaths up here. Sergeant Blakemore, it seems, has a one-track mind."

Either she was wearing black panties or Coswell was looking at pubic hair. Maybe her auburn locks came from a bottle. He struggled to concentrate on her question. "I'm not as convinced of Maggie's guilt as he is, but I have to admit that all the evidence points to her."

She smiled. "That's evading my question," she said. "It's

your intuition I'm interested in." She was waggling her feet now, a considerable distraction. Coswell shifted in his chair.

"It's more a negative thing," he said. "I feel that Maggie is innocent, but my intuition so far doesn't include the name of the guilty party."

The feet were hypnotizing him. Then, suddenly, the floor in Garret's cabin and the dusted footprint jumped into his mind. The outline of her feet showed clearly through the thin, worn soles—a perfect match for the print beside Garret's bed.

She continued to talk, but Coswell wasn't listening. Instead, his mind buzzed with the possibility that Bonny could have been Garret's killer. But the thought left as quickly as it had come—Bonny had been in Vancouver at the time of Garret's death.

"I'm sorry," he said, noticing her staring at him. "My brain just skipped a beat there. What did you say?"

"I said, do you still suspect my father?"

"He's the only other person who could tie together all three murders. I have to consider him."

She swung her feet off the footstool, stood up, rearranged her robe, and went over to the bar to pour herself another Scotch, mixing it with water.

"An old Scotsman friend of mine would have a heart attack seeing you dilute what looks like a single malt from Glenlivet," Coswell said.

She laughed. "You sound just like my father, although he emphasizes the price rather than the distillery."

She returned to her chair, this time leaving her feet on the floor. "It couldn't have been my father," she said. "Between us, we polished off an entire bottle of this stuff before we went to bed. I could hardly walk, and father wasn't any better. I'm sure he passed out as fast as I did. Ride across country, kill two men, and ride back before dawn? No way."

A strong argument, once more leaving him at a loss.

"Maggie's the only one capable of doing that," she said. "That's the bottom line, I'm afraid."

"I thought you were going to use the 'mystery third person or persons' defence."

She lifted her glass, saluted him, and took a swallow. "You give me somebody with motive and opportunity, and I'll jump at it. Meanwhile, I've already given her my best advice: own up to it and then I can plead drug-induced insanity or the like. That'll cut down prison time considerably."

"But if she is innocent and reasonable doubt can be established, she'll be acquitted and serve no time. As I said, there's a good possibility that she'll have at least one sympathetic juror in Quesnel."

She grimaced. "Ah, yes. So you did ... another Indian." Her mood darkened. A frown creased her forehead. "I'll discuss all the options with Maggie again tomorrow. Right now I'm going to finish this and have a pre-supper nap. I'm bushed."

Coswell took the hint and left. He was aware of her eyes following him out the door. A lot was going on in Bonny Hansen's head, and he would have given a lot to know just what. As he walked by the rolltop desk, he recalled how the key had still been in it when they'd found Maggie passed out. Another thought crossed his mind: they never did establish how the key got there.

***

When Coswell went back to the cabin, Richard and Maggie were sitting together on the bed. Richard got up immediately, embarrassed, perhaps, at being caught in an unprofessional position. Coswell smiled, remembering he had felt compelled to sit by her as well.

"As you were," he said and pulled over a chair for himself. "Something has been bugging me, Maggie, and I wonder if you could clear it up."

She looked at him with wide, innocent eyes, again making him question his objectivity. "Of course," she said.

"I want you to tell me exactly what happened when you went upstairs with Garret after he finally agreed to get you the methadone."

"I waited in the den while he went to get the key to the cabinet."

"And could you tell where he went to get it? You know every room in the house so I presume you had a pretty good idea."

She bowed her head. "Yes. I couldn't help it. He got it from the Hansen's bedroom, but I couldn't tell exactly where and I swear I didn't go looking for it afterwards. It was just there in the lock when I woke up."

Coswell almost shuddered to think what a prosecutor would do with that testimony. "When is your next dose?"

"Eight tomorrow morning."

Not just "tomorrow morning," Coswell noted—she had it to the hour. He glanced around the cabin and realized it didn't have much more to offer than her jail cell in Williams Lake—no books and no TV. Helga had cleaned out the magazines.

"Pretty tough for you to be stuck in here," he said. "Do you want me to try to soften Mr. Hansen up a bit?"

"Thanks, but I'll be okay and maybe Bonny will let me go riding with her."

"I'll bring you some books," Richard said. "What kind do you like?"

"I don't read much," she said. "But I like magazines."

"Good," Coswell said. "You need to keep your mind occupied." He doubted that Hansen would be keen on her going out riding with his daughter.

Richard's reluctance to leave was obvious, but Coswell wanted to get back to the hotel and he had no desire to sit around waiting for Hansen. He had a job for Blakemore.

"We'll be back tomorrow," he said, "when the dust has settled a bit."

As they drove out of the driveway, Coswell looked across the fields and thought he saw two horsemen coming down from the farthest pasture, moving slowly in single file. He debated telling Richard to stop but decided against it. Instead, he took his own advice to let the dust settle. There was no point trying to converse calmly while Richard steered the pickup over the potholes.

"This thing's sprung like an old covered wagon," Coswell said, bouncing in his seat.

"You're right about that," Richard said, "They use leaf springs in these old Dodges, but it'll still be rolling when those trucks with fancy new suspensions start falling apart."

"And probably roll better than my poor spine. Slow down, for heaven's sake."

When they pulled onto the pavement, the relief felt wonderful.

THE TRIBAL CRUISER WAS GONE when they drove past the village. "Probably over at Chief Isaac's," Richard said, "ingratiating himself now that the two sons are dead, which opens up the competition for band chief when the old man dies. He'd like nothing better than to control the tribal grants."

"Interesting. Daniels as the third party. I never thought of that."

"Pardon me?"

"Motive, Richard, motive. Who benefits from the Johnson brothers' deaths? And who has the perfect opportunity to bump them off and direct the blame to the Hansen ranch?"

Richard's eyebrows arched sharply. "Yes and he's certainly been working at keeping the arrow pointed in that direction, but why kill Garret? That swings the arrow towards a revenge killing, someone from the village or Anahim."

"No. I think he'd see it as keeping our focus on the Hansen ranch. When we started to look elsewhere, at Tom Porter and even the tree planters, he might have gotten nervous."

Richard thought it over. "The key left in the methadone drawer doesn't make sense. Daniels wouldn't have worried about Maggie hearing the shot. He'd be gone by the time she came over to investigate."

"That's a good point, but maybe Maggie crossed herself up with her story. Garret may have taken the key with him, intending to replace it in the morning. Then Maggie went out to the cabin, tiptoed in, found the key, and returned to the house."

"And didn't admit that she'd been out there a second time, knowing it would surely incriminate her," Richard said.

"Right, although it's hard to imagine she could think that clearly after just waking up from a shot of methadone."

"Possible, though," Richard said, obviously keen to adopt the theory.

***

Coswell posted Richard in the Anahim Hotel lobby while he went up to his room and phoned Blakemore. No waiting this time.

"Tell me you've solved everything," Blakemore said. "I'm starting to get bugged by the Quesnel detachment now. They tried to pull in backup from Prince George and were told to go piss up a rope. That leaves us, and since we've been informed that *we* started the whole damn mess, we're obligated to straighten it out."

"The stresses of command seem to be weighing on you,"

Coswell said, "but I'm afraid I can't help. I do have a job for you, though."

"Wonderful. Another job."

"Don't whine. I know you checked once for me but I want you to double-check that Bonny Hansen actually did board that plane to Vancouver the night Garret was killed. The ideal, of course, would be an eyewitness confirmation, not just some passenger list."

"What? Bonny Hansen? Jeez, if that's how far you're reaching, I'm doomed."

"Never mind the sarcasm. It's just routine police work. Remember your basics: all alibis need proper authentication."

"Okay, okay, but keep digging, will you? I'm getting nervous."

Coswell hung up and returned to the lobby. "That's enough for today," he said to Richard. "You head on home. I'm going to have an early supper and hang out at the bar for a bit. We'll get back to it tomorrow morning. I'll meet you here for breakfast."

"Early?"

"No. Get your beauty sleep. Eight o'clock will be fine." He picked up on Richard's disappointment. "And I guess I don't have to tell you that an evening tryst with Maggie would be a very bad idea."

Richard's eyes flashed. "No you don't."

"Just being cautious," Coswell said. "Not an insult."

"Okay."

***

Coswell slept in until seven the following morning, an hour later than his usual waking time, making him ponder his advancing age. Normally, the stress of his job affected his sleep very little, but then he decided that all that fresh Cariboo air and the unaccustomed travel had upset his metabolism. Age had nothing to do with it.

He took his time performing his morning ablutions before descending to the lobby to wait for Richard, who arrived ten minutes early.

"Easy, boy," Coswell said. "We've got time to burn this morning. I don't want to arrive too early. Let's go tie on the old feedbag."

Richard smiled. "You're beginning to sound like a native," he said.

They lucked into a window seat. The first wave of breakfasters had finished and were leaving. The waitress filled their coffee cups and handed them menus.

"Order lots," Coswell said. "Lunch may be a long way off today and that housekeeper of Hansen's doesn't sound like she appreciates extra work."

They both ordered the hungry man's breakfast: steak, eggs, hash browns, and two flapjacks. Coswell took a sip of his coffee and looked around the bar. He recognized a couple of the elders, but a younger man sitting with them rang a bell. After a moment, he placed him.

"I think that's one of the two ranch hands I saw helping Garret with the calf branding."

Richard followed his gaze. "Yes. That's Andy. Verne's his partner. Andy's been part-time at the ranch for years. Verne's newer."

"Andy's foreman now," Coswell said. "So I guess Sam Hansen's prejudice isn't all that bad."

"Necessity, I'd say, rather than desire ... on both parts. Andy probably needs the job and Sam can't find anyone else. Verne will come in on Andy's coattails."

Coswell pondered that information for a moment. "Those are names that we haven't considered," he said. "Maybe we've been missing something. Tell me about them."

"I don't know a lot to tell you. Verne's just a kid, younger even than me and a bit slow. If we had a special needs facility around here, he'd be in it, but he loves being a cowboy and hero-worships Andy. Wouldn't hurt a fly."

"And Andy?"

"He's a generation ahead of me, more Sam Hansen's age. We're acquaintances, really, and then only because I ran into him off and on at the Hansen ranch."

"That would make him a contemporary of the Johnson brothers?"

Richard thought about that for a moment. "He's a bit younger than them, but yes, I guess you could say they were contemporaries. I doubt if they had much in common, though. Andy's a quiet one and I've never heard of him getting into any kind of trouble."

"It may be nothing, but they're the only other individuals familiar with the Hansen ranch. Perhaps there was some animosity that hasn't come to the surface."

***

They passed the tribal police office just before nine. Still no sign of Daniels.

"Maybe he's out on patrol," Coswell said. "You'd better keep your speed down."

"On the way back, maybe, but right now he'll still be at his breakfast table."

When they reached the turn into the ranch, Richard slowed the pickup to a crawl in consideration of Coswell's kidneys. The engine barely turned over, and the absence of a dust cloud made for a relatively silent approach to the house. Hansen's pickup and Bonny's rental car were parked in front. They pulled up behind the latter and got out.

They saw no one outside until they walked to the end of the porch. The stable doors were open and Andy could be seen mucking out a stall.

"Why don't you go over to the cabin and talk to Maggie?"

Coswell said. "I'll have a chat with Andy before I go to the house."

Richard didn't need a second invitation. He was off.

Coswell walked over to the stable and stood in the doorway. It took a moment for Andy to realize that he was there. He stopped mid-pitchfork.

"Howdy," Coswell said, the cowboy vernacular slipping out.

Andy tossed the manure he was holding onto a crude sled, adding to a small pile already there. "Boss's over at the house," he said, barely glancing at Coswell before scooping up another forkful.

Like Garret, Andy had looked tall on horseback, but on foot he was actually the same height as the deceased foreman. His legs seemed disproportionately short for the mass of his upper body — broad shoulders and a powerful neck that appeared joined to his ears rather than his jaw. Pockmarks dotted his cheeks, and his nose looked like the front end of a bus.

"I'd like to speak with you first, if you don't mind," Coswell said.

The man's expression said he did mind, but he stopped what he was doing and leaned on the pitchfork, regarding Coswell with steady black eyes. "What about?" he asked. Only two words, but they conveyed a lot: belligerence, suspicion ... a challenge.

"You've worked with Garret a long time, I understand," Coswell said. "Men talk when they work. I thought maybe you heard him say something that might help us find out who murdered him."

"Like what?"

Ordinarily, Coswell dealt with hostile witnesses by putting the fear of the law into them but he decided that Andy's attitude could simply be racial. Best to tread softly.

"Oh, talk of someone out to get him, someone he really pissed off or maybe a gang-related thing like drugs or gambling."

"Nope. Nothing like that. Garret just told us what to do mostly. We didn't jaw a lot."

"What kind of boss was he? Fair? Tough? A son of a bitch? He's dead now, so you can say anything you like. I don't agree that everyone becomes a saint when they die. Assholes are assholes."

A trace of a smile. "He was hard, but you got to be hard to run a ranch."

Leading questions made for weak interviewing, but Coswell couldn't think of any other way to get through to the man. "Garret came across to me as being prejudiced toward your people," he said. "Did that come up when you were working with him?"

A real smile this time. "White man boss, injun worker? Prejudice is normal. You get used to it."

One might get used to it, Coswell thought, but more often prejudice generates hate and given the opportunity — retaliation. "Are you going to move into one of the cabins?"

"No. I got a house of my own."

The sound of galloping horses cut off their conversation.

"Girls are back," Andy said. He jabbed the pitchfork into the pile on the sled and walked quickly to the door, brushing past Coswell. Richard appeared simultaneously.

Bonny, on her father's Arab, and Maggie, riding Rusty, were pounding down the fence line, both horses running flat out. Bonny led by two lengths. They braked to a stop in front of the men, the horses' hooves spraying dirt. Coswell watched as the women dismounted. Maggie did so normally, but Bonny swung her right leg up over the Arab's neck and slid to the ground in one smooth motion while holding onto the reins. She landed with a thump on both feet.

"That was a rush," she said. "Nothing like an early morning ride."

Andy came over and started to undo the saddle—a cue for Richard. "I'll take Maggie's," he said.

"Ah. Big strong men do come in handy sometimes," Bonny said, "I've never been able to lift one of those damn things. But don't worry about the bridles. Maggie and I'll bring them back after we walk the horses to the pasture."

Coswell was glad to be left out of the procedure, not wishing to test his own strength on those masses of leather. He stood and waited for everyone. Arriving at the house as a group, he thought, might temper Sam Hansen a bit.

He watched Bonny and Maggie lead their horses to the pasture. The women were superb examples of the feminine figure, their rounded buttocks accentuated by skin-tight jeans. But his eyes swept past them to a familiar black shape just inside the paddock—Spook, Brent's horse. The animal stood near the gate, head up, obviously excited by the return of his mates—like a kid, Coswell mused.

Maggie opened the gate to let Bonny lead the Arab in first. She followed with Rusty and pulled the gate closed behind her. To Coswell's amazement, Spook came up behind Bonny and nuzzled the back of her head. Even after she'd pulled the bridle off the Arab and it trotted away, Spook stayed close to her. She gave him a pat while she waited for Maggie to let Rusty go.

Getting back through the gate created a momentary problem: Spook wouldn't leave Bonny. She solved the impasse by having Maggie shut the gate while she ducked under a fence railing.

Richard, having dealt with the saddle, had caught most of the performance as he walked back from the stable to stand beside Coswell. His astonishment equalled the inspector's. "I've never seen him do that before," he said. "But then, I was always with Brent. Bonny almost never went riding with us."

"Yes," Coswell said. "Obviously he's not a one-man horse. Seems to have room in his affections for at least one female."

***

Coswell assumed that they'd all go to the house, but Bonny had other ideas. "Father's in a foul mood," she said. "It's Helga's day off, and he had to make his own breakfast." She turned to Richard. "Why don't you two go for a walk out behind the cabin? There's a nice trail through the trees that comes out at the east pasture."

"Yes," Maggie said. "It's lovely."

They headed off, not arm in arm, but the affinity showed.

"Well, that's that," Bonny said. "Now let's go and check out the old bear in his den."

She set off at a brisk pace that Coswell had some difficulty matching.

"You don't seem to have lost any of your equestrian skills," he said, "despite your moving to Vancouver. University, law school, public defender's office, private practice. That's a lot of years out of the saddle ... literally."

"It's the old riding-a-bike thing, but the endurance is gone. I'll stiffen up later."

***

Hansen's mood was worse than foul. When Bonny and Coswell walked into the kitchen where he sat brooding over a cup of coffee, he met them with nothing but hostility.

"Shit," he said. "Might as well be living in Vancouver. Drug addicts and cops everywhere."

"And a good morning to you too, Sam," Coswell said. "But don't worry. We won't be staying long. Maggie seems to have settled in okay. I'll report that back to the powers that be."

"You do that," he said. "And tell those powers the sooner

298

they get her back in court, the better. I've had enough of all this."

And with that, Coswell, finally, had enough of him. "There's been a murder here," he said. "A man's dead, a man who supposedly meant something to you. You've tried, convicted, and hanged Maggie for it, but your enthusiasm in doing so appears excessive to me."

Both Hansens looked at him, taken aback by his outburst.

"I believe that Maggie is innocent—and perhaps is being used as a scapegoat. That puts you high on my list of suspects, and I'll bloody well come and go here whenever I feel the need."

Bonny responded first. "I thought you and I had agreed that father couldn't possibly have murdered anyone."

"Then you misunderstood me."

With that, he turned and marched out, leaving the two of them stunned.

***

He headed off after Richard and Maggie. He knew they'd be walking slowly enough for him to catch up with them. As he hurried along, thoughts were popping into his head with startling clarity.

Witnessing father and daughter together again, he sensed complicity. Bonny had taken pains to set up her father's alibi for the Johnson murders. She said he had been too drunk to kill anyone, but that was only her word.

Blackmail was the likeliest reason for Garret's murder. He probably did know who massacred the Johnsons. With his uncertain future at a ranch in some financial distress and if all the doom and gloom about the beef industry was true, the temptation to cash in on the opportunity would have been considerable. But who rode out from the ranch that night? Hansen, Garret, Bonny? Perhaps all three?

And then it came to him — sweat. A horse ridden hard enough to leave the ranch, gallop to and from the Johnsons' camp, two hours each way, would still be covered in sweat at six-thirty AM when Garret went to gather the mounts for the day's ride. He would have noticed.

Bonny's riding breeches were stained with horse's sweat — from riding bareback, Richard had said. She couldn't lift a Western saddle, but the padding in the breeches would have cushioned the ride. The black hair — Spook's — had caught in the breeches button as she slid her right leg down his mane while dismounting. No one would have dreamed that she could ride him. Or could they? Garret must have known, and blackmailing Bonny would have made sense. A successful lawyer meant money.

But how did Garret get shot? The obvious answer: Bonny confided in her father and he committed the actual murder — or maybe they were both in it from the beginning. It all made sense.

He fretted about their inability to find the murder weapon, but he was certain now that it was the grandfather's antique .38 revolver. Sam Hansen could have extracted it from the bundle of Mountie paraphernalia Garret had taken to the Kamloops museum.

His thoughts were interrupted by the distinctive sound of a helicopter coming from the direction of Anahim. He stopped and looked up as it passed overhead, wondering if Les were piloting it. Suddenly, two faces popped into his mind: Bert Neiborg, and his daughter Jean, Bonny's best friend from school days. Two bosom buddies, sharing all their secrets. Yes! Call Jean Neiborg. He had a couple of vital questions to ask her now.

He stepped up his pace. Richard had to get him to a phone — and fast, because the vulnerable person in all of this was Maggie. Her innocence, if it were proven, could cause someone a lot of grief, and he had an uncomfortable feeling he'd just been talking with two such people.

✳✳✳

Coswell waited until they reached the pavement again on the way to the village before he told Richard about his conversation with the Hansens and the concerns that came out of it.

"My God!" Richard said. "If you're right, we shouldn't have left her back there."

"A risk, I agree. Which is why I want you to step on it. I'll make the call to Jean Neiborg from your grandmother's."

Fifteen minutes of pushing the old pickup to the limit brought them to Gramma's. The old lady didn't react a bit to their obvious haste. She calmly put the kettle on the stove and began setting cups, cookies, and fixings on the table.

Coswell phoned the Department of Psychology at the university in Victoria and immediately became entangled in annoying bureaucracy.

"I'm sorry," the receptionist said. "We do not take calls for students."

"On this occasion, you will make an exception. I repeat: This is Inspector Mark Coswell of the Royal Canadian Mounted Police and I wish to speak to Jean Neiborg on an urgent matter. Now go get her."

Wrong approach. "I'm sorry, sir," she said. "I've been told that there are to be no exceptions to the rule."

"By whom?"

"My supervisor."

"Then I'll speak to your supervisor."

"She's on coffee break."

He exhaled in disgust. "Young lady," he said. "I'm rapidly losing patience. If I do not hear from your supervisor in the next ten minutes, I'll have a patrol car sent out, siren blaring, and two burly officers will come charging into your office."

He gave her the grandmother's phone number and hung up. Five minutes later, the phone rang. He answered. "Coswell here."

A chuckle. "Jean Neiborg here, straight from a stimulating lecture on the history of Gestalt psychology."

"Sounds fascinating," Coswell said. "Are there big ears listening in on our conversation?"

"No. Our darling administrative assistant has put her private office at my disposal. You obviously made an impression."

"I'll bet."

He'd debated with himself just how to approach Jean Neiborg. After all, she and Bonny Hansen were best friends. He decided to be direct. "I have to ask you some uncomfortable questions," he said, "but justice and a young lady's welfare stand in the balance."

"Sounds ominous, but go ahead."

"Did you ever see or hear about an old pistol belonging to Bonny's great-grandfather?"

Pause. Jean's mind was obviously turning. "Yes," she said. "But what's its significance?'

"Please. Just tell me. I'll explain later."

Another pause. "Bonny's grandmother had it. Part of the personal effects when the grandfather died. When Bonny turned fourteen, grandma gave it to her. Showed her how to use it too, and swore her to secrecy. Said a woman should always have a gun to make up for being the weaker sex. How's that for liberal thinking?"

"Charming. Did you ever see Bonny fire it?"

"Yeah. Fired it myself. We'd go way hell and gone into the bush and set up targets. Lot of fun, actually. Now, are you going to tell me what this is all about?"

"Another question, first. Did you ever see Bonny ride Brent's horse?"

"Spook?" she said. "Another secret. That horse loved

302

Bonny from the time it was a colt. She could ride him all right, and did ... when Brent and his father weren't around. Even then, we'd go up to the very end of the pasture and Spook would follow us. When we were out of everyone's sight, Bonny would ride him bareback. Brent shared everything with his sister, but not that horse. It gave him status, which he dearly needed ... with his father and even his friends, for that matter."

"Surely he grew out of that with time. Why continue to keep it a secret?"

"Seems silly, I agree, but Bonny wanted it that way. She had feelings for her brother that went way beyond the norm. You're the only person I've ever told."

"But Garret knew, didn't he?"

"I'm sure he did, but he never let on. His feelings for Brent went deep, too."

"Last question. Do you know where Bonny kept the gun? Is there a chance someone could have found it?"

Jean didn't have to be told. She got the whole picture. Her voice took on a tone of resignation.

"No. She had it hidden inside a cold air vent in her room. If that gun was the murder weapon, only Bonny could have supplied it." Her voice dropped even lower. "I've just sold my best friend down the river, haven't I?"

"I'm afraid I have to warn you not to relay our conversation to Bonny," Coswell said, dodging the question. "In court, that would be considered an act of impeding justice."

"You've answered my question, Inspector," she said. "I'll say goodbye."

He hung up and turned around. Richard and his grandmother were standing looking at him.

"One more call," Coswell said, "and then we'll go back to the ranch."

Thankfully, Blakemore was at his desk in Williams Lake.

Coswell fired orders at him the second he said hello. "You want *what*?" he asked, dumbfounded.

"No time to explain," Coswell said. "Now just get your ass and a couple of sets of handcuffs up to the Hansen ranch as fast as you can. Commandeer a helicopter."

He hung up before Blakemore could respond. He felt a twinge of guilt, but shifting the arresting officer role to Blakemore would save him a ton of paperwork, to say nothing of multiple Williams Lake court appearances.

***

Richard and Coswell were strapping on their seatbelts when a small pickup with a brush bar, oversized tires, and auxiliary spotlights pulled in behind them. Richard's friend Allen got out.

"What now?" Coswell muttered.

Richard rolled down the window as Allen came round to his side. "I just missed you at the hotel this morning," he said. "Had to charge up my dead battery before I could get the truck going. I heard something last night that you'd better know."

Coswell leaned over. "What's that?" he said.

"My uncle and Chief Isaac headed up to the hills early yesterday morning on horseback to do a traditional ceremony for Isaac's sons at the spot where they died. Communing with the spirits or something like that."

"I've never heard of such a thing," Richard said.

"Neither have I. That's why I'm telling you. I think they're up to no good."

"Oh, dear," Coswell said. "Are you saying they're going after Hansen?"

Allen looked down and stirred the dust with his foot.

"Maybe."

19

THE ONLY VEHICLE PARKED at the Hansen house when they drove up was the rental; there was no sign of Sam's pickup. The stable doors were wide open but nothing stirred inside.

"Pull up in front of Bonny's car," Coswell said. Richard gave him a quizzical look. "Procedure," he explained. "Slows a suspect's unexpected departure a bit."

Richard obeyed, and as he did so, Coswell looked out the passenger's window and caught a glimpse past the buildings into the far pastures. There, less than a couple of hundred metres from the upper treeline, sat the big Dodge and behind it, two figures loading hay bales. He grabbed Richard's arm to stop him from leaping out the door.

"Whoa," he said. "I just saw Sam and Andy within rifle range of our mountain trail up back. I smell an ambush. Andy could be setting the whole thing up. We have to get Sam away from there. Pull forward and hit the horn for all you're worth."

Richard moaned. "The horn doesn't work," he said, "and I'm more worried about Maggie. She's in the house alone with Bonny."

"I'll deal with that," Coswell said. He got out of the truck and gave an order. "You boot this thing up to that pasture and get Sam back here, where he's safe."

Richard hesitated, but just for a moment, and then slammed the vehicle into gear and sped off, the rear wheels spinning.

Coswell rushed to the house, threw the door open and shouted. "Anyone home?"

He heard a thump upstairs, and then the sound of hurried footsteps along the hall as someone moved from the den to Bonny's bedroom.

Coswell took the stairs two at a time. The door to the den was open and he could just see the top of a head lolled back on one of the leather chairs. Coal black hair — Maggie. Déjà vu hit him as he rushed into the room. But this time, Maggie was fully clothed, right down to her riding boots. On the floor beside her sat an empty glass. Magazines were piled on the coffee table. Coswell glanced at the rolltop desk. The drawer lay open and the key was stuck in the lock. He grasped her shoulder and gave it a shake.

"Maggie, Maggie. Wake up."

She didn't respond, but her chest moved normally with each breath and her colour was good. He heard Bonny's bedroom door open. A moment later, she appeared at the den door wearing a robe and rubbing her eyes.

"What in God's name is going on?" she asked, then saw Maggie crumpled on the chair. "Oh, shit. She must have sneaked into my bedroom while I was in the shower and taken the key out of my jeans pocket. I hadn't gotten around to putting it back after I gave her the methadone this morning."

"What is she doing in the den?" Coswell said. "Your father wouldn't be happy to know she'd come into the house."

"I took pity on her cooped up in that shack of Garret's. I left her here reading magazines while I went to the shower."

They were interrupted by the slam of the front door and the sound of someone running up the stairs. Suddenly, Richard burst into the room and when he saw Maggie, he rushed to her side, ignoring both Coswell and Bonny.

"She's okay," Coswell said. "Just drugged out. But how did you get out to that field and back so fast? You did do as I ordered, didn't you?"

"I didn't have to go far," Richard said. "I parked and just kept flashing my lights. When I saw that they were coming, I came back here."

Coswell smiled at the young man's ingenuity. His ability

to think on his feet boded well for his future in the Force. "Okay, Richard," he said. "Now I want you to stay with Maggie. Bonny and I are going for a walk."

"A walk?" Bonny said. "I don't feel like a walk. This is very upsetting."

Coswell looked at her and saw fear in her eyes. "Oh, but I think you'll find what I'm going to show you of considerable interest."

"All right then," she said. "I'll go get dressed."

"No. We're not going far. In fact, those slippers will be fine."

She grumbled. "This is ridiculous."

He took her arm. "You might not think so in a few minutes."

She blinked rapidly, but let him lead her out of the room. He could hear Hansen's pickup rumble into the yard outside, and when they stepped onto the porch, Sam came striding over. Anger flashed in his eyes. "What the hell is going on?" he said, then saw the look on his daughter's face. "Bonny?"

Coswell answered for her: "We're going to the paddock. I have a theory about the murders that I know will interest the both of you. Why don't you come along?"

Hansen looked as though he were about to argue, but sensed he should not. He called over to Andy standing beside the Dodge.

"Start unloading those," Hansen said. "I'll give you a hand shortly."

They made their way to the paddock. Coswell led the way, still holding Bonny's arm, and Sam Hansen followed on their heels. They stopped at the pasture gate. Spook came running.

"Your friend has noticed you, Bonny," Coswell said.

She remained silent. Coswell moved back a few steps. The horse came forward and reached his nose over the rail to nuzzle her shoulder. She didn't respond.

"If you check his hooves, Sam," Coswell said, "I think you'll see he's missing a shoe."

"So what? He's not the first horse around here to throw one."

"Forensics, Sam, forensics. A terrible thing for the guilty. We have casts in our Vancouver lab that I'm willing to bet match this animal's prints exactly and we collected those from the Johnsons' camp the day they were murdered."

Silence again.

"Bonny, you are the only person who can ride Spook,' Coswell said.

She didn't respond.

"We'll go back to the house now and I'm going to tell you both a little story while we walk."

He took her arm again and she went with him passively. Hansen remained at the paddock, staring at the black horse. After a few moments, he turned and caught up with them in time to hear Coswell speaking quietly to Bonny.

"I think that on the night you, Garret, and your father reminisced about Brent, your resolve to exact revenge emerged, perhaps aided by the alcohol. I'm guessing that Garret went to bed first, leaving you and your father to fan the bitterness. You began to water your Scotch down and when your father tottered off to bed, probably in the wee hours of the morning, you were almost sober — but not sober enough to temper your anger. You changed into your riding breeches, knowing you had a long, hard bareback ride ahead of you, and silently slipped out of the house."

Her eyes were fixed on the ground ahead. Her father looked stunned.

"You got a bridle from the stable, but not a saddle — too heavy to carry. You went to the pasture, bridled Spook, walked him a good ways before mounting, and rode at what must have been death-defying speed, even with the bright moonlight, all the way to the Johnsons' camp. They were asleep in their tent, but you wanted them awake to see what was coming to them. Hearing a female voice, they wouldn't be concerned about their safety, just curious. You shot them in cold blood with your grandfather's revolver and tried to make it look like a robbery."

They had almost reached the house. Coswell pointed to the porch. "Why don't we sit out here for a few minutes while I finish my story?"

Bonny took a chair facing the yard. Coswell did the same. Hansen stood beside his daughter, his hand resting on her shoulder. Coswell continued, looking steadily at Bonny.

"Light was breaking when you got back to the ranch. No time to rub down Spook. You put the bridle back in the stable, hurried to the house, and tiptoed up to your room. The next part's a bit fuzzy, but I think you probably just missed Garret coming out to get the horses for our ride. He sees you or notices the sweat on Spook."

She gazed out into the yard as though her mind were somewhere else.

"Sometime over the weekend, once the murders are discovered, Garret starts thinking blackmail. He gets you aside and makes his demands. You tell your father all that's happened."

Coswell looked up at Hansen.

"And that's where you come in, Sam," he said. "You're shocked, of course, but being a loving father, your daughter's welfare is paramount. You take over, tell her not to worry and leave everything in your hands. A plan forms in your mind. It begins by driving Bonny to the airport. You conjure up some business you have to deal with in Williams Lake that requires an overnight stay in the Clearwater Hotel, where you knew your check-in would be remembered. That done, you immediately drive back to the ranch, park the truck somewhere, and sneak in on foot.

Coswell paused for a moment, collecting his thoughts. He saw Bonny slowly shaking her head, but Hansen said nothing. Coswell continued, still directing his comments to her father.

"A number of things could have happened at this point, but somehow you see Maggie and Garret together and watch them. You soon spot the perfect opportunity to kill Garret and frame Maggie. Bonny has told you where the pistol is hidden. You tiptoe into the house to get it. On the way, you see Maggie asleep in the den. Your luck has gotten even better. You get the key to the methadone cabinet and put it in the lock. The rest is easy. The only mystery is why you didn't plant the gun on Maggie afterwards — but maybe something distracted you, so you ultimately returned it to its original hiding place. As an aside, I might tell you that a reliable source has told me precisely where that is."

Hansen's eyes were on his daughter now. Coswell tried to read his expression, looking for any indication of guilt or even denial, but saw nothing but sadness. He turned his gaze back to Bonny.

"But you weren't satisfied that all was settled, were you, Bonny? If Maggie got off, all three murders would still be on the books and the investigations continued. She had to be silenced just as Garret had been, but this time you would do the deed. Your father agreed, and created the ideal setting — Helga on her days off and Andy pulled to the very end of the property."

She finally stopped shaking her head and looked up at him as he continued.

"I think Richard and my arrival came in the nick of time. You were on the verge of shooting Maggie and placing the gun in her hand — just another native suicide. All the murders instantly solved and investigations brought to a halt. You and your father could rest easy."

Hansen finally broke his silence. "No, no," he said. "You've got it all wrong. I killed them all. The Johnson bastards needed to pay for Brent's death and you were right about Garret. He tried to blackmail me and I shot him just as you described. Bonny's completely innocent."

A tear rolled down Bonny's cheek and she began to speak in a low voice.

"I hated them all," she said. "That Bertha bitch, the Johnsons, even Maggie. Mother paid way more attention to those dregs of society that she hauled up here than to me and Brent. Even Garret, the evil bastard, threatening me like that. Father's lying to protect me. Just ask him where the gun was hidden. He doesn't know and it's back there right now with only my prints on it."

Hansen slumped into the chair beside Bonny. He leaned forward and put his head in his hands.

Coswell turned to face Bonny. He knew the whole story now. "You didn't get on that flight to Vancouver, did you?"

"No. I found a hooker who was happy to get a free one-way ticket and a hundred dollars to book in using my name."

"Why, Bonny? Why did you do it? You knew the law would deal with the Johnsons."

"The law? What a joke. You forget that I know exactly what the law does in cases like that. Manslaughter at the most, and if the tribal bastards had their way, they'd get nothing but a few hours in the healing lodge."

Her face contorted in anger. "They murdered Brent. They were two pieces of shit compared to him. My precious Brent." She began to sob. Hansen leaned across and put his arms around her.

Coswell felt nothing for Bonny, and he wondered at his callousness. Her life hadn't been easy: childhood bullying, inattentive parents, a brother whom she adored, murdered. But she'd ended up a bully herself — cold, calculating, and merciless. It would be interesting to see what white man's justice had in store for her. His deepest feelings, surprisingly, concerned himself. He'd been so certain of Sam Hansen's guilt. But why? It made sense, but where was his infallible gut instinct?

A rare bruise had formed on Inspector Coswell's ego ... and it hurt.

***

They were still on the porch when the helicopter flew in and Blakemore got out. Coswell went over and told him the whole story.

"Holy shit," was all Blakemore could muster. "Have you read her her rights?"

"No," Coswell said. "From here on, you're in charge."

He left Blakemore and walked over to the stable. Andy was sitting on a hay bale, smoking a cigarette. Coswell spotted an old three-legged stool beside one of the stalls and dragged it over to sit beside him. Nothing was said for a few minutes. Andy broke the silence.

"Lot of long faces over there," he said. "Somebody else die?"

"In a manner of speaking, I guess you could say that. Bonny Hansen's been charged with the murders of the John-son brothers and Garret Parker."

A flicker of surprise, then more silence. Finally: "You sure it was her, not her father?"

"Without a shadow of a doubt, I'm afraid. She's confessed."

Andy got up, threw his cigarette to the floor, and ground it out with his foot. He walked over to a corner where halters, bridles, and ropes were hung. He gathered one of each and then crossed to a railing where a half-dozen saddles were lined up. He chose one and swung it effortlessly onto one shoulder.

"Going out back for a ride," he said. "Might not be back for a bit. Tell the boss, will you?"

Coswell nodded and followed him outside. Andy looked across at the house only once, but it happened just as Blakemore led Bonny, handcuffed, to the waiting helicopter. He stopped for a second, and then continued on to the paddock without another glance.

Coswell walked slowly back to the house. Sam was standing on the porch, his eyes fixed on the helicopter as it took off and then sped east to Williams Lake and jail for his daughter.

A feeling of remorse swept over Coswell, evoked by the realization that he'd been too quick in his judgment of Hansen. He went over and placed his hand on the rancher's shoulder.

"Anything I can do for you, Sam?" he said.

Hansen pulled away and faced him. "You can get that squaw and her boyfriend out of my den. I need a drink and I don't want them as company."

EPILOGUE

Coswell watched the country drift below him as the Beechcraft 1900 flew west from the Williams Lake airport, then turned south to Vancouver, gradually climbing to 25,000 feet. He enjoyed this part of flying: humanity dissolving into two-dimensional images of spectacular beauty. Not a single cloud hung over the Cariboo that day. He could see rivers: some large, coursing headlong to the coast, others lazy, meandering in serpentine patterns as though reluctant to arrive anywhere. Ranches appeared below, their fields of dark green alfalfa and grass pastures burnt now to a light brown. He could make out buildings and even machinery, but they looked like part of a child's play set, not mundane objects of daily life.

The extent of the pine beetle scourge became more apparent as the plane gained altitude. The damage was even more pervasive than what he saw during his helicopter rides. He thought of Bert Neiborg and his crew racing against time to salvage as much wood as possible from the dying trees. His daughter Jean had answered another call and rushed to Bonny's side, a true friend.

He thought he could make out an RCMP cruiser on the highway at one point. It wouldn't be long before Richard might be its driver; he said he would request a Cariboo posting, and as a First Nations, he would likely get it.

Maggie probably came out of the whole mess best of all, considering where she'd been. Chief Isaac, of all people, used his influence to get her admitted to the Nengayni Wellness Centre on the Deep Creek reserve just north of Williams Lake, a band-directed drug rehabilitation facility.

Blakemore didn't fare quite as well. Ill feelings still lingered from his high-handed actions at the courthouse, but a sense of justice eventually prevailed, the score evened: an Indian girl saved, a white girl in jail. Two brethren killed, a white policeman dead, his father devastated.

Peace returned to the Cariboo ... for now. He knew prejudice still fermented in the hearts of the diehards and would likely erupt again, but he saw hope for the future. People like Richard Delorme and his friend Allen represented that hope. It would be their generation that would bring down the barriers. The memories of the Chilcotin Wars would fade as the elders passed on.

These thoughts failed to cheer him, though. He had been so confident of his brilliant solution to Garret's murder. He'd been wrong before, but never in the face of such certainty on his part. Sam Hansen's personality had caused a prejudice within him that, in truth, was no better than that of Chief Isaac and his cohorts. In a professional at his level, such an error was unforgivable. Perhaps he too needed to step aside and let fresh blood take his place.

But then Corporal James popped into Coswell's mind, bringing his self-flagellation to an abrupt halt. His mood instantly lifted. Another dinner at the Vicinage with his subordinate was in order. The young man would be relieved to have his mentor back in command.

The plane began its descent into Vancouver. The traffic leaving the city had almost reached gridlock status on Canada One. The real world rushed up to meet him.

END

ACKNOWLEDGEMENTS

Special thanks to board editors Don Kerr, who led me and Inspector Coswell through the first of the series, and Diane Bessai, who stood in for this one. It has been my great fortune to be taken on by the wonderful people at NeWest Press. Long may they continue to offer aspiring Canadian writers the opportunity to have their work recognized.

Natalie Olsen has been an absolute gem. Her covers are superb examples of just how valuable a graphic designer can be to a book's salability.

Thanks, too, go to retired Constable Peter Phillips, my source for information on all things police and the sometimes peculiar workings of the Canadian justice system.

Finally, thanks to the RCMP officers I have known and admired — men and women like you and me who must deal on a day-to-day basis with a society that has, perhaps, made itself too complicated.

ROY INNES is a retired eye physician and surgeon whose penchant for the arts, buried for years in the world of science, was rekindled upon retirement. His first Inspector Coswell novel, **Murder in the Monashees**, was released in 2005 and was followed in 2008 by **West End Murders**. Innes is an avid hunter, a lover of classical music, and, despite his skinny frame, a gourmand. He lives on British Columbia's lush Gabriola Island with his wife Barrie and his daughter's cat.